Not Far Away

Lyrics by Ann Narcisian Videan

Oh, my friend, I have a gift to give you.
Not something you can buy or touch
But one to live within you.
There are many things I could give you,
To show you that I care,
But nothing you can touch,
Can show you what is really there…
I am giving you my friendship to last throughout your life.

Also by Ann Narcisian Videan:

Rhythms & Muse CD – An accompanying music CD with five
original compositions inspired by the novel.

Rhythms & Muse

"Nothing you can touch can show you what is really there."

Ann Narcisian Videan

vIDEAn Unlimited Publishing
anvidean.com

Published in the United States of America through:
vIDEAn Unlimited Publishing, Mesa, AZ
anvidean.com • videanunlimited.com • avidean@videanunlimited.com

Library of Congress Control Number: 2010917368

ISBN-10: 0-615-38854-X
ISBN-13: 978-0-615-38854-0 (pbk.)

I dedicate this book to you Robert, Cutter and Codi. You marched on brilliantly while I spent so many hours away researching, writing and editing. You are the ones who made it possible to attain this lifelong dream of mine to become an author.

I love you each more than words can say.

Acknowledgements

My deepest appreciation goes to Kalisa Turanchik for her ongoing critique and input over the many years of this story's creation. This is almost as much her book as it is mine.

A core group of friends, plus talented writers and marketers contributed to this book in many ways. Cheers, you beautiful people!

Andrea Beaulieu – for your profound support and inspiration
Janet Drez – for your friendship and enthusiasm
Mary Fachman – for your insightful editing
Paula and Dane Graves – for your cozy writing space and hospitality
Harry and Madge Narcisian – for consistently reminding me I could accomplish anything if I just set my mind to it
Beverly Rosenbaum – for your professional manuscript editing ideas
Cherie Scott – for your bubbly joie de vivre and cheerleading
Kathy Stephenson – for your astute edits
Pam Swartz – for your valued publishing advice
Kris Tualla– for your publishing savvy and guidance
Christopher West – for your inspiration and remaining my friend these 40 years
Dr. Robert and Martha West – for access to your comfy cabin with its writing space and view of beautiful Cd'A
Cathy Yardley– for your professional query and synopsis editing ideas

I am also so grateful for the support received from my mastermind groups and other business contacts, church friends, the Desert Rose chapter of the Romance Writers of America, and my ALWAYS writers' tribe (Alliance for Literary Writers, Authors, & Yabbering Scribes). Your many tips and ideas appear between the lines on every page. Thank you.

Ah, I must not neglect my gratitude for The Coffee Bean & Tea Leaf. Its welcoming environment and delicious tea lattes fueled the writing of this story through many joyous hours.

May 2003: Alex

"No!" Alex whispered forcibly, sitting bolt upright in bed. She clutched her silver satin bedclothes to her pounding heart and felt a bead of sweat drip along her temple. She was instantly alert.

She heard the reassuring trickling of her Zen water fountain on the cherry wood nightstand beside her bed. *My own room...*she thought, struggling to control ragged breathing. *That blasted car dream again!* Every time she had it, its real quality left her with an unnerving, surreal feeling. Shaking her head to clear the dream's effects, she laid herself back onto the bed, pulled the cool coverlet over her head and waited for the weird feeling to subside. But this time it seemed to linger, as if leaving a message to decipher.

She moved the coverlet off her face and lay still for several minutes. She watched a new shaft of the day's sunlight on her bay window seat warming the velvet pillows from rich purple into burgundy shades. The light highlighted the floral brocade in the silver curtains and reached across the room. It glinted off the glass doors of her music-box case and lit up the engraved words "Alexandra Lauren" on numerous awards for her music education contributions, including her prized Grammy Award atop the fireplace mantel. Comfortable in her own surroundings, her hammering heart calmed and she was able to think objectively about the dream. She let it play again in her mind. It always started with her leaning her head partially out the car window and breathing the rushing air...

❖❖❖

Twilight sea salt and damp earth blasted her senses with the force of the passing wind. She ducked back in and watched an endless movie loop of vibrant succulent blooms blurring past the fender.

Maneuvering the contours of the coast, she caught another glimpse of the sunset behind cerulean waves. She could hear the waves crashing against the shore below, even above the thumping of Led

Zeppelin's *"Misty Mountain Hop"* from her VW Beetle's 8-track. Nothing could mar the rhythms of this glorious day.

Glancing in the rearview mirror, she saw a little red Mercedes 450SL fast approaching behind her. She pictured a handsome international spy at the wheel. It was the perfect set-up for a spectacular movie car chase. Menacing little sports car close on her tail. Narrow road along a high cliff. Her heart trilled with excitement.

Approaching a tight turn at the edge of one mountain outcropping, she imagined soaring off the cliff road onto the ocean thermals and landing safely on the deep sand below. If anyone could make a Beetle fly, an undercover agent's genius inventor could. She imagined the instantaneous, euphoric high of the flight, the freedom of escape, until a glint of white brought her eye back to the road ahead.

Distant, around the next curve, the setting sun flashed off an oncoming white car approaching at a dangerous speed. As it turned toward them, it smashed into the mountain slope on one side, veered and barely missed sliding over the cliff on the other. Her euphoric image of flight dissipated like steam into warm air.

Unease prickled her neck as the Impala careened toward the curve ahead, and her hands tightened on the wheel. Her heart quaked in her chest as the car quickly approached on a straightaway. The closer it came, the slower everything around her seemed to move. The images in her head slowed until the flow of motion seemed only to drip. Wildly onward the car approached, clipping railings as it advanced.

Her rearview mirror revealed the red sports car moving up on her, oblivious to the oncoming danger. Both cars closed in, looming larger and closer with each surreal, stop-action second. As they compressed the available road space, she realized she was about to be caught between them.

Heart pounding and hands trembling, Alex watched the white Impala move into her lane not 200 feet ahead. *I'm going to die,* she thought, scrunching up her eyes.

She didn't turn the wheel. She didn't brake. She didn't do any of the things she thought she'd instinctively do. She just drove blindly into fate, bracing herself for the oncoming impact.

In the next instant, she felt a small jolt as the white car clipped her front fender. She heard squealing tires and a hot blast of wind as the

*car blew past. Her Beetle spun backward 180 degrees into the deep
sand of the inside shoulder, shuddering to stillness.*

*She opened her eyes just in time to witness the white car smash
head on into the swerving red sports car. She instinctively covered her
ears to blot out the horrific noise as the huge impact of crushing metal
just yards away reverberated in her chest.*

*Mesmerized, she watched the impact send both cars spinning
across the outside shoulder and off the cliff. They seemed to hover
momentarily, spinning on the thermals above the cliff line, then
dropped from view. A moment later, she heard them crashing onto the
beach below.*

❖❖❖

Alex lay in her bed and analyzed the elements in the dream. When
she first dreamed it in high school, it had been fun; just a breezy drive
along the coast with no peril involved. The dream created a cool,
movie-like reality she'd welcomed. She'd even wished to dream it
more often. But as the years had gone by, it had unfolded into more of
a nightmare, filled with the sinister and scary fast-approaching cars
and imminent danger.

She pressed her hands to her forehead. She'd never dreamed an
actual collision before. *But, I was safe after the crash. Shaken, but
really safe*, she thought. Alex felt strangely and deeply comforted by
this impression. Somehow, the finality of this realization made the
dream feel complete to her. She just knew, somehow, she would never
have the dream again. It was done. *Weird.*

Looking around, Alex's surreal frame of mind dissolved into the
early morning light filtering into her room. But, as soon as her mind
registered the red digital 5:45 a.m. on her alarm clock, her stomach
squeezed involuntarily with the familiar pressure from managing her
daily routine.

She sighed, listening to the unusual, vast quiet of her house and a
spark of joy relaxed the tightness in her stomach. *Two whole blessed
days to myself!* Starting with giving all her staff the day off, her
assistant Madeleine had helped Alex cook up a plan to get away from
her daily pressures. It did mean Alex had to lie to her producer about

falling sick today, but she needed the quiet time so badly. *Madeleine Beauchamp, I'll love you forever for helping me make this happen*!

Alex imagined herself in just an hour or so behind the wheel and headed toward Santa Barbara, California, where a studio musician friend had offered up a private beach house for her use. Driving cross-country was one of Alex's favorite things. Pavement blurring by under her tires, new countryside to feast her eyes on, and R&B blaring from the CD deck... *Ah-h-h, heaven!* Excited to enjoy every moment of these all-too-rare days to herself, she tossed back the covers and climbed out of bed.

On her way past the fireplace mantel, she rubbed her fingertips across the gold gramophone topping her Grammy award. Following her morning ritual, she also ran her fingers along the inlaid rose in the lid of her old music box. This morning, she was tempted to pull out Matt's old school photo tucked safely inside. But, she resisted. Those precious items represented the two most important periods of her life: achieving her most desired career goal, and being in love for the first and only time. But, this morning, she saw them anew, suddenly wondering why she cherished them. The award had fulfilled a dream she hoped would fill her need for love, while the music box promised a dream of love that never was fulfilled. Neither had brought her the happiness she craved. Actually, it was that award that had trapped her in this unhappy lifestyle. Since the Grammys, her life had just not been her own. Sighing in frustration, she grabbed workout clothes from a cherry wood dresser drawer and pulled them on.

Alex pulled her hair into a ponytail and walked down the hall into her well-equipped exercise room. Even if her personal trainer wasn't coming today, she still needed endorphins to help her through the day. She plugged into her iPod and warmed up on the treadmill until sweat glistened on her forehead. Moving to the Stairmaster, she punched in her favorite automatic circuit. Three settings into the uphill workout the telephone rang. She hung her head, but didn't stop her routine. *They can all just wonder about me. I am not answering this early in the morning.*

She completed her 30-minute workout with a soak in her Jacuzzi and, toweling the back of her neck, walked to her gray-marbled master bathroom. As she washed her face, her frenetic daily schedule ricocheted around inside her head: always on the move, sun-up to sundown. It felt more and more overwhelming.

Just when her facial cleanser had bubbled soapy foam all over her face, the phone rang again. Her heart started racing immediately. She took a slow, deep, calming breath trying to ignore the voice mail message…a request for her participation in another fundraiser. She rinsed and dried her face, and hung up the hand towel, carefully centering the monogram.

As she went about her routine, a nagging thought lurked in the shadows of her subconscious, but she couldn't seem to bring it forward. She leaned her hands on the pink marble and studied the depths of her seashell-shaped sink. Perhaps the obscure message was simply some lingering emotion from her nightmare. She shrugged it off, straightening. Pulling her curls out of its band and forward over one shoulder, Alex stared at herself in the mirror, really seeing her face for the first time in many years.

This 40-something woman certainly wasn't the woman the teenaged Alexandra Lauren once had envisioned. Sure, she looked great on the outside, but nobody seemed to notice the dissatisfaction lurking behind her emerald eyes. The nagging message roiling in her subconscious bubbled up again and Alex dropped her eyes from the mirror. What was it? What was bothering her? Her age? Her lack of companionship? No, something else.

She closed her eyes and thought deeply about her current life. Quelling any impressions from her physical senses, she reached internally for clarity. Immediately a cold wash of sadness flowed over her from her forehead to her feet. She became dizzy and felt suddenly as if she was teetering on the edge of an abyss. She steadied herself with the cold marble counter, opened her eyes, and saw her very pale face staring back from the mirror. *What was that? …I have everything I want, do what I love to do…* She hesitated, realizing there was an unspoken "but" following that sentence.

She was forced to weigh what it meant. Yes, she had plenty of money, went anywhere she wanted, and shared her music with millions of people. It all seemed so glamorous. But, she'd discovered with the glamour came a whole raft of tiresome obligations. After all, hadn't she had to finagle a simple, quiet weekend by herself, just to escape those endless duties? With that thought, her lack of fulfillment overtook her, quickly followed by a wave of loneliness. It was as if she'd just opened herself up to reality. She felt resentment flooding in about how her record company sucked her energy dry, always trying to get more. More interviews. More concerts. More money.

And hadn't she just heard through the grapevine that her masseur was dropping her name to potential customers despite Alex's request to remain an anonymous client? So few of her staff showed real loyalty. She suddenly understood even her carefully selected hired help cared more about *working for her* than *caring about her*.

Even though it looked like she had control of her life, she was quickly approaching a precipice. Envisioning what it would feel like to jump off the cliff like the cars in her dream, a wave of nausea rolled through her and she dropped to sit on the edge of the tub. She clutched her knees as her hands began to tremble. Maintaining a life as a performer was no longer meaningful to her. *My life isn't my own. It's empty. But what do I do? Do I want to stop being a performer?*

The musical ring of Credence Clearwater's "Proud Mary" on her cell phone interrupted her thoughts. *Cig Gary's ring tone*, she thought, taking two deep breaths. The phone continued playing as she moved through the master bedroom and down the marbled hall into her music room. *Here we go.* With shaking hands, she flipped the phone open.

"Just a sec', Gary," she choked, feigning a cough and pressing the mute button. Steadying herself with a deep breath, she sat down on the piano bench and returned to the call. Clearing her throat, she said croakily, "Good morning."

"Just checkin' in to ask you to bring along your new song sheets to review at the meeting this afternoon." He paused briefly, as if the tired scratchiness of her voice had just registered in his mind. "You OK?"

"Gary, I can't make it to the meeting today. I feel terrible."

"What's the matter, chickadee?" he asked, with a moist sound indicating the relocation of his cigar to the other side of his mouth.

Suppressing the desire to tell her record producer just how annoying she found his habit, Alex said in a tired voice, "Just a virus. You know, fever, upset stomach. Nothing serious, I'm sure."

"You're sure you're too sick to meet today? Can't you take a couple of pills or something?"

"Pills won't help a virus, Gary."

"Oh yeah, that's right. I could get a doctor down there to attend you. Mad Bo can make a call for you."

"Thanks, I already talked to Madeleine about handling that," Alex said, rasping to clear her throat. "She's probably called the team to let them know I won't be there, and to reschedule the meeting, too."

"You sure we have to change it? You know, my on-call doctor is always willing to spend a day caring for any of my peeps. He'd load you up with the pink stuff and hold airsick bags for you."

Alex felt the usual frustration building in her. These people drove her crazy! They were supposed to have her best interest in mind, but wouldn't even allow her to be ill.

She cleared her throat. "Gary. I'm sick."

"OK, OK. We'll reschedule." Moist chewing noises again filled the airwaves.

Alex staged a coughing fit, astonishing even herself with how real it sounded. Eventually, Cig Gary broke in, "You need anything?"

"I'm set. I'll just take good care of myself so I get well quickly."

"OK, good idea. You do that. You need to be up for the LA concert this weekend, you know."

"I'm sure I will, Gary." She picked up a recently finished BJ Starr composition off the piano. "I'll practice up on those song sheets and bring them along when I see you next." She strangled out a cough.

"OK. You're going to be fine, I'm sure."

"It's under control."

"OK, then. Take care and we'll see you in a couple of days."

"Yeah." Alex faked a small burp. "I've got to go now, Gary."

He paused, but finally just said, "Ciao," and hung up.

Alex snapped her phone shut and blew out a long breath. She could tell from his worried tone he'd actually bought it. *Yes! Another step toward some freedom.* She enjoyed a brief moment of elation before remembering Cig Gary's comment about being fit for the upcoming LA concert. Her heart began to pound and she consciously worked to quell the mounting emotional pressure.

Her thoughts roiled as she stepped into her shower. Under the hot steam, she thought about her successful records. She'd sung them all

8

Ann Narcisian Videan

over the country. She'd won awards. So, why was she left with this hollow feeling inside?

She recognized how the egos of her producers were wearing on her, not to mention the constant travel. After 25 years, it just wasn't fun any more, especially the madness of the past year. *I'm burned out and need a rest.* She slammed off the water and stood there, dripping, for a long moment with her hand still on the faucet.

Eventually, she exited the snail shower, wrapped herself in a fluffy towel and leaned into the mirror studying her freshly scrubbed, pink face. *No self-pity, Alex! What are you going to do?* She leaned her forehead against the mirror. *Make plans.* She could use these next two days to think about what she really wanted: an emotionally rewarding, love-filled life.

Her thoughts immediately turned to her happiest days, right after moving to Coeur d'Alene, Idaho, for her senior year of high school. When she first knew Matt. It had been far too many years since she'd seen him. *My talented lone-wolf dreamer.* she thought, watching her lips meander into a smile as she remembered her very first day at Coeur d'Alene High...

September 1977: Alex

*A*lex's eyes popped open with a feeling of exhilaration tickling along her shoulders. She reached back and smoothed the pillowcase away from her neck with the back of her hand.

The image of the VW flying along the coastal highway lingered in her minds' eye. *Whoa, that was one realistic dream.* She stretched her arms long above her head. *Maybe that pretty ocean drive means I'm truckin' down the right road at this new school. Or maybe not!* She giggled out loud at the thought of believing in good omens.

Alex glanced across her bedroom to her new school clothes laid out across her beanbag chair. Throwing back her quilt, she reached over, flicked on her bedside transistor radio, and flopped out of bed.

As the strains of The Guess Who's "American Woman" filled the room, Alex gathered her curls forward over her shoulder and opened her window shade. She shivered, watching the early morning sun glint through the pine boughs outside her window. Tiny stripes of shadow and light patterned the glass, lighting up the rainbow colors in her peace-sign sun-catcher.

It is *so Boss here. Why does everyone keep telling me how dreary it is in Idaho? It just couldn't be worse than the "dry" heat in Phoenix.* She smiled to herself.

With a deep cleansing breath, Alex turned to pull on her peasant blouse and bell-bottoms. She looked in the mirror and picked up her brush, wishing her hair was as hip as her clothes. She attempted to part her unruly curls down the middle and have them lie smooth and straight. *Hopeless.* She fastened her favorite necklace around her neck, slipped on her clogs and clumped down the stairs feeling a bit shaky from first-day-of-school-in-a-new-town butterflies.

Alex received many not-so-subtle glances at "the new girl" as students trickled into the classroom. Standing by the desk where Mr.

O'Hanlon had asked her to wait, Alex remained as unobtrusive as possible. She composed her usually over-expressive face, as she self-consciously gathered a loose mass of curls over her shoulder.

She couldn't suppress a quick frown at Mr. O'Hanlon who was busy directing students to their new homeroom seating assignments. *You'd think he would have at least made time to assign me a seat*, she reasoned. *What a ridiculous thing to do to a new student; making me stand here at the front of the room like a sideshow freak!*

In an effort to suppress her unease, Alex thoroughly studied the classroom. She noted the typical smells of floor wax, cleaning solutions and new paint, barely masking the age-old musk of hundreds of active kids. But the decor made her almost believe she'd stepped into an earlier century. A bank of windows along one wall reached almost to the height of the unusually high ceilings. They provided a beautiful view of giant old oaks in the schoolyard and lent a nice airy feeling to the room, but their antique glass was wavy and dotted with air bubbles. The desks were wood and wrought iron, and bolted to the creaky wooden floors in rows. Each desk surface was attached to the back of the desk in front of it. But, the kicker was the round hole drilled in the desktop to hold an ink bottle.

I can't believe they still have Little House on the Prairie *desks. It is 1977, after all.* Alex felt someone's gaze and turned to see a handsome young man approaching. His head involuntarily jerked back as their eyes met, and he immediately averted his gaze. Alex's heart skipped a beat and she felt a powerful urge to reach out to touch his face as he passed. She clenched her fist and forced her arm not to move.

At that moment, a tall, dark-haired girl in jeans and a T-shirt walked in. The plump girl took in every detail of Alex's being, from her clogs northward. Just opposite Alex she stopped short. Her twinkly, chocolate-brown eyes snapped onto Alex's necklace and a smile rounded her rosy cheeks.

"Hey, I like your treble clef." The gal lifted a silver charm hanging from her choker and held it still for Alex to see.

"It's just like mine!" Alex said, fingering her own choker.

"I'm Suzanne. Do you sing? I'm a soprano."

"I'm an alto. I'm Alex. Nice to meet you."

"Hey, maybe we'll be in the Viking Swing Choir together," said Suzanne, distracted by the teacher who was motioning from across the room. Nodding, Suzanne added, "Looks like Mr. O'Hanlon found you a seat. But, catch up with me after class and we'll talk more, OK?"

"Great," Alex said, clutching her books tight against her chest. Mr. O'Hanlon walked her to a spot next to a gangly, red-haired, fellow grinning widely as he watched Suzanne take her seat across the room.

"Alexandra, this is Brett Thompkins," the teacher said. "And this…" he turned to Brett, gesturing as if to formally present her "…is Alexandra Lauren." "Keep the chatter to a minimum, eh, Brett," he added with a warning look.

Brett shrugged off Mr. O'Hanlon's comment with a grin equally as large as the one he'd worn watching Suzanne. Alex acknowledged him with a quiet, "Glad to meet you." She slipped into the desk and tucked her books under the hinged desktop.

Brett responded with a toothy grin and, in a southern dialect louder than Alex would have preferred, said, "I bet that root beer tan of yours brings you from somewhere south of here. Right?"

Alex almost laughed out loud at his thick southern drawl, but instead bit her lip in a smile. "Yes, Arizona, actually. And *you* aren't exactly a native, either."

"Nope. We moved up here a couple of years ago from Dallas and I've been buggin' y'all with this here di-a-lect ever since." He nodded his head at her like one of those bobble-headed Hawaiian hula dolls she'd seen on car dashes. "Yee haw! Now I've got another 'sunshine person' here to sympathize with me during all the dreary months."

"What?" Alex glanced out the window at the sun shining through the red and golden trees of Indian summer. "It's bitchin' here."

"Yeah? Just wait another couple weeks. The sun'll go under a cloud bank and you won't see it again until next July. I swear!"

Alex gave him a doubtful look.

"I *swear*!" he said, crossing his heart.

With a quiet laugh, Alex turned her attention to a rapping noise from the front of the room. Mr. O'Hanlon, now seated at his desk, was smacking his pencil so soundly against the edge of the desk Alex was amazed the pencil didn't splinter into pieces. When he had the class's attention, he abruptly began roll call.

Alex snuck a dubious look across to Brett, before turning her attention to the names that matched the faces of her new classmates. In response to, "Briggs, Suzanne" her soprano friend replied, "Here!" and smiled at Alex.

Alex acknowledged her own presence when her name was called and continued her study of each student during the roll. She noticed a faint familiarity about many of the faces. Some of them reminded her of Arizona friends, yet, with few exceptions, everyone here seemed to be pale and...well, kind of frumpy. She fingered her blonde curls, suddenly noticing that almost everyone else had long, straight, brown hair and wore straight-leg jeans and tee shirts. *No wonder everyone stared at me when they came in. I'm about the only blonde and really overdressed. So much for hip.* Alex sighed.

The name "Post, Daniel," called from the podium pulled her from her contemplation. "Right on!" a handsome, athletic guy loudly replied from the back of the room. He caught Alex's eye as she glanced back at him and he gave her an appreciative raised eyebrow and a slight purse of the lips.

She snapped her head back to the front abruptly. *Typical jock.*

The next name called was, "Roberts, Matthew." Alex rested her gaze on the lean, fair-haired fellow looking out the window at the bright September morning. It was the same guy whose face she'd wanted to touch earlier. Her heart skittered again. "Hey," he responded after a moment, not skipping a beat as his fingers absentmindedly tapped the desktop like a piano keyboard. He never removed his eyes from the window either.

While other names were called, Alex kept stealing glimpses of this guy Matthew. What was it about him that made her heart jump? Possibly sensing her glances, he turned once and looked right into her eyes. Alex felt an odd emotional jolt, a surge of recognition. She quickly looked away, blushing furiously.

He didn't look like anyone she'd known before. Still, she *knew* this guy. She felt it through a quick rush of intense emotion from deep inside her. She *knew* this perfect stranger, this Matt. Somehow.

September 1977: Matt

*M*att glanced twice at the new girl as soon as he walked into homeroom because he thought she was someone he knew. Besides, how could anyone miss that off-the-shoulder peasant top? Their eyes met briefly and he felt a shock go through him. He could have sworn she wanted to reach out and touch him. In that instant, an ache immediately started in Matt's chest; the same familiar twinge that arose every time he composed a new song. An ache filled with excitement, impatience, yearning almost, yet laced with a powerful innate contentment. The feeling always drove him to scribble lyrics and to jot hundreds of little black notes onto musical stanzas, which somehow captured, yet released, his feelings.

Matt took his seat, wondering how one glance at a person could so completely unsettle him. He glanced at her again. She was talking with Suzanne Post and admiring her jewelry. As he studied the new girl's angular face, lyrics flashed into his mind. He listened to his quickening heart rate, hearing a simultaneous beat, like a pencil rapping on wood. He started lightly drumming his fingers on his desk in time to the internal rhythms as he absently watched the morning breeze carry waves of amber and scarlet oak leaves to the grassy lawn.

Matt's reverie was interrupted as he became aware of the new girl's response to Mr. O'Hanlon's roll call. *Ah! Alexandra*, he thought.

He stared out the window as his fingers continued absently keyboarding with words flowing in tempo. Matt barely heard his name called, but managed a response, even though his senses were brimming with melody and poetry. *Alexandra...*

What's in your look, that sets the music flowing?
What's in your pose, that tells me you're worth knowing?
What's in your mind, that says it's worth exploring?
What's in your heart, that brings me thoughts adoring...

As "adoring" swam astonishingly inside his head, Matt felt a prickle at the back of his neck. The mental music stopped cold and he looked over, right into Alexandra's green eyes. She quickly averted her gaze, but one thought lingered with him. *Wondrous.* The word perfectly described how he felt as he observed her.

Who is *this chick? And why did music pop into my head as soon as I saw her?*

May 2003: Alex

D ressed for the morning's travel to Santa Barbara now, Alex sighed heavily as she packed her favorite flannel nightgown into her rolling suitcase and zipped it closed. *How different her life could have been if Matt had just believed in their love and been willing to accept fame.*

Matt certainly had the talent; nobody disputed that. He was going places…and she had initially worked hard to help him get there. But, she could never get him to move into the limelight. And, to this day, he'd never compromised his artistic nature for notoriety or profit. All the effort she'd put into their powerful love and friendship so long ago… Wasted. She frowned realizing he probably still hated her for "stealing" his music. Yet, he'd never given her the chance to explain.

The doorbell rang and she hurried barefoot to the front of the house and needlessly peeked out the window. What with all the gates, door codes and cameras on the premises, it was not likely to be anyone else besides her manager. A glimpse of inch-long, scarlet nails clutching a tray with tea and a pastry assured Alex it was Madeleine Beauchamp. *Bless Mad Bo for bringing breakfast!* She handled everything before Alex even thought of it.

Alex opened the door and immediately heard, "Grab it, quick!" Madeleine plopped a croissant in Alex's one hand and a tea latte in the other, and looked furtively toward the front gate. "I spied a paparazzo already. And don't look at any tabloids. Today, you're about to kill yourself over an ex-boyfriend."

Balancing her breakfast, Alex pulled her assistant in the door. "What would I do without you, Mad Bo?"

"Probably never wake up in the morning with caffeine and go blind from constant light bulb flashes."

Alex laughed. "So, is everything ready?"

"Here's a map to the Four Seasons hotel for tonight and your door cardkey. Car's ready in the garage. Everything's hidden in there for your 'getaway,' except your clothes. You packed?"

"Done," Alex said, impetuously hugging the woman. "I can't thank you enough for helping me get some time alone."

Mad Bo acknowledged Alex with a smug smile and nod, and fluffed her platinum blonde hair. "Before you go... Real quick... I told the team we'd meet the day after tomorrow. So that's all set. Oh, and I got a call from *The Late Show*'s people yesterday. So, when you get back, we'll talk about if you want to perform on the show again, OK?"

"Sure. I also got a call this morning about some tennis benefit thing you'll need to check into." Alex sighed. "I'd better enjoy this tiny break in the action while I can, eh?"

Mad Bo nodded. "You'd better. And, you work on staying safe, darlin', especially since your new bodyguard doesn't start until Monday. Don't you dare take any chances! I don't want to regret helping you do this, now."

"You won't, Madeleine. I promise to be extra careful." Alex hugged her manager again.

Madeleine refluffed her hair. "OK. I'll just make like a tree... As soon as I get your bag." She swooped up the hall, rolled Alex's luggage back down and cracked open the front door. She pushed her sunglasses up and glanced both ways before stepping onto the porch. "Be watchful as you leave, sweetie. Just one flash could ruin...well, you know." Blowing her famous charge an air kiss, she pulled the door closed behind her.

Alex twirled herself all the way back to her bedroom, careful not to drop her breakfast. Two days to herself! What would it feel like to have no driver, no bodyguard and, hope of all hopes, no paparazzi? It had been so long, she couldn't wait to be alone again, just to have time to think and to figure out why she had everything, but was still so deeply unhappy.

Alex took a few bites of her roll, sipped her tea, and deposited the rest of her breakfast on the nightstand. As she picked up her shoes and sat down on her bed, an unbidden memory of more peaceful days filled her mind.

It was her most special day with Matt. She'd never felt more loved or happy before or since that day in his secret meadow. They'd sat on a secluded pad of verdant, feathery spring grass with Matt listening to her childhood stories. She remembered exactly how he looked leaning across a tree-stump picnic table, eyes smiling into hers. She imagined his long blonde hair lightly shifting in the breeze as sunlight filtered through the trees and illuminated his dreamy, hazel eyes.

Alex's mind swam in the memory of those eyes and slowly came back to focus on the shoes now in her lap. Stroking the soft, intricately woven black leather with one finger, she wished she could think of a way to encourage Matt to talk with her again. Maybe they could finally iron out their misunderstanding. *I want to be happy again. Happy like I was then.*

An idea started niggling at the edges of her mind. It was time she did something for herself and if it could also benefit Matt... Well, she just had to do it, didn't she?

❖❖❖

Alex basked in the solitude and the beautiful California sunset as she traveled along the Pacific Coast Highway. She felt wonderful. Her escape from town, miraculously, had gone unnoticed. And, her solitary day at her friends' beach had been bliss. She'd had time to play in the waves, rest, and actually think through an initial plan for righting her life, and hopefully Matt's, too.

Grateful at the moment for the opportunity to drive alone, which always freed her creativity, she expected to enjoy every last moment of this day. Right through one long soak in the tub at her hotel suite and a quiet night all to herself.

Her thoughts drifted to Matt again. They had been so right at first. She wondered how he could have let it all go with no explanation.

Thank goodness for Suzanne. Her best friend's sage guidance had helped Alex make it through everything for the past 25 years, starting the very first day they met.

September 1977: Alex

*A*s promised, Suzanne was waiting for Alex outside the door right after homeroom. "So, I take it you're in the choir?" Alex asked with a grateful smile at her new friend.

"Have to get my dose of singing every day," Suzanne said. "I know I'm not that great, but I've loved it since I could sing nursery rhymes. You, too?" she asked, cocking her ear to listen while cradling her books in one arm and reviewing her class schedule.

"Yeah, we have enough home movies featuring my little performances to keep me on *The Gong Show* for a year," Alex said with an exaggerated wince.

Suzanne smiled knowingly at her and turned a wink on Brett as he left their classroom. The Texan turned a shade of scarlet only redheads can truly manage.

Suzanne snickered and turned back to her new friend. "Hey, let's walk and talk. Where's your next class?"

Alex studied her schedule, "Ms. Bonsuela, Spanish, room 107."

"That's handy. I have Spanish in 105. Come on. I'm headed that way. I'll show you a shortcut."

As they walked along dodging students in the hallway, their chatting was interrupted several times as Suzanne raised two-fingered peace signs to friends. Suzanne showed Alex out of a side door and into a courtyard. At the far end, a half circle of pine trees backed a circular asphalt slab with three flagpoles. Alex noticed the Coeur d'Alene High School banner flew at half-mast along with the U.S. and Idaho flags.

Suzanne stopped and gazed up at the flagpole with an expression of real pain and said, "We'll never forget the King, will we?"

Alex shook her head slowly. *What a loss. Mutton chop sideburns and sequined pantsuits, even fame and fortune couldn't make the King of Rock and Roll happy.* She looked back at the lowered flag with a twinge of sadness for the loss of that great talent.

Suzanne bowed her head reverently to the flags before motioning for Alex to follow her. They ducked under the branches of several tall pine trees dotting the courtyard and entered through a door on the opposite side of the green space. The hallway they stepped into was obviously in the high school's "new wing." It was like walking into a different era, even the sound of it. The old wing creaked with footsteps on linoleum-covered wood stairs. Here, indoor/outdoor carpeting dulled scores of conversations reverberating off gray concrete.

Every classroom door opened to a wide, curved main hallway. Peering through as she passed, Alex saw each classroom was tiered with rows of individual desks facing the teacher's desk and a blackboard low in the front of the room.

As they walked past several of the open doorways, Suzanne continued to wave peace signs at friends and teachers. "Geez, do you know everybody, Suzanne?" Alex asked.

"Well, I *almost* do!" Suzanne laughed.

"Anyone else from homeroom in the choir?" Alex asked.

"Like Matt Roberts?"

Alex's heart skipped a beat. *How did this girl know she wanted to know about Matt Roberts?* She covered her amazement with, "The long-haired guy by the window, right?"

Suzanne sniffed and rolled her eyes. "I saw you staring at him."

"When I first saw him, I felt like I knew him from somewhere."

"Well, that's not likely. He pretty much keeps to himself. When he's not taking care of his younger brother and sister, he's usually at a piano. He's *so* talented." As she waved to another friend, she added off-handedly, "He could have the pick of any chick in this school…"

"How can he keep to himself with girls hanging on all over him?" Alex asked.

"I didn't say he actually dates any of them. You know how girls are attracted to a loner. It's just part of…"

As she continued her phrase, Alex spoke along with her. "…his mystique." They caught each other's gaze in surprise.

"Far out!" Suzanne said, her eyes twinkling in acknowledgement of their shared thought.

"Being mysterious is cool and all that, I guess. But how can anyone have a relationship with a guy who is only focused on himself?" Alex asked.

"Oh, that's not it. He just mostly concentrates on his music. I think a 'date' for him is usually a hike, a picnic on the beach, or sailing on the lake. It's weird though, he's only seen a couple of girls and never more than once or twice."

Alex had a quick vision of sitting under a white sail with Matt gazing at her under the boom and an odd feeling of peace washed through her.

"He's quite a hunk in his way. Not as hunky as the King, of course. Rest his soul," Suzanne said, putting one hand over her heart. "Matt just doesn't much care what other people think of him. Music is everything. In choir, he gives Director Nelson fits because he only wants to play the music the way *he* hears it, not necessarily the way she *wants* it played. She only puts up with it because he's so talented."

Alex shook her head. Suzanne obviously was an encyclopedia of information about Matt Roberts. A small uncomfortable feeling started in the pit of Alex's stomach. She lowered her voice. "Suzanne, how do you know all this…?"

The disdainful look on Suzanne's face was answer enough. She giggled. "It's just that… Well, one of my old friends used to be…is…obsessed with him. Believe me, I've heard a lot of details about Matt Roberts."

She stopped and pointed to Alex's classroom number. She looked at her watch. "Shoot, the bell's about to ring.

This proved true just as Suzanne ducked through the next doorway. Alex moved into her own classroom and immediately saw Brett's friendly grin. He wildly motioned to the seat in front of him. She made her way forward, smiling, even if her mind was elsewhere. *Matt Roberts, I'm gonna find out what makes you tick.*

At lunchtime, Alex stood in the cavernous, gray cement cafeteria, her eyes sweeping the crowd for a glimpse of Suzanne. She barely heard her new friend's call above the familiar din. Suzanne waved and smiled as she slipped into the lunch line.

"How was the rest of your morning?" Suzanne asked when Alex fell in line behind her.

"Pretty good. No headlines yet."

Suzanne gave her a puzzled look.

Alex flashed all her fingers next to her head. "Headline! Young Arizona singer lost in dark recesses of new Idaho high school."

Suzanne laughed. "Do you miss Arizona? I've never been in the desert. What's it like?"

"Mostly, it's hot. Has some really great sunsets, too." The girls moved down the lunch line.

"What do you do for fun there when it's so hot?"

Alex highlighted a few desert summer survival techniques as the girls moved along the lunch line to order. She chose cheese pizza and strawberry gelatin with chocolate milk, and handed over her 35 cents lunch money. Alex followed Suzanne to a long table near the window.

"Maybe over here I won't be interrupted by friends right away," Suzanne said.

Alex obliged gratefully, taking a spot with a good view of the room. As Suzanne started in on summer gossip, including her family trip to Disneyland, Alex's mind wandered and her eyes roved the lunchroom for a glimpse of Matt. She just couldn't shake that stroke of familiarity she'd experienced when she first saw him and it nagged her to understand what it meant.

She finally spotted Matt's handsome profile about half the lunchroom away. He faced a lanky, plain brunette whose eyes were riveted to every word his lips formed. Whenever he paused, she giggled and nodded her head energetically. *She looks like a loyal puppy. Could that be a girlfriend?* Alex sensed a new emptiness in her stomach that wasn't hunger.

Suzanne, noticing Alex's attentive gaze, nudged her new friend. "The continued ogling of Matt Roberts by Kathy Sampson. Is that disgusting or what?" Suzanne shook her head, sadly. "If she was going to abandon all her friends for a guy, she could have at least picked a guy who returned her sentiments."

Alex gave Suzanne a quizzical look, but her friend just shrugged and played with the remaining salad on her lunch tray. "She's the reason I know so much about Matt. She was *always* obsessed with him. Last year, she just dumped everyone – including her best friend – and started hanging out with Matt."

Alex leaned in toward her dark-haired friend, "Kathy was your best friend?"

Suzanne nodded. "We met in National Honor Society, but she dropped that, too. Not too bright, huh?"

Alex studied the couple, frowning at Kathy's infatuation with Matt, obvious even from this far away. He barely seemed to see her. "You said Matt doesn't like her?"

"Not in *that* way, Suzanne said, "She, Daniel Post and Matt have been friends since they started riding tricycles down their block."

"Daniel Post, the blonde jock in homeroom?" Alex asked, recalling his predatory pursed lips and raised eyebrow.

"Yeah, he's a story for another day," Suzanne winked at Alex. "They all still live in the same neighborhood. Kathy's literally the girl next door. She's really a good person, but..." An expression of sadness and regret crossed Suzanne's face.

Alex cocked her head.

"She lost her mom last year. It's like the passing flicked a switch in her," Suzanne explained, frowning deeply. "The whole focus of her world, after that, became Matt...and Daniel, of course. When she's not hanging on Matt, she's moaning to their best friend about her unrequited love."

"But why does Matt put up with any of that?" Alex asked.

"He owes her a lot. She makes herself available to help care for his younger brother and sister. And, they *always* need a baby-sitter. She won't even let the Roberts pay her. She does it for Matt, I guess."

Suzanne responded to Alex's questioning look. "His parents are movers and shakers in the design industry; barely ever home. Those kids have pretty much been raised by Matt."

"Really? Yowsers."

"He's up for it, I guess. But, personally, I don't understand what Kathy sees in him," Suzanne said.

Alex watched the couple for another moment, understanding *innately* what Kathy saw in him. "She's obviously totally in love. He just doesn't notice?"

"Oh, he notices alright," Suzanne said, smiling at a large group of giggling friends headed their way. "He's just not interested, so he treats her like a sister." As the crowd of girls reached them and she stood up, she turned to add, "A sister so dedicated she even signed up for a cooking internship at the culinary institute to help make healthy meals for him."

That's pretty whacked, Alex thought as she mostly ignored Suzanne's loud greeting of her friends, and stared intently at Matt and Kathy. Suddenly, she realized Kathy was glaring back at her. Alex dropped her eyes and feigned great interest in the current color of her mood ring until Suzanne nudged her. She rose to meet the new friends, absently wondering why she was reacting so strongly to a couple she'd never even officially met. Whatever it was, she smelled a strong bond between those two. And, it reeked of a closeness she really didn't like.

❖❖❖

Alex's jealous feelings had all but disappeared by fifth period. Going into Concert Choir was like coming home. It wasn't just the acoustically deadened sound of the room, dusty smell of chalkboards, or the rows of orange plastic chairs and black music stands on broad risers that made her feel comfortable. It was the familiarity of the musical energy that flowed there. Every music room she'd ever been in felt exactly the same: positive, quietly energized, home.

That first day, Director Nelson began the hour sitting at the piano surrounded by several new students including Alex. In the typical first-day process, all the new students sang scales to help determine their vocal range. Suzanne, of course, was already sitting in the soprano section. She waved a peace sign at Alex as the new alto took her place lower on the risers.

As Ms. Nelson positioned herself in the front of the room and completed the tryouts, Alex looked around the classroom. From her vantage point, she was disappointed to discover the keyboard was turned away from her at the other end of the risers. With her piano training, she always liked to see the accompanist's hands on the keyboard while she sang.

At that moment, Alex noticed the accompanist slipping onto the piano bench. His face became visible through the triangular space under the lifted lid of the grand piano. It was Matt Roberts. She wondered where he'd come from. *How could I have missed him?*

With a rap of a baton on the black music stand, the hubbub of conversation subsided and rehearsal began. Alex concentrated fully on the unfamiliar notes and words charted on the music before her. She glanced up only to follow the director's motions.

At a break in the alto line, habit made her try to see the piano keys. She looked up, right into the curious hazel eyes that had detonated her psyche earlier. An emotional burn of familiarity seared through her. Outwardly, she simply managed a half nod and a slight smile.

Matt acknowledged her with a raised eyebrow and a slow blink and moved his eyes on to the next row of singers. Alex noticed he missed a couple of notes. *Did that have anything to do with her? Doubtful.* Surely, he was distracted by his intense study of her fellow musicians. Recalling her own close examination of classmates in her homeroom earlier, she smiled slightly, perceiving a shared curiosity.

September 1977: Matt

*I*n the split second when his eyes met Alex's in Concert Choir, Matt's mind left the accompaniment and a beautiful melody with more sweet lyrics ebbed into his brain.

He'd just sat in the bleachers with all the other choir members, watching the tryouts and feeling more than just a little curiosity. Now, with one look into those intelligent green eyes, a ballad filled his head again. A ballad that had nothing to do with the familiar choir music he was playing right now. His heart thumped and his palms began sweating. *It's happening again!*

Matt scanned the musicians in the bleachers, relying partially on their voices to keep his place in the accompaniment. He knew this choral music so well, but he struggled to keep his attention on it as the new ballad in his mind crescendoed. Distracted, his fingers actually stumbled over the keys for a few bars. The choir kept singing, although a few of the students, including Suzanne and even Ms. Nelson, shot him surprised looks.

Concentrate! he thought. He forced himself to look at everyone in the room, except Alex. *I can't let anyone get under my skin like this.*

Minutes later, he thought his struggle ended with the merciful bell signaling the end of class. But, in the crush to get out of the music room and on to the last class of the day, she literally bumped into him.

September 1977: Alex

A lex felt the pink rise in her cheeks as she became pinned briefly against Matt's chest moving into the hallway. She tried to ignore it by teasing him. "How can you learn a new piece of music while you're so busy looking around the room?" Not the most perfect introduction she guessed, but it was a start.

"Actually, it isn't new music to me." He shrugged and gave her a small self-deprecating smile, which formed a small dimple just above one corner of his mouth. "I had to do *something* to occupy my time."

I could occupy your time. Alex couldn't stop the thought as she watched the dimple smooth away with his smile.

"Besides, watching the singers helps me feel the emotion of the music," Matt added, running a hand through his hair as they squeezed through a crowded doorway and into the cool September air.

"Well, whatever you do, it's obviously working. I can tell you've been playing a long time."

"I started lessons when I was three… Thanks."

"Three? Really?" She stopped and looked up at him. She hadn't expected him to be so tall. Gathering her wits, she added, presenting her right hand, "Oh, I'm Alexandra."

"I know," he said, firmly shaking her hand. "I'm Matt." With a sideways glance, he released her hand and turned down the sidewalk, raising his chin at her in farewell. "Catch ya tomorrow morning."

As the look in his tawny eyes lingered, Alex felt a strong spark of attraction ignite. *Uh-oh…I'm in trouble.*

May 2003: Alex

Driving along the scenic coastal highway, Alex continued to build on her new strategy. She started a mental checklist of things she'd have to do to get her plan moving. She'd somehow have to get her record producers' blessing to do a benefit concert, and that wasn't going to be simple. They'd have to undo some recording agreements she was supposed to fulfill this fall. The toughest thing, though, would be getting Matt on board to perform with her.

She'd actually have to make a proactive move to contact Kathy Post to ask for her help. That meant her husband Daniel Post would have to be involved, too. Alex screwed up her mouth at the thought of talking to that manipulator again.

Overall, this whole thing was going to be touchy. Alex just wasn't sure about Kathy now. As a teenager, Kathy had been extremely jealous of Alex. But, she had apologized for it way back when. Plus, Alex had heard through the grapevine that, at Daniel's side, Kathy had changed immeasurably. Hopefully, she'd changed enough to completely get over her girlhood infatuation. Kathy, after all, was integral to the plan. Matt's life-long childhood friend would be the most likely to influence him. And that just meant interaction with Daniel, too. Alex sighed, remembering the man's ego.

September 1977: Alex

*A*lex left Spanish class and headed to her locker, needing to pick up her books for third-period Sociology. She bumped through the crowded hall, stopped at door #77, and proceeded to dial the combination. Just as she removed the lock, a muscular arm reached in and opened the locker door for her.

Alex looked up into one of the most handsome faces she'd ever seen. Unfortunately, she quickly recognized it and took a step back.

"I thought we could use an official introduction," he said, offering his hand. "I'm Daniel Post."

"Yes, I know," she said, not really wanting to take his hand, but giving it a brief shake. "From homeroom."

"So, I stand out in the crowd, do I?" A seductive glint lit his eye.

Alex covered her irritation with a half smile and a sideways glance and went about her business.

"So, why don't you let me carry your books to your next class?" Daniel asked, grabbing the volumes Alex had just pulled from her locker shelf.

"No, that's OK. I can manage." She tried to take the books back, but he quickly pulled them under his arm and started walking backwards down the hall. "I've got 'em for you. Come on. Chivalry's not dead yet, you know."

Alex had no choice but to follow. She slammed the locker shut, forced the lock closed and asked, "So, don't you want to know where my next class is?"

As she walked up beside him, Daniel turned and hooked her arm. "Nope. Got it covered."

"Really? And how do you know my schedule?"

He grinned broadly. "That's for me to know and you to find out. So, anyway, you already going steady with someone?"

After considering her response for a few moments, Alex suddenly smiled and put on her most wistful voice. "Well, at my old high school, I was going with a real hunk. Tall. Dark. Muscular. All the girls were crazy about him."

She glanced over and watched Daniel mentally checkmark his competitor's characteristics.

"Cristo was the star *every* sport season: football in the fall, basketball in the winter, baseball in the spring," she continued.

"Could he be my twin?" Daniel asked, sidling up against her.

Alex ignored his provocative smile and moved away. "Somehow, Cristo even managed to letter in track, too."

Alex saw Daniel's surprise as he turned to search her face. Recovering, he said enthusiastically, "At the same time as baseball?"

She continued. "And Cristo always made the honor roll."

He nodded knowingly. "Gotta admire jocks who always make the Principal's List."

Watching him from the corner of her eye, Alex added nostalgically, "Cristo is simply perfect. I don't know how I'll ever find anyone to match up." Alex stopped in front of her Sociology classroom door, cocked her head and gave Daniel an innocent, little smile. "Cristo was always kind to small animals and children. NASA even asked him to fly on the next mission to the moon."

With a manufactured sigh, she grabbed her books from him and pulled the classroom door closed behind her. The last image she saw was Daniel's stunned and slightly perturbed expression framed in the door's small window.

❖❖❖

Suzanne got a good laugh about it when Alex recounted the story as they walked to choir that afternoon.

"Gal, you harshed his mellow!" Suzanne said. "Daniel's pretty smart, especially for a jock, and a real smooth talker. Not many girls can leave *him* speechless."

"Ugh! His 'I'm so perfect' attitude just turned me off. Leaving him standing there with nothing to say was more delicious than a double-dip chocolate chip ice cream cone." Alex licked her lips.

"The only thing more delicious for me would be to find out the results of last week's Viking Swing Choir try-outs," Suzanne said as she pulled Alex toward the music corridor. "They're supposed to be posted today."

"Far out!" Suzanne said as they approached a small crowd gathered around the choir room doors. Heads bobbed up and down and bodies jostled as the students worked their way to the front where they could see the papers taped to the door. While a couple of students walked away with lowered eyes, Alex heard a girl near the front squeal. The girl's brunette head topped the crowd as she jumped up and down in excitement and cried out, "You made it, Matt!"

Alex heard Suzanne's small snort and a barely audible, "Like that's a surprise."

The crowd drew back slightly so as not to get jumped on, and Alex saw the brunette was Kathy Sampson, clutching Matt's hand and looking into his face. Alex felt a little chill ripple through her. But it trickled into nothingness when she saw Matt gently but firmly remove Kathy's hand from his.

Kathy self-consciously swept her brown eyes across the crowd and her plain face reddened. She quickly ducked through the group. Matt followed calmly, a few paces back, shaking his head. Recognizing Alex as he brushed past, he rolled his eyes.

"Some chicks…" he said under his breath, and Alex's heart leaped.

Suzanne had already discovered her name on the list and Alex approached to find hers, too. She took an extra few seconds to check for Matt's, just to be sure. When she turned away from the posting, Suzanne gave her a smile and a wink.

May 2003: Alex

O h, how many times Alex had been thankful for Suzanne in her life. Surely, her friend would help support her as she worked to return Matt, and some meaning, to her life.

As Alex neared Santa Barbara on the coastal highway, her plan began to gel. Action items raced through her mind at the same tempo as the patches of vibrant succulents rushing past her window in a brilliant blur. The shade of twilight magnified their colors and demanded her attention as she drove along the cliff-top highway.

Such beauty. The only thing more beautiful to her would be looking in Matt's eyes and seeing love again. She imagined what it would be like to meet him face-to-face and an image came to her from the last occasion they'd met. His expression filled with pain, hurt and anger. *What if I can't convince him I've been honest with him all along? What if my showing up in his life again, renews the pain and hurt? Is my plan a waste of time, a grand mistake?* Alex suddenly felt as if she needed some fresh air.

Cracking her window to breathe in the salt sea air, she caught another glimpse of the sunset beyond the azure waves below. *Déjà vu.* She'd felt the rhythms of this two-lane road before, in the twilight, and at exactly this stretch of road. A funny feeling started in the pit of her stomach and last night's dream flashed into her consciousness.

It's only a coincidence. That stupid dream is only in my imagination. And, besides, it's done now. I felt that this morning. Done and gone!

Still, needing a distraction to help her shake the uneasy feelings, Alex turned on the car radio. The station, tuned into one of her favorite alternative-format stations in LA, was tuned here to a California oldies station. "Misty Mountain Hop" blared over the noise of whooshing air streaming through her cracked window.

As she'd realized this morning, only twice had the Led Zeppelin hit played while she drove along the cliffs. In the very first dream and last night. Her heart immediately began pounding.

Warily, she looked in her rear-view mirror. She was unnerved to see a small red sports car gaining on her. *This cannot be happening.* But, looking ahead, she spotted a white sedan swerving almost off the road on the curve immediately ahead.

Alex didn't have time to think. The cars were already on her. There was nothing she could do. She closed her eyes and felt the oncoming car graze her bumper. She was jerked forward in her seat and her stomach lurched as the centrifugal force pulled at her body. Swept into the soft sand on the inside shoulder, her car spun slowly halfway around and stopped.

Alex pushed unkempt hair out of the way and opened her eyes just in time to witness the head-on impact of the two other cars. The inertia carried them both off the cliff, angled nose-to-nose. In a close reenactment of last night's dream, they seemed to hover momentarily against the sunset. A motion picture action-still a photographer could only dream of capturing. Then they fell.

She heard the horrible crash as they struck the hillside below and the inevitable splashing crunch into the ocean. Stunned, Alex sat along the roadside for several moments trying to make sense of what had just happened. *What does this mean?*

Suddenly, she realized there were people, or bodies, down there in those cars. With uncontrollably shaking hands, she was just able to turn off her car and dig in her purse for her cell phone. She didn't want to see what was down there at the bottom of the cliff. She knew the sight would haunt her, her entire life. But, she also realized she could not be the one to call 911 directly. Should it become know she was a witness or, even worse, nearly killed, the media hoopla could turn wicked. Better to see the crash, give Mad Bo as accurate an explanation as possible and let *her* call it in anonymously. That would provide another layer of safety for Alex, but it would never work unless she got the heck out of here before another car came along. Fumbling with the door latch, cell phone to her ear, she lurched from the car and crossed the street to peer over the cliff.

❖❖❖

Alex successfully snuck away without being seen near the crash site. She arrived at the beachfront Santa Barbara Four Seasons, found an unobtrusive parking spot and, using her cardkey to enter a side door, hurried unnoticed to her hotel suite. She closed the door and leaned hard against it, dropping her luggage, sunglasses and scarf on the floor. All she could think about was getting into that hot bath to soak away her frenetic thoughts. A shiver chilled her spine considering the accident she'd so nearly avoided, not to mention the potentially disastrous media circus.

A half-hour of soaking and stress-reduction exercises did the trick and Alex felt more relaxed. Now, with her emotions under control, she could think through the evening's horrific events. Wrapping her robe around her, she collapsed on the bed.

Breathing deeply, she relived the wreck and its parallel dream, all the way through. Her recurring dream had prepared her for the event, but Alex realized dreaming about an extraordinary car wreck and living through it were absolutely two different animals. *The dream told me what was going to happen, and I've been ignoring it for more than 25 years. Just like all the other intuitions and dreams Suzanne kept telling me actually meant something.*

She could not refute it now. This one had meant something. Something she had stubbornly ignored. It stirred a memory of another dream from long ago.

October 1977: Alex

*I*n the light of the street lamps, Alex was walking up a snowy hill with Matt's arm tucked around her waist. Breathing clouds of crisp coldness and displacing swirls of thick snowflakes as they walked, they listened to the deadened quiet of the snowy evening. Only the crunch of snow under their boots disturbed the silence.

They turned off the main street up an ever-narrowing lane. Alex looked up and saw a lone, rustic cabin with unusual windows, almost hidden in the pines. She somehow knew the small, rectangular, wooden structure would protect them if they could just reach the sunlight on its broad wooden porch. They headed toward the quiet haven, climbing steadily along the snowy path. The trickling of a creek grew louder as they approached the structure and she could see it flowed underneath the deck.

Her skin felt cold, but Alex felt an internal warmth flooding her body. She looked up and found Matt's eyes.

Alex shuddered and was immediately alert although, for a moment, she had difficulty convincing herself that the familiar Keep On Truckin' and Cat Stevens' "Teaser and the Firecat" posters above her bed were truly tangible. Awakening from such realism had altered her perceptions. She shivered again, realizing her bed covers had fallen to the floor.

What's with these dreams? They feel so real, but just don't make any sense! I barely know this guy, so why's he haunting my dreams?

At that moment, her mom called, "Alex! Get up! Breakfast is ready. We're all waiting for you!"

"OK, Mom!" Alex popped out of bed and ran to her closet, shouting over her shoulder, "Can't miss your Sunday-morning omelet! I'll be down in a sec'!"

Alex opened the pink "Sweet 16" music box on her dresser and, for a few seconds, watched its ballerina twirling to her tinkling music. She turned with a pleased smile and pulled on some sweats, ignored her hair and ran downstairs.

Her Cocker Spaniel Amber sat begging by the table. The dog looked up at Alex with wishful, hungry eyes and wagged her tail. Alex rubbed the top of the dog's furry head and sat down at the table where her mom's special ham and extra-cheesy omelet awaited. "Sorry, girl," she said to her furry friend. "This food's not good for you."

"Nice hair, Alex," her younger brother, Jake, said from across the table. "You see a ghost this morning that scared it to attention?"

"Nope. Just took one look at you," Alex retorted.

"You should talk, Jake," their dad said, putting down the slice of toast he was about to bite. "I'm surprised your mom didn't turn you upside down and use you for a broom this morning."

"Hey, I got my sense of style from you, Dad," Jake said, pointing to the ever-present cowlick at the crown of his dad's head.

They all laughed.

"Alright, you all, enough banter for breakfast," Mrs. Lauren said, taking a seat at the table. "So, what's on the agenda for today? Dad and I are going to be here all day putting up storm windows. Can you help us?"

"I promised the guys I'd meet them at NIC to play basketball at one o'clock," Jake said. He received The Look from his mom and regretfully added, "But, I can help this morning."

"I'll help this morning, too, Mom. But, remember I told you I was meeting Suzanne at Tubbs Hill for a hike around 1:30?"

"That works out. Alex, you can drop Jake off at the community college on your way, right?"

"You got it."

❖❖❖

After dropping her brother at North Idaho College, Alex buzzed along the long curve of dreary Coeur d'Alene Lake to the City Parking Lot. She saw Suzanne's sturdy form at the trailhead near the boat docks, so she parked, pulled on her sweatshirt and gathered her hiking things. Walking toward her sensible friend, Alex's mind was abuzz with her dream. She could barely wait to hear Suzanne's take on it.

They shared a quick hug and Suzanne started fuming immediately about a disagreement she'd had that morning with her mother. As Suzanne spouted, she stuffed her backpack with water and snacks, sunscreen, bug spray, a compass and a dozen other small articles you might need on a hike, even if it was only an hour long.

Alex, still preoccupied with her dream, was only half listening. After what seemed an eternity, Suzanne finished her rant, zipped in all her items, and straightened all the straps and buckles. She slung her backpack over her shoulders and smiled at her friend. "So, how's your morning?" she asked.

"I have to tell you about this dream I had," Alex told her friend as they headed toward the trailhead. She described the images of beautiful snow, the cabin haven with its unusual windows, and the creek trickling under its deck. Seeing the scenes as vividly as she had in her dream, she barely registered the steady crunch of rocks under their boots and their growing breathlessness as they wound their way up the sloping dirt path. Her clear mental images made it easy to share the powerful impact of the dream with her friend. "When I woke up, it felt real, Suz. Like Matt and I had been together for years." Alex stopped her uphill trek and listened to the breeze swoosh through the pine needles high above.

Suzanne walked up beside her and stood silently. Alex could almost hear the gears in Suzanne's head working through all the dream details. Eventually, her friend said, "Maybe you're just projecting how you'd like it to be if you really *were* with him."

Alex looked up into the clouded gray sky above the evergreens and savored Matt's lingering presence in her mind. "Probably. She expelled a large sigh to help normalize her shallow, quick breaths. "It felt *so* neat to be near him."

They both took off their packs to find canteens. As Alex let the water refresh her cottony throat, a cold breeze carried a waft of pine scent down past her nose. Even though Alex's heart was preoccupied, her other senses could only marvel at this environment. Through a break in the trees, she could just catch a view of the deep blue lake, now far below them.

The speedboats down on the water sent triangular, whipped cream wakes rippling against the dark water. A brilliant red, blue and yellow-striped spinnaker, billowing in front of a crisp white sailboat, moved across their line of vision. In the distance, across the large bay, Alex could just make out the outlines of various cabins dotting the rocky shoreline. From this viewpoint, she and Suzanne weren't even near the hill's crest still a hundred vertical feet above them, yet Alex felt on top of the world.

"The cabin in my dream was up on the side of a hill like this, not down on the shore like those," Alex said, thoughtfully, pointing across the bay. "I wonder why I was dreaming about a cabin?"

Suzanne snickered. "Intuitively, you're all ready to set up housekeeping, it sounds like to me."

Alex turned a fake glare on her friend. "I have too many goals to want to settle down at age 17. Especially with someone I just met two weeks ago!"

"Hey, it's *your* dream! I'm just trying to help you figure it out," Suzanne said in mock anger, offering Alex a handful of chocolate-sweetened trail mix to munch on.

After a minute or so, savoring the crunch of the "gorp," their breathing slowed. Taking a last sip of water, they stowed their canteens, slung on their packs and started up the path again.

"What's your big goal, anyway?" Suzanne asked.

"Well, I know it's probably a long shot, but I want to be a singer. It's what I've wanted since I could first carry a tune, wear a costume and entertain anyone."

"I'm not surprised. And, I don't think it's such a long shot."

"Really?"

"Well, you certainly have the talent. Plus, if anyone can make it, I'll bet you can. You have the confidence to totally take control of your life. You know what you want and you go after it."

"Yeah, I guess," Alex smiled self-appreciatively. "So, what do you want to do, Suz?"

To start with, there's college. I have to get through so I can find my perfect ad agency job."

"You want to design ads?"

"Nope, write them. For TV."

"You mean like, that anti-stomach acid commercial with the Italian guy sitting on the bed saying he can't believe he ate…'" Alex started.

Suzanne continued, "…yeah, yeah. …the entire bowl of spaghetti." She laughed. "Something like that."

"Well, I can't believe I dreamed this whole thing about Matt," Alex said, brushing nonexistent dust off her pants with one hand.

Suzanne cocked her head and gazed thoughtfully at her friend. "I wish your dream had continued on… I bet I would have been able to give you a better interpretation if you'd dreamt more."

"Oh, Suzanne. It's just a dream. I'm sure my subconscious is just making stuff up to deal with how Matt's and my chemistries clicked. That's all."

With this thought, Alex noticed a green dragonfly buzzing lazily along the path. It hung close to her side for several long seconds. She even had time to motion at it with her head for Suzanne to see. Eventually, it buzzed off, disappearing into a wildflower-filled gully.

Suzanne shrugged. "Seriously, I'd say there's more to your dream than what you're accepting, Alex. Dreams that mean nothing flit out of your head as quickly as that dragonfly. If your mind's still crankin' on the reality of a dream seven hours later, you'd better start figuring out what it means to your life."

Alex stopped and turned to her friend. "Suzanne, you and I see eye-to-eye about a lot of things, but… Well, dreams just don't have any real meaning."

It was Suzanne's turn to stop short. She looked at Alex in amusement. Or was it amazement?

"So you poured out all this to me, expecting me to tell you it didn't mean *anything*?"

Alex absently picked at the strap on her backpack, thinking. Eventually she said, "It felt – feels – so real. But…dreams are only dreams. Just the subconscious at work. I don't believe messages are lurking out there in the universe just waiting for me to pick them up." She looked hopefully back up at Suzanne.

"Odd that we don't see eye-to-eye on that. I truly believe what *Desiderata* says, 'No doubt the universe is unfolding as it should.' My advice is to start paying attention to what that subconscious of yours is trying to tell you."

Alex cocked her head and gave a short laugh. "You're an awfully deep thinker for an aspiring advertising copywriter, Suz."

Suzanne lifted her hands above her head and in evangelical style said, "I'm out to write ads that will change the world, sister."

Alex laughed. "How about if I give you some ideas from my dreams? Since you think they're around to change my world."

"Well then, you'd better start dreaming about funny, memorable, '...eating the entire thing' one-liners," Suzanne said, "so I don't end up writing novels instead of ad copy."

May 2003: Alex

*A*lex's supportive memories of Suzanne contrasted sharply with the loneliness and fear overtaking her tonight in her California hotel bed. She was so distracted she hadn't even thought to turn on her iPod to help her relax. Music, her eternal emotional elixir.

Alex suddenly felt an urgent need to talk with her sensible best friend. Suzanne could help her deal with the aftermath of her own dream portending a fatal car wreck better than any playlist. So, instead of reaching for her iPod, Alex rolled across the hotel bed and dialed Sedona, Arizona.

"Suz, you're there!" Her tone came across with even more relief than she'd anticipated.

"Alex? Suzanne answered. "What's the matter?"

Alex took a deep breath. This was probably going to sound unreal, even to her ardent New Age friend. "Suz, you know that car wreck nightmare I've always had?" She paused. "Well, this is really quite weird, but…"

Suzanne gulped air. "It happened? I knew it! Oh, my heavens…are you alright?"

Alex wasn't surprised Suzanne immediately understood the situation. Alex had always been so grateful for her friend's inexplicable mental link.

"I'm fine," Alex answered. Her throat constricted and her eyes stung with tears.

"You're not lying in a hospital bed somewhere, are you?! Do I need to come to LA?"

"No, I'm just a little unnerved it actually happened, that's all," Alex said, as a tear escaped and glided down her cheek. "Oh, and you can't tell *anyone* but I'm actually in Santa Barbara on a solitary retreat for a couple of days." She whispered and looked around the room as if someone might discover her there.

"You're always safe with me, girl. Now, take a couple of deep breaths, Lex," Suzanne said in calm support. "Take a minute to center yourself and tell me exactly what happened."

Alex took several calming breaths. Once she had regained control, she told Suzanne about the events of the last 24 hours.

"But that's exactly like your dream," Suzanne said, dazed.

"Yeah, well, I'm trying to figure *that* out. I was just so freaked out, I had to pull the car off Highway 1 at least three times to wipe my eyes and do my stress-reduction exercises so I could drive."

"Oh, geez, Alex. Are you OK? You sure you don't need me to fly over there tonight?"

"No, no. I just feel weird and need to talk with you." Alex suddenly realized she was calling past Suzanne's usual bedtime. "Oh, man, did I wake you and Brett up?" she asked.

"Brett's at a meeting tonight and I'm up working on questions to ask my spiritualist tomorrow. It wouldn't matter anyway; this is important, Lex." Suzanne made a little click with her tongue.

Alex answered slowly, "I have to admit it does seem you've been right about my dreams after all." Alex pressed one shaking hand against her forehead and added mostly to herself, "As weird as that is."

"So what are you going to do?" Suzanne asked.

Alex's legs suddenly began to tremble and she could no longer hold the phone steadily against her ear. "Suzanne, hold on a minute. I've got do my stress thing right now." She put the receiver down on the bed and closed her eyes. She visualized herself sprawled on the cool grass of a small woodsy meadow. She imagined the fluffy white clouds skirting by in an azure sky above the treetops. Mentally feeling a warm breeze on her skin and hearing the long chirping call of an osprey echoing across the nearby lake water, she immersed her being in the scene. She opened her mind to Love and let it fill her, seeing herself as calm and perfect with no outside influences.

She opened her eyes and picked up the telephone receiver again. "OK. Calm now."

"Wow, that only took like 90 seconds this time," Suzanne said.

"Yeah, well I've had lots of practice lately. Like three times already tonight." She inhaled deeply. A leftover tremble shuddered through her hand, but she pressed it to the bed, picturing it reflecting Love-filled sunlight. "OK, where were we..."

"I was asking what you're going to do now."

"Oh yes. Well, just move ahead with my life and plans, I guess."

"There's the whole cabin dream to consider now, you know."

Alex's mind filled with the image of the safe, snowy cabin she'd been trying to reach for years in her other recurring dream. The dream flickered through her mind like a fast-frame video, but she stopped it.

"I can't think about that right now or my brain will explode. My focus has to be implementing a new life plan I've been scheming. Something based in reality."

"A new life plan... One that might happen to include Matt Roberts?" Suzanne asked, knowingly.

Alex fell silent. Of course Suzanne would know that Matt was the focus of her plan.

Suzanne laughed at Alex's hesitation. "I was wondering when you'd get back around to needing Matt more than your fans. Think more about your cabin dream, Alex. I'm sure you'll realize that dream has more to do with your 'realistic' plan than you think it does."

"Thinking that *that* dream could come true, too, is freaking me out right now."

"At least that dream ends on a positive note."

Alex had thought that about the car dream, too...initially. "For now," she said.

Both women let a friendly silence hang between them over the phone line. Eventually, Suzanne ventured, "I think you're doing pretty well, considering. Still, girlfriend, you'd better get to bed."

"Yeah," Alex sighed. "Suz, thank you for being such a good friend. I don't know how I'd survive without you."

After she'd hung up the phone, Alex lay down in the darkness of her bedroom and dialed up a calming playlist on her iPod. Ear buds in place, she exorcised her remaining emotions from the car wreck and its correlative dream with beautiful ballads. On the emotional flow of the music, a stream of tears trickled down her temples soaking her hair, as early reminiscences flooded her mind.

October 1977: Alex

*B*y the end of her first month at Coeur d'Alene High, Alex felt quite comfortable in her new school. She had fallen into the rhythm of the days and especially loved starting each morning with the energy of Viking Swing Choir practices. Mrs. Nelson had chosen her as a member of this group and also to sing "I Don't Know How To Love Him" as a soloist in their upcoming Fall Concert. Alex loved the *Jesus Christ Superstar* movie soundtrack and was delighted to sing a song from it, But, mostly, she was thrilled Matt had agreed to accompany her on the piano. It gave her a legitimate excuse to spend time with him in the coming weeks.

For their first rehearsal, they agreed to meet after lunch in Music Room 19. As Alex walked down the barren, fluorescent-lit hallway dotted with numbered grey doors, she heard piano music growing louder and her heart stuttered. *Definitely Matt's touch.* Just outside #19, she stopped to peer through its windowpane.

The plain white room closed around an upright spinet piano, two chairs and a chalkboard, but Matt's music spilled from the sterile room with life and energy. Alex watched Matt at the keyboard. He held his head to one side with closed eyes, caressing the powerful tune from the keys.

"I Don't Know How To Love Him" was one of Alex's favorites, but with Matt's touch it resonated somewhere sweeter, deeper. She lightly bit her lip and put her forehead against the door's small pane of cool glass. Alex let the music flow into her like a river filling the ocean. She closed her eyes and listened, feeling her heartbeat swell with the melody. Its crescendos and decrescendos ebbed and waned in her soul and she lost herself in its richness. As the last notes hung in the air, she lifted her chin and opened her eyes right into Matt's quizzical stare.

The bottom dropped out of her stomach. *Oh, yowsers, he must think I'm such a goon!* Alex thought, quickly opening the door and stepping inside the room.

"Hi, Matt," she said hurriedly, pretending to feel normal. "Wow! That sounded boss! I bet you came up with that arrangement yourself." With a nervous laugh, she added, "I hope I can do it justice."

He returned his music to the first page, resituated himself on the piano bench and looked up at her with those richly lashed eyes. Bright hazel caught her gaze again for a long second. *Does that quizzical sparkle mean he's amused, or could it possibly be admiration?*

Matt shook his head slowly and said simply, "You will."

Alex quickly shifted her gaze to one of the chairs, deposited her books, and pulled her curls over one shoulder. "Thanks so much for helping me out on this," she said. Approaching the piano, she willfully shook off her unease. "I know we only have a little time, so shall we get to it?"

For the first few run-throughs, Alex peered at the music over Matt's shoulder. Once she was more comfortable matching the words with the timing of his rhythms, she moved away from the music.

Envisioning the audience, she positioned herself behind and to the side of the spinet, about where she'd stand in the curve of the grand piano during their upcoming performance. What she hadn't considered was having such a clear, unnerving view of Matt. A close-up image of his face from her snowy dream filled her mind for a brief second, bringing an immediate weakness to her knees. She grasped her hands behind her back to hide the trembling that immediately set in.

With her nod, Matt began playing the introduction and Alex sang the first stanza.

> *"I don't know how to love him.*
> *What to do, how to move him."*

As the words left her mouth, their immediate meaning hit home. She kept singing, but in her mind she imagined reaching over to gently gather a handful of Matt's smooth, honey-colored hair. She'd start at the temple, smoothing the full length of it through her fingers across her palm, as the back of her hand skirted his cheekbone, neck and shoulder. Jittered by her own imaginings, she stumbled on the words.

"Oh, yowsers, I'm sorry," she stammered. "Let's start again."

Matt played the introduction again and she actually made it to the second stanza before her gaze fell on the curve of his lips as he simultaneously mouthed the lyrics. She realized she had just started singing the wrong verse.

Matt stopped playing. "You're trying too hard, Alex. Let the music flow through you."

If only you knew how music flows through me when you play it, Matt. And how much I just want to look into your eyes. She said, "I know. I know. I guess I'm just nervous."

"Nervous? In practice?" He raised an eyebrow and almost smirked at her. "Am *I* making you nervous?"

She thought she detected a glint of hope in his expression. "No, of course not," she lied, clenching her hands. "You know, new girl, new school. Everyone's a critic, you know. So, will I do OK? Measure up? Stuff like that."

He looked full into her face for a long moment and shook his head. "Seriously, do you love singing?"

"Of course. I want it to make me famous some day." Her face rapidly colored as she realized she'd actually said that out loud.

He smiled at her, ignoring her pink face. "Then sing for the joy of it. Hang that critic junk."

That simple truth hit a chord. "Is that what you do?"

In a low voice, Matt said, "My music is my own, nobody can take it from me, even if they hate it. I create it for me and only me." He spread his long fingers out wide along the ivory keys and a faraway look of peace moved across his face. He lowered his voice until it was almost inaudible, "It's an outlet, my security, a haven." The peaceful look abated and his eyes snapped back to her face.

An expression of surprise took over his face as if he'd just blurted something he'd never said to anyone before and he shook his head. "Anyway," he said, "you heard it here first. Music is individual. It's yours for the making." He winked and said sarcastically. "And, of course, *I* make better music than anyone, so *I* would know."

"Yeah, right." Alex snickered, but asked, "What makes you such a philosopher anyway?"

A shadow flitted across Matt's face, despite his tight-lipped smile. "Experience," he said, glancing at his watch.

Alex wondered just what kind of experience made a 17-year-old sound like he was 30, but said only, "One full run-through before we get on to class. OK?"

Late afternoon the following Saturday, Alex sat next to her mom in the passenger seat on the way to Matt's house for another practice. They turned on his oak-lined street, vivid with fall colors. Several large, white houses lined one side of the street. Autumn leaves blew across the road through a wrought-iron fence and onto a public beach.

Her mom blew a low whistle. "Wow! He lives on *this* street, Alex? Look at the view of the lake from here. Lucky ducks."

Alex gazed at the second-story cupolas on the house they were passing. "Yeah, they're definitely not hurtin'."

"Hmmm, should I worry? Mixed up rich families, you know."

Alex snapped her gaze back to her mom's face. "Mom, you've been watching too much TV. Mr. Roberts is an architect and sits on the City Council. Mrs. Roberts is an international interior designer and glass artist. You've seen her work downtown in the bank."

"Being rich and well-known doesn't make you automatically nice." Her mom clicked her tongue and furrowed her eyebrows.

"Don't worry, Mom. Matt isn't an ax murderer." Alex smirked.

Her mom relaxed her eyebrows and smiled from the corner of her eyes at Alex. "Hey, I'm a parent. I'm supposed to worry about stuff like this."

"Trust me. He's a great guy." Alex carefully jammed her purse into her backpack.

"But how do you *know*?"

"I just know, OK?"

"Oh, I see. It's your intuition. A gut feeling?"

"Mom! He's a straight A student and a talented musician, for goodness sake."

Her mom sighed, giving a quick nod of her head which made her short blonde curls bounce. "Well, most of your musician friends *are* great kids. And, I trust your judgment, Alex. I don't suppose it hurts that he's a *hunk*, either," she added with a wink.

Alex rolled her eyes as her mom turned the car into a drive labeled with the named "Roberts" in stained glass which hung from the arm of a wrought-iron driveway post.

"Here we are. I'll be back in about an hour and a half, OK, Alex?"

"Thanks. Oh, and, Mom, if I'm not here when you get back, just barge in and look for the pieces of my body hidden under the grand piano lid, K?" Alex slung on her backpack and ran up the sidewalk.

❖❖❖

Alex rang the doorbell thinking, *I've never seen a doorbell button set in beveled glass before*. She also admired the stained glass window gracing the Roberts' front door until she heard footsteps approaching from inside. She wiped her palms on her jeans and tried to act casual.

Matt opened the door with a broad grin. Her heart melted like chocolate under the warmth of the sun. She quickly looked away and stepped inside.

Matt lingered in the doorway an extra moment to wave to Alex's mom whose car still idled in the driveway.

"Oh, she just wanted to make sure someone was home," Alex said, justifying her mother's protective tarrying.

"Lucky you."

As Matt closed the door, a middle-school-aged girl and boy ran down the gracefully curving stairway. Both kids stopped short at the bottom of the steps and stared at Alex.

Matt walked over and put an arm around the strawberry blonde girl's shoulder. "Alex, this is my sister Rebecca." Rebecca's pretty face turned up to Matt's with a happy metallic grin. "'Becka' for short," he said.

"Just call her 'metal-mouth' like I do," the younger brother said, turning to run.

Before he could bolt, Matt caught him by the arm and pulled him in for a noogie. "This is Davey," he said to Alex. "You get used to him." Davey escaped Matt's grip and skipped down the hall, laughing.

After a quick roll of her eyes at her younger brother, Rebecca turned straight to Alex. "Hi. You're pretty. Are you Matt's girlfriend?"

Matt poked his sister. "Becka!"

Alex giggled nervously. Her face glowing red, she quickly said, "No, Becka, I'm here to practice a solo. Matt's accompanying me in the Swing Choir concert in a couple of weeks."

"Oh, cool! Can I listen to you practice?"

Before Alex could answer, Matt said, "You know the rules, little lady. Better get your homework done first. You'll be able to hear us from your room anyway."

"I kno-o-o-w," Becka sighed. "Oh well, it was worth a try," she said with a smile. "Nice to meet you, Alex," she added, turning to go back upstairs.

As she ascended, approaching footsteps and a female voice sounded from the top of the stairs. "Davey, come back up and finish your homework so we can start making a fort." It was Kathy Sampson. She nodded tersely to acknowledge Alex. *Obviously, Matt forewarned her I was coming. I wish he'd done the same for me.*

Matt turned to Alex. "Have you met Kathy Sampson? She helps me with my brother and sister in the afternoons so I have time to work on my music."

Alex's stomach did a small flip, her face still pink. "Oh, hi, Kathy. I've seen you at school." The situation with a high-school student helping a neighbor of the same age take care of his siblings struck Alex as odd. She managed a smile, although she wasn't sure how sincerely it came across.

Davey came running around the corner and bulleted up the stairs. "I was starving!" he said to Kathy, waving the apple in his hand. "I'll race you!" he said to Becka as he bolted past her.

They took off along the upstairs hall. Kathy and Matt smiled knowingly at one another. Matt shook his head. "You guys have fun," he said to Kathy.

"You have a good practice," she said, her eye contact clearly showing her comment included only Matt. She moved down the hall after the kids.

During the next uncomfortable seconds, knowing the color hadn't faded completely from her cheeks, Alex didn't know where to look.

Anywhere but Matt's face would be good. Her searching eyes fell upon the richly appointed, entirely white living room. Alex couldn't help taking in a quick breath.

The late afternoon light shafted through colorful stained glass in nearly every window. It created a kaleidoscopic of incandescent, geometric, modern art, and lit everything in the room.

Glad for the distraction, all Alex could manage was, "Whoa!"

"It's my mother's glass work."

"I heard she was a gnarly interior designer and I've seen the window she designed down at the bank. But I had no idea…"

"Yeah, well…" His eyes swept the room and he shrugged before turning back to her. "You wanna get started?" he asked beginning to walk down a short, wide hallway. "The music library is back here."

"Sure." Sneaking backward glimpses over her shoulder as she followed Matt down the hall, she heard the phone ring. As they moved into the bright music library at the back of the house, Matt made some comment about Kathy answering it, but his words hardly registered. Alex stopped dead and stared around her.

She couldn't believe this expansive room actually existed in someone's home. It belonged in a museum or public hall, for sure. A sleek black grand piano gleamed in the bay window. No ordinary bay window either. Pane after pane of beveled glass stacked two stories high, refracting glorious light everywhere. Alex mentally calculated the hundreds of yards of lace it took to create the delicate draperies cascading from the filigreed curtain rods two stories above her.

The view through the wall of windows framed a section of the Roberts' backyard. Beyond a spacious wooden deck sloped an autumn lawn speckled with brilliant red, brown and yellow oak leaves shifting in the breeze. The lawn was outlined by stately, lush evergreens, contrasting sharply with the crisp, dark outlines of oak branches reaching their nearly barren arms into the gray sky.

Floor-to-ceiling book shelves flanked the shimmering windows. Matching leather-bound book sets lined most of the built-in shelves. These served as a rich backdrop for several glass cases displayed among the books. Each case held a different orchestral instrument: french horn, flute, acoustic guitar, violin…something from every instrument family. Showcased in the center of each wall and highlighted with special track lighting were two, large, shimmering glass sculptures. Both were faces of women sculpted in reverse within a two-foot block of glass. The haunting faces, carved into the center of each block, seemed to follow you as you moved around the room.

Alex caught yet another awe-inspired breath. "This room should be in a movie," she said.

Matt looked up and around indifferently. "Yeah, I guess," he said.

Alex saw Matt's look of near disgust. *How could he not be awed by the home he lived in every day?* As she studied his face for a clue, his eyes locked onto hers and she glimpsed there a single moment of controlled anger.

It dawned on her why Kathy's being here seemed so odd. Matt's parents weren't here. She remembered Suzanne's comment about his parents seldom being home and thought about Matt encouraging Rebecca to follow the rules and finish her homework. *Kathy must be here every day after school.*

With a pure thought as crystalline as the glass art surrounding them, she realized this beauty was just a facade. All this luxury was a substitute for his parents' presence.

Matt must have read understanding in her face because he looked, searching, into her eyes. His need for love reverberated elementally in her. Maybe, if she could just pull him close enough to her, he could somehow share the family love and support she always received and nearly took for granted. Heart slamming against her ribs, Alex resisted the urge to pull him to her. Instead, she broke their gaze. *What is it about this guy? I can't be near him for more than five minutes without getting all...*

Alex wiggled her fingers and shook her hands, anything to help disperse her longing to physically connect with him. She purposefully plopped herself into a plush, wing-back chair set in the curve of the piano and busied herself digging through her backpack, looking for her sheet music. *Face it, Alexandra, you're just being swept away by this house and this hunk because they are both so incredibly gorgeous. You can't see into his soul, or heal his pain.* She pulled her music from her pack. "Well, you sure can tell your mom is a designer!" Alex said.

He ignored her comment, situating himself on the piano bench, and asked, "So, you ready to get started?"

She nodded.

After running through "I Don't Know How to Love Him" a few times, the powerful meaning of the lyrics receded into Alex's mind and the words began to flow more effortlessly with his accompaniment. As Alex sang, she concentrated on her pitch and style, but her eyes roamed that amazing room. Not only was it beautiful, but it was functional. The piano was mic'd and connected to a sound mixing board and stereo recording equipment. The recording center was strewn with audio tapes cleverly hidden behind a short handsome bookshelf.

What kind of parents would create this luxury to surround their children, but never remain home to enjoy it with them?

❖❖❖

They had practiced for about half an hour when the doorbell rang.

Matt stood up. "I'll get it." Matt pointed to the mirrored wet bar at the back of the room. "Want a pop or something? Help yourself."

After he left the room, Alex pulled two cola bottles from the mini fridge behind the bar. She was pouring the soda into the fanciest disposable plastic cups she'd ever seen when she heard a male voice in the hall and a subsequent giggle. Matt returned, followed directly by Daniel Post and Kathy Sampson.

"Alex, you know Daniel, right?" Matt asked.

Alex's spine stiffened, but she tried to put a friendly look on her face while she exchanged light greetings with her hopeful suitor.

"He and Kathy both live on my street and we usually play Frisbee over at Sanders Beach in the afternoons," Matt explained. "Dan's dropped by to see if we want to go throw some disk on the beach."

Kathy had a smile pasted on, but Alex could see a competitive spark flashing in her eyes. "You're almost done here, aren't you?" she tested Alex in a sweet voice.

Daniel gave Alex a look of suggestive expectation with a lift of the eyebrows. Alex bristled. *Always the jock.*

She managed to keep her voice level. "You know, Matt and I only have a few more practice times left before the concert, and we really should make use of the time I'm here, before my mom picks me up."

"Your mom's picking you up?" Daniel asked, almost smirking. "What happened to your Bug?"

"Nothing. My mom was headed this way anyway for an appointment, so she just dropped me off."

Kathy smirked and said with too much sugar, "Wasn't that nice of her." She took Matt's arm, "I wish my mom would chauffer me around town. Don't you wish yours would, Matt?"

Matt looked at Kathy impatiently and replied matter-of-factly, "You know my mother has better things to do."

Kathy pouted a sympathetic frown at him while Matt continued, "Alex is right. We do need to keep pluggin' away. Besides, the kids aren't done with their homework, are they Kathy?"

She shook her head.

"Sorry, guys, we can't," Matt said.

"Ten-four, good buddy," Daniel said, with his eyes still on Alex. He turned to Kathy. "Let's stay and listen for a while. Wanna?"

Before Alex could object, Matt interjected, "Hey, that's a great idea!" He led Kathy, still on his arm, to an overstuffed chair backed against the short recording-center wall. She was all smiles as Daniel walked past her to sit inside the recording center.

"OK, let's hear it," Daniel said with a gleaming grin at Alex.

Alex's muscles tensed and, leaving the two colas unsipped on the wet bar, walked slowly toward the piano. She wasn't very keen on performing in front of Kathy and Daniel, but Matt was looking at her expectantly with a pleasant and proud smile. "They're gonna love us," he said softly, winking and starting the opening bars of "I Don't Know How To Love Him."

Kathy was leaning forward, studying Matt with expectant joy. As Alex started singing her first line, Kathy sat back, crossed her arms and settled into a stubborn expression which said, "I hope you forget your lyrics."

Alex burned inside, but she wasn't going to let the green-eyed monster fluster her. She was going to give them a performance they'd remember! Centering her focus on her heightened emotional energy as her voice coach in Arizona had taught her, Alex closed her eyes and allowed herself to disappear in the music. She let the gorgeous, flowing melody move her and the aching longing of the lyrics pull her heartstrings and flow through her vocals. Her voice lilted through the room, wafting through the books and art and reverberating off the beveled-glass windows.

As the final chord hung in the air, Alex opened her eyes to three stunned faces. Matt's face glowed and he turned around for his friends' reactions.

"Unreal!" Daniel said simply, with a sincere look of admiration. Alex let one corner of her mouth lift in a smile.

Kathy immediately covered her unguarded reaction by jumping up and running over to hug Matt. "Oh, that was so beautiful!" she gushed. "Play something else for us!"

He laughed at her and began shuffling quickly through some handwritten scores.

Alex noticed Daniel still staring at her. "Not bad, Ms. Lauren. You ever considered a career as a singer?"

"Well, I might have thought about it once or twice," she said, laughing lightly.

"Think more about it," Daniel said, shifting his gaze to Matt with a calculating look. "Got something else to share with us?" he asked.

Matt pulled several crisp scoring sheets from the pile he'd been searching and placed them on the piano music stand. "Here's one I just finished. You guys can give me some feedback on it if Alex will give it a shot." He begged her with sparkling eyes.

Alex immediately stepped toward him, unable to resist those gorgeous hazels. His chemistry drew her to him like a flower to sunlight. Witnessing their exchange, Kathy immediately stiffened and glared at Alex. She returned to her chair with a grim expression.

Matt began to play, his own warm voice providing the melody. Alex leaned over him to more closely study his newly penciled score titled "Like the Moon Pulls The Tide." A warm herbal essence wafted up from his silky hair, making her feel slightly lightheaded.

As he neared the end of the first verse, she reached across him to turn the page. At the same time, Matt stopped for her reaction and, as he turned, his lips brushed her arm. A thrill ran through Alex, making her knees softly buckle and the music sheets to shift off the piano. She caught herself deftly, stooping quickly to grab the music fluttering to the floor.

"Beautiful song," she managed to whisper. She nodded her appreciation at Matt with a forced smile. She barely registered his lingering gaze as she worked to recover her poise.

Matt seemed to remember where he was suddenly and dropped his eyes to the score in her hands. Gently taking it from her, he placed it back on the piano. He cleared his throat. "You want to try singing it?" he asked softly, tinkling along the keys.

Alex took a deep breath. "Sure," she said. He instantly began the song's opening bars and, now familiar with the melody, she focused on the lyrics and sang.

Something in the way she moves through the universe...
She walks in the room. His soul submerses in a wave.
He's drawn by the way she sets her head; the sway of curls, falling.
Stolen from his normal space, he'll never leave her world.
She moves him forward, grace absorbed.
And back, into her eyes.

She draws him like the moon pulls the tide
Into the depths of the most beautiful creation
A place where music plays when flowers grow
Where love hangs like dew in the air
Where energy illumines darkness
And scents of joy fill warm breezes.

She loved the song's qualities: a beautiful, romantic ballad; a rich love song weaving a tale of destined lovers. As they reached the instrumental interlude, Alex wondered about his lyrics. They seemed so full of emotion, as if he truly was taken over by this woman the first time her saw her.

Just like I felt the first time I saw him. As this spark lit her mind, she glanced over at him. She realized Matt wasn't looking at his score. He was staring at her as she sang. Staring with such penetrating awe it startled her.

Alex's eyes snapped back to the lyrics and, as she performed the words, she searched for their underlying meaning. Her heart thrummed as she sang.

She may be young, but sends him to a creative place
Where he only dreamed he could go
The inspiration wells forth a bubbling brook of harmonies.
It fills his mind and completes his soul
Until he can no longer see reality, only the spirit of their souls
combined, forever entwined.

"Whoa, Matt!" she said with a quiver in her voice as the song ended. She quelled a strong urge to reach over and touch his cheek.

Daniel broke her out of her introspection. "You really *aced* that song, Alex. Do it again!"

"Yeah, I'd like to hear you sing the whole thing again, Alex," Matt said huskily. "You make my song sound like real music."

"Real music? Are you kidding? This is such an amazing song!"

Matt's eyes glistened and color rose in his face as he turned back to his music to explain how he intended the vocal inflection to fall during the chorus.

Kathy sat quietly watching them with an expression of smoldering anger. Alex took no small satisfaction in Kathy's jealous silence.

Behind the recording-center wall, Daniel pulled off his coat like he planned to stay for awhile. He moved some equipment around and dragged a microphone out beside her.

"Do we really need all that?" Alex asked, turning from Matt's instructions to watch Daniel's efforts quizzically.

"You want this done right, don't you?" Daniel asked Matt. "It's a primo song and it deserves the right amplification."

Matt just laughed and shrugged. "Whatever, Dan. Knock yourself out. Alex, just pretend you're in a huge music hall, singing to thousands of adoring fans."

Alex shook her head, but she thought it might actually be fun to be mic'd and really knock Kathy's socks off.

Daniel busily moved equipment around, messing with the volume controls and other buttons, while Alex received her last few instructions from Matt. They did a quick sound check to make sure the equipment was working, Daniel gave the sign that everything was set, and Matt started the accompaniment.

Alex found it easy to get caught up in Matt's flowing melody and she made every effort to do it justice. She felt the afternoon sun shining in on her and imagined its warmth melding with her tones. She sang the words Matt had written and imagined him crafting them specifically for her, line by line. That allowed her to put every ounce of controlled emotion she could into their meanings. Totally in the moment, Alex was reluctant to hear the last chord and see Matt's fingers stilled.

Daniel jumped up, whistling and applauding wildly. Kathy turned around and glared at him while Matt and Alex laughed at his over-enthuiastic response.

"Dan, get a grip!" Matt laughed.

Daniel stopped his antics and smiled. "That's a song the world should hear!"

Matt raised his eyebrows at him. "Even though you can actually understand the lyrics and there's no head-banging going on?"

"Yeah, Dan," Kathy piped in. "That doesn't seem to fit with your Black Sabbath collection."

"Hey, I can appreciate other kinds of music besides metal," he retorted, "especially when it's sung by someone as talented as Alex."

"I just sang it, Matt *wrote* it," Alex said, slightly embarrassed.

"Ah, he's too competitive to ever give me any credit," Matt smiled, shaking his head at his friend.

Daniel grinned back and shrugged. "Hey, I am who I am."

At that moment a glass clock behind the wet bar chimed the hour and they all turned to it.

Kathy gasped and stood up abruptly. "I better check on the kids." But, as soon as she turned, she saw them peering into the room from the hallway.

"Wow! Your voice is *boss*," Davey said, coming into the room.

"I bet you're going to be famous one day," Becka gushed.

Alex laughed. "No more than your brother. It's *his* song."

Kathy shot a perturbed look at the youngsters and glanced at the clock again. "Hey, Dan," Kathy asked, "weren't your parents expecting you for dinner about now?"

"Parents, schmarents," Daniel replied, messing with a few buttons and switches in the audio center, closing everything down. He put on his coat.

"It was great to hear your song, Matt," Kathy said, her eyes not budging from Matt's face.

"And to hear it so beautifully presented, Alex," Daniel added, swooping an exaggerated bow toward her.

Matt and Alex laughed and expressed their appreciation.

Daniel punched Matt on the arm. "Catch you on the flip side…for Frisbee tomorrow." He darted an I'd-like-to-catch-*you*-now look at Alex. "Come on, neighbor girl," he said, nudging Kathy with his elbow so she'd start bustling the kids back down the hall. "Let's let these two 'ar-tistes' do their thing."

He picked up the two colas on the wet bar as he went by. "You don't mind if we have these, do you, man?" he asked. Matt waved him on, shaking his head in mock irritation.

Along with Daniel's nonchalant manner, Alex wondered if there wasn't just a small glint of smugness in his eye as he left. Whatever that was all about, she didn't care. She fully intended to make the most of the rest of her time with Matt.

November 1977: Alex

*A*fter the Fall Concert, Alex parked her VW Bug, setting the parking brake against the steep slope of the hill next to the pizza parlor. Before opening the door to the crisp air, she laid her head back against the headrest and let the evening's performance slip through her mind once more.

It couldn't have gone more perfectly. She had worked through her nervous pre-concert jitters and succeeded in remembering every lyric during "I Don't Know How To Love Him." But the highlight came just after her bow, seeing the look in Matt's eyes as she turned to him with her arm extended, encouraging the audience to acknowledge his perfect piano accompaniment. Matt's eyes had literally glittered with admiration as he took his own bow. Only, he had inclined his bow toward her, rather than toward the audience.

Alex sighed. Leaving her quick reverie, she opened the car door to the chilly November night air.

Pappy's was a two-story, wooden restaurant built into the side of a hill just around the corner from downtown Coeur d'Alene. Alex shivered across the parking lot and opened the double doors on the upstairs level. She immediately felt warmed by a sea of red, yellow and orange shag carpet, not to mention the cheesy tang of pizza filling her nostrils. *Everything* looked like pizza at Pappy's, including the pepperoni-hued counters, dark mushroom-tinged paneling, and Mozzarella-shaded lighting fixtures hanging over each table.

Alex saw a row of her choir friends seated downstairs, reflected in the building's three-story, inward-slanting, plate-glass windows. Leaning over the railing, Alex caught Suzanne's eye and waved. Once Suzanne waved, arms sprouted like drab swaying poppies along the long picnic table and she was greeted with a chorus of hellos.

Alex descended the stairs, registering Queen's "Somebody to Love" playing on the jukebox, and that Matt was nowhere in sight.

"Alex, you were the most!" Brett drawled, grabbing her hand and pumping it in congratulations as soon as she reached the group. "I could have sworn it was the real Mary Magdalene crooning at me from the stage. Well, the real Yvonne Elliman's movie version anyway."

Alex laughed, but before she could comment, she was engulfed in a giant bear hug from Suzanne, accompanied by a loud, "Far out, girl!"

The continued praise from her other choir mates made Alex glow with relief and pride inside, but she felt her face go lobster red. To cover her embarrassment, she placed her hands behind her back, laid her cheek on one shoulder and dug her toe into the carpet. "Ah, shucks, guys. Thanks," she said.

Alex slid onto one of the picnic benches next to Suzanne, added a few dollars to the pizza fund piled on the table and easily joined into the lively post-concert evaluation. Between bites of pizza and laughing about backstage gossip and on-stage mishaps, Alex kept an eye peeled for Matt. Suzanne had warned her he didn't do large groups and parties much. But she couldn't believe he wasn't here somewhere.

At one point, Alex raised her cup to drink but only got drops from melted ice. She realized asking for a pitcher of cola would be impossible over the din of conversation, so she got up and walked to the other end of the table where the server had placed the pitchers. Just as Alex reached for a pitcher she spotted Matt.

He and Kathy were sitting at a table just visible around the corner. He held a piece of pizza in one hand while Kathy monopolized his other arm. She was talking excitedly with her face inches from his cheek. After one bite, Matt pulled his head back to smile and acknowledge her comment.

Disappointed, Alex started to turn away. *Obviously, this isn't a good time.* At that moment, Matt saw her. So did Kathy.

Matt looked at Alex half expectantly and she acknowledged him with a little half wave. She included Kathy with the rest of the wave. *How can he be so happy spending time with that girl? I wish I could crawl into that head and find out what he's thinking.*

Alex reached partway for the cola pitcher, wishing Matt was alone. Realizing she may not be able to catch him away from Kathy all evening, Alex felt a strong urge to retreat. Instead, she pulled her hand back from the pitcher, steeled her nerves and walked to them.

November 1977: Matt

*O*nce Matt realized Alex was approaching, his mind shut out everything else. The weight of Kathy leaning on his arm melted away. The jukebox music and babble of conversation faded. No taste. No smell. Just the presence of Alex, making each moment register in pristine clarity as she moved closer.

Just look at the way she walks, like she's out to conquer the world. He watched her blonde curls flow and bounce around her shoulders as if in slow motion. He absorbed how the line of her cheekbones met the corner of her arched lips and how her green eyes flashed. "These Eyes" filled his head. She'd told him once during practice that was one of her favorite songs by one of her favorite bands, The Guess Who.

As she came closer, a powerful image from her performance earlier that night flooded his thoughts. It wasn't the performance itself that had reached him so deeply. Sure, the rich tones of her warm voice always moved him. And, she definitely had rapport with the audience. Yet, it was something more than performance ability. It was what he had felt as she acknowledged him during the applause. Her quality of soul reached out, flicked on a switch inside him and flooded him with peace. He wondered if she affected everyone that way. Once again, the only word that perfectly described her came to mind. *Wondrous.*

Simply nodding acknowledgement to Kathy, Alex said, "Hey, Matt." She reached out to shake his hand. "Thanks for helping me get through tonight."

He gave her a dubious look. "Get through it? I'd say it was a pretty damn memorable perf…" he curbed his enthusiasm, glancing at Kathy, "um…concert."

Kathy obviously caught the near compliment, as she quickly pulled her arm from his and a flash of anger moved across her face.

Turning directly to Kathy, Alex asked her, "So, did you enjoy Matt's performance?"

Kathy stiffened and answered coyly, "Yes, it was...*memorable.*" At the last word, she shot a sideways glance at Matt. He ignored her.

Still looking at Alex, he said, "Ms. Nelson said she was pleased with everyone's performance. Why don't you sit down with us for a minute and we can compare notes?" He gestured to the bench across from him. As soon as he said it, he wondered what in the world had compelled him to. *There I go losing my composure around her again.*

"I have a better idea," Alex said. "The gang's just around the corner already discussing everything about tonight. Why don't you guys join us over there?"

Against his better judgment, still unable to resist Alex's spell, Matt stood, reached for their pizza and fixed Kathy with a questioning look.

While she picked up her drink, Kathy's attention moved to the "jocks" table at the end of the room. She nabbed her food and turned away abruptly, saying over her shoulder, "I'll come over and join you in a while. I want to go say hi to Dan."

As Matt and Alex moved toward the choir group, he snatched a glimpse of Kathy greeting the athletes. Kathy placed her hands on Daniel's shoulders and massaged them while she giggled at something the guys said in greeting. She directed a smug look back toward Alex, who abruptly turned away. Matt shook his head, deciding to ignore his old friend. After seeing Alex seated, he tucked his legs under the table next to her.

Brett bent low across the table with his arms outstretched, palms down, in a bow toward Matt. "You're the piano Messiah to Alex's Magdalene." Brett straightened up and with a huge grin, drawled, "You do play one outta sight keyboard, pal."

Alex grinned knowingly at Matt. He sniffed self-deprecatingly and looked toward the ceiling. "Forgive him, Father, for he knows not what he says," he said.

"And to what do we owe the honor of your presence at this lowly affair, oh, Lord of Lords?" Suzanne pushed her palms together and bowed her head in Matt's direction.

"Knock it off, Suzanne. I know you hardly ever see me at these post-performance events."

"*Hardly* ever...?" She batted her eyes at him.

Matt laughed. "OK, so it's a first. What're you gonna do, nail me to a cross for it?"

"Oh-h-h! Oh-h-h-h!" Brett groaned. "Enough of the *JC Superstar* theme! Enough already, ya'll."

"I say we dump the Messiah thing and just make Matt into a Superhero instead," Alex said. "How about SuperMatt, Musician of the Universe...erse...erse," she mimicked an echo, which faded quickly into a giggle.

The group laughed and Matt just shook his head. "Well, if we're talking key characters in the universe," he smiled impishly at Alex, "we'd have to make you Princess Alex Organa, wouldn't we?"

A wave of giggles passed along the table, as Matt continued, "I can see it now, 'Long ago, in a distant galaxy...' there lived a princess whose voice was so beautiful and soothing, no one could do anything evil around her. One warning beep from her trusty sidekick Suz-3PO," he nodded at Suzanne, "and the Princess starts her song. Within minutes, Brett the Emperor Palpitate has cancelled Death Star construction and called the Vader boys over to boogie the night away."

By the end of his delivery, the whole table was loudly laughing.

"Holy hero worship!" Brett exclaimed. "I don't wanna be Palpitate, I wanna be *Brettman*. Whenever bad singing occurs on the Earth, I see the Brett signal reflected in the clouds and jump in the Brettmobile to save the world from noise pollution!"

Brett moved down the row of choir members along the table, giving each an appropriate superhero name. Matt, amused, watched the proceedings. Brett was definitely on a roll. So while the redheaded Texan's drawl held everyone's rapt attention, Matt tried to study Alex without being too obvious. At one point, he met her gaze and gave her a friendly wink. Her return smile warmed his heart.

When Brett ran out of friendly superheroes at his own table, he began scouring the room for unsuspecting victims.

"Now, take Dan The Man over there. He's always trying to lure girls into his web. He's sly." Brett started singing, "Slyer Man, Slyer Man. Tells whatever quick lie he can..." As he continued, the rest of the group joined in. Soon they were singing the knock-off TV theme quite loudly over and over.

Bemused or perturbed faces throughout the restaurant turned to look at the group. Matt almost joined in, but stopped himself when he noticed Dan's glare and Kathy's disdainful look from across the room. When the singers wore out, Matt saw Kathy lean back over her table and make a comment causing the athletes to laugh loudly as they looked across the room.

"Ah, now there's a tough one," Brett drawled. "What about Kathy Sampson. Hmmm…"

"How about Poison Ivy?" suggested Suzanne. Turning to Matt, she teased, "She's always trying to poison your mind with her constant attention, isn't she, Matt."

Matt's relaxed smile faltered, but he countered, "She's actually more of a mother figure, rather than a superhero."

Brett let out a huge guffaw. "Your Mama!"

Matt smiled slightly, but his eyes were serious. "Kathy's always there for her friends with support and love."

Brett almost had time to gape at Matt's comment before Suzanne pitched in, "He's right, Brett. Look, she's surrounded by all her little dorks right over there. Anyone of them would be glad to have her in their little cottage cooking and cleaning for them. See?" She started pointing one by one to the jocks. "Doofy. Dippy. Dweeby. Dullard…"

While the rest of the musicians rolled with laughter, Matt sported a closed-lip smile. He was thinking about Kathy. *They can think what they want about her, but she is sweet and smart, but naïve.* He gave a mental sigh…*also stupidly jealous.* He moved his gaze to Alex, who quickly looked away and shook her head at Brett and Suzanne. Those two were still bantering about additional names for the athletes.

Matt's attention stayed on Alex. *She's always so strong and in control. I'd have to be someone like Han Solo to deal with a woman like that every day.* Alex looked over at him. "You actually *are* a lot like a Princess. You could rule the entire world," he said.

Her eyes widened, but he didn't have time to say more. At that moment, Kathy walked up behind him.

His friend said curtly, "You know I've got to be home before 11:00, Matt, so Dan's offered me a ride. See you later." She turned to leave, but Matt stood up, caught her arm and threw a concerned look at Pappy's' giant wall clock. Just above its face, he also saw Daniel's handsome form on the stairs watching the little drama unfold with a patient smirk.

Matt turned back to Kathy. "I'm sorry, Kath. I lost track of the time. I'd be glad to take you home if you need to go now."

Her demeanor softened slightly, but he was sure she wasn't about to give in that easily. "No, go ahead and hang out with your friends. I'll just catch you later."

Matt watched her go impassively. Turning back to the table, he said quietly to Alex, "Good thing the charming prince showed up." He smiled ruefully and sat down again, and quietly sipped his drink while the music students' laughter and conversation continued around them.

When the lively talk had lulled into quiet one-on-one exchanges, Matt gave Alex a regretful look. "It is getting late and Brett is actually quiet. Must be time to go."

"I suppose. I've got an early morning tomorrow, anyway."

"May I walk you to your car?"

She nodded appreciatively.

Matt was acutely aware of Alex's nearness as they walked across the parking lot toward her Bug, and he fought a strong urge to reach down and warm her hand in his. He watched her breath hang in the brisk air as she shouted goodbye to Brett. Crazy Brett was waving madly, hanging out the passenger window of Suzanne's departing car. The ludicrous sight made them both laugh. Matt felt the little cold spot, always in his heart, warming slightly. It expanded the new, deep peace he'd felt earlier that night during Alex's performance.

As Alex unlocked her car door and turned to say goodbye, Matt put his hands on her shoulders. "Alex, I want you to know your performance tonight was very special…" He searched for just the right words, but all he could muster was, "It meant a lot to me. Thank you for letting me be part of it."

Alex looked up into his face. "No. *You're* the inspiration, Matt." She pulled one of his hands from her shoulder and lightly held it.

Matt covered her hand with his and looked questioningly at her.

Cocking her head to one side and giving him a friendly smile, Alex paused and added, "You just have star quality written all over your future, SuperMatt."

He laughed at her superhero reference.

"I know you'll be famous someday," she added.

He cringed internally at the thought, but gratitude filled his heart at her confidence in his talent. He looked down at her and squeezed her hand. "Thank you, *Princess*." Alex laughed and her fingers squeezed back in farewell.

As she climbed into her car, Matt fought the strong urge to pull her back out of the driver's seat onto her feet and kiss her. Instead, he simply turned to go.

"You fill up my senses…" John Denver's "Annie's Song" lyric slid easily into his head. He put his hands in his pockets and walked away quietly humming the country tune, halfway hoping she'd hear and recognize it.

May 2003: Alex

A lex turned her head on the unfamiliar pillow and a cold patch of wet from her tears broke her reverie. She dully realized "Annie's Song" was playing on her iPod and chills ran down her arms. *No wonder I was thinking about that time with Matt.*

She sniffed, set aside her music and got up to retrieve a tissue from the bathroom. On her way back to lie down, she grabbed the hotel's complimentary *Los Angeles Times* newspaper from the table, thinking it might be a good distraction to help her fall asleep. Settling down into the comforter and against her pillows, she shuffled through the paper. She set aside sections carrying all the horrific news she couldn't handle at the moment, until an article about music programs in the Northwest in the "Life & Leisure" section caught her eye.

The main photo showed a group of middle-school-aged kids on risers in a beautiful pine-paneled music room. They surrounded a handsome man smiling across a piano at the camera. Alex's heart leapt and her hands started trembling. She'd recognize those eyes anywhere.

She hadn't seen Matt in years except her mind's eye. A bit of gray streaked the ponytailed hair. He sported new creases around his mouth, which deepened his single dimple, but he looked essentially the same.

The article featured him and a number of children from his Coeur d'Musique Camp who had been selected to perform at the White House later in the year. It said he was currently in Santa Barbara drumming up interest in the school.

She lowered the paper slightly. Here he was, featured in a newspaper she never usually saw. And here she was in a hotel chosen by her assistant, seeing the article on this particular day. The same day she'd started plans to connect with him again. The same day he happened to be here…in the town of Santa Barbara. Where she was. *This cannot be coincidence.*

"What do I need to do, Matt?" she asked out loud to his photo. "Just tell me and I'll do it." She pulled the image closer and looked into those hazel eyes as if he was really here with her. Her eyes blurred, spilling tears, and the image before her morphed in her mind into the school photo that started it all.

November 1977: Alex

Alex always loved the day school portraits arrived and this late November Thursday was no exception. All day, students searched out their closest friends, eagerly signing the backs of their personal images with the usual witty prophecies or sappy declarations of friendship.

Alex stopped after choir to find a bench where she could privately jot down one last special message. Disappointingly, Matt hadn't been in choir that afternoon. *Drat! Of all days for him to be gone,* she thought, furrowing her brow.

As she took out her portrait and a pen, she saw Suzanne's picture smiling up at her through the transparent plastic of the zippered pencil bag. Alex smiled at the thought of her friend's message: "If I'm still around in 50 years, I'll still be your friend. And never forget, "The King Lives!" AFA (a friend always) – Suz."

They did have such similar ideas. She'd scribbled on the back of Suzanne's picture, "May we still be friends when we're old and gray! AFA – Alex."

Exactly what to write on her photo to Matt had been troubling Alex all day. It had to convey how much he meant to her, but in an indirect, not-too-serious way. The right idea simply popped into her head, inexplicably, moments ago while listening to the sopranos' melody line for "Penny Lane."

Alex penned it. "'These Eyes' will be watching you. I ♥…Guess Who. – Princess Alex Organa." She liked its double meaning. Would he catch how the heart symbol from the New York ad campaign related to him? Would he understand she was watching for any indications of his increased interest in her? It was cute and light enough, yet implied she really liked him. *Now, if I could just bump into him.*

Sighing as she neared her sixth-period classroom, Alex stopped short and her heart flipped. *Fab!* Matt appeared unexpectedly beside her. He didn't say anything, just widened his eyes at her expectantly. With hands on hips, she asked sarcastically, "And so where were you in choir, SuperMatt? Flying around saving the world?"

"No, *Princess Alex*," he said. "Nothing so heroic. I just had to take Becka to a dentist appointment."

Alex was amazed his parents would actually make him miss school to take his sister to an appointment. Her voice softened and she said lightly, "Well, that is pretty *super* of you."

Matt laughed. "All in a day's work, Your Royal Chickness."

"Not for most of us," Alex said, casting down her eyes so he wouldn't see the anger and pain she felt for him. Matt was silent, obviously struggling for a response to her sudden serious mood.

Alex mentally rummaged for the right words, for a transitional phrase that would allow her to give him her photo. Finally, just to end the uncomfortable silence, she said, "Well, I'd better beat feet to math class." She turned on her heel to walk into her classroom door, but Matt caught her arm tightly.

"What? No school picture for your favorite superhero today?" Alex saw a look of eager interest in his face.

"Oh!" the surprise blurted out before she could even think. Collecting her wits, she used her best sickeningly sweet Southern Belle imitation, "Why, SuperMatt, *dahling*. Of course you are the *only* one to whom I'm giving my photo this year." She cocked her head, curtsied, and gave him a wide, fake smile and handed him her inscribed picture.

He immediately shifted his armload of books to accept her offering. He gazed at her two-dimensional face, read her comment on the back and, with a glint in his eye, slid the picture into one of his books. "Thank you, Miss," he said in a formal tone accompanied by a deep bow. Straightening up with a serious expression mocking the sarcasm, he reached for Alex's hand. He turned it palm up and delicately laid his own wallet-sized face into it. His touch was surprisingly tender and Alex looked up questioningly. As their eyes met, her deep personal connection with him stirred again. In a split second the moment was gone and his eyes darted with mischief.

"It's a riddle for you," he said, smiling with a look of anticipation. Turning, he abruptly disappeared down the hall.

Alex looked down at his handsome paper face staring up from her hand and felt a rush of excitement. She actually now held something he had given her. She turned the picture over and saw the "riddle" scribbled in his raw script. It was a list of consonants strung in rows across the small space.

TFTEISYF
ITTSRIYE
ATMASWTGYG
TTDATEOTS...
...AIKOJWFTE
ALTTEOT, ML
TFTEISYF
YF, YF, YF.
– SuperMatt

The sixth-period bell rang. *Yowsers! I'll have to decipher this later.*

Within seconds of leaving the building after school, Alex came face to face with Daniel. "I need to talk with you, Alexandra," he said. "Just for minute.

Beaming at her playfully, he put two firm hands on either of her shoulders and pushed her back gently against the cool block wall of the building.

"What do you think you're doing?" she asked.

"I can't let you get away before I give you a school photo." Blocking her way, and with determination lining his face, Daniel pulled a picture from his shirt pocket and handed it to her.

The inscription read, "I would do anything for you. Take me up on it. *Forever* yours, Dan."

Alex stared at the small piece of paper in her now sweaty palm. This was the first time anyone had thrown a pass at her using his school photo. Speechless, she furrowed her eyebrows.

Daniel moved in closer until he was almost nose-to-nose with her. Although she didn't feel threatened, he was inside her personal space and her instinct was to back away. Unfortunately, she was trapped against the wall.

She stared angrily into his eyes. But what she saw there took her aback. A deep fire burned inside those azure blues. His sincere passion sent a trill down her spine. She knew she should be angry with him, but suddenly became more than aware of those handsome features and his sheer magnetism. Catching waves of emotion from him, an unbidden flame ignited deep inside her.

Obviously unaware of the effect he was having on her, and bent on making his point, Daniel said. "You know, Alex, I have goals for my life. I don't plan to be just a football player. I'm too smart to waste my time on sports alone. I'm going to be a lawyer some day."

"And this has *what* to do with me?"

"When I get my law degree, Alex, I expect to have lots of money and lots of power. I want someone talented, smart and beautiful to share it all with."

"So?"

He continued to stare at her until his meaning sunk in. "And you think that's me?" she asked, incredulous.

"You know it is. I've never met anyone like you."

Struggling to shake off the slow burn he'd started in her, Alex stared him down. "You mean, that *looks* like me?" she said.

He laughed. "Your looks aren't all of it, Alex. We're both strong people, we're in control of our lives. We're meant to make our mark on the world, to be together. I can offer you everything you want...help you become a star."

Alex stared at him, but she couldn't stop a flicker of hope kindling in her heart. "You barely know anything about me. How can you offer me *stardom*?"

"My family has connections, you know."

Alex pushed her hands against him until he let her by. No longer trapped, and more in control of her feelings, she turned to face him.

"Look, Daniel, it's solid of you to care enough to help me but, frankly, you're only 17. We both have a lot of things to experience and people to meet yet before we figure out who's right for us. Besides, you didn't even ask what *I* want."

Daniel pulled his lips tight against his teeth. "I know you have the hots for Matt," he said. "But our musical friend is a dreamer and a loner at heart. He'd never make you happy."

"You can't possibly know that," Alex exclaimed. "You don't even *know* me!"

"I know him."

Alex dropped her head and put one hand on her forehead. Suddenly a strong need to get out of the situation hit her. "Look, Daniel, this is crazy. We don't know one another and I can't believe we're even having this conversation. I've got to go... I need to take Suzanne home." She started to leave.

Daniel straightened up and grabbed her arm. He regarded her with a wry expression. "Mark my words, Alex. Some day, when Matt hasn't come through for you, you'll turn to me to help fulfill your dreams. I know it, just like I know smiley faces will never really go out of style. But, I'll be here for you when you're ready."

Alex just nodded and walked away, her mind swimming with confused emotions.

Alex did not mention the encounter with Daniel to Suzanne as she drove her friend home that afternoon. She needed time to sort out her feelings and thoughts before discussing it.

In the passenger seat, Suzanne was hunched over Matt's picture trying to figure out his encrypted message.

"Could it be a code?" Suzanne wondered.

"Don't you think that would be *too* difficult?"

"Well, maybe they're just words with all the vowels missing."

"No, I thought of that. In Math, when I was supposed to be listening to Mr. O'Land's equation explanations..." Alex giggled guiltily, "...I tried deciphering it that way. No luck."

They lapsed into silence. In a few minutes, as the car approached a stoplight, the girls' eyes suddenly fastened and they said in unison, "They're acronyms!"

They laughed. Alex wondered why she hadn't figured that out right away. "Spaz," she said, smacking herself on the forehead.

"But what secret message would he want to share with you, Alex?"

Alex wrinkled up her nose at her friend and said, "It's probably just some superhero slogan or something." But, even as she said it, somewhere deeper Alex realized his message offered more meaning. The letters were strangely familiar, but she couldn't quite place them.

They pulled up in front of Suzanne's house and she handed Matt's picture back to Alex. "Lex, if you figure it out, I'd better know about it as soon as I get back from my cousin's wedding. Deal?" she asked, climbing out of the car.

"Deal," Alex promised. "First moment I see you."

"Check ya later!" they said at the same time. Both were smiling as Alex put her Bug into gear and drove down the street.

In homeroom the next day Matt approached Alex.

"Have you figured out my little riddle yet?"

She shook her head.

"I guess 'A' only stands for 'Alex' and not 'admirable.'"

She recognized the hint, but didn't acknowledge it. "Don't worry, SuperMatt. When I have a chance to think about it a little, I'll let you know." She didn't let on his message had been the main focus of her last 24 hours, or that the desire to know his secret message was driving her crazy.

"Well, how 'bout a hint, Princess?" he asked.

Alex feigned disgust. "I don't need your clues, SuperMatt. I just haven't had a chance to think about it! Bug off, or I'll throw the ugly thing out!"

"You wish!" he said brusquely. But Alex saw a shadow move into his eyes. Was he disappointed that he may not be able to string her along in his game? Or was he really concerned that she didn't care enough to figure out his code? She desperately hoped it was the latter.

Saturday morning, Alex lay on her family-room floor, headphones couching her ears. She lay there listening only half-heartedly, with her mind drifting.

She keyed into the last few phrases of a Roberta Flack hit, singing along quietly. "The first time ever I saw your face, your face, your face... your..."

She stopped.

She said it slowly, "Your face. Y-F."

Song lyrics. Were they really song lyrics? *Yowsers! Had he written a love song on the back of his school picture to her? Was it possible?*

Alex ripped the headphones off and ran over to the piano bench. Up went the lid, out came the sheet music she'd played a billion times before. She quickly read through the lyrics. It had to be!

She ran upstairs into her room, grabbed Matt's school picture and sat on the bed comparing the first letters of each of the words.

She read silently. *The first time ever I saw your face...* Speaking aloud, she compared. "T-F-T-E-I-S-Y-F." Reading and comparing, she went on, tracking every letter.

She whispered the last phrase. *"'Your face.' Y-F.* Whoa!"

Alex sat on the edge of her bed, one hand limply holding Matt's picture, the other empty, its music fallen to the floor. She froze there for a moment of eternity, trying to quiet and organize her thoughts. *How could this be? Does he really feel this about me? If he does, what am I going to do?*

Alex spent the rest of that day worrying what she was going to say to Matt about his riddle. Every conversation she imagined made her stomach flip as she rehearsed and re-rehearsed possible scenarios in her bedroom mirror.

If only Suzanne hadn't gone to California for her cousin's wedding. She would have known just what I should say to him.

As it turned out, her words didn't matter.

Monday morning, as Alex walked expectantly toward homeroom, she saw Matt standing in the hall just behind the classroom door...with Kathy. He held both of Kathy's hands, and his forehead pressed against hers. Kathy was looking down at a smattering of teardrops spotting the linoleum.

Alex quietly slipped through the doorway and sank into her desk with an iron heart. She had just witnessed Matt's true feelings for

Kathy. She now knew his riddle to her was just another of his creative exercises, or something. She kept her eyes on her book until the starting bell rang so she wouldn't have to see Matt walk past her desk to his seat. Thank goodness he didn't stop and give her the usual morning greeting. He was certainly preoccupied, and perhaps slightly embarrassed with her now.

She pretended to be interested in Brett's chatter, yet her mind was deadened behind a forced smile. The entire class, she avoided looking across at Matt, afraid if their eyes met he would see her heavy disappointment. If she could just avoid him for a while longer, she would be able to get herself under control and discover something within her leadened mind to say to him. When the bell rang again, Alex fairly sprinted to the door and into the crowded hallway.

Somehow, she made it through the morning. By lunchtime, when she turned down the hall toward the cafeteria, her head had finally begun to clear. As she walked through the double doors, Matt almost ran into her. She could see he was startled to see her, but he quickly recovered and stopped. She felt his gaze following her as she continued on into the lunchroom. After her retreating form, he asked, "Hey, Alex. So, what did you think of my riddle?"

Alex's knee-jerk reaction was sarcasm. She stopped, turned to face him and, without thinking, said, "It's just what I would expect from you, SuperMatt…more Flack!"

She spun on her heel, barely catching his delayed chortle. She sighed in relief and continued on her way.

May 2003: Alex

A slight smile formed on Alex's lips at the memory, cracking salty tracks from her drying tears. She set aside the newspaper article with Matt's picture and hung her head for several minutes, thinking. Suddenly, she felt extremely tired. After taking several deep breaths, she wiped her face with the back of her hand and reached for her iPod to dial up her "New Age" playlist. She lay down with a long body stretch and a wide yawn, and closed her eyes. Picturing solid black behind her eyelids, she shut her mind to any other memories and, in that meditative state, slowly drifted to sleep.

In the light of the street lamps, she was walking up a snowy, pine-tree-laden trail. Breathing clouds of crisp coldness and displacing swirls of thick snowflakes as she strode along, she listened to the deadened quiet of the snowy evening. Only the crunch of snow under her boots disturbed the stillness.

She turned onto a narrowing lane where, barely visible through the thickening snowfall, she could just make out a winding path. She followed its bends through the forest's alternating dense darkness and small, open clearings revealing the forests' secrets.

She wandered alone for a time, peeking through the gaps in the trees trying to discover...something. A powerful unknown force was drawing her upward along the path. Suddenly, Matt was with her. With a warm smile, he tucked his arm around her waist. She felt safe next to his solid, warm body. He hummed a quiet song as he walked along, which she thought might be the "Moonlight Sonata."

They walked through the wintry night for a long time, soaking in each other's presence, feeling completely at one in their snowy world. At one open vantage point in the forest, she looked up the hill and saw a lone, rustic cabin high in the pines. Its unusual porthole-shaped windows drew her attention. A creek wound under the cabin's wooden deck and trickled down the snowy hill forming white, glittering ice crystals on the felled-tree branches dangling in the water.

She felt a strong pull to reach its broad wooden porch. She turned to Matt and he took her hand, pulling her steadily along the snowy lane toward the quiet haven. But, suddenly he broke away and hid behind a tree, playfully peeking out once as she approached. But when she got there, he had vanished. Moving back to the lane, she called his name repeatedly, peering through the veil of snowflakes for some sign of him. She suddenly felt incredibly alone.

The trickling of the creek suddenly grew into a roaring river. She began to cross a bridge spanning the river, but stopped as the power of the cold spray from its whitewater stole her breath and stung her face. Dizzy from watching the rushing water, she began to reel and a distinct feeling of unease overtook her.

Blinking against the river's watery spray, she saw Matt on the far side, kneeling by a loose tree stump, carving something into its flat surface. He finished his knife work, smiled at her sadly, lifted the wide stump with great effort, and heaved it through the misty spray. The stump splashed with a loud kerplunk into a deep pool just below the river's rapids. It quickly surfaced with a watery boom and bobbed erratically against the river rocks until it caught in the current. As it flowed away, she glimpsed letters carved in the flat top of the stump, but couldn't quite make them out for the thick snowflakes and speed of the water.

When she looked up, Matt had again disappeared. As she stood searching for any sign of him behind the white misty spray, pricks of cold crystal began to hit her face. The snowflakes fell faster and heavier, collecting in folds around her. Within minutes, snow had drifted onto her, covering her form in the shape of a long, flowing white dress. Larger snowflakes clung to the bodice and shoulders like lace. The lengths were dotted with shining ice crystal rhinestones. Down her back, gauzy snow lightly dusted her long hair in a veil.

She looked up to see a shadowed stretch of winding pathway ahead. It appeared long, steep, lonely and cold. But, she knew at the end lay the warmth and safety of the cabin. She felt so alone. All that was left was the allure of the structure, and her heart yearned to reach its safety. As soon as she moved up the icy path toward it, the snow dress fell from her in one swift avalanche of powder. Leaving the frosty pile behind her, she hastened up the path. The going was steep and she slid back one step for every two she took. After what seemed like hours of hard toil, she reached the final stretch of path leading to the cabin's broad, welcoming, rustic porch.

A brilliant beam of light pierced dense snow, falling directly onto the center of the wooden porch. Was that Matt's face she saw reflected in it, or was it just a trick of the light? Alex knew if she could just get into that beam of light, she'd be safe. Panting with exertion as she approached, she heard the faint tinkling sound of music and a voice singing. Looking for the source of the sounds, she walked into the sunlight. Its power radiated through her body and she raised her face into its warmth.

Alex awoke with the hotel's soft, fleece blanket across her cheek. Through half-mast eyes, she peered into the early-morning sunlight trespassing into the dark room between the curtains. Music tinkled delicately from an alarm radio in the front room of the suite. *The cabin dream again.* Thoughts of yesterday's car crash began filtering into her slow-moving thoughts. Images of broken and bloody bodies amid the wreckage cleared Alex's mind rapidly. She shuddered and rubbed her fingertips across her forehead.

She got halfway out of bed, resting her elbows on her knees to hold her head in her hands. After a few moments clearing her mind, she cooled her bare feet on the suite's Saltillo-tiled floors as she crossed to the wet bar and started a pot of tea. After running a brush through her curls and washing her face, she went back to empty a packet of sweetener into her tea. Balancing her mug, she carefully opened up the French doors to the stone balcony and, stepping out, placed her cup on the table next to the cushy lounge chair.

A salty breeze blew off the Pacific Ocean, tantalizing her nasal passages and tickling her hair against her shoulders as she stood at the stone railing. She briefly raised her face to the sun. A smooth expanse of water opened up in front of her from a horizon of distant fog. Alex gazed down across the beach to the frothy waves lashing at the yellow sand stretching below her. Their calming noise suddenly became overshadowed by the mental vision of two cars falling to another beach. Alex purposefully banished the image, but her heart beat faster with the recollection of the previous day's events. A chill sprang along her spine.

The car wreck had actually come true after dreaming it for all those years. It had moved from her dream-state into her reality in one unavoidable occurrence. *How bizarre was that?* And then there was Matt's photo appearing in the paper here.

Alex pulled her hair over her shoulder, turned to settle herself in the lounger, and picked up her tea. She often knew what people were going to say before they said it, or what people would do before they did it. She'd always thought she was just using good common sense and well-developed power of observation to see things about to happen. How could she have disregarded so many everyday instances of her keen intuition? *All these years, I should have listened to my internal voice.* Not simple coincidences after all, they were messages.

And, now, what about her dreams, where her deepest intuitions lived? She lay back in the lounger, closed her eyes and let the cabin dream replay in her mind. She searched her snowy mental adventure with a fresh perspective.

She began to recognize how Matt's appearances and disappearances in the dream had metaphorically corresponded with his actual presence in her young life. He'd shown up initially by putting a love song on the back of her school picture, but disappeared "into the trees" when Kathy Sampson had needed him. She couldn't help the swelling emotion in her heart remembering the second time he showed up in her life, starting with that crazy dance invitation from Brett…

November 1977: Alex

One afternoon the week after giving Matt her "more Flack" comment, Alex left choir and discreetly watched Matt meet up, yet again, with Kathy. Just as he had every day for a week, he placed his arm around Kathy's shoulder and they walked down the sidewalk, talking intently.

Alex struggled with her aching feelings and wounded ego as she started toward the parking lot. How had she so widely misinterpreted his photo message? It had seemed direct, but was obviously something else. He showed his creativity mostly through music, but it seemed somehow out of character for him to make light of a love song like this. Apparently, she had wanted so much for him to like her she read too much into his riddle's meaning. "Blast!" she said half out loud.

At that moment, she heard Brett shout her Spanish-class nickname. "Bonita!" He quickly crossed the withering lawn and caught up with her. "Hola. ¿Que paso?"

Usually Alex laughed when this good ol' Texas boy tried his southern drawl in a Spanish accent. Managing simply a smile, she replied, "Nada, mi amigo."

Brett abandoned the Spanish. "Hey, did you catch all of the story Señora Bonsuela told in class today?"

"Yeah, most of it."

"She talks so fast. I missed about half of it, per usual." Brett looked around uncomfortably and nervously wriggled his fingers as they headed toward the car lot. Alex eyed him curiously. She'd never heard him speechless. Brett usually had more than a week's worth of words in any given conversation.

He suddenly stopped walking. "Do you think Suzanne watches *The Love Boat*?" he blurted.

Alex almost laughed. "I have no idea, but I doubt it. Honors classes' workload doesn't allow much time for TV."

"The Captain and Tennille were on the show a couple of weeks ago. Do you think she likes their music?"

"She mostly listens to the King. But, I do know she knows all the words to 'Love Will Keep Us Together,' 'cause I've heard her sing it..." She looked sideways at him. "Why?"

"Oh, just trying to get an idea of what type of music she likes," he said. The funny, hopeful, look on his face made her wonder what was making him so nervous.

"Something on your mind, Brett?"

"Well, yeah," he said with unusual speed, even for him. He set his shoulders. "I was wondering if you'd ask Suzanne for me if she'd come to the Holiday Dance as my date. But, you have to come with us, too!" he added impulsively.

He looked so completely eager and scared, Alex almost laughed. She bit her lip and asked, "You're uncomfortable going with her all alone to the dance?"

He nodded with a pained expression on his face. "If you come with us, it'll be more like being there just as friends. She can sorta warm up to the idea of being with me, ya know." Brett studied his shoes and kicked the brown grass against the sidewalk, glancing up nervously every few seconds as he waited for her reply.

Just days ago, Alex would have bet money she would be going to the dance with Matt, but obviously that wasn't happening. She exhaled. Was she willing to be the third wheel so Brett could be with Suzanne? *Better than staying home alone.* She put one hand on his arm. "Hey, OK, it would be fun to go with my good friends. I'll set it up with her."

He gave a little hop of joy and smiled his big, goofy grin. "Thanks, Alex. You are far out!"

"Backatcha!" Alex laughed. "We'll talk details in class tomorrow, OK?" She watched the lilt in his step as he walked away.

"Alex, there's no way Matt would get together with Kathy after sending that message to you," Suzanne said that night as they climbed the stairs to Alex's bedroom. "There's no way! Something else is going on we don't know about."

Alex sighed and closed her bedroom door. "You're just trying to make me feel better. What else could it be?"

They dumped their bags on the floor and plopped onto the bed. "No way, Alex. Something else is up. Trust me."

"You know I trust your opinion, Suzanne. I just don't want to believe you and then be disappointed again."

Suzanne stopped and looked at her friend, an amused lift at the corners of her mouth. "Alex, you're in love with him."

Alex stared at her friend and panic welled in her. "Don't you think the "L" word is a bit too strong at this point?"

"Chick! Your dreams! The weird car-chase dream you keep having. He's in that sometimes. And you said your cabin dream was one of the most vivid dreams you'd ever had."

"Yeah. So?"

""Lex, you're having recurring dreams about Matt. To the max! Snowflake wedding dresses… You're obviously not paying attention." Suzanne sniffed loudly. "*You* don't see the expression on your face when he's around. You should have known *I* wouldn't miss *the look*."

Alex relived the powerful feeling of the dream Matt's warm arm around her as they walked up the snowy path. She felt the comfort of his soul seeping into hers as he had quietly hummed Beethoven's "Moonlight Sonata."

"I guess I do have some pretty strong feelings about him. It just seems so out-of-control to be so swept away by someone I barely know." Alex studied her fingernails. "OK. I admit to being infatuated. But L-O-V-E? That's so far from where I am."

"Re-e-eally?" Suzanne leaned forward until her forehead almost touched Alex's. She stared straight into Alex's eyes. After a few moments, she sighed and backed off. "OK, well, you're obviously not wanting to see it yet. Just think about it. Something in your subconscious is telling you how special Matt Roberts is to you… He's going to make a difference in your life… It's chemistry. A sign. Don't you get it?"

Alex's stomach clenched at the thought of actually believing those three little words. *Could I really be in love with him?* Was she subconsciously thinking of *real* love when she'd written that message to Matt on the back of her own school picture? She'd thought it clever and whimsical but, on another level, could it have meant more even to her? She shook her head and looked up cautiously at her friend. "You *know* I don't believe in that stuff. I'm just confused why Matt started hanging with Kathy right after his whole 'Y-F' message to me."

"It's all in the timing, Lex. 'No doubt the universe is…'"

"'…unfolding as it should,'" Alex finished. She smiled and rolled her eyes.

Suzanne hugged her friend. "Lex, I'll do what I can to help you… even third-wheel it with you and Brett at the Holiday Dance when I'd rather have him all to myself." She shook her head but, presently, her face brightened. "You will let me dance with him at least half the time, won't you?"

"You got it!" Alex laughed and hugged her friend back.

November 1977: Matt

*O*n Saturday night two weeks later, Matt sat with Kathy in a roomy back-yard porch swing, looking out at the Post's silent, moonlit yard. The frosty evening air chilled his face each time they swung forward. The faint scent of pine wafted down to them as a breeze filtered through the boughs far above, and a few needles fell across the face of the moon and landed silently on the grass. Matt tucked cold hands under his legs and pictured the decorated high school gym. He wondered what was happening at the Holiday Dance; what Alex was doing right now. He clenched his jaw. *I've got to escape this dinner party soon!*

The back door slid open and Daniel came outside, buttoning his jacket. He sat down on Kathy's other side, athletically backing into the swing's forward motion without breaking the rhythm of its sweep. "Things are heavy in there," he said, forcing the swing into a wider arc with his feet.

"All that parental drivel about great reasons to move to Europe," Kathy said, peering back inside the house. "It's so bogus! I had to book it out here, too."

At the forward point of the swing's arc, Matt could see Kathy's father through the sliding glass doors as he conversed animatedly with Mr. Post across the kitchen table. The glass door framed an image of Mr. Sampson, glowing with expectation. On the backward swing, he could see Mrs. Post through the kitchen window, busily washing up dinner dishes and talking over her shoulder to the men.

"I found the adult conversation to be *most* stimulating," Daniel replied sarcastically.

Kathy crossed her eyes at him. But when he puckered his well-turned lips at her, she pulled back. "Flirt!" She let out a long slow sigh. "I wonder what everyone's doing at the dance right now?"

Matt glanced over at her.

"Dancing," Daniel replied, staring out into the darkness.

"Don't *you* wish we were actually there, too?" Kathy asked, turning to Matt impatiently.

If only you knew how much. The mental image of Alex dancing with Brett, or any other guy for that matter, made his hackles rise. He shook his head.

Daniel snorted. "What? And miss this heartfelt, family farewell dinner for your dad?" He smirked at Kathy.

Kathy lowered her voice. "Why did my father have to accept that stupid job anyway?"

Daniel stopped pushing the swing and tucked his arm behind her coat collar, giving her a sideways hug.

"Beats me."

She sighed. "Dad's been so lost since Mom passed away. I'm glad he's got something to be excited about, but…" she said with a catch in her throat, "…why did it have to happen *now* during my senior year? Right in the middle of my catering internship. And when I only have a few more months to hang out with all my friends. I don't want to leave! This should be the best year of my life!"

Her vehement whisper pulled Matt's thoughts back from the dance and into the present conversation. He grasped her hand and leaned in close to her. "Don't worry, Kath, we're going to find you a place here to stay."

"You're high, Matt! We've looked all over town. Nobody's going to let a 17-year-old rent an apartment without her parent's consent."

"We'll work on your dad to give over." Daniel's eyes gleamed knowingly. "Or, maybe we can just come up with a creative solution he can't refuse."

Matt studied Daniel out of the corner of his eyes. *If anyone could come up with a solution for her, Dan could.*

Kathy arched her eyebrows. "You cookin' up one of those crazy, underhanded schemes again, Dan? You're not going to get me in any trouble, are you?"

Daniel feigned extreme hurt, his hand on his heart. "What do you mean underhanded? You know what a good guy I am. I can't help it if I'm resourceful."

Kathy smirked. "You mean like sneaking a copy of a certain love-interest's school schedule so you could walk her to class?"

Daniel shot a warning glance at Kathy and looked quickly at Matt.

Matt ignored him with the passing thought, *so Dan's chasing yet another chick.*

Daniel moved his gaze from Matt and smiled reassuringly at Kathy. "Naw, all that took was a little distraction and charming of the student office assistants." He leaned back in the swing with a smug expression and folded his hands behind his head.

"What are you dreaming up, Dan?" Kathy asked.

Daniel shrugged. "Nothing I'm ready to talk about yet, but I have some things to work on." He pushed the swing again with one strong, fluid motion.

Kathy gripped the swing's hanging chain and shook her head. They sat silently, listening to the rustle of wind in the treetops. Kathy glanced at Daniel's face as if looking for more clues, but his expression had changed.

"I wonder what *is* going on at the dance?" he asked. "I bet Alex is dancing with Brett and every other guy there."

Matt's eyes widened. "Why do you say that?" he asked.

"Well, let's see, where to start. Amazing singing voice. Beautiful hair. And her figure…" Daniel said, raising his eyebrows.

Anger welled up inside Matt, but Kathy's indignation burst forth before he could get his thoughts together. "*That's* what you care about, Dan? A body? Do you think you could be any more shallow?" She leapt from the swing and walked to the edge of the back porch. Matt leaned forward to study his friend's face.

"C'mon, Kath," Daniel said, "Alex doesn't compare to *you* in the brains department, but she isn't any dummy either. It's just not brains guys want to dance with…"

Kathy turned to face him. "She's all hair and trendy clothes. How can you *stand* that?"

Matt coughed. "Kathy, that's not fair! You don't even know her."

Daniel laughed and shrugged. "Hey, I'm a guy. We like a little style." Daniel turned to Matt as if for support, not quite masking the gleam in his eye.

Matt leaned back in the swing, realizing Daniel's interest in Alex. His heart thumped hard in his chest.

Kathy spun back around to the frosty lawn and stared upward. "Why are all men insane?" she asked the cold moon. "Always drawn to the conceited babe with the beautiful hair and cute figure. Add on a great voice and, well, who can resist!"

"Kath…" Daniel began, getting up, grabbing her arm and trying to turn her toward him.

She resisted, wrenching her arm away. Anger sparked her eyes. "Just go ahead, everybody fall for the cute blonde who moves to town. Never mind the really smart, dedicated friend who is always around to help you. Just ignore the one who's always there to care for your brothers and sisters, and supports you when your parents ignore you…" She stopped abruptly, suddenly remembering Matt was there.

Matt abruptly stood up. "I appreciate your help more than you know, Kathy. But, you're wrong about Alex. She is not conceited and is much more than a cute blonde."

Daniel nodded his head knowingly at Matt. "So, you are interested. I thought as much from our little gathering at Pappy's the other night."

Matt glanced at his friends and moved to leave. Kathy caught his arm and asked in a pleading voice, "Matt, why are you wasting your energy on *her*?"

That was simple. "For some reason, I know she and I are meant to be together."

Kathy snorted. "Meant to be? Like cosmically?" She dropped his arm. "More like Katie and Hubbell in *The Way We Were*!"

He returned a disgusted look. "This isn't the movies, Kath. This is real life."

"I know it is," she said sadly, lowering her eyes. "Every time you look at her, I can almost hear the poetry in your head churning out those iambic pentameters from our last English assignment." She pressed her fingers against her temples and sighed. She looked up at her him, eyes glaring. "Guys. Neither of you see what's right in front of you. I don't suppose, Matt, you've noticed the way Dan's eyes glaze over whenever Alex shows up?"

Daniel's eyes darted to Kathy in surprise, but quickly returned to Matt's wary glance. Daniel raised his chin in defiance and a familiar spark of competitiveness flashed across his face.

Matt immediately understood his designing friend's expression. "You may think it possible that Alex is meant for you, Dan, but I'm not sure Alex is feeling that way." Matt's hand found the sliding door's handle. *And I'm outta here right now to find out for sure.*

Daniel snickered under his breath. "That will be Alex's decision, won't it?"

"Definitely," Matt said with a glare at his overconfident friend. "I'm sorry to bolt, but I just realized I have someplace to be." Matt nodded farewell to Kathy and slipped into the house to say his thank yous and goodbyes to the Posts and Mr. Sampson.

December 1977: Alex

*W*alking into the darkened gymnasium that Saturday night, Brett looked like the proudest Texan who'd ever graced Coeur d'Alene High. He puffed out his chest, proudly showing off his boutonniere and promenading a beautiful date on each arm.

A live band blasted Aerosmith's "Walk This Way" across the balloons, blue-and-white crepe paper, and formally attired students, while teachers and parents stood sentry by the dancers and punch bowl. From one corner, flashes from the obligatory, sunset-background portrait setting continually broke the darkness. Couples lined up anticipating yet another glassy-eyed, photo-album memento.

The trio found a table to share and Brett brought punch to the young women. When they'd greeted other friends and drained their punch cups, Brett took Suzanne's hand and turned to Alex. "Do you mind if I take this other beautiful woman out on the dance floor for a spin? Your turn next, Alex. Deal?"

"Deal." Alex smiled and, with a pang of sadness, sat down at a nearby table and watched them jostle out onto the darkened gym floor to jive with the other dancers.

As the evening wore on, Alex danced a few times with Brett, taking turns with Suzanne. She even received other dance offers, but turned them down. After a while, the feeling of loneliness built up in her heart and she excused herself to go get some fresh air.

Instead of heading outdoors, she sought out an inconspicuous spot halfway up the dark bleachers rimming the gymnasium. She looked around again for Matt. Halfway grateful not to have to see him with Kathy, she contented herself by watching overdressed, twisting, wiggling bodies trying to catch the beat. Their movements would have been almost funny, if she hadn't been feeling so sorry for herself.

Although she knew she had no real right to, she missed Matt. He had been so preoccupied recently he'd barely said a word to her. He'd skipped choir again today and, rumor had it, Kathy wasn't in school that afternoon either. One would surmise they were out together doing, well, whatever. Alex's hands clenched at the thought.

Oh, how she wished she were out there on the dance floor with Matt right now. Their chemistry was so tangible she just couldn't believe he didn't feel it, too.

As the band started playing Roberta Flack's "Killing Me Softly," Alex flashed on the notation Matt had scrawled on the back of his school photo to her. She blinked her eyes rapidly to keep tears at bay, glad she was sitting in the dark so no one could see her fight her emotions. She watched the crowd intently, concentrating on the lights, the musical arrangement, anything but the opening words. She watched Brett pull Suzanne into a slow-dance clinch. They began dancing the repetitive, slow circle requisite of all high-school dance partners. Suzanne put her head on his shoulder. Both closed their eyes. Alex saw just a hint of a smile bloom on Suzanne's face. They were obviously having a great time.

They do make a great couple... She sighed and hung her head. *Just like...* Before the dark thought could fully form, Alex felt a hand on her shoulder.

"Here you are!" Matt said. "I've been in every nook and cranny in this gym looking for you."

"Matt!" she blurted. Pretending she'd not been startled, Alex looked around cautiously for Kathy, "Why are you looking for *me*?"

"To ask you to dance, of course. Can't resist sharing more Flack with you," he said with a wry smile. "Come on."

Matt pulled Alex onto the gym floor and took her in his arms. Thoughts of Kathy receded from her mind as her body absorbed the warmth of his chest through his suit coat. Resting her head on his shoulder, she reveled in the smoothness of his fingers at the base of her neck and the calming sound of his humming as they danced. The familiar lyrics washed through her as the song played out. *But, what am I going to say after the song ends?* She squelched the thought, concentrating on Matt's arms holding her. They encompassed her in a world where the future didn't matter.

As the song ended, she opened her eyes and just caught the smug, I-told-you-so look on Suzanne's face as she lifted her head from Brett's shoulder. But, there was no time for a response as Matt took

Alex's hand and firmly drew her toward the back patio. Without saying anything, Matt pulled her out into the crisp, December night. He led her to the farthest corner, past two other snuggling couples, and sat her down on a freezing cement bench. Alex inhaled the fresh, natural smell of icy pine trees. She was glad for the cold. Maybe Matt would take her emotional trembling for shivering.

Matt held her hands and looked into her face. "Alex, I know you've been wondering what's going on."

"No. Not really," Alex lied, gulping a breath to open the tightness in her throat. "A riddle's a riddle, right? It's nothing to take seriously."

"But I really wanted you to take it seriously," Matt said quietly, leaning forward.

Her confusion turned rapidly to anger. Fire searing her stomach, she pulled her hands away and lashed out, "And where, pray tell, is Kathy tonight, Matt? Wouldn't she wonder where her constant companion is?" She stood up and turned her back to him.

"Ah, you did take me seriously then. Good," he said, getting up and turning her to face him. "I have an explanation, Alex. Will you hear it?"

Alex said, "What are you talking about, Matt Roberts?"

"It's not all good news, but hopefully it will help you understand. Come on back here and sit down," he said, leading her back to the bench and taking a deep breath. "Kathy's dad has gotten a sudden transfer and is moving to Europe at the end of January."

Alex stared, the fire in her belly quickly cooling to embers. "So, she's leaving?"

"No-o-o... Kathy doesn't want to leave her friends. Plus, she's in the middle of her culinary arts internship."

"Couldn't she get even better training in Europe?" Alex asked.

"Probably, she doesn't want to blow this great opportunity here. Chef Max has been her dad's pal since their middle school days. She knows him well and he's willing to be flexible with her schedule." Matt paused momentarily and added almost inaudibly, "She doesn't have the confidence to go start again with an international chef anyway." Bringing his voice back up, Matt continued, "Kathy needs the support of her friends to help her find a place where she can afford to stay. So, I spent all week helping her find something."

"*You* skipped school to help her scout jobs and apartments? What about her dad? He didn't help?"

Matt looked sad and played with the back of Alex's hand. "He's been worthless since the loss of Kathy's mom about a year ago. But, since he's gotten this job offer, he seems to have a new lease on life. Still, he's just not supportive of her staying here."

"He's her dad. Of course he wants her to be with him."

"Of course." Matt laughed sardonically. "His mistake was telling her if she could find an apartment on her minimum-wage salary, she could stay for the rest of her senior year."

"I'm sure he's banking on her not being able to find a place."

"Probably. And, we haven't found her anything yet. But, I know one thing, our clever friend Daniel won't put his closest friend on a plane to Europe against her will, without a good, sly fight."

"Has he been helping?" Alex asked.

"As much as he can around school and basketball practice."

"He'll probably take the easy route and try to get your parents to take her in," Alex said

Matt laughed. "Sounds like something he'd do."

Alex's heart suddenly leapt. She bit her lip and squeezed his hand. "So, if you've just been helping her find a place to live, that means, you really aren't..." She stopped and gazed up at him.

Matt's eyes bored into hers and he whispered, "No, I'm not interested in Kathy as anything but a friend, despite what she wants of *me*." He leaned in closer to Alex. "I promised her dad to help watch out for her. I'm sure you got the impression I really liked her, but it was *you* who got the lyrics, wasn't it?"

Alex's heart expanded with joy. "Oh, Matt. I'm sorry. I was so amazed by your message I didn't know what to think. Then I saw you two together... I..." She stopped.

"I know. I'm sorry. The timing just stunk. But my message is real. The first time ever I saw your face, Princess..." He ran one finger along her jaw line. "I knew you were going to be someone special to me. I know you felt it, too." He looked at her questioningly.

"The *very* first time..." she answered, reliving the jolt of recognition she'd felt when she saw him that very first morning. Suddenly there was nothing more to say. For a long moment they studied each other's faces and Matt leaned in as if to kiss her. Instead, he just pulled her tightly to him.

After lingering in his arms, Alex pulled back to soak in the contours of his handsome face. She realized they'd begun a journey neither could or would have avoided. Her shiver broke the moment, as the cold penetrated even her inner warmth. She grabbed Matt's hand, pulled him back toward the gymnasium door, said, "Come on, you have to help me explain this to my date."

They went back inside to search for Brett and Suzanne, and quickly discovered the couple making out in the darkness of the bleachers. Upon Alex and Matt's approach, they jerked apart. Even in the dim light, Alex could see both their faces flush darkly. But, as soon as they realized Alex was holding Matt's hand, they smiled.

"Looks like I have a different ride home tonight, OK, guys?" They just grinned at her.

May 2003: Matt

*M*att sat in the balcony chaise lounge, sipping coffee and reviewing his music camp's positive coverage in yesterday's *LA Times*. He still hated the public relations work required to support his Coeur d'Musique camp, but complimentary articles like this one, resulting from this last week's media tour in LA, would certainly help guarantee full classes this summer.

Staying in Santa Barbara the last night of his trip – his sister Becka's inspired idea – had also given him time to relax after his whirlwind LA media tour. In the quiet of his hotel room last night, he'd even succeeded in laying down a few solid reference tracks for a new composition in his GarageBand software. Still, he was eager to return home to Coeur d'Alene later today.

He sighed with relief and focused again on the stillness of the ocean in the new daylight. He wondered how so much water could possibly remain so smooth. Its glassy barrier spread to the horizon, seeming to hold the fog at bay.

Something about the ocean was so calming and connecting. Some people looked at the moon to feel close to their world. Matt chose water. There was nothing like a great expanse of water to point out how small your problems really are, along with everyone else's. A hollow feeling bloomed in his chest, but he soaked in the gorgeous ocean view until the feeling dissolved.

Directing his focus just up the beach, he could see his hotel's sister property, a four-star masterpiece with cascades of fuchsia and yellow bougainvillea gleaming down the building's terraces in the early sunshine. He wondered why more of the "rich and famous" over there weren't out enjoying this glorious morning and connecting with every element their world offered.

He smiled as a woman came into view and stood against the railing of the distant property's top-most balcony. *Nice to know someone who can afford the Penthouse suite can also afford time to take in the scenery*. He watched her grasp the railing, lean back, and raise her face to the sun. She gracefully leaned out over the railing and slowly moved her gaze across the horizon. She was far enough away he couldn't make out her features, but he could see the wind catching her blond curls. After a particularly strong gust of wind, she pulled her hair over shoulder in a hauntingly familiar way. He started. Alex had always done that when she was agitated or thinking hard.

Matt laid aside the newspaper and got up. *Could that possibly be Alex?* He watched her for quite a time. She had a very similar form and moved like her. But, what would be the odds? *It couldn't be her.*

Still his heart pounded. What if it were? If he ran into her, what would he say? "Why did you have to get sucked in by Dan's schemes? Don't you know I think of you every day, even though you stole my music? I've never been able to find anyone who compares to you, even though I've tried to banish you from my psyche? Every time I try to write a love song, it's your face I see in my mind? I'm a fool for letting you go?"

He turned away once he realized his thoughts were running away with him, and forcefully quelled the ache in his heart. He ran both hands through his hair and leaned back against the railing. Better to let bygones be bygones. He didn't want to see her. Didn't want to even imagine it was her over there. He was happy with his life now. He did what he wanted. He didn't answer to anyone but his clients. But... the niggling hole in his insides gaped open again. Why had feelings for Alex started showing up again?

Matt moved his lounger to face away from the woman, sat, and tried focusing on the ocean again to calm his mind. But, the vision of that woman – so much like Princess Alex. *Princess!* He hadn't thought of his nickname for her in years. A sharp ache panged through his heart and he dropped his head in his hands.

He couldn't stop the memories from flowing. ...seeing Alex win her Grammy on TV. Her laughter as Brett provided everyone with superhero names that long-ago night at Pappy's. ...the silence in the home studio after she sang his "Like the Moon Pulls The Tide" composition for the first time. And Dan's reaction. Matt tensed, thinking of it. Right before his own eyes, Dan had taken the opportunity to steal Alex's heart with the promise of fame.

That conniving Daniel stole her from me. And, he roped her into stealing my music rights. Thank goodness I found out about their deceit early on, or I might have lost everything. He glanced at the article he'd dropped and pictured his beautiful music camp and its promising students. He immediately felt calmer.

He was doing what he loved and was making a difference in the lives of so many people. He didn't need Alex. The feelings coming up recently were just old garbage he hadn't really ever dealt with, and didn't really want to deal with now. Realizing he needed to just continue moving forward with his life, he strode purposefully to the sliding door and went through into the hotel room. As he closed the door behind him, he couldn't resist a glance back across the beach. No one stood over on the balcony now.

Gone. Out of my life. Both she and Dan. He sighed thankfully. Even with his inner pain reappearing after all these years, neither Alex nor Dan could manipulate his feelings any longer. He simply wouldn't allow it like he had when he was a teenager...

December 1977: Matt

*M*att sat at his grand piano, bent slightly forward, eyes closed, urging resonance from the keys. Lost in his world, he barely registered the sudden dull thud and simultaneous vibration through the piano. Matt jerked his hands off the keyboard, leaving harmonic notes hovering in the air. His eyes flew open to see elbows plunked on the piano and Daniel's grinning face not more than a foot away.

"Psyche! Dan. Where'd you come from?"

"Through your front door, down the hall and into your private sanctuary, Jive Turkey." Daniel straddled an upholstered wooden chair and gave Matt a cheesy smile. "Becka let me in."

Matt shook his head and mockingly scowled down the hall. "She'll just let any riff-raff in. I'd better have a talk with her," he said sarcastically, while lightly fingering the piano keys.

He looked intently at Daniel. His friend held a fake grin. *So, Dan, you're going to act like nothing's happened; like you haven't noticed Alex and I are together.* Matt narrowed his eyes as Daniel sat back in the overstuffed chair and too casually steepled his hands. *I'll play along, Buddy, but I'm watching you.*

"Speaking of letting any riff-raff in," Daniel said, "I hear you and Kathy still haven't had any luck finding her a place to stay."

"Nice to see you, too, Dan. Are you sure there wasn't something you *really* wanted to discuss with me?" Matt asked, shooting a wry expression at his friend. Matt frowned down at his hands, stretching tight fingers against his thighs. His mind recapped the endless apartment managers' offices he and Kathy had left, disappointed, over the past three weeks.

Daniel took a seat in the upholstered chair in the curve of the piano. He pressed his fingertips together and cocked his head.

Matt sighed. "She really is in a tough spot. I wish I could do more to help her."

"Maybe you can." Daniel raised his left eyebrow and his mouth slid into a lopsided smile.

Matt explored his friend's face and waited for the bomb. From Dan's expression, he knew he wasn't going to like it.

"Kathy's done a lot to help you, hasn't she?" Daniel asked. "Helped babysit the kids… Always there you when you needed moral support…" His voice trailed off and he looked questioningly at Matt.

Matt replied warily, "So…"

"Well, maybe it would work out for her to help you even more by living here all the time to help with all your family responsibilities."

"Here?"

"She'd pretty much do anything you want," Daniel added. "You know how crazy she is about you."

Matt's mind jumped to an image of Kathy sitting across the dining table from him, following his every move with her puppy dog eyes. He grimaced and ran his hand through his hair.

"You'd have your own Stepford wife, just like those guys in that movie a couple of years ago who changed their spouses into perfect women robots," Daniel said, raising his eyebrows.

Matt dropped his head and looked at Daniel with disgust. "Just what I need," he said. "Kathy doesn't need any more work. What she needs is a place to live."

"That's exactly what you, Becka and Davey could provide her. It would be just like a little supportive family. Everyone helping out in their own way. Imagine how much it would mean to Kathy to live here with your family." Daniel leaned forward and lowered his voice into calming tones. "Think about it. If she's living here with you, you'll have a fallback. More time to practice your music. Really make some headway on your composing."

Now, that *was* tempting. Matt imagined everything being taken care of while he spent hours sitting at the piano pouring his soul into his music. No kids interrupting him with homework questions. Help with cleaning up the kitchen after the kids went to bed. Someone else to take his parents' incessant business and social phone calls, explaining to his siblings why they wouldn't see their parents *again* tonight. But, his daydream bubble burst quickly with one fleeting image. He saw himself bumping into Kathy as he left the bathroom wrapped in his towel. He shuddered.

A little knot started forming in the recesses of his gut and he studied Daniel's face intently for his real purpose. "You're awfully eager to see this happen, aren't you?" Matt asked.

Daniel leaned forward, resting his elbows on his knees, and donned a reproachful expression. "You don't want her to be happy?"

Matt returned Daniel's look with a dubious expression and asked impatiently, "You haven't already asked Kathy about this, have you?"

Daniel threw up his hands. "Do you think I'm stupid? Get her hopes up before it's all settled? Of course not!"

Matt stared at his friend. After a few moments, Matt stood and walked to the beveled bay window. He leaned against the windowpane and stared out into his back yard. "And, my parents. What do you suppose they'd say?"

"Oh, I happened to run into your mom at the art gallery this afternoon," Daniel said casually. "She thought it could be a great idea to have someone else around the house to help, especially our dear Kathy. She said she'd call your dad and Mr. Sampson to see if it could be arranged."

Anger welled up in Matt's chest. "You just happened to 'run into' my mom at the gallery? Since when do you spend afternoons downtown during basketball season?"

"Hey, man, this is a good thing. Why are you getting your skivvies all in a bunch?"

"Just 'ran into her'?" Matt repeated, turning to glare at Daniel and clamping his lips tightly together.

"C'mon, man! OK, I left practice early to talk to your mom. Hey, I'm just trying to come up with a solution for Kathy here."

Matt quickly turned again to the window. His hands started shaking. As he struggled to gain his composure, Matt realized it wasn't Daniel who had sparked this flame. *She thought it was a great idea.* How very typical of his *thoughtful* mother not to take even a moment to consider her son's feelings. She'd just go ahead and make plans no matter how they affected him. Again!

He watched a bird dart from a tree limb and swoop high into the wind, and the powerful final movement from Tchaikovsky's "1812

Overture" began hammering silently in his skull. He watched the bird soar higher and higher. He imagined himself as the bird, the mental music lifting him like the crisp autumn air beneath the bird's wings. The music crescendoed in his mind as the bird became a little speck and disappeared into the gray winter sky. Musical stanzas carried him ever higher, ever freer from the bonds of reality.

A ringing phone shattered the image and Matt plummeted back to Earth. He glanced at Daniel, who was staring patiently at him. As he moved across the room and answered the phone, Matt realized his nerves were no longer raw. *Bless Tchaikovsky.*

"Hello, mother," he said. After a short, informative conversation in which he reacted as little as possible, Matt hung up the receiver and turned to his friend with a calm smile. He felt even better now.

Daniel looked at him expectantly.

"Looks like our parents have solved the dilemma for us, ol' pal. Kathy will be staying with *your* family."

Daniel stared, incredulous. "*My* family?"

"Guess my father wasn't really up for having a full-time house guest, so my ever-resourceful mom convinced Mr. Sampson it was in Kathy's best interest for *your parents* to take her in for the rest of the year. They already worked it out." Matt laughed a heartfelt laugh.

Daniel just sat there, stunned.

Matt put a hand on Daniel's shoulder. "Sorry for getting my hackles up earlier, Dan. But, I think you'll deal much better than I would with your own Stepford wife."

May 2003: Alex

*W*hen Alex opened her eyes, she realized the sun was much higher over the beach now. She set aside her cold tea and took stock of her dream comparisons, looking for answers. No matter how much time had gone by, Matt was still an important influence on her life. Unfortunately, the rhythms of their relationship had left them with no steady cadence for spending their lives "happily ever after."

Still, at the beginning of their relationship, as in the dream, Matt had shown up as a powerful and meaningful force in her experience. Some strange energy had drawn them together. From that first moment in homeroom, before they had even been introduced, she and Matt had shared an immediate, unspoken bond. As they'd discovered their mutual love of music and become friends, their connection had become palpable. The remembered warmth of their early, shared chemistry flowed through Alex, sparking one of her favorite memories…

January 1978: Alex

Alex had hardly seen Matt for the past two weeks during their holiday break from school. The time had flown, what with studying for final exams, Matt's Christmas-carol accompaniment gigs in local nursing centers and private homes, and Alex's family Christmas activities. Today, a healthy layer of snow deposited by the previous night's snowstorm provided the perfect excuse for Alex and Matt to get together for snow tubing.

As the couple trekked through the deep snow toward Alex's favorite neighborhood sledding hill, Alex finally was able to detail to Matt the "grilling session" her parents had put her through the morning after the Holiday Dance.

"I can't believe you didn't get grounded," Matt said.

"Yeah, well, my folks don't believe in grounding. They use a *special* technique to scare us into submission, otherwise known as my dad. One serious, half-hour conversation around the kitchen table with my dad's psychology and…well… you'd admit to murder."

"How's that work?" Matt asked, slightly out of breath. He'd stopped at the top of the hill and turned to search her face. "I thought grounding was every parent's favorite form of punishment."

Alex stopped, her inner tube nudging the back of her calf. "Not *my* folks. Dad has this way of leaning across the table at you, piercing your soul with his scowl, and asking a bunch of super-pointed questions. He deliberately phrases the questions so you really have to think to keep yourself from digging yourself in deeper. He just wears you down until, eventually, he makes you admit in your own words just how stupid you've been. Very annoying."

"You're lucky your dad cares enough to keep tabs on you," Matt said almost inaudibly.

She smiled a wry smile at him and, looking around, took in some deep, slow, gulps of the crisp air until she could draw her breath evenly and naturally.

She and her brother had discovered Fairway Hill after the first snowfall that season; a clear, vacant field just up from their house. Almost invisible behind a thick patch of young pine trees, it lay across the street from the public golf course. The slope of the hill was steep enough for cars to get stuck on, on snowy days and, as Alex had discovered months earlier, steep enough to get you really winded on a bike ride. She was relieved to see no one else had disturbed the beautiful, pristine blanket of dry powder on the slope.

Alex wrinkled her nose at Matt. "Thank goodness mom got to know you through our Fall concert practices."

"What? Your mother's talked with me maybe four times in her entire life."

"Well, in our conversation when I got home from the dance so late, she said you seem like a 'fine young man.'" Alex looked disgusted. "She's always had a thing for musicians. Don't *even* get her going on the 'Peace Train' of the handsome and talented Mr. 'Moonshadow.'"

Matt laughed.

"Anyway, mom wasn't really mad once she found out *you* were my excuse for breaking curfew, so dad wasn't *too* hard on me."

"They didn't even give you grief about my long hair? My parents could care less, but most parents automatically think I'm a hippie and wouldn't let me within sight of their daughters."

"Yeah, well, I don't think it was your hair, but I did get dishwashing duty all week. My brother's thrilled for the time off."

"I still say you're lucky you didn't get grounded.

Alex grinned at him, and suddenly plopped backward into her inner tube and slipped down the hill. Matt didn't waste a second in following her.

Like ice on tile, they glided in consecutive synchronization down the steep slope. Moments ahead of Matt, Alex hit a large, mid-hill bump. With a shriek of laughter, she became airborne, then landed heavily in a sideways skid. As she continued to drop down the hill, Matt hit the same bump, landing in an opposing trajectory. The hill's natural contours moved them in long sweeps from left to right across each other's paths, like children on invisible, intertwined slides.

They landed at the bottom of the hill, both breathlessly laughing. Alex struggled out of her tube. She finally stood, hands on her knees, gulping giggles and watching her breath hang in the cold air.

Matt tramped toward her through the knee-deep snow drifts they'd landed in. "Hey, not bad for an Arizona Princess!" Matt teased between breaths. "You looked like an old pro."

"Don't they teach you anything here in Idaho, SuperMatt?" Alex pretended to scoff. She folded her hands primly, looked off into the distance and said, "Arizona's climate zones range from tropical desert to *sub alpine*." Turning back to him and dropping the feigned tone, she asked, "Something you don't understand about the word 'alpine?' There's a whole bunch of it just two hours north of Phoenix in a city called Flagstaff."

She pretended to get huffy and stomped up the hill. Matt just laughed. In a few quick strides, he caught her hand and held it as they walked. Their tubes bounced along behind.

After half an hour of nonstop sledding, they decided to take a last trip down the hill together on one tube. Matt let his tube glide empty to the bottom of the hill and climbed onto the center of Alex's tube. She sat on his lap and gripped his knees while his arms held her around the middle. Unable to steer the unwieldy tube, they plummeted and careened wildly down the hill.

Hitting the big bump just the wrong way, they went flying scarves over boots. Alex landed on her back in a sideline snowdrift with a great thump and a fit of laughter. Moments later, Matt flew through the air and landed on top of her, his face just inches away from hers. He rubbed his red, cold cheek against hers.

Alex yelped. "Ahhhh! Stop it! You're freezing!"

"Like you aren't!" Matt said, looking down into her face. "Why don't I just see if I can warm you up a bit."

She felt his arms push through the snow up under her shoulders and pull her against his chest. Alex held her breath with anticipation as they held each other's gaze. With an almost audible click, Alex felt the emotional bond spark between them. It snapped them together as they looked into each other's faces, a bond of knowledge and awareness forged by their emotions. He looked deep into her eyes and slowly lowered his lips toward hers.

Sudden, distant screams and laughter broke through the pines from the snow-laden golf course across the street. Matt closed his eyes and, with an almost imperceptible shake of his head, pulled back from Alex to look in the direction of the noise.

Alex's bubble of expectation burst. She let out a long breath. The noisy disruption certainly meant the appearance of a golf course greens-keeper. Alex envisioned the sledders scattering at the sight of the "greenie" – an explosion of toboggans, boots and laughter disappearing into the wooded rough. She knew if the kids wanted to keep sledding, they'd most likely show up shortly in the field where she and Matt currently lay. She craned her neck backward in the snow to see what was happening. Matt gently rolled off her and stood up.

"Let's go before anyone else shows up. I'll fix you some hot chocolate and really warm you up," Alex said, lifting her head back where she could see only him.

"Deal. But, whatever you put in a mug will never be as sweet as this." He grabbed her hand and pulled her up into a quick embrace.

They gathered their tubes and took three steps toward Alex's home before Kathy and Daniel burst breathlessly out of the woods nearby.

"Hey, fancy meeting you here!" Daniel said slyly, dropping his toboggan rope. "I could use some warming up and you're just the ticket," he said. He walked up to Alex and engulfed her stiff body in a bear hug.

Over Daniel's shoulder, Alex saw Kathy's eyes flash at her, then turn a sweet smile on Matt. Ignoring that fact that he was staring angrily at Daniel, Kathy walked up to Matt and took his arm, "That lazy greenie showed up, but didn't even try to chase us. Can you believe they're still protecting their precious fairways in the middle of the winter?" she asked, looking up into his face.

He didn't take his eyes from Daniel, who still had his arms around Alex, but replied, "They *are* paid to keep the grass in good shape, and there's not much else for the groundskeepers to do when there's snow on the fairways, is there?"

Alex pushed Daniel away, embarrassed and angry. She stepped back with her palm outstretched toward him and turned to Matt.

The young men stared at one another and a long silence ensued. *Daniel is coming on to me right in front of his "best" friend. He knows*

Matt is interested in me, so what is he doing? To break the uncomfortable silence, she said the only thing that came to mind. "Matt and I just finished sledding. We're leaving."

Kathy stood shaking her head at her guy friends. A small smile lifted her lips and she dropped her hands from her hips. Turning to Alex, she said, "So are we, thanks to that greenie. Say, don't you live just down there, Alex?" she added in a too-sweet voice. "Could we impose on you for a little break from the cold?"

Anger sparked in Alex's gut. She knew Kathy could be pushy, but to invite herself...?

At that moment, Brett and Suzanne rushed through the woods just above them, dragging sleds behind them.

"Hey, ya'll! Did I hear something about a break from the cold? Would that include hot chocolate?" Brett asked. "Mmmm-mmmm! The perfect thing to settle us down from our meanie-greenie scare."

"We couldn't resist the good sledding snow you told us about," Suzanne added breathlessly. "But, we really didn't mean to interrupt you guys." She looked apologetically at Matt and Alex.

Alex's face brightened as her anger subsided a bit. "I *suppose* I could rustle up something warm for *you*," Alex said, pointedly addressing the two newest arrivals. "If I know my mom she'll already have the hot chocolate on. Everybody come on down," she said, circling one arm forward in the direction of her house.

January 1978: Matt

When Alex's smiling mom opened their front door, the tinkling piano notes of Beethoven's "Für Elise" and smell of freshly baking cookies wafted outside with her. "How neat that you're all here in our neighborhood. Hot chocolate and cookies for everyone?" Mrs. Lauren asked, ushering the group inside.

Everyone answered enthusiastically and filed into the Lauren's tiled entryway. Alex quickly pulled off her coat and mittens and placed them on a wooden drying rack. "I'll help you, Mom," she said, starting toward the kitchen behind her mother.

Suzanne gestured to Kathy. "C'mon, Kathy, we can't be lettin' them make hot chocolate without the Sampson Special Spice recipe and the Briggs' Mondo Marshmallow treatment, now can we?" Kathy looked questioningly at her former best friend and turned to Matt. He nodded his approval.

"Hey, wait for us!" Suzanne called after the Laurens. She bounced out of her snow pants and proceeded to tug a reticent Kathy down the front hall.

Matt finished hanging up his wet clothes and followed the sound of the music into the living room. The warmth of the hardwood floor, red braided rug and overstuffed furniture in the room contrasted against the cold, towering, snow-laden pine trees visible through the front wall of country-curtained windows.

A junior high-aged boy with a mop of curly blonde hair matching Alex's looked up from the baby grand piano against the far wall. He immediately stopped playing.

"Don't stop," Matt said. "Piano's my favorite thing in the world."

"It seemed like it from how great you played at the Fall Concert," the boy said. "You're Matt, right?"

"Yeah." Matt walked up next to the piano bench and held out his hand. "And, you're Alex's brother Jake?"

The boy shook Matt's hand with a shy smile. "Yeah."

"Beethoven, eh?" Matt asked, gesturing at the piano music.

"Yeah, it's for my recital in a couple of weeks." Jake's blue eyes swept to the group of students meandering into the room and he nodded quietly as they greeted him with waves and hellos. "If you guys are stayin' a while, I'll get a fire goin'," he said.

The students gathered in the comfortably open room. Matt slipped onto the piano bench, while Daniel helped Brett pull up chairs in a semicircle along one side of the hearth. Brett fell with a sigh into one of the wing chairs, while Daniel plopped himself on a couch just under the long bank of white-curtained, front windows. Kathy came back into the room with a plate of warm cookies and passed them around before taking a seat inconspicuously next to Daniel.

Soon, Jake had the large, brick fireplace crackling and popping with flames and the pungent scent of burning pine permeated the living room.

"You ready for the recital, Jake?" Matt asked.

"Almost, except one part in the second section," the boy said, moving back toward the piano. "It's so fast!"

Tinkling a few keys, Matt said absently, "This baby has a really nice tone."

"Will you play us something, Matt?" Kathy prompted. A brief look of regret came over her. "I always wanted to take piano lessons, but never had the talent." She shrugged at Daniel's sympathetic smile.

"You have your own talents, roomie," Daniel said, eyes twinkling. "Such as baking the lightest puff pastries known to man and admiring hunks like me!" He plopped down on the couch beside her.

Kathy punched him in the arm.

"Hey, Matt, would you play "Für Elise" so I can hear how you'd play it?" Jake asked.

"Sure."

Jake pointed out the section giving him trouble, and Matt began playing without even looking at the sheet music. As the music filled the room, Mrs. Lauren, Suzanne and Alex quietly passed around mugs of hot chocolate.

The women took seats in the chairs by the fire and listened as Matt played the difficult section three times through. He stopped and turned to Jake for a reaction. Jake nodded. "OK. That really helped. I can hear it now."

Mrs. Lauren beamed at Matt. "You do have a gift, Matt," she said.

Matt smiled at her in thanks. "OK," he said to Jake, "your turn. Lay it on us." He got up and stood behind the piano bench.

"Oh man, you're gonna make me practice in front of everyone?" The color in his cheeks rose.

"You're going to have to play it at your recital. You might as well practice in front of an audience."

"Oh, man. That's a drag." He looked over at his mom, but she made scooting gestures with her fingertips encouraging him onto the piano bench.

With cajoling from everyone else, he eventually sat down and played through the piece. His face glowed red as he played, but he only stumbled a couple of times in the second section.

"You've almost got it," Matt said. "I think if you work on your fingering here," he pointed to the music, "you'll have it." He leaned in to demonstrate on the keyboard exactly what he meant. "OK, now, try playing the section again."

Jake obliged, playing it perfectly.

"You've got talent, Jake," Matt said, slapping him on the back. "You come from a musical family or something?" He winked at Alex who grinned at her mom.

"I told him he'd better not get more famous than me," Alex said with an exaggerated glare at her brother.

"Matt's the one who's going to be famous," Kathy said.

Suzanne nodded and shot a thumbs-up to Kathy, who smiled knowingly back. Alex privately agreed with both of them, surprised she and Kathy could actually see eye-to-eye on something.

Matt consciously fought the desire to clench his jaw. "All that matters to me is that I get to keep doing it," he said, taking a mug of hot chocolate from Mrs. Lauren's tray.

"Well you certainly have a knack with kids," she said. "Jake's been working on that section for weeks. Today, he played it better than he ever has."

Matt smiled at Jake and moved his gaze out the window toward the cold landscape. "Thanks," he said, gears in his head turning. *Who knows? Maybe someday I'll be able to put my talent to good use helping young guys like Jake here.*

He sat down by Alex and contemplated the idea while Mrs. Lauren asked the students questions about school and their extracurricular activities. Her genuine curiosity carried the conversation for a long time. But, eventually the pace of her questions started to slow and Kathy suggested to Daniel it was time they headed on home. This started a chorus of agreement, followed by a round of thanks to Mrs. Lauren as everyone gathered their belongings and headed out.

February 1978: Alex

O ver the next several weeks, Alex and Matt became inseparable. They spent much of their time around a piano preparing Alex for her solo at the State Band and Choral Competition, a much-coveted, three-day field trip to "State," in Moscow, the home of the University of Idaho.

Every student who earned a spot on the bus had tried out locally, earned judges' ratings and was selected because they had successfully demonstrated high levels of expertise in their musical area.

Alex was delighted both she and Suzanne had been selected, and that Ms. Nelson always included Matt to help accompany the singers. Alex was looking forward to a wonderful three days away from school with her friends, doing the thing she loved best.

The night before the trip, Alex packed a duffle bag, filled her backpack with a tape deck and headphones, her competition music, some snacks and water, and laid out her favorite comfortable bell-bottom jeans and Coeur d'Alene High Vikings sweatshirt to wear on the bus. Despite a stomach ruffling with butterflies, sleep came upon her quickly.

Matt looked into her eyes as they walked through the snow with their arms encircling each other. Peace and comfort brimmed Alex's heart as they approached a cold waterfall crashing into the river by the familiar, rustic cabin. She tore her eyes from Matt's as a loud thump emanated from the pounding water. A tree stump hurtled over a large, jagged rock in the midst of the waterfall. The stump flew through the misty spray and splashed loudly into the river rapids. There, it bobbed against the river rocks, turned roots down and suddenly caught in the current. Alex could see letters carved in the flat top of the stump, but couldn't quite make them out for the thick

snowflakes and speed of the water. She watched the stump ride the current into the white distance.

The moment the stump disappeared Alex felt a freezing chill, a twinge in the tangible bond with Matt. She turned to him for assurance, but he was gone. She searched the river and the forest, but she could longer feel his presence. She stopped and watched the stark snowflakes melt into the rushing water, as an unrelenting wind swept around her head, until a sudden chill on her cheek shocked her system.

Alex's eyes flew open. Her dog Amber was rubbing a cold nose on her cheek and panting a morning welcome. Alex let out a sigh of relief and pulled Amber into a hug. The animal's warmth helped her shake off the weird sensation left from her snowy dream.

What's with this dream I keep having? Before she could dwell on it, her alarm clock rang. *We're leaving for State today!* She jumped out of bed.

An hour and a half later, Alex was sitting next to Matt in a musky-smelling bus rumbling down the highway toward Moscow. Suzanne sat in the bench just in front of them.

Alex's stomach fluttered as Suzanne described the fun activities they could expect over the next three days. Suzanne and a handful of choir members had qualified for the competition in Moscow in years past, so she described bowling in The Commons student union building, locations for the tastiest cafeteria food and the most accessible junk food stops.

When she started in on the best places to sit and ogle college guys, Matt shot her a look of mock disgust and stood up. Gripping the overhead storage rack with one hand to keep his balance as the bus bounced along the road, he rummaged in his duffel bag, bringing down a shoebox.

"Whatcha got?" Alex asked.

"Just brought along a few goodies to help keep you occupied on our trip. I'm hoping they'll distract you from all the college guys." He winked at Suzanne, gave Alex the box and said, "Open sesame."

Suzanne waved Alex on with an expectant look and leaned over the back of the seat. Alex opened the lid and pulled out a lump of something swathed in tissue paper. Unwrapping it quickly, she discovered a kazoo.

"A good back-up in case I forget my words? Thanks *so much* for your confidence in me, SuperMatt." She wrinkled up her nose at him.

Matt snickered. "Actually, Princess, I thought we might get bored on this long bus ride and you could serenade us."

"No! Give it to me!" Suzanne grabbed the small instrument from her friend and practiced a few notes of the "Hokey-Pokey."

"I could accompany you, Alex, while you 'put your left foot out' for all of us." She directed a hopeful smile at her friend.

Alex ignored her, looking back down to unveil another packet from the box.

"A rabbit's foot?"

Matt's eyes glinted merrily. "To bring you good luck during your judging session."

Alex darted him a thankful smile. "Nice. Thank you."

Alex continued to unwrap items: two candy bars and a pack of gum, a vending-machine necklace in a domed plastic container, and two vibrant, floral "Keep On Truckin'" and "Flower Power" stickers. The last and largest packet revealed a simple, lacquered music box with a rosebud inlaid in the lid.

She opened the box and held it up to her ear to hear the tinkling music over the bus noise. She could barely make out the melody of the "Moonlight Sonata" over the rumblings.

She looked up at Matt, a slight pink rising in her cheeks. "You are too sweet." She closed the lid and admired her shiny treasure.

"Well, I thought maybe it might help calm your nerves before you go in to perform." Matt gave her a doubtful glance and reached over to run a finger absently across the rosebud design.

Alex couldn't take her eyes off of it. "How did you know I collect music boxes?" she asked.

A look of surprised delight hit Matt's face. "I didn't!" He reached for her and they exchanged a long hug.

"Nifty idea, Matt," Suzanne said, reaching out for the box. She held it up to her ear and closed her eyes for a moment. "Love it. You'll let me borrow it before my performance, won't you, Alex?" she asked, handing it back to her friend with a grin.

Alex agreed, cupping the box in her hands even as someone at the front of the bus started singing the old "Kookaburra" folk song.

Matt and she joined in, and Suzanne grabbed Alex's new kazoo as accompaniment. The song quickly became a round, lasting for several minutes. Next, they started a round of "Row, Row, Row Your Boat," which launched the group into laughter and led to the singing of several of their performance songs.

After an hour of singing and conversation, the rolling motion of the bus got the best of the students and most settled down into talking quietly or napping.

February 1978: Matt

*M*att could never sleep easily in moving vehicles. He gently prodded Alex's fluffy coat back up under her head as she leaned against the cold window, deeply asleep. He watched her blond curls swaying in rhythm with the bus, noticing the strength in her features and the determined set of her mouth even as she slept. She reminded him of a beautiful warrior.

His heart began to thump in his chest and a powerful feeling of attraction set his nerves on edge. He felt an almost uncontrollable urge to pull her to him, but a warning nagged at the back of his mind.

She's totally in control of her life. She goes after everything she wants and seems to get it. Even me; she's already got me giving her sentimental gifts.

As he looked down at the music box still tucked in her hands, he realized what he'd just done and his heart started to pound. He'd never given a sentimental gift to anyone before, even to his sister and brother. Which made him think of children again. Ever since helping Alex's younger brother Jake with his recital piece, Matt couldn't get music and kids out of his head. He'd had the idea to start a music school for talented youth, built somewhere in the mountains to provide inspiration, of course. *Playing music every day and sharing it with kids? What better way to improve the world?* Warmth spread through him as he thought about it.

But, if he was going to have a successful music camp and make a living at it right after high school, he was going to have to concentrate only on that. He'd have to find significant funding and good people to help him. He couldn't afford any distractions in his life, away from his plan. Not his parents, not his siblings, not college, not even a girlfriend. The cold thought pierced his internal warmth. Matt ran his hand through his hair as he focused again on Alex's tranquil face. His muse. His first real love. The familiar strains of music her presence always prompted drifted into the back of his mind, but he squelched them before they carried him away.

As strong as his feelings for her were, he suddenly realized he just couldn't fit anyone into his plans, even Alex. He'd just spent too many years trying to create his music around his parents' schedules. Their busy, selfish lives left him to take care of Davey and Becka, when all he wanted to do was compose. *Blast!* He wasn't about to put himself in a situation where he'd have to work around someone else again; especially someone as strong as Alex. His heart thumped a deep bass drum warning. *If I'm going to make my dream a reality, I've got to go it alone. No room for anyone else, especially a muse who disrupts my rhythms so completely. But...* He looked across at her sleeping form. *I love her so much, even if I haven't told her so.*

At that moment, Suzanne reached over the back of the seat and touched Matt's arm, snapping him back into reality. She looked over at the still dozing Alex and asked in as quiet a voice as could still be heard on a bus, "Matt, can I ask you a personal question?"

Searching Suzanne's eyes for a sign of her usual mischievousness, but seeing only straightforward concern, he nodded warily.

"Sorry for being so blunt, but are you in love with Alex?"

Matt's stomach lurched. He paused and responded evasively, "Is she in love with me?"

"Well, I just know Alex has some kind of unexplainable connection to you and I don't want to see her get hurt."

Matt ran his hand through his hair. "Connection?"

"She never told you about her dreams, then?"

"Dreams?" Matt's brow furrowed.

Suzanne pulled back and Matt wondered if she was going to continue or not. She pursed her mouth, contemplating. Suddenly, her expression cleared and she leaned again over the seat.

"Look, Matt, Alex is very intuitive. She has powerful dreams, but she's ignoring their messages."

"You believe dreams give you messages?" Matt thought about making light of her comment. But, before he could even so much as snicker, Suzanne looked him directly in the eye and said matter-of-factly, "They do."

Matt stared back at her.

"The fact is that Alex has recurring dreams that foreshadow what's going to happen in her life."

Matt gave Suzanne a doubtful look and the warning tattoo inside his chest pounded louder.

"She's having some very strong dreams about you and your relationship, and I think you'd both better pay attention to them."

"Yeah?" Matt asked cautiously. "Why's that?"

Suzanne thought for a second and said, "Your family has lake property, right?"

"Yes..."

"It has a cabin on it, right?"

"If you can call a big wooden box a cabin."

"Exactly, a rustic cabin with a wooden porch out front, porthole windows and a creek that runs under the porch."

As soon as the words, "Yeah? So?" came out of his mouth, Matt realized neither Suzanne nor Alex had seen his family's cabin. "How do you know what it looks like?"

"Alex saw it in one of her dreams."

Matt stopped, surprised. After a moment, he said, "That doesn't prove anything. There are plenty of cabins that look very similar."

Suzanne looked over at her still-sleeping friend. "Any others have porthole windows and a creek under the porch."

"Well, not that I know of."

"Exactly. She described it all in great detail with only her dream images to draw on."

That's weird," Matt said, lowering his eyes.

"She also saw you in her dream, Matt. Caring deeply for her and protecting her."

His insides squirmed. "She saw that?" The idea of Alex having premonitions made him feel scared and vulnerable. "These dreams obviously mean something to her if she's telling you about them," he said. "Why wouldn't she tell me?"

Suzanne sniffed and shifted her gaze out the window to the passing landscape. "She wants to be totally in control of her life. She doesn't want to believe something mystical and intangible could be directing her. She's shared the dreams with me because they seem so real to her. They're very powerful and really affect her emotions. But, as I said," she looked directly into his eyes, "she's not listening to the messages. She's not thinking about why they focus so much on you. She thinks they're just a result of her overactive imagination or something."

"Maybe that's all it is," Matt replied hopefully. "You know her creativity. The way she talks, thinks…sings."

"Perhaps. But I still think you both should pay attention."

"C'mon, Suzanne, you really believe that?" He said this as much to convince himself as her. Still, the increasing tightness in his stomach told him what Suzanne said felt true. His unusual connection to Alex did have a mystical feel. *Were they destined to be together? Was he tied to Alex?* He sat back in the bus seat and stared at the honest face in front of him as the world closed in around him. Trapped by an image of completely losing control of his destiny, his heart pounded a drum solo inside his chest.

Suzanne put her head to one side and looked concerned. "You all right, Matt?"

Matt took a deep breath and straightened up in the bus seat. "I'm fine. It just all seems a little spooky."

Suzanne raised her hands next to her ears and wiggled her fingers at him. "Don't worry. Yo-o-o-ou have been forewar-r-r-rned," she said in a light voice. "Now that you know to pay attention everything will work out the way it should." She winked at him and turned back around to face the front of the bus.

Matt worked to control his ragged breathing as he watched Suzanne arrange a travel pillow against the window and lean into it, presumably for a nap. He glanced over at Alex and felt an immediate urge to change bus seats. Willfully overcoming the feeling, he moved his gaze out into the blur of fields whizzing by the bus windows. He took deep, slow, quiet breaths and tried to understand his feelings.

He knew Suzanne pretty well. When she was hanging out with Kathy all the time before Mrs. Sampson's death, Suzanne had always impressed him as sensible and worldly for her age. She'd always given sound advice to her friends and seemed very stable in her own life. It made him wonder why she believed in all that *woo-woo* stuff. "No doubt the universe is unfolding as it should?" *Sheesh!* he thought. But his mind whirred along.

How'd Alex know about their cabin? That's really weird. And why was he in her dream as her figure of love and support? What if Alex's dreams really were driving her destiny? What if being in them tied him to her *life goals? As strongly as he already felt about her, would he be able to resist, to pursue his own goals?* His stomach sank. It was the same trapped and burdened feeling he got when his parents flitted off, leaving him to manage the household right when he was in the middle of composing a piece of music.

Blast if I am going to let anyone else control my life or ruin my goals when I am so close to being on my own. He looked over at Alex again, but with hardened eyes and a distinct musical void in his mind. He thought about taking the music box from her hands, but resisted. *I will not be magnetized by her or sucked into her dreams, imagined or otherwise. I've got to fight my feelings for her.* His heart seized at the thought, stilling the pounding beat, but he was determined.

February 1978: Alex

*A*n hour later, the bus pulled up in front of the University of Idaho. Matt was among the first off the bus when Ms. Nelson enlisted the guys to pull the music stands and heavy instruments from the bus storage compartment.

Suzanne waited with Alex, letting the bus aisle clear for a minute or so before they gathered their belongings. With a contented smile, Alex carefully wrapped up her music box and other gifts to tuck into her purse.

Outside on the sidewalk, all the students grouped around to hear Ms. Nelson's instructions for the day. With her stomach pinched from hunger, Alex was delighted to hear lunch was first on the agenda. She looked across the group to find Matt, but he and the other guys already were carrying the musical equipment down the sidewalk toward the music building.

She shrugged off her light irritation that Matt had left without even a wave goodbye, accepted Suzanne's understanding smile, and took off for The Commons with the rest of the group.

They purchased their cheeseburgers and sodas and sat at one of the cafeteria tables. "I told Matt about your dream," Suzanne blurted.

Alex stared at Suzanne, dumbfounded. She leaned back in her chair and gathered her curls over one shoulder.

"Just thought I'd tell you before he brings it up."

Alex's heart quickened. "Why'd you do that?"

"He needed to know."

"Know what? That a girl's fantasizing about him in her dreams?" She laughed. "Like that never happens."

"You think your dreams are typical fantasies? I already told you I don't think so."

"They're not that big a deal, Suzanne." She sent an exaggerated frown across at her friend.

"I told him *you* didn't think they meant anything. But, you two should talk about them."

"Well, that'll be about a 12-second conversation." Alex shook her head in exasperation. "So, who needs enemies when they have friends like you, anyway?"

Suzanne just laughed and bit into her cheeseburger.

Alex knew her friend was well intentioned, but Suzanne had just forced Alex into discussing this with Matt. Well, she'd just explain that the dreams were realistic, but didn't mean anything to her. They *certainly* didn't forecast anything important. *Maybe only an eight-second conversation.* She allowed herself an inward smile.

Just as they were finishing their meals, the choir guys finally returned. As they stood in line at the cafeteria counter, Alex caught Matt's eye. He lifted his chin with a slight smile, but continued his conversation with the tenor next to him in line.

The girls gathered up their trays and deposited them on the kitchen-bound conveyor belt. Alex turned to scan the room. Spotting where Matt sat, she motioned to Suzanne to follow and walked over to his table.

"So did everything get set up?" she asked, including Ms. Nelson and the other guys in her gaze.

"We're ready for our practice," Ms. Nelson said. "Just meet on the sidewalk outside The Commons' main entrance at 1:30, OK?"

"Great." Putting a hand on Matt's shoulder, Alex asked, "Want company while you eat?"

He didn't look up, but he stopped eating and Alex saw conflict shade his face, followed by a steeling of his features. "We'll be done here in just a couple of minutes. You guys go on outside and catch rays while you can."

Alex felt a cold wall go up around him. Something was eating at him. *Was it something to do with her dreams?* She took in Suzanne's frown, tipped her head toward the door and said goodbye.

Once they were out of earshot, Suzanne said with a worried look, "I guess my little conversation with Matt freaked him out."

Alex tsked. "I'll set him straight."

❖❖❖

Alex had completed her individual practice session with Ms. Nelson an hour ago. It had gone smoothly and quickly. Even though she felt ready musically for her judged evaluation tomorrow morning, a glimmer of the usual butterflies fluttered through her stomach. She peeked into her purse and placed her fingertips on top of the music box. Its smooth lacquered surface and thoughts of Matt immediately calmed her.

Rubbing her hand along the rough and worn finish of the old wooden chair, Alex noted a light musty smell seeping from the textbooks and music scores lining the music library bookshelves. Old wooden study tables lined the interior of the room. A smattering of college students sat at them, reading and taking notes. She wondered how the students could effectively study here, what with the whispered conversations and muffled, confused dissonance of numerous instruments echoing in from the hallway.

Ms. Nelson popped her head in the door to call her last student to his practice session. As Alex looked around, she realized everyone else was now back here in the library. Everyone but Matt. After a few minutes, Alex realized he must still be in a practice room using precious available time to play his own music. She had just enough time to go find him.

She wandered down the hallway, peering in each door's narrow windowpane. She listened to music growing louder as she approached each door and fading as she walked beyond it. Alex paused momentarily when she spotted Ms. Nelson and her final student running warm-up scales in a room. She quickly moved on, wincing as the alto attempted to screech out a high F-sharp.

She moved along the corridor until she heard Matt's familiar touch on piano keys. Typically beautiful. She lingered outside the door to watch and listen.

He was composing, using only his right hand to create a simple melody. Alex recognized the minor key and wondered at its sad sound. He repeated the notes several times and paused. After less than a minute, he began playing again. It was the melody he'd composed moments before, but complete with a beautifully complementary musical arrangement. He paused again, relaxing his still fingers lightly on the keyboard as he turned to gaze out the window.

Alex could only stare in amazement. Had he just written this mysterious, sad piece? He could only have had a short time to create it before she arrived. *That would have taken me hours to compose.*

Matt turned his attention back to the keyboard. He played only the melody, but also sang lyrics he'd obviously just drafted in his head.

Alex could only catch a couple of words.

"…Dreams of another…" "Cling and smother."

Her heart dropped. *Is he writing a song about dreams?* Alex wondered. *About* my *dreams?*

Matt stopped playing, pulled both hands into his lap and dropped his head in concentration. He paused like that for several moments, then took a slow breath, brought his hands back to the keyboard and confidently began playing and singing a polished creation.

Through the door, Alex could just make out the lyrics:

> *Dreams of tomorrow*
> *I just can't borrow.*
> *Dreams, not surreal,*
> *I truly feel.*
> *My dreams, I find*
> *Can't be intertwined*
> *With dreams of another*
> *Who'd cling and smother…*
>
> *I need to call my dreams my own.*
> *I want to own the dreams I've sown.*
> *I'll strive to own my future.*
> *No other's goal can fill my soul.*
>
> *I am torn by swift, engulfing passion.*
> *I must focus, in my solo fashion,*
> *To stay true to my seclusion,*
> *Not to follow your illusion.*

What? Alex quickly retreated from the door's windowpane. *That song* is *about my dreams!* She leaned her back against the door and closed her eyes, her thoughts pounding even louder than her heart.

Is this the same guy who I rode the bus with just a few hours ago? Who gave me my precious music box?

Just because of her stupid, meaningless dreams, he was putting up barriers so he could reach some unknown future goal? Her dreams weren't a threat in any way to Matt or his goals. *They're just dumb dreams!* She didn't even knock, she just walked in and stood there in exasperation as he turned toward her. Tones from his abandoned music hung lost in the air.

Alex watched his expression move from immediate surprise and embarrassment into raised hackles. "Alex," he said coldly, "I'm working here."

"Working on something that's not fair."

"Alex, this is private."

"Not when it has to do with my stupid dreams. Look, Matt, I know Suzanne told you I'm having some sort of prophetic visions. They aren't reality, you know. They're just *dreams*."

Matt looked flatly into her eyes and didn't reply.

She continued quickly, "Everyone has dreams. They're wild, wacky, horrifying maybe, but they're not real. They don't reflect what's happening in life!"

He shook his head. "You're not paying attention."

"What?"

Matt looked at her levelly. "Suzanne thinks your dreams do reflect what's going to happen in your life."

Alex snapped her head forward in disbelief. "You're swayed by the opinion of the chick who thinks 'Desiderata' is the answer to everyone's life?"

"Suzanne is a very wise person, Alex."

"I know that, Matt, but she isn't a guru or anything! She can't make dreams come true."

Matt got up from the piano bench and walked to the small room's narrow window. He leaned against the glass and heaved a deep sigh.

"Alex, you know I have a lot of responsibility at home, right?"

"Of course."

"Well, you see," he said quietly, "my parents are *never* around. It's amazing to see them even 15 minutes over breakfast, or to get a 'good night' before we go to bed. And, it's not just the care for Becka and

Davey. It's everything else. Who do you think buys the groceries? Who cleans up after the kids? Does laundry?"

The frustrated sadness in his voice took the angry wind out of Alex's sails. She wiped her sweaty palms on her jeans and said contritely, "I didn't realize the full..."

He paused, turning toward her. "Every day I have less and less time for me, my schoolwork, my music."

"But you manage it all so well."

"Yeah, well that's why my parents expect me to keep doing it all. That way, they can forget all their real responsibilities and go off to pursue their own interests and diversions," he said angrily.

"I'm sorry, Matt," Alex said, moving a few paces across the room. "But I really don't understand what this has to do with you turning away from me because of some stupid dreams I'm having."

"Alex, they can't be stupid dreams. Think about it. Think about our connection. I felt it the very first time I saw you. Dang it, music started flowing through my head! I know you feel it, too."

"Yeah. So?"

"We have some kind of connection that's not like other people's."

"Yeah. So? Isn't that a good thing?"

Matt folded his arms and looked out the window. After a moment he turned back to Alex.

"OK. Describe for me the cabin you saw in your dream."

Alex looked at him quizzically. She hesitantly started to describe the lone cabin, surrounded by tall pines, with the trickling creek.

His expression grew intense. "As you face the cabin, where was the creek."

"On the right side."

"Where did it flow?"

"It ran from right to left, underneath a wooden deck on the front of the cabin."

"What made the cabin different from other cabins you've seen?"

Alex hesitated before answering. She said warily, "The two unusual windows. They almost look like ship portholes."

He stood up straight and stared at her. "They are portholes," Matt said, amazement tinged with fear growing on his face. His voice was tight. "You've never actually seen my family's cabin, have you?"

"No," she said, dropping her voice and fighting rising fear.

"Yeah, well, in your dream, you saw it perfectly." Matt visibly shuddered and looked away.

Alex pushed aside the eerie feeling gnawing at her insides. *This was just a twist of fate.* She scoffed. "C'mon, you actually think that some coincidental image in my head about how a cabin should look is some cosmic message?"

"Alex, our cabin is not all that normal looking. How many cabins have you seen that have porthole windows?"

"I knew you sail, my mind just put that together and added portholes to your cabin." She stomped her foot for emphasis. "It doesn't mean anything."

"I'm telling you, Alex, these dreams are a part of our connection. Doesn't it scare you somehow?"

"No! I don't think we are linked by my stupid dreams."

"Well," Matt looked away. "It feels that way to me. Big time."

Her stomach tightened and anger nudged against her fear. "Even without my dreams we have a strong connection. That's good, right?"

"On one level it is. But, I'm thinking about the future, Alex. We're only 17 and, by whatever force is behind it, we're getting tied together tighter and tighter. Knowing your dreams show you things you've never seen before... Knowing they include me... It makes me feel smothered, constricted. It feels out of control to me and I don't need my life to be any more out of control than it already is."

"But, if we're together, I can help you with all your responsibilities."

He laughed lightly. "You're going to buy my family's groceries?"

"No, maybe not that. But, I could help pick up the kids from school or take them to their lessons, or something. Like Kathy does."

"I know this is going to sound ungrateful, but that sounds like one more person in my life that I have to manage, Alex. It feels like more responsibility."

Alex studied her fingernails, her mind racing.

Matt continued, "I have goals, Alex. I can't accomplish them if I'm tied down."

"What kind of goals?"

Matt looked out through the window at the clouds skirting the leafy treetops and his brow smoothed.

"I want to start a music camp for kids. It's something I have to accomplish…" He looked down at his shoes, then back outside. "For myself." He held himself very still as he spoke, like he was focusing his whole being on his future.

"I know how important goals can be," she said quietly, trying to ignore the confusion and anger welling inside. "But why does your goal have to exclude you from becoming close to anyone?"

He turned burning eyes on her and said with measured words, "I have to break away, to focus completely on creating this camp without any distractions. It's something I have to accomplish by myself, for myself. If I fail, I'll still be in my parents clutches and I'll be lost."

The force of his words unnerved her. *What the heck do I say to that?* Her heart started pounding so wildly its beat visibly pulsed her clasped arms. Closing her eyes, she consciously calmed her breathing.

After a moment she ventured, "Look, Matt, I don't believe my dreams mean anything. Do you really think I'm *clairvoyant*?"

Matt gave her a defiant look. "No, but dreams are a reflection of your subconscious. Suzanne thinks your dreams are trying to help guide you, but you may not be totally aware of it. And, if that means guidance that pulls me in, then…" he paused. With a pain-filled glance, Matt turned back to lean against the window frame and dropped his voice, "…I have to pass."

Alex clasped her shaking arms close to her body. "So, you're going to choose to believe some spiritual hooey and just pretend we don't mean anything to one another? But, you just gave me the music box." She paused and lowered her voice, "My most precious gift."

He tightened his jaw. Eventually, he broke the hanging silence with a quiet, "It really has more to do with me than with you. I just have to do this on my own. I'm sorry, Alex."

The way he concentrated his gaze out the window reminded Alex of the first day at school. She re-experienced her emotional reaction to her first glimpse of him and her heart flooded with dull pain. "But, Matt, what about 'The First Time Ever I Saw Your Face?'"

He dropped his head, but at that moment, there were some quick raps on the practice room door and Ms. Nelson popped her head inside. "Time to go, you two. The bus is waiting!"

Alex shot a sorrowful, frustrated glance at Matt's bowed head and left the room. *This conversation isn't over yet.*

May 2003: Alex

*A*lex wondered what might have happened all those long years ago if she had just taken him at his word after that first breakup. She supposed it didn't matter. Matt was lost to her now, anyway, except in her dreams. A familiar sadness and longing for him filled her heart. She'd never really felt complete without him.

She sucked in a lungful of damp sea air. So, what could she do now to change their fate? How could she reach the safe haven of the cabin with Matt and make the dream become a reality? If Matt was one thing, he was a loner. Still unmarried, according to the *LA Times* article. He'd had personal life goals from which he didn't want to be distracted, even by his perfect soul mate. As their relationship unfolded, other emotional and physical obstacles had kept it from fully developing, especially his misunderstanding about her involvement with Daniel over the single's music rights. Maybe, in the dream, the trees, snow and his disappearances represented these obstacles.

Yet, the dream always ended with such promise, with a glimpse of his face in the light, followed by the tinkling singing voice and the ray of light on the cabin porch. She knew in her dream that everything would be all right if she could just reach the cabin. Did that mean she *did* need to go search out Matt?

I know we are meant to be together. I just know it! But, Alex rubbed her hands absently along the smooth ceramic of her teacup as she thought of facing him again. The image made her heart race. He'd been so angry with her the last time they'd seen one another…so long ago. He'd been irrationally furious, blaming her…

She remembered now that, in her exhaustion right after their final altercation, she'd had the cabin dream and reached the shaft of light for the first time. Her reasoned reaction at the time was to move forward alone with her music into her own brilliant spotlight. Could it be she had just rationalized herself out of 25 years with her one true love? What if she'd known then to pay attention to a more metaphysical meaning? If she'd taken the images in the dream literally, she might have interpreted it differently. After all, his reflected image shone in the dream light *before* the tinkling music started. Maybe she should have stayed and fought to find the light together with him through their music. Maybe she should try doing that now.

But isn't that what I'm already planning? She suddenly realized the plan she'd concocted in her unhappy state before the car accident, centered on finding Matt. And, now she'd come full circle to the same thought after reinterpreting her cabin dream. This was obviously a message. She must take action on the plan she'd developed.

A warm sense of promise spread through her body and she stood up with renewed energy. There was no time to delay in putting her plan into action.

June 2003: Alex

*A*fter a month of strategizing and schmoozing, Alex's plan was finally coming to fruition. She now stood at her fundraising event, absently twizzling her club soda with lime. She peeked out from behind a large bronze sculpture at the buzzing crowd. Hundreds of cocktail-attired, California entertainment industry peacocks meandered the Museum of Contemporary Art lobby, each trying to out-do the other in designer glitz. Tuxedoed servers peppered the room, trailing wafts of delectable barbequed meats, spicy sauces, and sweet, buttery pastries as they sauntered through the crowd.

She glanced at Reginald, her new bodyguard, lounging against a near wall, and grimaced. How she hated the constant presence of someone watching her. It just rankled. Still, Alex did appreciate Reg. He was a good man and expert at his job. *What a job. Hanging out with beautiful people but never talking with them. Watching delicious food pass by and never tasting it. Putting up with the boss's crazy whims...like mine.* Regs eyes never stopped darting; he never missed a movement. Alex started as a swirl of red satin and matching nails suddenly arrived beside her. Surely nobody in the room missed the movements of Mad Bo.

"Find 'em yet?" her manager asked, the train of her dress whooshing to one side as she stopped. "Or too busy hiding?"

Alex shook her head. "Just got here."

"Can I get you anything? Another club soda with lime? An egg roll? Veggies? A tasty date? I could drum up a boyfriend up for you faster than a speeding bullet." Mad Bo nodded at a drop-dead-gorgeous young actor across the museum lobby standing in front of a bold, wall-sized acrylic painting.

Alex laughed. "That's the guy who plays the teenage Clark Kent on *Smallville*, isn't it? Dang, he's tall."

"Yee-e-e-s-ss," Madeleine said, appreciative eyes studying him from the tip of his long eyelashes to the well-buffed leather of his huge dress shoes. "Simply gorgeous. And named one of *People Magazine's* 'Breakthrough Stars' last year." She turned abruptly to Alex. "It might be good publicity for you to hang out with him."

"Madeleine, get a grip. He's way too young for me."

"I suppose so." She sighed heavily. "He's married anyway."

Alex shook her head. "How *do* you know all this stuff?"

"It's my business to know the business, mon cher."

Alex watched the young heartthrob extend his hand and flash a brilliant smile at a beautiful, dark-haired woman who looked faintly familiar. The woman's teal dress beautifully complemented the vibrant purple in the painting behind them and Alex noticed her graceful mannerisms. Alex's attention turned from the lovely woman to the man now shaking the hand of popular culture's new Superman. She knew too well the grin of that drop-dead gorgeous lawyer. Daniel Post.

Vivid memories of a younger Daniel careened into her mind and she pulled her curls over one shoulder.

April 1978: Alex

Alex was walking across the school campus to her car. She was reliving Matt's prevalent and successful avoidance techniques during the rest of their Moscow trip: excuses to eat meals late, made-up reasons to be elsewhere when Alex tried to talk with him, aloofness while accompanying her during her competition. He'd even managed to spend an entire return bus trip sitting next to Ms. Nelson talking musical theory. Worrying over Matt, Alex barely even remembered earning her "A" rating in the competition.

For the first few weeks back to school, she'd tried everything she could think of to get him to discuss the situation. After a while, though, Alex had tired of his evasiveness and, in frustration, began ignoring him. Still, the pain in her heart continued, always with her as a significant aching weight.

Every school day she saw Matt at least three times: in homeroom, at lunch and in choir. Each time their paths crossed, she'd exchange surface pleasantries with him, while their inexplicable connection tugged at her soul.

Suzanne was still apologizing for causing their rift, and periodically hounded Matt to be open-minded and to talk with her abandoned friend. Alex knew Matt was too internally focused to listen to Suzanne's advice. Suzanne certainly knew it, too, but wasn't giving up easily.

Alex shrugged off the emotionally charged environment her friends were causing, choosing to fully concentrate on schoolwork and music. She knew if she'd just push it all out of her mind for a while, she'd eventually think of something to remedy the situation.

As she walked along, images of Matt bombarded her thoughts. *I'm obsessing about him again.* She immediately forced his face from her mind and willfully began reviewing for the next morning's Spanish test. She pictured the conjugations of "caminar" on the windshields of the cars in the school parking lot. Just as she pictured *"caminamos"* on the windshield of a yellow Camaro, she felt a hand on her shoulder and heard Daniel's voice croon close to her ear, "Hey, Foxy! Fancy meeting you here."

Alex twitched and glanced around for a quick escape. *Yowsers.* No one within 50 yards she could feign to catch up with. Not even a tree near enough to dodge behind. She gave him an impatient smile. "Hello, Daniel."

"What? Not happy to see me?"

"I'm as happy as I always am to see you, Daniel," she said, fluttering her eyelids at him.

"Well, you're going to be after this conversation."

"Am I? How's that?"

"I have something you want."

Alex stopped walking, opened her mouth and eyes as wide as possible and threw one hand up to her cheek in mock surprise. She exclaimed with exaggerated joy, "You're moving to Timbuktu! Oh, I am *so thrilled*!"

Daniel paused close beside her and gave her a patiently disgusted look. "So are the girls in Timbuktu," he said, raising one eyebrow. "No, really..." He flashed his brilliant smile. "You won't be able to resist this."

"Let's see. What could you possibly have that I could want? A million bucks?"

"Better."

"Really? Two million bucks?" she asked, looking distractedly around the parking lot as if searching for her car.

"Think about the hardest concert tickets to get and who might have access to backstage passes."

Alex's gaze snapped back to Daniel's face. *Could he really have...?* "No way!"

"Yep, The Entertainer himself!" He cocked his head. "You can close your mouth now, Alex."

She snapped her lips together and shook her head, as turmoil churned her insides. *BJ Starr, wow!* Was she going to let backstage passes to BJ Starr sway her to go on a date with this admittedly gorgeous but overgrown hunk of arrogance?

"I got four tickets and convinced Brett and Suzanne to come, so why don't you just tag along with us?"

Alex stared at him in stunned disbelief. It was obviously a ploy. She shook her head to clear it. "Suzanne and Brett agreed to go to the concert with *you*?" she said, trying to lighten her accidental emphasis on "you."

"Alex, it's BJ STARR! Who wouldn't want to go?"

"Me," she said, her heart pounding.

Daniel reached out and laid his hand lightly on her arm. "C'mon, Alex," he said in a sincere tone Alex had never heard him use before. "I know you've been hurting since Matt pulled his loner gig with you. I've tried to give you some time to heal by not pestering you. But, this would be just a date. You'll be with your friends and you'll get to *meet* the ultimate piano balladeer of all time. How often are you going to get this chance?"

If she hadn't known his type so well, Alex might have sworn this was a completely different guy. *You manipulator*! She clamped her books closer to her chest and tensed her muscles against the warmth of his touch on her arm. "I'm sorry I just can't go," she said with resolve.

Daniel pulled back and stared at her in disbelief. A long moment passed and Alex watched a painful change move over his face. "What do I have to do to get your icy heart to melt, Alexandra Lauren?" he asked, his eyes pleading. "All I really want is to spend some time with you so we can get to know each other better. Maybe then you'd see how much I..." He turned half way away and lowered his eyes quickly, but not before Alex caught a glint of moisture in them.

Alex was taken aback at his turn of emotion. Where had the cocky, self-assured jock gone?

She watched him straighten his back and lift his head. He cleared his throat, turned back to her and said, "I'm not a musician and I'm not a poet. I know you admire those things. But, I am not a loner, either, and I wouldn't pull away from you for any reason in the world, especially without fully explaining it to you."

Alex just stared at him, conflicted. That was not at all a comment she had expected from Daniel. But, realization hit her with force. *Faking the emotion or not, he was right*. With Daniel, what you saw is what you got. With a sigh, she looked up into his face. What she saw there now surprised her. Honest need. *Is it possible I actually mean something more than a trophy to him?* She was seeing Daniel anew. Maybe she had been so focused on the jock stereotype she'd always worked so hard to avoid, that she hadn't seen him as a real person.

She studied his smooth, chiseled face; his clear, eager, blue eyes framed by soft, light blonde, feathered locks. The words *total hunk* came to mind and a rush of attraction unexpectedly surged through her. Reticence flowed away. *Maybe I should get to know him better...*

Daniel reached into his pocket, pulled out two tickets and expectantly held them out to her. The draw of those tickets was powerful, but it was the slight tremble in Daniel's hand that pushed her over the edge. She gently reached out and took the tickets.

"OK, Daniel." She dropped her head to one side and looked up at him resignedly. "Let's see what happens."

Was that self-satisfaction she saw flitting across his face? Whatever it was got lost in an exuberant jump and giant whoop. Daniel bundled Alex and her armload of books in a big bear hug and bounced her up and down until the books nearly slid out of her arms.

Alex pulled away, laughing at his impetuous response. Calming himself by letting out a long breath, he looked down at her with a broad smile. "OK. Cool. I'll call you tomorrow and we'll make plans. Keep those tickets safe. You won't regret this!" he said, grinning back as he walked away.

Alex stared, motionless, at the tickets in her hand for several moments, turning over in her mind what had just happened. She witnessed Daniel's emphatic, "Ace!" with a fist in the air, from the other end of the parking lot. She shook her head. Daniel had manipulated her into a date. But it *was* just so irresistible. Besides, it would show Matt. He could just stay at home with his precious piano, while she partied with Daniel...and *BJ Starr*!

Alex's stomach was filled with excited butterflies. Here she was 20 miles into Washington State at the Spokane Opera House, just minutes from seeing BJ Starr perform and hours from meeting him backstage! It felt almost surreal, like it was happening to someone else and she was watching from the outside.

So far the evening had been pleasant. They'd shared a quick pizza at Pappy's before the drive across the state line and into the city. Good music on the stereo and Brett's constant drawl kept them entertained throughout the half-hour trip.

Daniel now led the foursome single-file through the Opera House lobby toward their aisle entrance. Thousands of noisy, jostling students jammed the carpeted hallways, and Alex felt the tug of Suzanne's grip on the sleeve of her gauzy gypsy dress. Suzanne, in turn, dragged Brett by the hand through the crowd behind her. In order not to get lost in the crowd herself, Alex held onto Daniel's back jean pocket. With distracted pleasure, she sensed his athletic muscles moving under the denim and along her fingers tucked there. *Definitely a hunk.*

As if he'd heard her thought, Daniel turned and raised his eyebrows at her. Alex felt pink rising in her cheeks but, luckily, at that moment spotted their curtained portal hallway. She pointed to it and Daniel quickly turned to break a path through the crowd. They descended the steps to the main floor and crept through the rows of excited fans, finally locating their seats in the center of row 11.

From their position near the stage, evenly spaced between the huge stacks of sound monitors, "canned" music pounded through their chests so profoundly Alex could barely think, let alone talk. From her vantage point, she had a perfect center-stage view of the grand piano ivories. She fleetingly wondered whom Daniel's family knew to secure such fantastic seats.

Within minutes, the opening band was introduced, played several songs and took their bows. The black-garbed roadies spent an eternity restructuring the stage in preparation for the headliner. Finally, the lights dimmed and thousands of people leapt to their feet and exploded with one giant bellow of expectation. Lighters, held high in the air, lit up the darkness around them.

"Ladies and gentlemen!" the announcer's voice descended upon the crowd. "It may be winter in Spokane, but it's gonna be hot in here tonight!" The crowd roared its approval. "This is the winter night you're going to remember for the rest of your life! Just the memory of this evening's music, from ballads to rock n' roll, will melt the cold of every future winter night! This is the night you are going to meet one of the greatest entertainers of your lifetime. This is the night to experience…BJ Starr!"

At that moment a huge bank of fireworks shot up along the edge of the stage in a gigantic explosion. The crowd thundered in response, girls' screams piercing the roar. In the momentary blast of pyrotechnic light, Alex saw several musicians taking their positions onstage and a driving rock beat began. The stage lights flooded on and she saw BJ Starr standing at the piano right in front of her, pounding the keys like there was no tomorrow.

Immediately, BJ Starr's amazing piano technique, the power of his music, swept Alex away. Time seemed to stop. The din and activity of the fans around her faded into shadow. To her senses, Daniel, Suzanne and Brett blurred into the rest of the surrounding shadows. She registered only faint impressions of jumping and dancing nearby, and of muffled applause. But the only image clearly focused in her line of vision was BJ Starr at the piano just above her, playing solely for her while she sang. She barely noticed the growing fatigue in her vocal chords. Even through the ovations after every song, Alex was transfixed. She became cognizant of a slow-motion Suzanne clapping and mouthing something toward her during the din. Alex hazily responded with a smile and a nod, but focused right back on the stage.

In what seemed like only minutes, the second encore ended and BJ Starr left the stage. The clear roar of the crowd flash flooded her senses. Suddenly, she realized there were people all around her jumping and screaming, applauding with their hands in the air. Finger whistles sliced her eardrums.

Along with the blast of house lights filling the auditorium, came the realization that Daniel's hands were on her hips and she was leaning her back against his chest. She quickly pulled away, startled. *How long had they been standing like that?*

She shook her head vigorously in an attempt to clear her head of the lingering music. Reddening, she caught Suzanne's knowing smile and Brett's exaggerated wink.

"Hello, Alex," Suzanne said. "Glad to have you back with us." Suzanne's voice sounded odd through the ringing in Alex's ears.

"Yeah, you'll have to tell us what concert you saw that we didn't," Brett added.

Alex looked back at them, still slightly befuddled. She flashed back to being transported to the same distant mental plane when she'd first heard Matt play "I Don't Know How to Love Him" from outside the music room door.

Daniel turned her around and placed both hands on her shoulders. His eyes shone as he looked into her face, he asked, "You OK?"

"Fine," she said making an exaggerated effort to wiggle her forefingers in her ears as if to clear the ringing. She forced her voice into a light tone. "Fine." She took a deep breath. "It was an awesome concert. I just... well, I love his music so much."

"Obviously." Daniel winked at her. "I was there to support you."

Envisioning the recent warmth of his body against her back, Alex flushed an even deeper shade of red.

"If you reacted like this just watching BJ Starr's performance, are you sure you're going to be okay meeting him backstage in person?" Daniel asked.

This immediately cleared the emotional fog, as a spark of chagrin flickered in Alex. *I've got to get control here!* Aloud, she said, "It's not the man that gets me, it's the music. Just don't let him sing to me any more and I'll be perfect." They all laughed.

"Good, let's get going then," Daniel said, pulling Alex behind him into the chaotic ant rows of people working their way down the aisles and out of the great hall.

Daniel navigated Alex, Suzanne and Brett backstage and presented their badges to Security. A guard ushered them to a large, cold room in a lower hallway of the Opera House. It was filled with several pockets of people lounging on cushioned couches and around the bar and a large snack table. Several long-haired musicians and black-clad roadies were scarfing food. They sat around on sound monitors reverberating with the concert sponsor's radio station. A baby grand piano sat in one corner flanked by a silver drum set and several guitars and music stands; a perfect set-up for jamming.

A man in a business suit came through the door behind the teens. He introduced himself as BJ Starr's publicist and encouraged them to help themselves to some food and drink. He assured the group BJ Starr would be coming in soon.

140

As the teens moved toward the refreshments table laden with meat platters, fruit trays and chafing dishes filled with steaming appetizers, Brett looked at it longingly. "Ya'll ever seen anything as far out as this?" he asked loudly over the radio music. "I can't wait to sink my teeth into one of them egg rolls!"

"Looks yummy," Suzanne added. She nudged Alex and inclined her head toward Daniel.

Daniel's eyes were fixated on a fidgety group of halter-topped, miniskirted groupies flirting with members of the warm-up band.

"See anything worth sampling?" Suzanne asked pointedly, looking directly at Daniel. He snapped his gaze back to her and quickly lifted his eyebrows twice.

"Nah," Daniel said, suddenly turning to Alex and pulling her toward him in a sideways hug. "I only bother with the choicest morsels," he said licking his lips.

Alex's insides quivered as she watched his mouth, but she masked her emotional reaction by slugging him lightly in the stomach.

"Kiss-up," she teased.

They filled their plates with goodies and attempted to eat while Daniel dragged them over to a group of BJ Starr's band members who had just come in.

Daniel stuck out his hand to the lead guitarist. "You were really on tonight. Some really nice riffs. Thanks for the great show."

"Thanks!" the guitarist said, shaking his hand. "So how'd you guys score backstage passes to this gig?" he asked looking the teens up and down, his eyes lingering on Alex's hair.

Daniel put a protective arm around Alex's shoulders. "My mom's law firm handles legal stuff for KISS-FM, the concert sponsor. They took care of her," Daniel explained.

"Whoa! Lucky man," said the guitarist, his eyes wandering to a red-haired groupie passing by.

At that moment, the door opened and BJ Starr came into the room. Everybody's head turned, a roadie ran to turn off the radio, and BJ Starr's publicist moved quickly to his side. BJ Starr paused briefly to scout out the territory and, with the publicist leaning into his ear, walked right over to his group of musicians and the teens.

Acknowledging his band with a nod and "'nother great show," he turned to the teens and asked in his slurred British accent, "So, did you have a good time tonight?"

Alex's heart was in her throat. She swallowed a couple of times in an attempt to speak, but Daniel spoke first. "It was *so* fine, Mr. Starr. Thank you."

"Oh, buggers!" he said. "Mr. Starr? Just call me BJ."

They took a moment for introductions and handshakes all around, during which Suzanne stood dumbstruck, looking up into BJ Starr's face. When Daniel introduced her, her mouth started to move, but nothing came out. Brett watched her in silent amusement.

BJ Starr just shook his head and smiled at Suzanne while addressing the rest of the group. "Well, I'm glad you're here having a good time."

Alex's finally gained control over her excitement and responded, "I feel so very privileged to meet you. You've been my greatest inspiration ever since I figured out I could carry a tune."

"Which was yesterday," Brett teased. They all laughed, but he added, turning to BJ Starr. "It really was the best concert I've ever heard...uh..." he said, smiling over the word, "...BJ. 'Course your greatest fan here," he drawled, pointing a thumb over his shoulder at Alex, "only had eyes for you onstage. I don't know where she was, but it wasn't with us."

Alex grimaced good-naturedly. "Couldn't help it."

BJ Starr laughed. "It's Alex, right?"

"Yes. Alex Lauren."

"So, a vocalist, are you?"

"One of the best you've ever heard," Daniel interrupted. "Do you want to hear her?"

"Daniel!" Alex whispered, embarrassed. "I'm sure BJ doesn't have time..." She looked at BJ Starr apologetically.

"Hey, I remember what it was like to be eager for someone to hear my stuff. I hear a lot of people's work and, honestly, I don't hear much that really has potential. Still, I'd be willing to listen to yours. Besides, I love jamming to help wind down after a performance," the star said, turning to Alex. "You want to give it a go?"

Alex's heart stopped. Jamming with BJ Starr? Could she really do that without totally choking?

"But…but…don't you have something more important to do? Aren't you hungry?" she stammered, glancing over at the bounteous food table.

BJ Starr laughed good-naturedly. "Nah. Can never eat right after a concert. Too much adrenaline going on in here." He pointed one finger to his head and one to his stomach. "C'mon, Alex! Do you know Billy Joel's beautiful tune "New York State of Mind?" he asked, waving them across the room with him to the piano bench.

Alex looked to her friends for guidance, but everyone already was gravitating toward BJ Starr. Everyone except Suzanne. Her friend stood immobilized, sporting a dumb stare. *She's completely star struck. Totally hopeless.* For some reason, this buoyed in Alex's courage and she laughed. She grabbed Suzanne's hand and dragged her toward the piano, whispering, "He's not the King, Suz, just BJ Starr." Following the pop star, she said with faux confidence, "Sure. 'New York State of Mind.' It's actually one of my favorites."

Alex wasn't about to look like a fool in front of the great BJ Starr. She latched on to a quote from *Macbeth,* which she'd just read in English class. She suddenly realized exactly what Shakespeare meant by "screw your courage to the sticking place." Alex took her spot next to the piano.

BJ Starr smiled up at her expectantly as he started pounding out the song's bluesy opening bars. "I'll sing the first verse, you come in on the second," he suggested. Alex glanced quickly around again at her friends. Daniel sported a proud smirk, Brett a broad grin, and Suzanne just stared at her in horrified fear.

Looking back at BJ Starr when he began to sing, Alex felt as she had when they had first entered the Opera House, like she was standing within a dreamlike slow-motion movie of the scene around her. His earthy tones fit the song perfectly.

Her hands shook as the second stanza's lyrics loomed, so she laced her fingers together behind her back. She timidly voiced the first few notes, but her love of the song's rhythms quickly drew her in. Within several bars, she barely noticed anyone else in the room and wove a warm rendition as if she'd been at home listening to and singing along with BJ Starr on vinyl.

When they came to the musical bridge, BJ Starr sang along with her, but he let her sing the last verse alone. As she fought to still the pounding of her heart, she noticed him staring up and smiling.

Well, I guess I can't be too bad, at least he's not frowning. She finished the verse as he lost himself in playing the keyboard rhythms of the song's final bars.

As the notes of the last chord dissipated, the room erupted in applause. Alex gulped air; she'd totally forgotten there was a crowd backstage. *He really is an amazing musician.* She began applauding with everyone else.

BJ Starr sat back from the keyboard and looked at her for a moment. He reached over and closed her clapping hands within his and said quietly, "This group wouldn't bother applauding for me in a backstage jam. They're applauding you, m'dear."

Ice crept through her limbs. The only part of her body she could seem to move was her eyes. They swept the room, taking in the expressions in the group: enthusiasm, admiration, jealousy. She felt like she was looking though a telescope at a newly discovered universe, exploring its excitement and wonder, yet overpowered by its significance. *How many unreal moments can someone experience in one night?*

BJ Starr sat back again. "Can you make me a tape I could take to my record company?"

Alex stammered and blushed, hardly comprehending what he was asking. Daniel grinned widely and handed BJ Starr an audiocassette.

"I was hoping to give this to you tonight," he said. "She's one talented woman, is she not?" he asked, swinging his gaze to his currently speechless date.

BJ Starr laughed. "Indeed. I see why you came prepared with this," he said, placing the tape in his pocket.

BJ Starr's publicist approached, followed by a woman sporting a Press Pass, a notebook and a tagalong photographer. He signaled to the rock star they were ready for an interview. BJ Starr sighed. Getting up from the piano, he said apologetically, "Would love to jam some more, but I've a previous gig with these blokes. Gotta go. Sorry."

The students each shook his hand and thanked him. When he reached Suzanne, he leaned forward and kissed her on the cheek. This made her surface from her daze and, with a crimson blush, stood smiling at him with one hand on her cheek.

He shook the audiocassette and said to Alex, "I do hope this reflects what I just heard. It would be a pleasure to sing with you again," he said, taking Alex's hand and bowing low to deposit a light kiss upon it.

Alex's mind was whirling as he walked away. She stared at Daniel's grinning face.

"What in the world is on that tape, Daniel?" she whispered.

"You. Singing."

Alex, incredulous, just stared at him.

"At Matt's. I recorded you singing his "Like The Moon Pulls the Tide" composition.

Alex's mind flashed back to the practice at Matt's house when Daniel sat at the recording desk. She remembered his insistence that she use the microphone.

"You plugged in a tape and moved that mic in so you could record us?" she asked angrily. "You didn't tell us?"

Daniel smirked and raised his hands. "Hey, babe, I was doing you a favor."

"So you think I owe you?" Alex asked. Anger nibbled at the surface of her incredulity.

"I saw the potential in that song, that's all. Now, BJ Starr has it." Daniel put his arm around her shoulder. "Alex, I just wanted to help. That practice showed me how talented you are. I knew I had to lay the recording down so I could help you make a name for yourself."

"But you never asked if that's what I wanted," Alex said.

"But it is," Daniel said confidently with a wry smile.

It *was* what she wanted. She couldn't deny it, or the fact that Daniel Post had made it happen. Her anger simmered lower.

"So, what're you freakin' about? BJ Starr likes your singing and has your tape!"

Alex didn't know whether to slap Daniel's face or give him a bear hug. Instead, she leaned against the piano, her mind reeling.

"Alex, come with me," Daniel said grabbing her hand.

She didn't have the fortitude to resist him, so she tagged dutifully behind, watching the way his light blonde hair swayed against his broad neck. *He really is an amazing guy. In charge, smart and looking totally choice tonight.*

She felt the trailing gazes of musicians, guests and roadies on her as she and Daniel passed by. A couple of people complimented her. "Thanks," was all she could muster from her numbed state.

Next thing she knew, Daniel had pulled her behind a changing curtain. He grinned at her and took her hand.

"I really want to help you celebrate this great success, Alex. The best way I can think of is to do something together that we'll always remember." His eyes sparkled at her.

"Something more important than tonight?" she asked, a faint warning tickled the edge of her mind. "Something, we'll always remember…?" An instant image of Daniel leading her into a hotel room flitted through her mind and her focus immediately cleared.

"Like what?"

"Like allowing me to totally pamper you when I take you to our Senior Prom."

This was certainly the last comment Alex had expected from Daniel at that moment. Taken aback, she was unable to muster a response before he continued.

"We could have dinner at The Cedars on the Spokane River before the dance and I'll hire up a limo to take us everywhere."

Alex's immediate reaction was wariness, but she thought about what Daniel had just done for her, getting her tape in front of BJ Starr. What else could she say?

"That'd be great, Daniel," she said. "That sounds like a great way to repa… I mean, celebrate together."

May 1978: Alex

*T*he following month, Alex found herself leaving a black stretch limo and walking into the decorated gymnasium with Daniel and a secret. The bass beat of The Isley Brothers' "Shout!" reverberating in her chest from the DJ's sound system, helped mask the nerves hammering her heart. She tried not to grip Daniel's arm too tightly as they moved into where the Senior Prom was in full swing. She looked around, hoping she wouldn't see Matt right away. She still didn't know how in the world she was going to approach her adversary.

At least she could count on that small boost in self-confidence that dressing up always provided. She smoothed the satiny flounce over her narrow, sapphire blue skirt. She and Suzanne had spent hours shopping for their dresses and Alex loved the gown Suzanne had discovered for her. Its fitted, princess bodice accentuated her shapely neckline and narrow waist, and the emerald sequins patterned down the satin sleeves mirrored the sparkle in her green eyes.

It didn't hurt that she was at this dance with *the* school hunk, either. No tuxedo could hide Daniel's muscular lines Alex observed as her eyes followed the shirt pleats hugging his chest. She admired his soft hair and the set of his high cheekbones, and met his clear blue eyes, which now smiled down at her questioningly. Realizing she was staring, Alex smiled self-consciously and quickly looked away, feeling slightly lightheaded.

In keeping with the senior theme "Reach the Highest Heights" the Senior Prom Committee had transformed the cavernous space into a respectable replica of a Swiss Alpine Village. The main cause of her giddiness was a spinning blizzard of bright, tiny, light flurries – an alpine storm of darting reflections sprayed around the room by the suspended mirrored disco ball. Drops of light dipped in and out of the punch bowl like confused fireflies on the refreshments table at the far end of the room.

Alex recognized one of the school cheerleaders waving coyly to Daniel from the dance floor. Once he'd nodded to acknowledge her, the girl's eyes moved over him. In one daring sweep, she took in everything from the tips of his shiny patent leather shoes to the curve of his long, light-brown eyelashes. Her eyes jumped to Alex's face and her hungry expression turned immediately icy. Daniel hadn't missed the cheerleader's reaction. As he and Alex passed by her, he didn't look at the girl, but lifted his chin slightly and a smug smile tugged his lips. His apparent pride in Alex took her rather by surprise, causing another self-conscious twinge.

To cover her unease, Alex turned away to scan the other side of the dance floor. Nervously scrutinizing the twisting throng, she hoped again she wouldn't see Matt just yet. The crisp blending of cologne, perfume and sweat hit Alex as she and Daniel stopped to watch the dancers during the softer bridge section of "Shout!" The DJ sang along, encouraging the dancers to crouch lower and lower until the music started its crescendo again.

Alex's eyes moved beyond the dancers and swept back along the well-crafted facade of wooden chalets framing the bandstand. About halfway to the refreshments table, a handful of Daniel's athletic friends walked up and greeted them. Alex said hi and pretended to be able to hear what they said over the blaring music. But, her attention wandered when a sudden cold chill swept across her bare arms. The breeze, generated by a large oscillating fan, blew intermittent blasts of air across tubs of ice. Moving back and forth, the cool air ruffled an expanse of paper snow drifts against one wall of the gym. She looked up at an impressive, icy-toned, bas-relief mural of the Alps, certainly the Art Club's contribution to the senior's big night. Its silver-glittered paper snow banks twinkled like pristine snow crystals in moonlight. Spotlights in front of the Alps lit a mock ski-lift set where the photographer was snapping commemorative photos. Alex glanced through the line of students waiting patiently for their turn in front of the camera.

Daniel leaned in to ask if she'd like some punch. She nodded and he walked away, promising to return quickly. At that moment, the song ended and Alex saw Brett and Suzanne approaching. Suzanne looked like a graceful princess wafting toward Alex with her fluffy pink taffeta dress, her hair pinned atop her head with a glittering hair clip. Brett, on the other hand, looked only slightly less than hokey in his powder-blue tux with a ruffled shirt. Alex covered a smile, as she pictured them dancing a slow dance looking like pastel bubble-gum ice cream swirled together.

"Nice threads, Alex, you're lookin' goo-ood!" Brett greeted her loudly, pressing his shirt ruffles against her in a friendly hug. "If it weren't for my Suzie-Que, here, you'd be the belle of the ball," he added, giving his girlfriend a sideways squeeze.

Suzanne gave him a light bump with her hip, but she kept her eyes on Alex. "You do look foxy, girl!"

Alex smoothed her tense fingers down the satin fervently wishing the clenching pain in her stomach would subside. "Thanks. And you look like a princess!"

Brett leaned in to Suzanne, winked at Alex and said, "I'll be right back. Nature calls."

"So, have you told Matt?" Suzanne said as soon as he'd left. She looked around the gym.

"I haven't seen him yet." *Thank goodness.*

Suzanne gave Alex an impetuous hug. "I can't believe you're even here. You should have called him immediately and stayed home to pack for LA!"

"Don't rush me now. We haven't even ironed out all the details yet. Besides, I promised Daniel I'd come to the prom."

Suzanne cocked her head and surveyed her friend with mock disgust. "What's with you? Aren't you over-the-moon excited? You get to record a song..." she overemphasized each word, "...for – a – major – record – label!"

Alex's heart leaped at the thought, but she answered as pragmatically as she could. "I'm just trying not to get too enthusiastic about the whole thing. It's not a deal unless Matt's on board." She pulled her hair over one shoulder with a trembling hand.

"Oh, come on, he's not going to turn down an offer like this, even if he does have to partner with some *sorceress* singer like you," Suzanne joked.

Alex raised an eyebrow at her friend. "You know how focused he is on making his destiny on his own. The record company wants us both, and if I can't convince Matt to follow along with my dream, even though it's not his... Well, then there's really nothing to be excited about." Alex rubbed her hand on her stomach. "Besides, with Daniel behind all this, who knows what's real? What if Daniel's parents just called in a favor with some contacts at the record company and they don't think we have any real talent anyway?"

Suzanne frowned. "BJ Starr loved you! Besides, they wouldn't call and give you an offer if they didn't think you had some talent!"

"You've heard about record companies, Suz. They mostly care about their artists, only as far as there's money in it for them. Maybe Daniel's folks are donating money to them or something."

"That sounds too bizarre," Suzanne said. "Jinkies, lady, you and Matt make some beautiful tunes together. Everyone who's heard you knows it."

Alex scoffed. "I hope I can remind Matt of that for long enough to at least attend a meeting with the record producer."

Suzanne spotted Brett approaching them and she quickly leaned toward Alex to whisper, "You know, a dance is the perfect place to work magic. If I had a Matt voodoo doll, I'd give it to you to pamper. Then he could never say no to you. For now, just concentrate on having fun tonight. You're here with the most *gorgeous* guy in the school!" Suzanne said, as Brett came up behind her and put his arms around her waist. She quickly adding, "Not counting my present company, of course." Suzanne exaggerated her coquettish remark by blinking her eyelashes at Brett over her shoulder.

"Yeah, well, there's nothing like a guy in a tux," Alex sighed, appreciating Daniel's form, still with his friends near the refreshments.

Alex watched Daniel, punch cups in each hand, engrossed in what appeared to be a hysterical conversation with one of the other jocks about his date's frou-frou dress. She was animatedly spinning and curtseying as her date pointed to the abundant floral attachments, lace and ribbons. Each time he pointed she flounced and another peal of laughter rang from the group.

Brett spun Suzanne toward him. "I hate to interrupt your boy talk, ladies, but... Suz, c'mon and dance with me," he pleaded.

Suzanne pretended to be perturbed and, putting her hand to one ear to signify the distinct lack of music filling the gym at the moment, asked, "To what music?"

Brett grinned broadly at her and waved a hand at the DJ. Immediately, "Killing Me Softly" began playing. Alex recognized it as the song playing when they first danced together at the Holiday Dance, right next to Matt and her. Alex imagined being in Matt's arms for the first time that now long-ago night and a twinge of pain squeezed her heart.

"You requested our song!" Suzanne gushed. Realizing the song's meaning for Alex, too, she shot her friend an apologetic look. Brett pulled her off onto the dance floor, his eyes shining. As Alex watched them, she caught a perfect view of Matt and Kathy in an embrace on the dance floor. She exhaled sharply.

At that moment Matt's eyes locked with Alex's. She turned away, her heart pounding.

June 2003: Matt

*M*att peeked out from behind a pillar on the perimeter of the teeming main gallery of the Museum of Contemporary Art. He scanned the room for Alex, pulling his tinted glasses slightly down his nose and raising the brim of his fedora to get a better view. He finally glimpsed her profile halfway across the room taking refuge behind a large bronze statue. She started to turn her face his way and he ducked back behind the marble column. His hands shook. *What the h*** are you doing here, Matt? You want to be done with her. You're more than a fool!*

He had carefully snuck into the corridor edging the main room and dropped his contribution check into the designated box with a nod to the security guard. He'd avoided anyone he knew, including Alex…and especially Mad Bo. That flashy talent manager never missed a trick and, if she recognized him here… He shuddered involuntarily and closed his eyes. That would be a true disaster. She'd have him in front of Alex within seconds. He glanced around again nervously for the whirlwind in red satin. *Ah!* There was the back of her brilliant dress, its short train shimmering behind her as she conversed animatedly with a circle of powerful-looking men.

With Mad Bo distracted for the time being, Matt set his full attention on Alex, the reason he'd come here. She was the only woman for whom he'd ever felt deep feelings, but that had been so long ago. Simply, he couldn't resist the temptation to show up here tonight to find out if his strong attachment to her had now diminished. *Blast that entertainment reporter at the* Times*! Why did she have to go and tell me Alex was planning this fundraiser anyway?*

Warily, Matt peered around the room, noting Dan's and Kathy's positions so he wouldn't have to deal with them, either. His gaze returned to Alex, who absently frowned at her bodyguard and stirred her drink. *What could she possibly have to frown about? Talented.*

Rich. Perhaps more mature, but still, oh, so very beautiful. He wiped a drip of perspiration from his temple with one finger.

Suddenly, Mad Bo appeared at Alex's side and Matt drew back, feeling like a mischievous kid hiding from his mother. *Was this really worth the trouble? Just to see Alex again?*

Matt peeked again and saw Mad Bo point out to Alex a tall, handsome man Matt thought he'd seen on TV. Dan was shaking hands with the young actor.

Matt watched Alex's face as she recognized the lawyer from across the room and immediately pulled her hair over her shoulder. Matt's pulse raced. Her nervous habit was disturbingly reminiscent of the woman's he'd seen on the hotel balcony last month in Santa Barbara. He now knew that woman actually could have been Alex.

Not a week after he returned home from last month's Los Angeles media tour, that nosy *Times* entertainment reporter had called wanting to know his connection to Alex. The reporter had referred to Matt's recently printed music camp article and wanted to know if he'd be in touch with Ms. Lauren about some joint fundraising? She'd explained how Alex had just publicly announced her new cause supporting children's music programs, including a sponsorship of this fundraiser at the Museum of Contemporary Art.

Matt had said he applauded Alex Lauren's efforts, but would not be collaborating with her. But, the reporter had very casually pushed, mentioning some details about the paper's photographer passing Ms. Lauren driving on the Pacific Coast Highway near that fatal wreck covered so thoroughly in the news. The reporter had innocently asked, "Didn't that accident occur near to the hotel where you stayed that very weekend in Santa Barbara?" She also wondered about his and Alex's former music partnership…and how they'd recorded "Like The Moon Pulls The Tide" together in the late 1970s.

When he acted noncommittal about the relationship, the reporter had hinted, not so subtly, about him possibly rekindling a relationship with Ms. Lauren. The caller's words still rang in his head. "I heard through your mutual friend and the fundraiser event planner, Kathy Post, that you and Ms. Lauren were an 'item' at one time. Not to sound like a tabloid, but… Well, Ms. Post said herself that she had been in love with you back then, too... So, anything you'd like to share to clarify how the old love triangle stands now?"

That was exactly *like tabloid news.* No wonder he'd always been wary of journalists; they never left well enough alone. He didn't remember exactly what he'd said about that all being old news, but he'd gotten off the phone as quickly as possible. Unfortunately, the call stirred up some familiarly powerful longings he thought he'd buried years ago. And, they had unexpectedly been eating up his insides for the past few weeks.

Matt sighed heavily and brought his focus back into the moment just in time to see Dan's second-take as he glimpsed Alex. Matt also wondered at the amazement that bloomed across Alex's face as she, in turn, acknowledged Dan and recognized Kathy. Her reaction meant she hadn't actually been involved personally in planning this little shindig with Kathy. Had she actually learned how to take a back seat and let others do things for her? He mentally kicked himself. Of course she had. She didn't do her own work anymore. Alex was a star. She had "peeps," like Mad Bo, to do her work now.

Mad Bo! He gave the room a quick scan. Luckily, she still had her back to him, continuing her conversation with Alex. Matt adjusted his position slightly to better see his songster. As he stared, he felt her familiar charisma drawing him. She barely looked older. Same beautiful curls, same glinting green eyes. She was still so...wondrous. What was it about her that tugged at his soul? He felt his control slipping and music started playing out in his head.

That took him by surprise and he pulled back again into the shadow. Taking several deep breaths, he let the ache of longing subside until his mind cleared. He peered back out and moved his focus across the room to Kathy, who was watching her husband approaching her former nemesis. The woman actually had a smile on her face.

Surely cultivated under Dan's tutelage, Kathy had become the epitome of "gorgeous" and "gracious." She shone with confidence, from the tip of the glittering clip in her shiny dark hair, past her brilliant smile, all the way to the pointy toes of her sparkling teal pumps. Everyone noticed her. Their reverent expressions unwittingly acknowledged her statuesque beauty and refined charm. Still...

He couldn't stop himself from briefly comparing her to Alex. Seeing them both so near, he realized that Kathy – no matter how lovely and talented – just could not compare, at least in his mind. Yet, he had to admire how his friend had transformed. How far she'd come from the loyal, but overly needy, friend who helped him have a life in his younger years.

Lord knew she'd been a great friend to him. He'd always tried very hard to be a good friend to her. But, he never could dredge up any romantic feelings for her, even when that jerk Dan stole her away from her job at the camp and married her. Still, from his very first glimpse of Alex in high school, she had completely overshadowed Kathy. With that thought, a series of early images of Alex raced through his mind. Alex bumping into him in the choir-room doorway. Alex singing. Waterskiing. Certain expressions. Her laugh. The images stopped abruptly as he jumped to a memory of Kathy's stricken face when Alex interrupted their senior prom date, and guilt pinged through him.

May 1978: Matt

*K*athy's arms clenched tight around Matt as they danced. Usually, he would have wanted to pull away, but tonight he was grateful for the undivided attention. Kathy's solid friendship gave him balance in his recent confusion. His world just hadn't seemed right since he'd split with Alex.

For years, he'd been clinging to his dream of finding an escape from the responsibility his parents had thrust upon him. His recent vision of a children's music camp was the perfect answer to that dream. But, somehow his vision had paled since he'd broken up with Alex. He'd lost his focus.

He still felt distracted by her, just as he'd written in his lyrics, "*She draws him like the moon pulls the tide.*" The closer he got to her, the more he was drawn toward her. The more he pulled away, the stronger was the pull to return. She formed the rhythms of his life. Acted as his muse. Every time he tried to write music, thoughts of Alex flooded his mind, and every time he saw her the music came flooding in.

Awakening from his daydream, his eye caught Alex's at the edge of the dance floor. She immediately looked away, but he couldn't take his eyes from her lovely form. He still felt her powerful pull and more lyrics came flooding in…

> *Like being ripped from Earth into the glory of clear Light,*
> *Unknown and terrifying, but ultimately right.*

As the words drifted from his consciousness, his mind was filled with images of holding Alex. His heart beat so hard against his ribs he thought Kathy might feel it. *Kathy's head on my chest.* He started, realizing she had snuggled in while he was mentally with Alex.

Kathy looked up at him adoringly. He returned a slight smile, but immediately broke free from her just as "Killing Me Softly" ended. "Let's take a break from all the noise," he said, escorting her away from where he'd seen Alex. Kathy gave him a puzzled look, but followed him out into the gymnasium's empty foyer.

He closed the double doors behind them, mostly silencing the DJ's latest pick, Bread's "Everything I Own," blaring through the gym behind them. Matt looked back through the door window and glimpsed Alex smiling appreciatively up at Daniel as she handed him back an empty cup of punch.

Kathy followed Matt's gaze, withdrew her hand from his and turned away.

"You OK?" he asked, noticing the look on her face.

"You're still in love with her aren't you?" Kathy asked.

Matt dropped his gaze. How could he say what he needed to without hurting his friend?

"What is it about her?" The pitch of Kathy's voice rose with each word, echoing off the entrance hall's block walls. "What hold does that witch have over you? Haven't I done enough to prove how much you mean to me? Why don't you love *me*?" she accused him, her eyes bright with tears.

Matt moved forward and gently took hold of her arms. "Kathy, you know how much you mean to me."

"Not *that* much," she said, punching a thumb toward the gymnasium door and Alex.

Matt sighed. "Kathy, I can't possibly thank you enough for all you do for me. So many days your help with Davey and Becka was the only thing that made it possible for me to work on my music. You're the best friend I could possibly have."

Kathy narrowed her eyes. "Best friend...?"

"More than that," he added, switching his weight from foot to foot. "I love you like my own..."

"If you say 'sister'," she interrupted, "I'm booking!"

"Come on, Kathy, I can't help..."

A blast of music drowned his words as the foyer doors opened. They slammed shut behind Alex and she tentatively approached them. "Hey, guys," she ventured.

Kathy shot Matt the most hurt look he'd ever seen on anyone's face. She turned on her heel and stormed back into the gym without even a glance at Alex. A blast of dance music came through the door as she left. Through the small window Matt watched Kathy's layered lace flounces jerking as she retreated across the gym floor. He made a move as if to follow, but the pain he knew he'd caused her immobilized him. Instead, his body tensed and he turned to face Alex.

"I'm sorry I interrupted your date," Alex said, nervously rubbing her fingertips together. "But, I…"

"Where's *Daniel*?" Matt asked.

"I told him I had some business to discuss with you."

"Business?" he asked.

"I need to talk with you, Matt. It's important." She laid a hand on his arm.

Matt stared down at her hand. Alex immediately withdrew it and scanned his face warily. What she saw there surprised her.

Desire.

It had been weeks since she'd stood face-to-face with him, and her soul unwillingly sank right into the hazel pools of his eyes. Immediate waves of passion washed over her, melting her resolve like cotton candy in water. Her rational acceptance of their breakup for the past weeks had been vanquished with one simple touch. She was awash in an emotional current. She unconsciously reached out her hand to touch his face.

Matt pulled back and gave her a guarded look. "What do you want?" he repeated in a ragged voice, taking a step back and jamming shaking hands in his trouser pockets.

Alex snatched her hand back, forcing her mind back up to the surface, to reality. Her purpose for interrupting him came back in a rush and, ignoring her flaming face, blurted, "I got a call from BJ Starr's record label last night."

Matt stared blankly at her for a moment before his eyes widened. He started to speak, but Alex held up her hand to stop him. "I know this is going to seem too amazing, but they want us to record a single of "Like the Moon Pulls The Tide."

His expression turned from shock into pure skepticism. "Yeah, right. We all know nobody's heard that song. I needed a good practical joke today," he said, turning to walk away.

Alex grabbed his coat sleeve to stop him. "I'm serious, Matt!" She haltingly explained how Daniel had made the secret recording and finagled the tape into BJ Starr's hands, and ended with, "There's no deal unless you're in."

Matt stared at her. He searched her face, but it held no hint of jest or malice, just honest anticipation and fear as she bit her bottom lip. His mind reeled and he blurted out a last-ditch effort to find truth. "After ignoring me all these weeks, the best you can do is dig up this scheme as an excuse to talk with me?"

Alex's mouth dropped open. "You know I didn't!"

Her astounded look told him everything and his heart skipped several beats. *They want my song!* "You're *serious*," he said.

She nodded and pulled her curls over one shoulder.

He ran one hand through his hair and scanned Alex's expectant face as silence yawned between them. "But, BJ Starr? Recording a single? How the heck...?" He pictured Daniel handing BJ Starr *his* song and a flash of jealousy punched Matt's gut, but he shook it off. "Yeah, this sounds exactly like something Daniel would do."

Alex smiled a small smile. "His intentions were good for a change," she said.

Good for us maybe. But, what will he get out of it? "I can't believe they want to record my song," Matt finally said with a slight waver in his voice.

Alex laughed quietly and nodded at him. "And me to sing it," she said, equally unbelieving.

The world around Matt seemed to slow its pace while his thoughts swirled. On one level, this was what he wanted most. If he could get some money from this song, his plans to start his music camp would be all the more feasible. But he realized this meant a close working relationship with Alex and that scared him. He lost his focus so easily with her, even when he *wasn't* around her.

Alex broke into his contemplation. "I talked with the producer last night on the phone. If you agree to it, they want to meet next Saturday to talk everything over."

Matt blinked away from Alex's face. "OK, a meeting sounds like a good first step."

"You're sure?" she ventured, with a wary glance. "What about your wanting-to-follow-your-own-dreams-with-no-one-to-distract-you thing?" She was almost able to keep the hurt out of her voice.

Matt shifted his weight away from her and heaved a sigh. He looked back into her hopeful green eyes and felt the faint shimmering of that familiar music forming from the depths of his soul. The thought of spending time in a studio with Alex was intoxicating, and this would further his own plans as well. He was almost surprised that no internal warning flags went up. Something about this felt right.

"Well, if I don't at least look into it, I know I'll regret it," he said.

Alex sighed in relief. "Far out!"

"Did you tell Daniel already?" Matt asked.

"I didn't want to tell him until I'd talked with you, Matt. Anyway, there'd be nothing to tell him if you'd said no." Matt fought an overwhelming urge to reach out and crush her to him. Alex added, "Matt, I'm really glad. Your music really does deserve to be heard."

"And people should hear you sing, Alex."

At that moment, Daniel burst through the foyer doors, pulling a reluctant Kathy behind him.

His eyes flashed at Matt. "I found this friend of ours in there looking for a way to get home." He pulled Kathy next to him as she wiped at her eyes and gave her a little push toward Matt.

"You guys have been friends your whole lives. Time to talk it out," he said.

Alex cleared her throat. "I'll call you with details, OK?" she said to Matt as Daniel grabbed her hand and pulled her back into the gym.

Matt fisted his hands, barely resisting the urge to grab Daniel and punch him in the nose. *You have no right to be mad at Dan. You're the one who broke up with Alex.* He took a ragged breath and turned to Kathy. He took her reluctant hands. "I'm sorry, Kathy."

She just glared up at him.

"You can't stay mad at a rock star, can you?" he asked with a crooked smile.

"What are you talking about?" She stomped her foot in frustration.

"Alex interrupted us only to tell me we might have a record deal for 'Like The Moon Pulls The Tide.'"

Kathy hesitated and a look of pure amazement lit her face. "Your composition?"

Matt couldn't stop the grin. "Yes!"

"But how'd they get it?"

"A Daniel scheme, of course."

"For real?" He nodded and she hugged him tight. "Maybe now you'll be able to fund your music camp."

Matt hugged her back. "We'll see," he said pulling away and looking into her eyes. "Kath, I'm going to need my friends now more than ever. Please don't give up on me." He watched an instant of doubt and pain shadow her joyful expression, but she nodded and hugged him as if she'd never let him go. And he hugged her back.

May 1978: Alex

"So'd you get your business finished?" Daniel asked Alex sarcastically just inside the gymnasium door.

"Yes, I did," she said.

"Anything that concerns me?" Daniel asked in a fuming tone that brought Alex back into the moment.

She quickly rubbed her palms together and turned her face up to his. "Actually, yes," she said.

"What business was it? A plan to drive a permanent wedge between Kathy and Matt?" His voice shook.

Alex widened her eyes. *That's more like something* you'd *do*. She was flying too high to buy into his anger. She looked sideways up at him and admired how handsome he looked with his eyes flashing like bright blue sparks. "No one can separate Kathy from Matt."

A knowing expression crossed his face. "Then, what was so pressing that you had to abandon me and infuriate Kathy to talk to Matt tonight in the middle of our dates?" he asked.

"Kathy made *herself* mad." Alex waved a hand in dismissal. "The little green monster has a permanent grip on her when it comes to me." She paused. "I needed to ask Matt if he would go with me to talk with BJ Starr's record producer next weekend."

"What?"

"They want us to record Matt's single."

"Your single? The one I gave BJ Starr?" Daniel asked, his anger vanishing. When she nodded, he shook his head, slapped his thigh and gave a hoot. "It worked?"

"Yeah. Thanks to you." Her heart soaring, Alex gave him an impulsive hug.

Not letting go of her completely, he turned her toward the dance floor as the synthesized opening of Gary Wright's "Dream Weaver" wafted its melody throughout the gymnasium. "This calls for a slow dance, girl. I want you to whisper every detail into my ear."

Alex held tightly to Daniel as they slow danced, but her mind moved in different circles. *What does this mean to Matt and my relationship? And what about Daniel? How am I going to deal with it?* Her heart hammered in her chest.

Daniel's hands moved to either side of her face. "I don't hear any details being whispered here. You daydreaming about being a rock star?" he asked. "Or can I hope your heart is racing like that because you're in my arms?" He licked his lips and moved his face closer as if to kiss her.

Alex pulled back. "No," she gasped.

Daniel stopped dancing, but kept a firm grip on her face, while his eyes questioned her. "What? No thank you for getting your song in front of the big guys?"

Did he really expect a reward? She dropped her gaze. "Just too much to deal with at once. "I'm sorry, Daniel."

One hand slid under her chin and he raised it until she looked into his eyes. "I can be patient. For a time." He held her gaze for a long moment. "Just know I *will* be there with you every step of the way." She nodded, and he turned to lead her from the dance floor.

May 1978: Matt

*T*he following Saturday, Matt sat in Mr. Post's legal offices with Daniel, Alex, her parents, and BJ Starr's recording label producer Gary Grandberg to discuss recording terms for their potential single.

Mr. Grandberg, a handsome bespectacled man whose wiry frame belied his lack of height, seemed permanently attached to an unlit cigar. It dangled from his teeth as if it might fall at any moment. He impressed Matt as being very sharp, demanding and straightforward. Still, whenever something pleased him, he flashed a ready, wide smile that brightly lit his face above the precarious cigar. Mr. Grandberg sat in a tan, leather, wing chair to one side of the room's expansive mahogany desk.

Daniel's father, who sat behind his desk, had generously agreed to let them meet in his firm's spacious Spokane office. Meeting here, rather than in Los Angeles, was a concession by Mr. Grandberg. Mr. Post had persuaded the producer to come to Spokane so Matt and Alex wouldn't have to make a whirlwind weekend trip to LA during the last few weeks of their senior year.

As the contract negotiations rolled on, Matt focused on the overstuffed chocolate-brown leather furniture and mahogany paneling giving the room a rich, warm feeling. Brass highlights brightened the atmosphere, and numerous potted plants softened the edges of the two, large, fifth-story picture windows.

Matt looked over at Alex, a smile playing at her lips and excitement sparking her eyes. In eager concentration, her head moved back and forth as she followed the conversation. *I wouldn't be sitting here if it weren't for her*. A little trill ran through his heart, but he ignored it.

He turned his attention to Mr. Post who was explaining what Matt hoped would be the final contract detail. Matt had no idea there would be so many items to discuss just to lay down one single track of music, but at least they'd lumbered through the main points already. He looked briefly over at Daniel, who had been strangely silent and exceptionally attentive to the details of the meeting. His friend's rapt attention currently fell on his father.

Matt forced himself to concentrate on Mr. Post, too. The lawyer was reiterating that they could each bring only two friends or family members with them into the recording studio. Matt nodded his head in agreement, as did Alex.

Matt knew his personal interests were foremost in Mr. Post's mind, as he'd specifically asked Mr. Post to handle his contract separately from Alex's. Matt was just more comfortable not treating this musical endeavor as a duet, but rather as two individual performers collaborating. His future freedom could be compromised if he didn't keep their financial arrangements separate. He hadn't discussed this with Alex, but she and her parents must think it was a good arrangement since none of them had raised an argument.

Matt's eyes wandered over to Alex's supportive parents, sitting together on the leather couch opposite Mr. Grandberg. Mostly observers today, the Laurens had pitched in only when they felt the teenagers' schedules or other needs might be taking a back seat to the record company's demands.

Matt resented his own notoriously absent parents. He'd thought he might have seen actual regret in his father's eyes as he told Matt an architectural conference conflicted with this record-deal meeting. His mother had been very excited for him, but the meeting conflicted with her sales pitch to a client in San Francisco. Her excitement had faded quickly, though, when she realized she'd have to find someone to stay with Becka and Davey. But, of course, she hadn't made the arrangements anyway. *My precious mother couldn't even find the time to make one simple phone call. God bless Kath for coming to my rescue again. I wouldn't be here without her. Or our scheming Dan for that matter.* Matt glanced over at his long-time friend. *He's the reason we're here at all.*

Matt's conflicted feelings about Daniel bubbled up again. *Can I blame him for pursuing Alex?* Matt studied Alex's beautifully animated face. *I just need to think of her as a friend.* He inhaled deeply. *I just need to get control of my jealousy and realize they are all just my friends. And every friend is a gift.* The thought immediately sparked lyrics and his mind took off on an accompanying tune. It emerged nearly fully formed in his mind.

> *Oh, my friend, I have a gift to give you.*
> *Not something you can buy or touch,*
> *But one to live within you.*
> *There are many things I could give you,*
> *To show you that I care,*
> *But nothing you can touch,*
> *Can show you what is really there...*
> *I am giving you my friendship to last throughout your life.*
>
> *The world is a circle and some feelings that you feel*
> *Go 'round in the circle to show you what is really real...*
> *That's why I'm giving you my love to last throughout your life.*
> *So, you'll remember that I care,*
> *And seek the way*
> *On the wings of air*
> *Not far away.*
> *A friend is there.*

He jotted the words on his notepad as they came to him, and mentally tucked away the inspired melody to flesh out in a composing session later. He finished just in time to catch Mr. Post's and Mr. Grandberg's summary.

"So, I'll look into an initial recording session in the studio here at Frankie B. Crosby's former Hayden Lake estate, where Alex and Matt can lay down the reference piano and vocals," Mr. Post said. "If that goes well, we'll sign the final papers and you'll bring the kids back to Los Angeles after their graduation for a final recording session with the studio musicians, right?"

"Great. Now, if your local studio doesn't work out for some reason, we'll make arrangements to do all recording at our LA studios. I'm hoping for 'Frankie's' place, though," Mr. Grandberg said, his unexpected smile lighting up behind the cigar. "Recording at the home studio of my all-time favorite crooner – rest his soul – would be a rare privilege, not to mention the great PR it would make for the single."

He turned to Alex with a bright smile and asked, "All this sound good to you, my little chickadee?" She nodded enthusiastically. "And, you son?" he asked Matt. With Matt's assent, Mr. Grandberg rose to shake hands all around. "We'll prepare the final paperwork and see you in a couple of weeks," he said, noisily moving his cigar to the other side of his mouth. With a broad wave, he strode from the room.

After expressing their gratitude and farewells to Mr. Post and Daniel, Matt and the Laurens left, also. Alex was the last to exit as Matt held the legal firm's front door for everyone. She paused as she went by, placing both of her hands on his arm and smiling at him. Green eyes sparkling, contagious excitement radiated from her and he caught its energy. She only lingered with him a moment before rushing to her waiting father. Matt watched her curls bounce around her shoulders as she looked up gratefully at her dad.

Matt tried to quell the pull of attraction welling inside him, but was unable to draw it back. His energy flew out and away toward her, entangling in the blonde ringlets caressing her face. The music started up again at the back of his brain. He couldn't fight it. He couldn't prevent her influence on him. She was his muse. He ran a hand through his hair, looking back up at the building as he walked away. Daniel stood at the fifth-story windows staring down at Alex's retreating form. *I'm sure I can get through this if I can keep that muse – not to mention the little green monster – at a distance.*

June 2003: Alex

*A*gitated by her vivid memories from what seemed a lifetime ago while here in the art museum, Alex twizzled her drink a little too enthusiastically and the iced liquid splashed onto her hand. It brought her abruptly back to reality where she found Mad Bo staring at her with slight concern as she dabbed at the spill with a napkin. "You tripping down memory lane with your hosts, mon cher?"

"Afraid so." Her gaze fell on Daniel again. He apparently hadn't changed much. Here he was at his wife's event, schmoozing funds from the likes of that young television heartthrob. Alex glanced back at the beautiful woman in the teal dress. *His wife's... But that means the woman with him...* "That's *Kathy*?" she gasped.

Mad Bo followed Alex's gaze. "What is your deal, hon'?"

She shot Mad Bo a quick glare. "It's just... It's been so long since I've seen Kathy, I didn't even *recognize* her."

"Rightly so, you've been very preoccupied with your career during the years that Daniel's gone all *Pygmalion* on her. He's actually made her into a believable socialite."

At that moment, Daniel scanned the room. His eyes passed Alex, and she imagined hearing a screeching noise as they jerked back to her face and narrowed. She met his gaze straight on and watched a smile grow on his lips. He immediately excused himself from his wife and the tall young actor and turned toward her.

"You want me to stay here for moral support?" Mad Bo asked as the lawyer approached.

Alex squared her shoulders. "Thanks, but I can take care of him, as always." She also glanced at Reginald whose countenance had changed from relaxed attentiveness to near-pounce readiness; his usual stance as anyone drew near her. "Reg has my back," Alex added. She nodded and winked at Reginald to let him know Daniel was a friend. Still, she couldn't stop a twinge of irritation, though, even if she did know Reg's bulky presence was only there for her protection. She exhaled involuntarily.

"OK then." Mad Bo winked as she stepped away, "Try not to start a public row with Daniel while I'm 'mixing' to find your next gig, OK?" She gave Alex a half smile, fluffed her hair, and flounced away in a shimmer of red.

Alex turned her head, right into Daniel's lingering kiss on her cheek. "It's been too long since I've seen you, m'lady. You avoiding me?" He lightly rubbed his hands along her shoulders.

She smiled slightly at his continuing persistence. "It has only been a year or so since I've seen you, Daniel. And, as I'm sure you know, I'm a very busy working girl." She took his hands from her shoulders, squeezing them in a friendly manner, but letting them drop.

"A Grammy, no less."

"Oh, yes. Thanks for the telegram." She dropped her eyes and ran a finger along the rim of her cup, scowling.

He leaned forward to look up into her bowed face. "Ah, the pressure… Looks like you need a rest."

"Probably do." She stared unseeing across the room as her finger continued to circle the glass, and said quietly, "A nice quiet place where no one has a camera and people respect my privacy. Now that would be seriously nice."

The handsome lawyer peered into her face and suddenly lit up. "What you need is a lakeside escape…to our little Coeur d'Alene. You know, it's a few months away, but our graduating class is planning a 25-year reunion."

"Really? Is there one? Has it really been 25 years since graduation?" She was pleased it sounded as if she really didn't know.

"You should go back for it. The hometown would love to see their girl return to them. A day or so of public appearances and then a week tucked away on the lake. Somewhere where even Reginald doesn't know where you are."

How can he possibly know my new bodyguard's name? Good thing to know Daniel hasn't changed. She was counting on that. "Oh, imagine all the hoopla. I'm not sure that's a good idea."

"Sure it is!" he said, checking over his shoulder.

Following his gaze, Alex saw a confidently smiling Kathy moving briskly toward them. "What have you done to Kathy, Daniel? She's not even the same person."

"I know. I'm proud of her. She's..." He watched his wife approach for a moment and turned to stare into Alex's eyes. "She's *almost* like you now," he said. His eyes glistened with a familiar light.

Alex recognized that hungry stare. It had been in his eyes almost every time he looked at her in those early days, at least until the recording session.

June 1978: Alex

*H*er very first recording session ever and she could barely keep her mind on the music. Alex sat behind the mic with her eyes closed. The sound techs were working on Matt's piano track, but she found herself shivering.

Blasts of icy spray from the river misting her face in her dream last night had sent similar frissons through her. Reliving the intense shaking took her right back into the dream...

She felt so lost scanning the woods for any sign of Matt. As she began crossing the bridge, the sheer power of the rapids stopped her. Its cold spray stole her breath, stung her face and sent a blast of unease down her spine. Dizzy, she began to reel from watching the rushing water. Expecting to tumble into the river at any moment, she closed her eyes. Instead of a dizzying fall, she felt a hand on her arm steadying her, spreading warmth into her.

When she opened her eyes, Matt was there with a penetrating stare. He pulled her close against his chest and held her. They stood on the bridge for many moments, arms encircling one another. Alex drank in Matt's essence. Was it her imagination, or was a beautiful faint melody hanging in the air, muffled among the snowflakes?

The studio music crescendoed, abruptly interrupting her reverie. She focused on the sound booth's padded mic just inches from her mouth and reminded herself of her immediate reality. She was here in Hayden Lake, Idaho, in Frankie B. Crosby's former home, listening to the final take of the piano and vocals reference tape she and Matt had lain down over the past few hours. She consciously shook off the dream's lingering influence.

Now fully aware, she peered through the glass windows dividing the booth from the mixing room/lounge. As their playback ran, she focused on the extensive, remarkable collage of "Frankie's" personal family photos and album covers gracing the walls.

Who knew the crooner would have a recording studio inside his house? Luckily, Mr. Post had discovered it when the celebrity had passed on the previous October. Frankie had left the home to his son, a client of Mr. Post's. A phone call was all it took to allow the students to record their song here. The son was happy to have a reason for someone to use the house while it was yet unoccupied.

Mr. Grandberg, whom the students had secretly dubbed "Cigar Gary" or "Cig Gary" for short, was overcome by the idea of recording there. Everyplace he wandered in the home, an unshakeable smile backlit his tobacco roll. He randomly ran his hands along items he passed as if trying to soak in the famous singer's missing presence.

At the moment, Alex could see Cig Gary just above the large, black, sound-mixing console. He paced back and forth with a light step, gliding along with the music, and his hands tapping the beat along chair backs and recording equipment as their music played.

Alex was proud. *This really* is *beautiful music.* She looked for a reaction from the row of friends and was shocked to see Kathy staring at her in admiration. The dark-haired girl's expression snapped off as soon as she realized Alex had seen her, but it was unmistakable. Regard, not jealousy.

Alex averted her gaze immediately, too. It landed on the shaggy-headed sound technician, a "mixer" named Kurt. Alex couldn't see his hands, but her friends' fascinated stares monitored his nimble motions. Her friends sat along a line of burnt orange couches, attentively watching Kurt manipulate the many buttons, sliders and knobs. With treble and bass input and output, volume, background noise and so many variables captured in a recording, Alex couldn't imagine how sound guys could ever remember which buttons did what. Just the 88 keys on a keyboard had been hard enough for her to learn.

Except for the few minutes when she'd slipped into last night's cabin dream, Alex had never been happier in her life. Most of the day, she had been in her element, singing her heart out to Matt's lovely music while Cig Gary and Kurt made shrewd observations and creative suggestions to draw out their best performances. Alex felt good about her vocals, but Matt amazed her. She was continually awed by his flexibility and instant creativity when asked, on the fly, for a specific tone or change in his arrangement. The only thing more incredible than Matt's ability to showcase his skills was her opportunity to share the experience with him.

Alex's heart quickened watching Matt across the small studio as the final track played out. He leaned back with his hands on the piano bench, his eyes closed. His cocked head caused shiny locks of honey-colored hair to fall over one shoulder.

As Alex watched him, her mind swam with the music, and strong feelings bubbled up. She would have given anything to go over and run her fingers through those honey strands. Realizing she was breathing erratically, Alex's eyes darted back to her friends beyond the glass partition. Had anyone noticed her staring at Matt? Her eyes immediately met Daniel's penetrating gaze. He looked away nonchalantly, but Alex noticed an unusually ruddy hue to his face.

A lump fell into Alex's stomach. How could she still have these feelings for Matt? She was dating Daniel now because Matt didn't want to be with her. Despite her first impression of Daniel as a "typical jock," he had proven charming, attentive and generous. There was no doubt about their mutual chemistry, either, but something about him still made her wary. She couldn't quite put her finger on it... No matter. She needed to get more in control of her feelings for Matt.

The recording came to an end and Cig Gary paused, eyes on the ceiling, considering what he'd just heard. Positioning his cigar further into the corner of his mouth, he leaned over Kurt to push the intercom button. "Nice work, kiddos. Why don't you all feast on the good eats Kathy so thoughtfully provided? Kurt and I will work on some of the recording levels here," he said. With a smile, he nodded at Matt and Alex, and turned back to the soundboard, already back at work.

Matt motioned to their friends to meet them in the adjoining studio kitchen. In the midst of a flurry of hugs and praise, Alex saw Kathy run up to Matt, hug him for a long moment, and pull away to ogle him with unconcealed admiration. Alex didn't know whether to be peeved, or relieved Kathy was completely ignoring her. She did wish Matt had asked Kathy to baby-sit his siblings today, instead of inviting her to practice her skills by catering their recording session. Alex scanned the fresh food and handsomely presented table. Begrudgingly, she had to admit Kathy had a knack.

Kathy asked Suzanne and Brett to fill cups with ice while she asked everyone what they wanted to drink. The others grabbed plates and piled sandwich fare and brownies from the trays lining the oversized table.

Just as Alex reached to take a plate, Matt grabbed her hands and turned her toward him. He gave her a long look and pulled her into a tight hug. He didn't say a word, but she immediately felt his unspoken thanks and the wonderment neither could fully express in words. She nodded at him and smiled her understanding as she pulled away.

Alex suddenly realized Daniel wasn't in the kitchen. Through the door back to the recording studio, she saw him still sitting on the orange couch, watching her with a wry expression. She moved to the doorway, popped her head into the studio and asked in a light voice, "Want a turkey roll, Daniel?"

"No thanks. Not hungry," he said, looking away to the activity at the soundboard.

He's jealous, of course. Her stomach gave a heavy turn. What if she stumbled into revealing her true feelings about Matt and made things worse? The longer she waited to address the situation, the worse it would get. She went into the studio and sat next to Daniel. With sweaty palms, she nonchalantly cocking her head to one side, she asked, "Everything OK?"

He glanced through the kitchen window at Matt and Kathy. Daniel returned his gaze to Alex and stared directly into her eyes for a moment. Giving an airy snort, he got up abruptly. "I'm fine. Everything's fine," he said and walked away.

Alex didn't get up to follow him. She sat, staring down at her clogs. Daniel was in love with her. She was in love with Matt and so was Kathy. Matt was in love with his dream. The Fates certainly had woven them into a complicated design. But Alex knew there was a way to unwind the tapestry spun around her friends. If she could just help everyone to get a grip on their emotions and mellow out, starting with herself.

June 1978: Matt

*M*att heard Alex offer a turkey roll to Daniel and watched her walk back into the mixing lounge to sit by him. He quickly looked away when Daniel caught his eye, but not fast enough to avoid seeing the pain lurking in his steely blues. In all their years as friends, Matt had never seen Daniel be anything but "on form," too busy scheming on his next conquest or meeting his next goal to let any situation faze him. Especially when it came to girls. Even when Daniel had been eight and had broken his arm while "tightrope walking" between Matt's tree house and rooftop, his eyes hadn't shown pain like that. This had to be Alex.

She doesn't even try to get under your skin, but she lives there anyway. How well he knew it. She was so different from other girls, with all their manipulations and schemes. Alex simply took a part of your psyche with her every time you met. Each time you encountered her, just because she was who she was, she pulled at you until you unwillingly gave her a tiny bit of yourself. And, after a while, you didn't feel complete unless you were with her. He'd felt the sensation today during the recording session. With plenty of time to sit and listen while she recorded vocals over his taped piano playback, her warm voice had soaked into his soul, the tones filling every fiber like butter over warm popcorn. She pulled at him and completed him. *Irresistible. Delectable.* Wondrous.

Dang it! He shook his head to clear his mind. *There I go again!* Refocusing on his surroundings, he caught Daniel's upward nod as he passed by. Daniel walked up next to Kathy. He angrily jammed a slice of roast beef on a small roll and popped it in his mouth.

Kathy looked up at Daniel with a worried expression. She shot a mean look at Alex in the next room and, excusing herself from Matt with a sweet smile, took Daniel's arm and maneuvered him away to a corner of the kitchen.

Matt knew something had to be done to ease the tension between all of them. *But what?* Maybe if he discussed with Alex how much this means to him – how it's helping him reach his goal – she'd understand better why he was even here today. He could say he was glad she's seeing Daniel. Of course that would be a lie, but it might take the pressure off her. Maybe just a conversation getting everything out in the open would help us all get back on even footing. *It's worth a try.*

With resolve, he put down his partially eaten plate of food and strode over to Alex. She looked up at him, surprised and he took her hand. "Can I borrow you for a minute?" he asked. She allowed him to pull her up and lead her through the studio's outside door onto a wooden porch overlooking the lake.

The deck was partially secluded by pine boughs, which provided some privacy, but still afforded a pleasant view of the water below. Pine forest framed the placid lake in deep textured greens, broken intermittently by rocky outcroppings and sandy beaches. In the approaching twilight, the water's boat-dotted surface captured reflected remnants of bare sky and fluffy gray clouds. They stared out at the mountainous scenery, and Matt felt grateful for the beautiful view, which almost filled their uncomfortable silence.

"You feeling good about what we're doing here?" he asked.

She looked askance at him, a slight tinge of pink coloring her face. "You mean with the music?" she asked cautiously.

"Yeah. The music," he said with a shaky laugh. Clearing his throat, he added, "You think we have something here?"

She looked back out at the water. "Yes, I do."

Unsure of where he wanted to take their conversation, he blurted, "I'm glad we're doing this together, Alex." His face colored as he realized how she might take that comment and he hurried on, "I mean, this really is an amazing experience. Recording our own single. Frankie's studio…"

"I'm glad, too, Matt. It is pretty much a dream come true."

"Yeah. Well. It's nice we're including our friends, too."

Alex nodded slowly, apparently pondering whether that was true.

"I'm sure it means a lot to Daniel. Since it was his idea and all. I…I'm…I'm glad you're seeing him." *Geez, no transition at all. I'm such a spaz.*

Alex glanced quickly over at him as if to see if he was serious. "You're glad?" She looked slightly surprised.

"Yeah. Well. He can give you the attention you want."

"Hmmm," she said, folding her arms and turning away. "*His* focus is definitely on me."

I guess I deserved that slam. Matt worked to gain control of mounting jealousy. Hoping she wouldn't hear the pain he was struggling to keep from his voice, he said, "Daniel needs someone like you, Alex."

"So he's told me."

"And, you need someone like him?" Matt continued, trying to keep it from sounding like a question, but not quite succeeding.

"I guess I do," she said, tightening her lips and blinking quickly.

Did he perceive an element of doubt in her tone? "Daniel seems perfect for you."

Alex turned back to him and stared him down, slowly shaking her head. "That's what he tells me." She said it so quietly he almost missed it. Matt looked intently at her, trying to understand her unexpected reaction.

"Where are you going with this, Matt?" she asked. The emerald pools of her eyes glinted with tears and Matt perceived deep, unchecked pain reflected there. He immediately realized Alex did not think Daniel was perfect for her. *She thinks* I *am!* The concussion of this realization sent a wave of remorse crashing through him. He had hurt her more than he had ever imagined. In all the recent weeks that they'd barely spoken, she had not shown any sign of sadness about their breakup. He figured she'd just taken it in stride and had moved on. After all, despite the seeming strength of their chemistry, they hadn't been together very long. Plus, she'd quickly started dating Dan.

Matt had no idea that she still wanted *him.* The knowledge knocked him backward and he actually took a step back, desperately fighting the urge to draw her against him and bury his lips in her hair.

This was not at all what he had expected to happen by starting this conversation. Not even remotely. He was losing his focus again, allowing her to nibble away at him. Only this time it didn't feel like just a nibble. It was a massive, unrecoverable chunk.

The brilliant, overwhelming relief he felt that she still loved him immediately obscured his solitary goals. Weeks of rationalizing that he was right to pull away from her washed away in a sea of feelings. How could he have been such a fool? He wanted her. And she wanted *him*. His thoughts must have shown on his face, because Alex grasped his hands and pulled his arms behind her. She laid her head on his shoulder and he felt her trembling against him.

"Princess," he whispered into her hair, holding her to him. With their embrace, weeks of frustration and needless angst flowed out of him and dissipated into the dusk. Music formed at the back of his mind, and he knew they were back together now, no matter what goals he had.

The studio door opened unexpectedly and they both jumped. "There you..." Daniel said, stopping short. His eyes narrowed and he immediately turned to leave.

"Daniel!" Matt and Alex cried out simultaneously as their friend slammed the studio door behind him. Alex bit her lip, looking up at Matt. He lightly squeezed her arms and gave her a feeble smile before retreating quickly after his friend.

June 1978: Alex

*A*lex stepped back inside just after Matt and, with both hands over her mouth, watched Daniel power through the studio sound room. Without missing a step, he grabbed his and Kathy's jackets from the couch. Ignoring Matt on his heels, Daniel marched through the kitchen doorway, blowing right past Kurt and Cig Gary, who were still at the mixing board. Daniel removed Kathy's plate from her hands and flung it on the table.

"We gotta go," he said into her astonished face. He shook off Matt's hand on his shoulder, grabbed Kathy's hand and pulled her toward the front door.

"What do you think you're doing?" she cried, trying to wrench her hand from his. She glanced back into the studio where Alex still stood, and at Matt's stricken face. "What's going on? I'm not ready to leave, Daniel." She tried breaking his grip.

"You may not think so, but you are. Neither of us needs to stay where we're not wanted."

Over her loud protests, Daniel drew her toward the front door. As Matt moved to follow his friends. Suzanne caught his arm with both hands. She spoke quietly, but forcefully, "Just let them go. You can work it out when everyone's cooled off." Matt jerked his arm away and glared at her, but he did stop. Suzanne's slightest of nods toward the sound room brought Matt to his senses. The men had stopped working to stare at the students with annoyance.

"I'll go see what I can do to cool things down," Suzanne told the room. She flinched as the front door slammed. Giving Alex a thumbs-up and Brett an apologetic glance, she hastened toward the front door.

As soon as Suzanne slipped outside, Alex turned her gaze to Matt. Her heart thudded against her ribs so hard she expected it to bruise. Matt tightened his lips and stared back at her. She caught waves of pain, frustration, anger and lingering desire emoting from him.

The sheer power of it made Alex catch her breath. *No time to give in to any of that now. We've got to address this with Mr. Grandberg.* She walked up to the producer and looked into his face with no remorse. "We're not crazy musicians, Mr. Grandberg, just students with high-school issues. None of this needs to affect our work today."

She gestured at Matt to come over. He straightened his shoulders, donned his performance face, and walked over to stand by her. "What's next, Sir? We're ready to get back to work." His voice was steady, but Alex could see his hands trembling as badly as hers.

Mr. Grandberg switched his cigar from one corner of his mouth to the other and back again, as his eyes followed the same pattern from one teenage face to the other. "Nice recovery," he said eventually with a smile nudging his lips. "I think you're done for now. Kurt and I have what we need. We can tweak from here without you."

Alex hesitated, but had to ask, "Are you pleased with what we've recorded so far?"

"You've done a great first take, kids. Thanks for your hard work." He smiled and slapped Matt on the shoulder. "Go ahead and get something to eat and you can leave whenever you're ready," he said turning back to the mixing board.

Matt took Alex's hand and they walked slowly into the kitchen. Brett sat at the table holding two pieces of bread piled high with meats, cheeses and vegetables and dripping mustard and mayonnaise. Alex saw his eyes flick toward her hand joined with Matt's and return to his Dagwood sandwich. "Drama always makes me hungry," he said, chewing around an enormous bite. He held his meal out toward them. "Want some?" They couldn't help but chuckle.

They stayed until they heard the crunching of Daniel's car tires on the gravel driveway fading away.

That evening, Suzanne sat cross-legged on Alex's bed twisting her mood ring on her pointer finger.

"I knew it was just a matter of time before you and Matt got back together, Lex," Suzanne said.

"Yeah, well, I didn't expect it and neither did Matt. It just happened." She rubbed her hand along her forehead. "I'm sure Daniel is royally miffed. I have no idea what I'm going to say to him."

"The truth is always good," her friend suggested. She made a regretful face. "He *was* pretty steamed."

Alex gathered her hair over her shoulder, grabbed a pillow and hugged it to her chest. "You followed Daniel and Kathy outside, right? You have to tell me what they did…every detail."

"OK, but some of it's not pretty. You sure you want to hear it?" Suzanne asked. When Alex nodded, she repositioned a pillow behind her to lean against the bed's footboard. "OK, so, when I followed them outside, I saw Daniel practically dragging Kathy to the car. She was trying to fight him off. I didn't want to get in the middle of that and make him madder. So, since they didn't notice me, I half hid on the porch behind a bush. I wanted to be ready to leap out and help if things got out of hand, though."

She looked at the bedroom door as if to make sure it was closed and continued. "So, as they got to the car, Daniel let her go and went to unlock her door. But Kathy stood in front of it. She crossed her arms and pretty much yelled at him, 'You're not unlocking this door until you tell me what's going on, Daniel Post!'"

"Daniel just glared at her and told her to picture the one man she loved most in the world locked in a back-porch embrace with the woman he loved most in the world. He asked her if that was reason enough to leave?'"

"Oh-h-h-h-h no." Alex plunged her face into her pillow.

"I know," Suzanne empathized, "but the worst comes later. OK, so, Kathy asked Daniel if he was sure of what he saw and he assured her he was 'dead certain.' She asked if you guys could have just been sharing a friendly moment since you guys have a history."

"I think his exact reply was, 'Kathy, I'm not a fool. I know what chemistry looks like when I see it.'"

Alex's heart dropped into her stomach. *Poor Daniel. He really is in love with me.* She raised her head and gave Suzanne an imploring look so she'd continue.

"You wouldn't have believed the crushed look on Daniel's face. Kathy must have felt bad for him, because she laid a hand on his arm and asked how she could help."

"He calmed down but got really sarcastic. He suggested they should take out a contract on their 'so-called friend' Matt." Alex's expression tightened. "But, Kathy said she didn't think a contract was the answer. Then, right after she said that, Daniel went to lean on the car, looking away up the road like he was thinking about something. Suddenly, he slammed his hand against the hood. I really jumped and almost gave myself away. He said something like, 'Yeah, a contract. That's it!'"

Alex sat up straighter and lowered the pillow to her lap. "Was he actually serious?

Suzanne laughed. "Kathy had that same reaction. She looked at him like he was insane. Daniel just laughed and said not to worry, that he wouldn't have him killed off. But he did have that devious look on his face."

"Kathy said Matt was sometimes stupid but he had been a good friend for a long time, so she warned Daniel not to do anything illegal. Daniel said he wouldn't, but he knew you guys were really in love and it was going to take something major to change that."

Alex's heart sank. "He's going to try to split us up?" she looked imploringly at Suzanne.

"Yep. He said he'd just thought of a way to cause a break-up without either of you knowing what happened. You should have seen his smug expression. He wanted Kathy to help him, but she just asked why he thought she'd want to be involved in one of his devious plots. His response was weird. He started almost coming on to her, moving in really close and twirling the ends of her hair between his fingers. He told her she was just as interested in splitting them up as he was."

A blaze flared in Alex's heart. "She agreed to help him?"

Suzanne shook her head. "I could tell she was tempted. But, to her credit, she started walking back toward the house and told him she wasn't doing anything until she knew what he was up to. Daniel called after her that that was too bad, and now she'd just have to sit on the sidelines and 'watch the master at work.'"

Alex dropped her jaw. "That scuz bag!"

Suzanne nodded and said, "Then he drove off. I had to go in to retrieve Brett, so I went around and came in the back door so it wouldn't seem like I'd been eavesdropping."

"Smart girl." Alex leaned back against the headboard. "Matt and I booked pretty quickly. We must have just missed you coming around back, since Matt's car was parked out there and we left on the lower road. Thank goodness for that. How did everyone react in the studio?"

"No one talked much. We had the distractions of the recording playing in the background and cleaning up Kathy's catering."

"So what do you think I should do, Suz?"

"Move ahead with your music with Matt and your relationship, if it feels right. You'll need to explain to Daniel, but be cautious. He's totally in it for himself."

June 1978: Alex

*D*aniel carefully avoided Alex over the next couple of weeks. Every time she tried to approach him, he'd avert his gaze or walk away. They needed to talk, but she still hadn't fully formulated what she was going to say to him. Besides, Alex hadn't been able to focus fully on the situation. She'd been so keyed into the recording and having Matt back in her life. Plus, studying for her finals and SAT test required extra time, not to mention graduation preparation, and making plans with family and friends. All were good excuses, but not good enough to excuse putting off her discussion with Daniel.

Matt told her he'd tried several times to contact Daniel, but he had made himself scarce from the neighborhood after school and wouldn't take Matt's telephone calls.

Kathy had gotten over her surprise and hurt since Matt had talked with her, and had decided to remain the ever-understanding friend. Discussing it later with Suzanne, her friend agreed this was just Kathy's continuing ploy to try to win Matt over with her puppy-dog, I'll-always-be-here-for-you act. Alex could tell Kathy had no intention of forgiving her. She threw burning glares at Alex whenever she was within eyeshot.

Alex had consciously put all relationship issues out of her mind until after today, their graduation day. She was determined not to ruin this, of all days, with the inevitable and painful.

The late afternoon ceremony, held on a stage on the school's football field, went smoothly. Alex watched faces in and around the sea of blue and white robes as the boring speeches actually touched proud fathers and caused much dabbing of the eyes by many moms, including hers.

During diploma presentations, a few students pulled high jinks, flashing shorts worn under their gowns, or yelling, "Hi, Mom!" or other comments while crossing the stage. When it was her to turn to accept her diploma, Alex crossed the stage with as much grace as her platform clogs would allow and turned, center stage, to grin and wave at her family before exiting. Luckily, there were no streakers or other more newsworthy events to mar the day.

Afterward, all the families gathered on the Coeur d'Alene Public Park lawn for a picnic dinner, sponsored by several local restaurants. Matt sat with Alex at her family's table. His parents had made it to the ceremony earlier, but had bowed out from additional graduation activities citing other obligations. Alex had gotten a glimpse of the elusive pair for the first time. But she hadn't had an opportunity to meet or talk with them. They looked nice and seemed loving, if not overly affectionate, with Matt. Not at all what she'd expected.

After the meal, Matt and Alex roamed the grounds talking and laughing with friends and gathering memories on film. Camera flashes punctured the twilight, capturing families and friends with their gowned, mortar-boarded students against the lake backdrop and an ornamental June sunset.

Alex saw Daniel snapping pictures with his parents, and with Kathy and her father, who had returned from Europe for his daughter's big event. Later, she saw Daniel sitting alone with Kathy on the beach wall, talking. Both times, Alex quickly turned the other way.

After dark, a band played for a couple of hours. Alex and Matt thoroughly enjoyed gathering big groups of family and friends for each fast-dancing set on the spotlighted grass dance floor. At one point, Matt asked Kathy to join the group of dancers when he found her alone along the edge of the dance area.

It was during this music set that Alex caught Daniel staring at her from the perimeter. His face held such guarded pain it jarred her. When he realized she was looking at him, his expression turned quickly to a smirk and he walked away.

Something about his look made Alex decide to talk with him right then and there, no matter whether she had the right words to say or not. Matt was dancing in their group of friends and across from Kathy. Alex yelled in his ear. "I have to go talk with Daniel."

Matt gave her an inquiring look. "Right now?"

"I can't wait any longer." She looked at Daniel's back disappearing into the park shadows.

Matt stopped dancing. "Yeah. We should all talk."

"No, let me talk with him first."

He nodded at her slowly. Alex glimpsed Kathy, still dancing with the group, glaring across at her. Alex glanced up at Matt, but he hadn't noticed Kathy at all. With eyes glowing, he pecked her on the cheek. "Good luck," he said and started to dance again.

Accepting his support with a smile, Alex walked quickly away in the direction she'd seen Daniel go.

After a few moments of searching the dark edges of the party, she found him leaning against the bark of a giant pine pulling apart a pinecone. He looked up when he heard her approach, his manner easy, yet blue eyes penetrating. *Why does he have to be so handsome?*

He turned his attention right back to his little project. "Tired of dancing already?" he practically sneered.

"Daniel, we need to talk."

"Do we?" He dropped the pinecone, folded his arms and looked straight at her. "There isn't anything to say, Alex. I recognize infatuation when I see it."

Alex paused. *My attraction to Matt isn't infatuation; it's real.* "Well…I'm not sure that's it, but I do owe you an apology for the way this happened."

"No apology needed. I'm moving on." His blue eyes bored that notion into her with an intensity she felt right in her gut. *Why does that bother me?* In the past three months, as she'd gotten to know Daniel better, she'd had to admit she found him intriguing and disarmingly charming. As she hesitated, she watched his eyes. Attraction washed through her. After a few uncomfortable moments, Daniel grasped both her arms and pulled her face close to his. Alex held his intense gaze and felt a charge of excitement.

A glint of pleasure came into his eyes. "Not completely sure you've made the right decision after all?" he asked.

"That's not it, Daniel," Alex said, trying to physically wrench away, even as she fought the temptation to stay.

Daniel held her firmly but gently and forced her to look at him. "You need to make a decision before I move completely out of your reach, m'lady. Let me help you…" He leaned in, nuzzling her neck while inhaling her scent.

Alex felt her knees weaken and her head begin to spin. Daniel lifted her chin. He positioned his mouth close to hers and whispered against her lips, "Our chemistry is just as strong as our personalities, Alex. Maybe stronger."

Even as she tried to stop her reaction, Alex's body fell against his chest with an overpowering longing. He continued in a fierce whisper, still brushing her lips with his words, "You were meant to be with me, not a lonely dreamer. Get rid of him and come back to me."

An image of Matt's dreamy hazel eyes suddenly flew into Alex's mind and she jerked her head away.

"What are you doing, Daniel?" she asked breathlessly.

"Trying to show you you're moving in the wrong direction."

"I most certainly am!" she retorted, shaking her head to clear it. "Getting rid of Matt would be like getting rid of music in my life."

"You can't deny your reaction to me," he said, stroking her face.

She shied away. "I don't deny I'm attracted to you, Daniel. But I'm not having prophetic dreams about you." The fact that she'd actually said this out loud shocked her into an abrupt silence and she put one hand to her temple. *Why did I say that? I don't even believe in those dreams.*

"Oooo, prophetic dreams. That sounds groovy."

"Don't make fun of me, Daniel. I know Matt and I are meant to be together. Forever."

"Really? Sure hope he feels the same way…now."

Alex stopped short, thinking of Matt's initial emotional departure once he'd learned about her stupid dreams. Daniel must have seen the internal doubt cross her face.

"Not really sure about him, eh? Well…" He leaned in and whispered seductively in her ear, "Consider what you're feeling here with me."

"I'd just as soon forget it."

"Yeah, good luck with that. I'm not forgetting it anytime soon," he said, lazily running a finger across her lips. He raised one eyebrow. "And, to help you remember, it looks like I'm just going to have to be around a lot more. As a matter of fact, I think I'd better go right now to patch things up with my friend Matt." He turned and walked toward the party.

"Daniel…" Alex tried to think of something to say that would stop him, but nothing came to her. He ignored her call and kept walking. She was suddenly aware of the chill in the air. Shivering as much from trepidation as the cool temperature, she took a deep breath to cool her emotional state, and lagged behind him as he walked out of the shadows toward the dance floor.

This had not gone at all the way she wanted. But there was nothing she could do. She watched Daniel approach Matt and Kathy, who were now sitting at a table at the edge of the dance area. Behind them, the band was breaking down their equipment. Kathy's hand rested partly on the back of Matt's chair and partly against him. She was listening intently to something he was saying and moving her fingers slowly along his back.

Alex's stomach squeezed and she stopped. She certainly was not emotionally strong enough to go there right now. Spotting Suzanne and Brett sitting at a table across the way, she caught Matt's eye and pointed to her other friends to let him know she was going to sit with them for a while. He nodded and turned warily to encounter Daniel.

❖❖❖

Alex slumped down in the chair next to Suzanne.

"Pal, that attitude's not cheerful enough for a graduation night celebration," Brett exclaimed.

"Oh, guys, I just talked with Daniel."

"Jinkies! I take it, it didn't go well?" Suzanne asked.

Alex shook her head. "Confusing."

Suzanne looked across at Daniel who was now involved in an intense conversation with Matt as Kathy looked on. "Daniel's really good at that."

"At what?" asked Brett, looking from one friend to the other.

Suzanne and Alex said it at the same time, "Manipulation."

"Well, if ya'll are *sure*," he said, laughing. Alex and Suzanne turned small smiles on one another.

Brett's smile faded, "I guess I do believe you, considering what I heard earlier."

Suzanne cocked her head at him, widening her eyes. "What did you hear that I didn't?"

"It was while you were taking family pictures. Mr. Post was talking with one of his cronies, bragging about what a great lawyer his son is going to be."

"Daniel's father? What did he say?" asked Suzanne.

"Oh, he was just saying what good ideas Daniel had while working with the law firm on Matt's music contract."

"Daniel was involved in the details?" Suzanne asked.

Well, Matt's parents weren't any help," Alex said. "He had to rely on somebody."

"Yeah, and why's that a big deal? Mr. Post was the one who signed off on everything, right?" Suzanne looked back and forth between Alex and Brett.

Brett shrugged. "Sure. But there was some comment about Daniel's innate ability to negotiate what people really wanted. Mr. Post sounded like he was going to burst with pride about it."

"Why?" Suzanne asked.

"No idea. But, it sounded like all Mr. Post did was tweak Daniel's wording and create the actual paperwork."

"Daniel wouldn't actually be able to write up the contract. He'd need to have passed the bar exam," Alex said.

"Whatever they did couldn't be too suspicious. Mr. Post could lose his license if they did anything illegal, right?"

"Yeah," said Brett, with a funny face, "But you know how Daniel likes to be 'creative.'"

Suzanne looked pensive for a moment. "Daniel's big idea to split you guys up had something to do with a contract, remember? Do you know if Matt's contract is different from yours, Alex?" Suzanne asked.

"I don't know. Our lawyers drew them up separately. I didn't think to ask to see his as long as I was happy with mine."

Suzanne shook her head with a worried look at Alex.

"I'm sure it's fine," Alex said. "My parents and I looked everything over. Matt and I have separate bank accounts for the record earnings and everything. No use worrying about it now. It's all done."

At that moment, an announcement blared over the loudspeaker announcing the start of the midnight volleyball tournament. Alex watched Kathy lean in behind Daniel's shoulder and point toward the volleyball courts where they'd be drawing names for the teams. Daniel stood up, said something with a smile to Matt as they shook hands. He slapped Matt on the back as he and Kathy turned to leave the table.

Matt came over to Alex, Suzanne and Brett. They arrived during a flurry of activity as students bade farewell to family members. In the midst of gathering up of belongings and younger siblings to head on home, Alex's parents came to say goodbye.

"Now, you call us if you get too tired to pull this all-nighter, Alex," her dad said. "We'll come get you any time, OK?"

"OK, thanks, Dad," she said, squeezing him. She hugged her brother and mom, too, before they left.

Alex's little group walked over to the courts where everyone was gathered to draw teams. She was thrilled to be paired with Matt, Suzanne and Brett in the "A" tournament while Kathy and Daniel were selected for the "B" tournament.

Daniel watched her as his crowd of "B" competitors moved across the park to their separate tournament area. He raised his eyebrows, pursed his lips and blew her a kiss with two fingertips. Her breath cut short. She slipped her arm around Matt's waist and quickly turned away. And, the last thing she saw was Kathy's jealous expression.

June 2003: Alex

No inkling of jealousy appeared in the chocolate-brown eyes of Daniel's "new and improved" wife tonight, though, as she moved gracefully across the crowded art museum lobby toward Alex and Daniel. Kathy nodded and exchanged short pleasantries with guests as she walked along until she arrived at her husband's side. She put one arm through Daniel's and held out her hand to shake Alex's. "It really is good to see you, Alex."

Kathy was breathtaking up close. Her lithe form glittered in teal satin and diamonds. Her brunette hair shimmered as it swooped over her forehead just enough to hide her sailing accident scar and to fall in waves behind an intricate diamond hair clip. Her overall glow suggested great comfort with her current place in life.

"Kathy, you look amazing."

"Marriage agrees with me," Kathy said, looking over at Daniel with heightening color. "Even after 14 years."

"She's not only beautiful, but she's the mastermind behind all the trendy parties...your fundraiser here not withstanding," he added, squeezing his wife's hand against his arm. "Her parties have become the talk of the town."

Alex couldn't tell whether his expression held simple pride in his wife or actual love. "So Madeleine tells me," Alex said, smiling honestly at Kathy.

"I totally enjoyed working with Madeleine. She doesn't miss much, that one," Kathy smiled.

"Well, you've both outdone yourselves. This truly is a stunning event. Thank you."

"No. Thank *you*, Alex. I'm honored to be included in your 'inner circle.' You rub shoulders with some very glamorous people at some pretty outrageous gatherings."

Alex smiled humbly and nodded in agreement. *If only you knew what a bore those glitter people and their parties are.*

Daniel turned to his wife. "Alex and I were just talking about the reunion. If we can convince her to come back, she'd be the piece de résistance in your reunion party plan." He turned to Alex and winked.

Alex feigned a dubious look at Daniel, but her heart leapt. *Perfect!* "Interesting," she said. She paused for effect and said, "You know, I've been planning to do a benefit concert in the Northwest to help out some educational arts programs for children. Maybe I could do it in conjunction with the reunion?"

Daniel beamed at her and Kathy clasped her hands together. "That would be fantastic!" Kathy said. "We could make it the main event."

Despite her excitement, Kathy's eyes strayed momentarily to a bouquet of flowers on a cocktail table several paces away where a large sprig of baby's breath lopped to one side of the spray of roses. Her eyes returned to Alex, then flicked back to the bouquet. Kathy was obviously fighting the inclination to go fix it immediately. But, Alex wasn't about to let her go yet.

"Kathy, last I heard you were working at Coeur d'Musique music school… What have you done with yourself since then?"

"Well, since Dan and I got married, we've just been working to grow my event planning business."

"It's obviously flourishing," Alex said, acknowledging their current environment with a nod.

"Thanks to Dan," Kathy said, squeezing her husband's arm. "And, I have to give credit to Matt, too."

The power of his spoken name jolted through Alex, leaving residual tension. She worked to keep her face still, but noticed an uneasy look fleetingly cross Dan's face.

"Matt's camp gave me a venue to hone my event management skills," Kathy said, her eyes remaining pointedly on her husband. She turned to Alex, "His – our – success at the music camp gave me the confidence and contacts to move on."

Daniel half snorted and looked disgusted. "Matt hasn't changed a bit; still a loner and a dreamer. He's barely taken a step out of town since he opened his Coeur d'Musique Children's Camp. He bought the land adjacent to his cabin with his inheritance and built quite a nice complex on it."

"I hear it's quite popular," Alex said, ignoring how hard her heart was pounding.

"It is!" Kathy said. "A couple of his protégés have been asked to perform at the White House at an arts-awareness event later this year."

"Really!" Alex smiled and nodded as if she hadn't read that in the *LA Times* article.

Kathy continued, "Matt's also selling a number of his original songs to vocalists. And his recording studio at the camp is attracting bands from all over the world."

"Yes, I know lots of independent artists who contract with him. They've found him even without much publicity," Alex said.

"It's all word-of-mouth," Kathy said. "He's not interested in attracting business from big labels."

"That translates into lower margins for him," Daniel said, earning him a wry glance from his wife.

"You might be able to help him find supplemental funds to change that, Daniel," Alex suggested innocently. "If you were able to go to Washington with him to help lobby for arts funding…" She paused and brightened her face as if she had just registered a new idea and said, "We might even be able to jump-start that by honoring him and his music at the reunion concert."

"He's still publicity shy, you know," Daniel said.

"True," Kathy said. "But he surely knows the value of good PR by now. He'll have to be coerced, though."

Alex blanched internally. His absence from the event would defeat the whole purpose of her plan. "You do still talk with him, Kathy?" she asked as innocently as possible.

"Actually, I haven't seen him in years. But, we communicate sometimes through email."

"Perhaps you could talk with him about being honored in-person at the concert, Kathy? He's bound to listen to you," Alex said.

Kathy nodded slowly. "I'd be glad to give it a try." She turned to Daniel. "Alex's D.C. lobbying idea is great, babe," she said, biting her lip in a hopeful smile at her husband.

Daniel's gaze moved between the women and he shrugged. "It never hurts to have more contacts there. I suppose I could offer him help in Washington. "

Alex stifled a sniff. "I thought you weren't talking with Matt."

"I'm not...yet." He met his wife's gaze.

"Matt is always going to be my friend, Dan. He should be yours, too," she said pointedly. She turned to Alex, "Maybe you should work on that, too, Alex."

Alex's eyes flew open involuntarily. "I haven't spoken to Matt in 25 years, Kathy. I wouldn't exactly call him a friend."

Kathy rolled her eyes and smiled. "Precisely what he has told me about you."

Matt talks to Kathy – to anyone – about me? That was a shocker.

"He might come around...with the right incentive," Kathy said. "I'll work on him."

Alex was hoping for exactly that.

Kathy turned back to her husband. "You need to make up with Matt, Daniel. It's way past time and, now that you can mutually benefit, you have no legitimate excuse to keep..." She glanced at Alex and paused as if about to say one thing, but finished with another, "...to keep pretending you're strangers."

"Hey, you know, dear, it wasn't me who has kept his friend at arm's length all these years. I've tried to reach him."

"Only by email? That delete key is all too handy. Besides, it's time for you to eat some humble pie and put your clever mind to the task of making us all friends again." A light went on in her eyes and she turned to Alex, "You in, Alex?"

My dearest wish. Alex swallowed slowly to help keep her tone nonchalant. "That would be a nice silver lining, but the goal of this reunion concert would be, foremost, to benefit children and the arts."

"Of course!" Kathy said. She sighed. "We'll have to get started soon if we're going to pull off a reunion *and* a fundraiser concert in just a couple of months!"

"Yes, there will be a ton of details to work out with my people. So, how about if I have Madeleine call you and set a meeting to iron out all the details."

Kathy nodded and smiled in excitement. "Perfect," she said, her smile quickly turning to a frown as she watched a passing waiter's shirttail peeking out from underneath his tuxedo coat. Returning her gaze to Alex, she said, "If you'll excuse me, I need to attend to a few details yet tonight." She kissed her husband on the cheek, held out a hand for Alex to shake and hurried off after the server, stopping momentarily to tuck the errant baby's breath back in its bouquet as she went by.

Admiring the now-perfect floral arrangement, Alex suddenly flashed on the wildflowers circling Matt's secret meadow. All this talk of the past, seeing Kathy and Daniel again... She couldn't stop the memories flooding in. They transported her immediately to being in the secret meadow with Matt for the first time.

June 1978: Alex

With overstuffed backpacks, Alex and Matt rode their bikes through town to the Coeur d'Alene Lake marina. As they whizzed past, the flower gardens and shady front-lawn trees gave way to scrubby fields brimming with wildflowers. Alex breathed in their musk of freshness and new life, grateful to be sharing her 18th birthday with Matt on this beautiful summer day. A few puffy white June clouds gave depth to a wide blue sky, and the springtime buzz of insects flew past their heads as they skirted the town toward the lake.

Had it only been a few weeks since they had gotten back together at the recording session? It seemed like a lifetime. Their previous sorrows now felt like something that had happened to other people.

A brief thought of Daniel brushed her mind, but she pushed it away. He and Matt had worked out some form of truce at graduation, but neither had shared details of the conversation with her. *It's between them. I don't need to get involved.*

She and Matt pulled up to the marina docks and walked their bikes down to the Roberts' boat slip. Alex looked in amazement at the tall mast sticking out of the boat cover. "A sailboat? I thought we were going canoeing."

"Yeah, another tax write-off my dad never uses. Perhaps you and I can take it out later this summer. Deal?"

"Deal! I've only been on a catamaran, never in a big beautiful mono-hull like this one. It would be great to try comfortable sailing for a change."

"We'll get you out there," Matt smiled at her. He tugged at the nylon tarp covering the aft of the sailboat. "Just pull off that end," he instructed, nodding at the far tarp corner. "The canoe's under here."

Alex quickly finished locking the bikes and ran over to help uncover the aft of the sailboat. They carefully dragged the canoe off into the water, tied it next to the dock and tossed in backpacks, lifejackets and oars.

Dropping himself into the canoe and balancing it with legs spread, he reached his arms up to her. "Here, let me help you."

Alex hesitated. "It looks pretty topsy-turvy. You sure it's safe?"

"Of course. Just keep your weight to the middle and it'll be fine."

She trusted the assurance in his eyes and stepped in. The tiny boat swayed dangerously with her first step and she began to fall, but Matt caught her and controlled her descent onto the second of three wooden seats spanning the canoe.

"See, Birthday Girl, I told you it was safe," he said as the boat rocked unsteadily. He untied the dock rope and sat down on the canoe seat just behind hers.

Alex raised one eyebrow at him as he handed her the rope, which she coiled and tossed into the stern. He shoved off the dock with one oar and smoothly maneuvered the canoe through the boat slips into the open lake. Once out in the main channel, Matt handed her an oar and, with his instructions, she quickly learned how to steer the boat.

Alex loved lakes. Her family had owned a motorboat back in Arizona, and she could think of nothing more lovely than skimming a placid evening lake on a single water-ski. But, her strong skiing arms were out of practice and half an hour of paddling took its toll.

"Can we take a break, Matt?" she asked rubbing one shoulder.

"What? I thought waterskiing built mighty arms," he teased, squeezing both of her biceps. She playfully wrenched her arms away.

"Hey, Coeur d'Alene's rainy spring weather doesn't allow for much skiing, you know," she said. If I was back on Lake Pleasant, by now I'd already be in great shape."

He laughed. "You're just not used to canoeing. Paddling uses different muscles. Anyway, this gives us a good chance to drift for a bit. Slide on back here with me," he said, motioning to a spot on the floor of the canoe just in front of him.

Alex carefully moved back. She propped her arms up on his legs and leaned her head against his taut stomach. He slowly rubbed her shoulders and she moaned comfortably.

The late morning air was unusually warm for a northwestern June. Whenever a soft breeze bounced along the smooth water's surface, the bright sun danced off the resulting ripples like brilliant sparks. In the distance, a monk's fringe of piney dense forest rimmed the beaches and coves. It could have been a postcard, Alex thought. So green and lush...and so unlike the desert cactus and rocky lake-scapes she was used to in Arizona.

Matt started humming softly as he kneaded her shoulders. Alex recognized it as Joe Cocker's "You Are So Beautiful." She wondered if Matt had picked this song specifically for her, or whether he was just humming something that had come to mind. Either way, the lovely lyrics and melody made a comforting backdrop to the scenery.

Alex watched screeching seagulls swooping above them. One was balanced on a single leg atop a tree-trunk post nearby, watchfully jerking its head back and forth. Numerous birds perched on two long rows of these posts following the line of the lakeshore off into the distance. A chain of floating logs connecting the posts resembled floating train tracks.

"What are the rows of telephone poles for?" Alex asked.

"You mean the pilings?" He pointed. "When lumberjacks cut trees, they float them on the lake and use the pilings to help channel the logs to the sawmills downriver."

Alex visualized hundreds of tree trunks floating down the lake to the Spokane River, bumping and crashing along between the pilings on their way to the sawmill.

After a few quiet minutes, Matt lightly caressed one of her arms and pointed to a twiggy-looking mass set precariously atop one piling. "See that pile of branches up there? It's an Osprey nest. Keep watching and I bet you'll see the mom fly back in a few minutes with a fish for her chicks."

Sure enough, within minutes, a large-winged, hawk-like creature dangling a small fish from its beak descended on the nest. It delighted and enthralled Alex.

"If you look closely, Princess, you can see our family cabin up there on the mountainside." Matt pointed the other direction to the far shore. "It's not too big a place, but it's a great getaway."

She strained to see it, but couldn't make it out. "Is that where we're going?" Alex asked.

"No, not today. I have a special birthday picnic site for us just around the bend. Are you rested enough to get going?" he asked.

In response, she deftly moved back to her canoe seat, pulled up her oar and began paddling.

They alighted on a scrubby shoreline. Wild grasses dotted with yellow and purple wildflowers spread upward toward the line of pine trees 20 yards from shore. They walked through the aromatic grasses and into the dense woods for several minutes. Suddenly, just past a particularly thick section of trees, the forest opened up into a miniature, natural meadow of green grass. A nearby trickle of water from the top of the hillside fed the site…creating a patch of verdant softness. The whole oblong meadow, closely ringed by old forest and batches of jaunty wildflowers, was just wide enough for two people to sprawl on the grass. To one side, a broad tree had been sawed off. The remaining trunk graced the space like a natural table decorated around its base with sprigs of colorful wildflowers.

Alex caught her breath and fell to her knees rubbing the surface of new grass. The green carpet was soft, lush and warm from the noontime sun.

"It's only like this for a few days in June. The grass and flowers get just enough light and run-off," Matt said, light glowing in his eyes. "In the winter it looks desolate, a tiny simple clearing, surrounded by gray and deadened trees. Not that impressive to anyone who didn't know where, and when, to look. My secret spot," he said absently, his eyes roving the tiny meadow.

Alex sat back on her heels. "No one else knows about it?"

"As far as I know, no one has been down here since the first winter my family bought the land. My parents have barely ever been to the cabin itself, let alone the surrounding woods. Becka and Davey don't have much reason to leave the cabin and beach. So, it just belongs to me…and you," he said, pulling Alex up to him.

"It's absolutely perfect," Alex whispered.

"I knew you would love it," he whispered, lifting her chin with his finger and gazing long and deep into her eyes. "I wanted this to be the place I first kissed you." He paused with intense expectation in his eyes. "May I?"

She caught her breath, nodded shyly and lifted her face. Matt leaned down and tenderly pressed his lips against hers. Alex felt her mind go numb except for the soft, comforting sensation he inspired. Her mind began sliding into an abyss where musical notes swirled on light waves like leaves on the wind.

Matt pulled away and the motion stopped. She opened her eyes, working to focus on his face. His eyes were on hers, but they looked through her into some unknown space of inspiration. He blinked and refocused on her face. He followed another light kiss with a powerful hug and a heavy sigh.

"Happy birthday, Princess..." he said, holding her close.

She could hear his heart beating and wondered if he could feel hers thundering inside her chest. She cherished his warmth until he slowly pushed her away to arm's length. Taking her in with his eyes, he cocked his head to one side and winked. "I'm starving! You?"

Alex's whole being wanted more of his kisses, but she also felt relieved he was taking it slowly. "Food? Yes!" she said, willing herself to follow his casual lead.

As they propped their brimming backpacks against the tree stump, Alex noted its vast number of rings. "This was one old tree," she said. "I wonder why someone cut it down?"

Matt laughed. "It was already dead anyway, so I chopped it down to let the sun in to help the grass grow. Plus, it makes a great table for a picnic," he said, spreading two checkered cloth napkins over the expansive surface.

They distributed the picnic fare atop the tree trunk. For the next several minutes, they savored chewy hunks of bread, cheese and ham; popped green grapes in each other's mouths; and relished chocolaty brownies washed down with sodas.

Alex munched on the last brownie, giggling through her family story about Buttercup, her only childhood pet. The chicken had hatched in an incubator in her brother Jake's kindergarten class. Buttercup had lived in a chicken-wire coop in her family's garage and, somehow, each night, managed to find its way up onto Jake's bed to nestle underneath his warm chin. During daytime examinations of the Lauren's backyard, the chicken also developed a healthy taste for the aphids in her father's prized rose garden, which pretty much destroyed the roses. This unfortunate interest eventually earned Buttercup a new home on an Arizona farm.

As Matt listened and laughed, he busied his hands carving letters into the surface of their picnic stump. Alex finished her tale and looked at what he'd carved. "AL + MR = ∞."

Alex traced her finger along the infinity symbol and smiled over at the man she hoped she would be with forever. He took her hand and scooted her down onto the soft grass. Warmed by the sun filtering through the trees, they lay side by side looking up at the tips of the towering pines.

"So, is this a choice birthday picnic spot, or what?" Matt quietly ventured into the silence.

"Perfect," Alex whispered, enjoying her prone perspective. She rubbed the smooth worn bark on the tree stump next to her. *How many years has this place been in the making?* She pictured the hundreds of rings across the tree stump's surface and looked up at a stream of fluffy clouds skirting across the treetops like whitewater along a green riverbank. The stump and water imagery merged in her mind and Alex gasped. This was the stump from her cabin dream. Why hadn't she recognized it immediately? She quickly sat up.

Matt sat up, too. "What is it?" he asked, nervously looking around.

Alex pictured the stump crashing down the waterfall in her dream with the illegible letters carved on its top. She looked over at the new carvings. It was exactly what she'd seen in her dream. Her breaths came quickly. If she recognized this stump from her dream, would she recognize his family's cabin, too? She had a burning desire to ask him to take her there now. No, she couldn't risk that. She couldn't tell him she'd seen his precious tree stump in a dream. He'd think it had some important meaning and get all freaked out again.

"Oh, I just remembered something I promised my mom I'd do," she said. She lay back down with her heart pounding.

Matt stared down at her, quizzically. "Anything I can help with?"

"No. No thanks. I'll just take care of it tonight." She forcibly pushed the dream from her mind and concentrated on calming her heartbeat. "This is a very special place," she said to change the subject and her mood. "Thank you for sharing it with me, Matt. I love it."

Matt moved in to cuddle against her. He propped himself on one elbow and looked down at her. He seemed to be debating whether to say something. Presently, he whispered a tentative, "You know, Alex... I... I love you."

Alex's stomach flipped and any misgivings vanished from her mind. The guy who had pulled away from her because she might interfere with his life goals had disappeared. *This* was the guy who'd given her the music box, and with whom she shared life's destiny. She reached up to place a hand on his cheek. "I love you, too, Matt."

He leaned over her and kissed her lightly. She reached her arms around his neck and pulled him closer. When they came up for air several minutes later, Matt rolled over and pulled her beside him until her head lay against his shoulder. She closed her eyes and, in her self-imposed darkness, her other senses sharpened. Soft, moist earth beneath her back; quiet lapping of water on the shore; fresh pine trees and wildflowers on the breeze; distant moanings of boat motors.

They lay in the warm grass for almost an hour until Matt leaned over, gave her a peck on the lips and sighed. He rose stiffly and stretched his arms over his head. "As much as I would love to stay here forever and hold you, Princess, we'd better get going. If you row fast, I'll have just enough time to get home and take Davey to his Little League practice." He winked at her.

Alex didn't want to leave. She looked at him plaintively while he helped her to her feet. "So, has this been a good 18th birthday?" Matt asked, hugging her close.

"The best," she said, pecking him on the lips in thanks.

He smiled and turned to clean up. As Alex carefully placed leftovers into her backpack, she felt a sense of magic around her. *It's our secret meadow now; our own little magic spot.* She glanced back one last time at the newly carved tree-stump and her heart gave a small tremor. *It's real, Daniel. Not just infatuation, after all.*

July 1978: Alex

On the beautifully clear, if somewhat cool, morning of the Fourth of July, two weeks after Alex's birthday, her family drove her down to the city docks to meet Matt. Alex was truly excited about his invitation to make good on their promised sailing excursion. For a whole weekend, too…even if her parents did have to chaperone.

As they carried their tote bags toward the water, she recognized the line of the Roberts' sailboat bobbing against the wooden dock with Matt waving from its bow. She thought she recognized Suzanne and Brett waving vigorously from the cockpit, while Becka and Davey stopped pulling boat bumpers to look up at her. Before she could wave back, Matt counted loudly to three and they all yelled, "Surprise! Happy birthday again!"

Alex stopped short and looked questioningly at her mom and dad. "You were in on this?" They nodded, both grinning broadly.

"Happy belated birthday, honey," her dad said, giving her a squeeze. "You needed some kind of big bash. You only turn 18 once, you know."

"Besides, it's a perfect way to celebrate your successful recording session in LA last week, too," Mrs. Lauren added, putting her arm around her daughter's shoulder and giving her a squeeze.

"Decent!" Alex beamed, clasping her beach towel tightly to her chest. A crisp breeze lifted her curls as she looked out with anticipation along the shoreline of Tubbs Hill at the low swells crisscrossing the bay.

Her mom gave Alex a hug and a light push toward the sailboat. "You go ahead with your friends and we'll meet you over at the Roberts' cabin. We just have to visit the motorboat rental office first."

Alex gave a little squeak, involuntarily jumping to her toes. "We're gonna water ski?"

Her parents nodded and laughed.

"You are such a spasmo," Jake said, shaking his head. As Alex mock frowned at her brother, her dad put his arm around Jake's shoulder and, smiling back at Alex, steered the boy away toward the boat rental office.

She greeted her friends with excited chatter as they settled in for sailing. As the boat slipped away from the dock, Alex sat in the sailboat cockpit next to her friends and raised her face to the sun. Reveling in its warmth, she closed her eyes and listened to the fading laughter of children playing nearby, the revving of powerboat motors in the distance, and the crackling snaps of the sails above her as they adjusted in the breeze. The fishy tang of lake water at first made her wrinkle her nose, but the boat's gentle slicing motion distracted and lulled her into a peaceful, expectant mood.

Alex felt the warmth of Matt's hand on her knee. She realized from his expression that he shared her calm eagerness for the day. He graced her with a small smile and turned to gaze back out over the deep blue water ridged with dark patterns from the delicate wind.

In the light draft, it took quite a while to reach the other side of the bay. Matt, at the helm, handled the sails and ropes with minimal help from his siblings. The couples sat across from one another in the cockpit, chatting and enjoying the warm sunshine and breeze.

"We can swim, ski and sail, picnic on the dock, lounge on the beach…whatever you want to do," Matt explained. "It's your weekend, Princess."

"I owe you one, SuperMatt. It's a great way to spend Fourth of July weekend!" She enveloped him in an impetuous hug, which knocked the tiller and set the boat leaning temporarily. He straightened the boat and grinned.

Watching the diminishing city buildings nestled at the edge of the water behind them, she pictured fireworks bursting over the buildings that night. "We will be able to see fireworks from the cabin, won't we?" she asked.

"We'll see them from our dock. But if you want to get closer to the fireworks barge, we can always go out and float around on the boat."

"The fireworks barge?"

"Yeah, didn't you know they shoot off the fireworks right from the lake, on the Coeur d'Alene fireworks barge?" Suzanne said.

Alex laughed. "Really?"

"Yeah, and half of Coeur d'Alene turns out in their boats to see it; a traffic jam of boats."

"Bashing, bouncing, bobbing…" Brett said with a snort.

Suzanne giggled, "Yea, that pretty much describes it."

Alex looked around at the surrounding lake water and envisioned fireworks bursting above hundreds of boats floating in the dark. "Is it safe? Don't the fireworks fall on them?"

"Nope, the rumor is that sparks usually fall on the barge itself and catch *it* on fire," Matt chuckled.

"You're joking," Alex responded. "It really catches on fire?"

"So they say. But we're not expecting it…or the usual rain."

"Rain? It doesn't look like rain," Alex said, looking up at the blue sky dotted only with a few small white powder puffs.

"No, it doesn't for a change! It's a perfect Fourth," Matt said, leaning across the tiller to peck her on the lips. At this, from atop the galley hood, Becka giggled and Davey groaned. Matt reached into the swabbing bucket by his feet and threw a sponge, which bounced off Davey's chest.

Shortly afterward, Matt maneuvered the sailboat near the dock below his family's cabin, even as the boat bobbed and swayed tenuously on the waves. Matt gave mooring instructions, the boat became a flurry of activity.

"Release the jib," he yelled, and Davey yanked loose the rope holding the front sail tight.

"Brett, drop the bumpers over the side, there," Matt instructed, pointing to the white, rubber-coated foam cylinders tied to the deck on short ropes.

On her older brother's order to loosen the boom vang, Becka tugged the rope under the boom holding the bottom edge of the sail.

Even as he barked instructions, Matt kept a watchful eye on the positioning of the waves, the dock and the boat. He managed multiple sail, mast and boom lines, plus the helm, with a deft hand. Alex watched his actions with fascination, impressed with his confident focus and control.

Ultimately, the starboard side came smoothly alongside the dock and Matt snapped all the ropes loose from their stops. "Davey, untie the halyard and drop the main sail," he said calmly. Davey scurried to the mast and unwound its vertical line. The siblings scrambled from bow to stern clearing lines and dropping and rolling sails until all were safely secured.

Alex stepped down onto the dock's long, grain-textured boards, smoothed by years of water and wind. The dock bounced beneath her, supported by its old yellowing Styrofoam floats. She checked her balance and lingered to take in the rustic atmosphere. The dock stretched toward land at a right angle to the boat slips where she stood. A wide plank covered the last few feet of lake water, ending on one end of a short, but deep, sandy half-moon beach. Beyond the beach, a line of shrubs and trees started the forest. At the far end of the sand, a well-worn footpath cut into the forest, following the rise of the hill. After a dozen yards it veered, disappearing into dense foliage obscuring the path's destination.

Matt loaded them up with sleeping bags, groceries and other gear. He picked up the last two duffle bags and stepped across onto the dock. "We're walkin' the plank, mateys," he growled in a pirate's voice and headed toward a narrow wooden bridge leading from the main dock to the sandy beach. Becka and Davey giggled.

"Aye, Captain," Alex said with a grin at her other friends. She followed Matt along the slanted boardwalk, gingerly balancing grocery bags. Where the plank met the shoreline, they stepped onto a sandy, flat footpath crossing the beach.

Alex watched Matt's golden-brown hair shimmer in the sunlight and his hamstrings flexing so tantalizingly as he navigated the boulder-strewn footpath. She also marveled at the many facets he'd revealed today. Where had the introverted loner gone? He'd been in total control of everything on that boat. The day's plans, the sailboat, its navigation, trip supplies, his friends and siblings. *A quiet leader. No wonder his parents put him in charge of the kids*.

As they walked along, Brett teased Becka and Davey for lagging behind under the weight of the cooler they carried. He threatened loudly to tickle them, which alone made them break into peals of laughter. Just as they gained control again, Brett "accidentally" bumped lightly into each of them, making them hoot with laughter and stagger off the path. The kids could barely hold on to the cooler handles due to their hobbled efforts to avoid him and their shrieking giggle fits. Suzanne tried to restrain Brett, but ended up laughing at his antics, too.

The path quickly turned into a rocky incline as they moved into the woods. It wound up the hill until they were engulfed in a forest of old trees. The growth was dense enough to obscure the view of either the lake or their cabin destination, but periodically opened upon small pinecone-laden clearings.

At one open patch, Alex looked up and saw high above them in the pines a lone, rustic cabin with porthole windows. Underneath its broad, wooden porch, a small creek bubbled and gurgled over stones and moss, eventually losing itself downhill in the depths of the forest. She caught her breath; it was the exact cabin in her dream. How could she have so totally put it out of her mind? Seeing it in reality caught her by surprise, just like the tree stump. Why hadn't she expected this?

Matt stopped. "You alright?"

Alex gathered her composure around her pounding heart. "Nothing but fine." She couldn't possibly remind him that she'd seen this cabin in her mind's eye. Her realistic dreams were exactly what had caused trouble between them before. She managed a quick cover up, with a breathless, "Your cabin. It's just so beautiful!"

His eyes flicked to Suzanne and he turned back to Alex with a wary look. Luckily, he simply turned toward the cabin and restarted his ascent.

As he continued along, Suzanne pulled Alex up beside her and stopped. She scoped out the cabin, deck and creek and turned an I-told-you-so look on Alex. Alex furrowed a warning brow at her friend. Suzanne just nodded and laid a finger on her lips.

As soon as everyone reached the cabin's deck, Brett released his armload of sleeping bags and ran over to tickle Becka for real. She collapsed in laughter, and Davey dropped the cooler to run over to pry Brett's tickle fingers away from his sister.

With an amused shake of his head at the ruckus, Matt reached above the doorsill and pulled down a key. He opened the door, ushered Alex inside and looked around the simple, cozy room.

"This is *decent*!" she exclaimed.

"It's my home away from home, for sure." Wistfully he added, "I wish I could live here even in winter, away from everything…school, the city."

Alex laughed. "Good thing you never *really* lived in a city, SuperMatt. You would want to live here full time!" Her mood softened and she added, "I wouldn't mind having a little haven like this."

"You're welcome anytime," he said, pulling her into a hug. "Were you surprised?" he asked.

"You mean about this weekend? No idea! We're going to have such fun!"

"If I have anything to say about it, we will."

The cabin door opened and their friends traipsed inside, still laughing. Within a short time they had put away the food and supplies, picked the girl's sleeping spots on the indoor cots, and divvied up the guy's deck space for their sleeping bags. After Matt smeared sunscreen on his siblings, everyone else except Alex grabbed a beach towel and trooped back down to the beach.

Waiting for Matt to put away the sunscreen bottle inside, Alex moved into the welcoming sunshine on the deck and her heart again filled with anticipation. Just off the sandy beach below, Suzanne and Brett were already splashing around with Becka and Davey who were attempting to escape on their inflatable rafts. Alex stood at the edge of the deck admiring the beautiful Coeur d'Alene skyline nestled in its cove far across the lake. A motorboat came into view approaching the dock below and Alex waved, certain it was her parents and brother arriving. But only two people sat in the boat.

Alex's stomach tightened as she recognized Daniel and Kathy. *What were they doing here?* She turned questioningly to Matt who was just coming through the screen door.

"What's up, Princess?" he asked, reacting to her stare.

She clenched her fists. "You invited Daniel and Kathy?"

"For sure."

She glared at him.

"Daniel's family has a *boss* waterskiing boat."

Alex continued to stare at him.

"What's the big deal?" Light exasperation tinged his tone. "They're our friends."

"*Your* friends."

"C'mon, Alex, we're all 18 now. Adults. Petty squabbles have to be put behind us."

"Petty squabbles? You know how Kathy hates me."

"She needs to learn to appreciate you, and she can only do that by spending time with you. You can just ignore her. I'll keep her in line."

"While you ignore *me*?"

Matt cocked his head in understanding. He moved to her and said quietly, "Oh, I see what it is." He pulled her into a hug and asked, "How could I ignore the most important person in my life?"

"They'll change everything this weekend, Matt." She fought the tears welling in her eyes.

"Only if you let them," he said. "You're better at controlling your feelings than anyone I know. Just don't let them bother you."

Alex pulled away and looked down at the beach where Suzanne and Brett were greeting the newcomers. As they turned to move up the path, Suzanne looked up at Alex with an uncomfortable, knowing expression. Alex set her jaw.

She watched the unwanted newcomers ascending along the windy path, disappearing periodically behind dense sections of trees. Kathy's eyes always stayed on the path, but Daniel looked up and stared at her every time they moved into clear view.

His penetrating gaze brought up an image of their encounter in the park just after graduation. She pressed her fingers against her mouth to stop the feeling of his lips brushing hers as he vowed to win her over. "You have no idea what Daniel has in mind," she said to Matt.

"I actually have a pretty good idea of what he's after," he responded with a nod. "Listen, I didn't really know it would bother you so much to have them here. But, we're still gonna have fun, Princess. Trust me."

"I trust *you*. Just not them." Alex raised her chin and walked into the cabin to fix some sandwiches and gather her self-control.

❖❖❖

Daniel and Kathy entered the cabin minutes later. Alex greeted Kathy coolly, simply nodding in her direction. She gracefully accepted Daniel's kiss on the cheek, ignoring how his eyes danced with mischievousness and his hands lingered on her shoulders.

He immediately offered to help her with the sandwiches.

"Actually, I'll just let you finish them up," Alex said with a sardonic smile, handing him a mayonnaise-laden knife. "I forgot something in the boat." She turned on her heel and, barely catching Kathy's stifled snort behind her, disappeared through the screen door.

As Alex hurried down the path, heart pounding, she heard another motorboat approaching. Looking up, she saw Jake standing at its windshield waving wildly. Alex laughed despite her mood and waved avidly back. She had a quick flash of escaping the cabin, skiing off across the lake next to her brother on a single ski. She ran out onto the dock. As soon as her family was within earshot, she yelled, "Hey, Jake, how about a double slalom?"

"Right now?" he yelled back.

"Yeah!"

Jake turned to his parents. His dad, at the wheel, nodded. He quickly turned the boat and cut the motor so it floated a few feet away from the dock.

"Suzanne," Alex shouted back to her beach-bound friend, "We're going out on a skiing run."

"Far out!" Suzanne called back. "Come back for us when you guys get tired, OK?"

Matt was standing on the deck of the sailboat with a relieved look on his face when they returned in an hour. Behind him, Alex could see the expectant faces of Kathy, Daniel, Brett and Suzanne.

"You guys have a good time?" Matt asked.

"Loads!" Jake yelled. "You going sailing now?"

"That's the plan. Lunch is on board and everything's ready. Do you all want to join us?" Matt asked the Laurens.

Alex's dad eased the motorboat up to the side of the sailboat.

"Sorry," Mrs. Lauren said, throwing a knowing look at her husband. "We've got to get our boat unpacked."

"She'll obviously need my brawn," Mr. Lauren said. He grinned, flexed his bicep and poked it with a finger. "I'd better stay."

"And I've got some beach time coming," Jake said, looking longingly toward the sandy beach.

"I want to stay, too," Becka said, pointing to a pile of floats on the beach. "That green float over there has my name on it."

"Nuh-uh! The green one's mine!" Davey yelled, scrambling down the dock. His sister followed close on his heels with a screech.

"We'll keep an eye on the kids, Matt," Mrs. Lauren said quickly. "You all go have fun."

"I really appreciate that, Mrs. Lauren," Matt said, with a smile. "How about you, Alex?"

She looked at the five friends already on the boat. An hour of hard skiing had taken the edge off of Alex's anger about Daniel and Kathy. The exercise had relaxed and rejuvenated her and she felt ready to take on whatever those two had to dish out.

"I'm cool," she said. She climbed up on the front hood of the motorboat and took Matt's hand as he helped her across. The sailboat bobbed and shifted under her weight and Matt stabilized her with a hard squeeze of her hand and a warm smile.

Brett gave her a sideways hug as she boarded, and Suzanne's bright smile gleamed at her from within the boat's shaded galley. Kathy huddled aft, near the helm, keeping her eyes on Matt. Matt raised his eyebrows at her and nodded slightly in Alex's direction. With a quick frown, followed by a look of resolve, Kathy met Alex's gaze and said almost warmly, "Hi, Alex. Happy belated birthday."

"Thank you," she replied, darting a glance at Matt.

She heard Daniel's swarthy voice above her. "Arrrrr, Fair Maiden boards the vessel." He was leaning out from atop the boat, shirtless, one hand grasping an angled mast stay for support. The image of a modern-day, swimming trunk-clad pirate filled Alex's mind as she looked up at him. His hair blew across his face in the now quickening breeze and he held a tempting soda can in his outstretched hand like a handful of beckoning silver. He bowed as low as he could without letting go of the mast cable and stretched forth the soda to Alex. She couldn't help but notice how his well-toned chest muscles rippled.

"M'lady? Some refreshment? The Captain of the Vessel has instructed us to treat thee with the utmost respect this weekend. We dare not sully thy birthright celebration, or we may find ourselves in Davey Jones's locker. Arrrrr!" he said, squinting one eye.

She pictured Matt's "walking the plank" earlier in the day. *What is it about guys and pirates?* She smiled in spite of herself and gave a deep curtsy before taking the soda. "Thank you, fine sailor. We dare not disobey the captain's wishes now, do we?" She turned to catch Matt's reaction.

Matt simply smiled and shook his head. He abruptly turned and called over to Alex's brother on the dock, "Hey, Jake, loose the sailboat line and give us a shove, will you?"

Jake grinned and wrestled loose the stern line. He yelled to his father, who had just finished securing the motorboat to the dock, to help push the sailboat out into clear water. They waved to the teenagers as the boat drifted out just far enough to reach a growing breeze. Matt tightened the lines to pull the sails in close. The wind snapped into the taught white cloth and the receptive boat quickly glided forward.

As they moved away from the shore, they heard Mrs. Lauren's call, "Don't forget to put on your life preservers! And, be back by 5 o'clock so we have time to eat before the fireworks."

"Moms…" Brett's voice wafted up from within the galley, "Talk about 'sullying the celebration of thy birthright!' Who can have fun with a life preserver on?"

Matt pulled two puffy orange vests from a storage box beside the tiller and tossed them down into the galley. "*We* can have fun making fun of the way you look in it, Brettman."

"What? You're gonna make us wear these, pal?"

He threw vests to everyone else. "We get pulled over by the Coast Guard without vests on and we get a big fat fine. Neither my folks or yours are going to like paying for our stupidity."

Brett held the orange thing up and regarded it with disgust.

"You get used to his boat rules after a while," Kathy said. "He only wants to keep us all safe, you know."

Brett gave them both a resigned look and pulled on the life preserver. Suzanne immediately threw her arms around him. "You're

like my own, big, orange teddy bear," she said, embracing him. Brett's
head lolled to one side and he donned an exaggerated look of ecstasy.

Alex popped the last bite of bread into her mouth and brushed
crumbs off her lap. *Somehow, ham sandwiches taste so much better
flavored with wind and sun.* She turned into the breeze and breathed
the lake's damp smell deep into her lungs.

"Why don't you go sit on the bow…up front," Matt suggested,
briefly taking his eyes off the sails and water to smile at her. "The
view's best up there."

Giving him a thankful squeeze, she started forward just as a gust
hit the sails. The boat heeled quickly to starboard and she almost fell
across the cockpit onto Brett.

"Oops! I'm sorry, guys," she said, grabbing Brett's outstretched
hands for balance as the boat continued to heel.

"Some people would do anything to be near me," Brett drawled,
quickly pulling Alex down onto his lap. Alex giggled. Brett wrapped
his arms around her and tucked her cheek next to his while he grinned
at Suzanne.

Suzanne reached over and methodically unwrapped his arms from
her friend. "Brettman, you're dreamin'. Only crazy people want to be
near you."

Brett feigned exaggerated horror. "But…but that makes you…" He
squeaked and cowered backward. Alex took the opportunity to get up.

"Yeah-h-h-h," Suzanne replied, maniacally moving her head back
and forth in front of his face. She grabbed his head in her hands. "It's
your devastatingly cute drawl. It drives me wild," she said, kissing him
hard and quick.

For once Brett was shocked into silence. Everyone laughed.

"OK. I gotta go now," Alex said with a fake smile, backing away
on tiptoes. "I'll just go meet up with all the sane people at the front of
the boat." With a backward wave, she adjusted her balance to the sharp
slant of the deck and gingerly edged forward along the port side, using
the mast stays and other vertical lines for support.

"Quite a heel," Daniel said, winking at Alex as he climbed up out
of the galley behind her.

She shot him a questioning look.

"Not your dear friend Brett, Fair Maiden. I meant the angle of the boat," he said, leaning on the midsection railing and studying her.

She simply raised an eyebrow at him and continued along to the bow. Ignoring the feeling of his gaze lingering on her, she sat and dangled her legs over the side. After a moment, she turned to smile at Matt at the far end of the boat, carefully avoiding Daniel's gaze. With the heightened wind, Matt's eyes roved everywhere but to her. She watched him examining the angle of the sails, slack in the lines, direction of the wind and approaching waves, position of oncoming boats and the increasing heel of the boat.

Next to Matt, Kathy was white-knuckling the side railing. Over the noise of wind and water, Alex barely heard her ask Matt, "We're not going to tip over, are we?"

Matt gave Kathy a quick, reassuring look. "Now, have we ever tipped…" The rest of his comment was lost in a gust of wind.

Alex was glad to hear the assurance in his voice. A heeling boat was more than a little disconcerting. She felt much more stable now that she was sitting firmly on the deck. It was actually quite exhilarating to sit high above the water as it slipped away below her.

She closed her eyes and relished the feeling of the warm sun on her skin, cooled by the spray of waves. Combined with the forward motion of the boat and the lake scents on the wind, she was quickly lulled into a calm reverie. Soon, a solid warmth moved against her arm and she leaned into it, absorbing the sensation of Matt's touch. *But who was steering the boat?* She opened her eyes.

"Daniel!" Alex blurted, jerking away.

"Mm-hmm."

"I thought…"

"I know." He grinned.

She gave him a perturbed glare, but he just leaned harder against her. She scooted away, but he moved closer. With the next scoot she bumped up against the center post at the tip of the bow railing. He snuggled in right next to her.

"What do you think you're doing, Daniel?"

"Keeping you warm, Fair Maiden. We can't have the birthday girl getting chilled, you know."

"I'm perfectly fine," she said.

"Yes, you are," Daniel said quietly, blue eyes boring seductively into hers.

Avoiding his eyes by looking out over the lake, she asked, "Aren't you uncomfortable hitting on me right in front of your best friend?"

"This wind is keeping him too busy to notice us. Besides, he knows I'm a harmless flirt."

"He doesn't know your real intentions here."

"Not fully. But *you* do. And that's what matters."

She narrowed her eyes. "You really are a scuz."

"I just know what I want, that's all."

She looked him full in the face. "Even though you know you are never going to get it?"

"You might be surprised at how often I get what I want," he said, placing a hand on her bare thigh.

Alex quickly pulled up her knees, starting to stand. At that moment, the boat lurched from a massive wind shift and she heard Matt yell, "Watch out!"

Alex turned just in time to see the main sail fill from the opposite direction and its supporting boom swing wildly across the boat. For as much cloth weight as the length of metal carried above it, it moved with surprising rapidity. In an instant, its bulk veered right into Kathy's head. She dropped like a bag of sand to the deck.

Stunned, no one moved until Matt went into frantic motion. Within seconds, he loosened all lines to under-power the sails, jammed the tiller to stall the boat and tied the lines off. The boat slowed and stilled until it simply bounced around like a large buoy in the water.

Suddenly, Daniel was down in the cockpit cradling Kathy's head on his lap. With one arm outstretched, he yelled at Brett to throw him a beach towel hanging from the boat railing.

"I'll get the first aid kit," Matt said, ducking his head, jumping the small stairs down into the galley and disappearing into its shadow.

As Daniel leaned over Kathy, Alex saw near terror in his face. He held his hand against the gash in her forehead trying to stem the steady flow of blood trickling between his fingers.

"Kathy?" he asked loudly. "Kathy!" He pressed the towel Brett handed him to the wound.

She fluttered her eyes open. "Ow."

Daniel pulled her against his chest in relief. "I bet." He let her back down and looked closely into her face. "Look at me, Kath. What do you see?"

"Your ugly face." She smiled wanly and grimaced.

"Only one of my ugly faces?"

"Yeah."

"Good." Daniel glanced up as Matt set the open first-aid kit on the deck next to Kathy.

"Her eyes aren't dilated are they?" Matt asked, leaning over his friends with concern.

"Open your eyes wide, Kath," Daniel said, peering down into them for a long moment. "No. Thank God." He peeked underneath the blood-soaked washcloth at her wound. "You're gonna have a nice big knot on your noggin, Fine Lady, but you're gonna to be OK."

"I'll head on back," Matt said, starting toward the tiller. Daniel looked up and nodded. As Matt passed Suzanne and Brett, he asked, "You'll help Daniel while I get us going again?"

They agreed and Matt quickly moved back to the helm. He continued to glance over at Kathy and Daniel even as he expertly maneuvered the lines and tiller until the sails caught the wind and the boat moved forward smoothly and quickly.

Alex marveled at Matt's calm and command, while her own heart still pounded nearly out of her chest. Still at the bow of the boat, Alex watched Daniel methodically asking Suzanne and Brett for supplies as he disinfected Kathy's head wound, stopped the blood flow and carefully bandaged it up. He undoubtedly had lots of experience treating sports injuries. Daniel showed such concentration, tenderness and concern. *He must really care about her to treat her so gently.*

Once Kathy was sitting up leaning against him, Daniel started telling jokes and stories. With prompting and support from Brett, he kept everyone laughing, holding Kathy's hand the whole time. Between stories, he checked on her, stealing concerned looks at the large bandage covering her forehead. Jealousy pricked Alex's heart.

At one point, she watched him throw back his head and laugh at his own joke. The white flash of teeth as his smile chiseled perfection into the handsome lines of his face made her unexpectedly weak. Alex had to admit, she was attracted to him. And, as much as she consciously hated his forced attentions toward her, they emotionally flattered and moved her. His focus on her, too, had seemed to keep Kathy in her place. But now, she suddenly realized Kathy was very important to Daniel, and Alex felt that twist her gut.

She willfully buried the emotion. *Stupid, you're in love with Matt!* She looked back at her sailor as if seeing him would validate her feelings. At that moment, Matt sought her gaze. He provided her with a reassuring wink and a nod. Anger flooded her and she instinctively averted her eyes.

The unexpected reaction confused her. What had Matt done to make her mad? *Nothing.* She turned her face into the wind, allowing the cool force to blow away the emotional cobwebs trying to tangle her mind. She dropped her head into her hands, curls falling through her fingers and fluttering frantically around her face. For a long time, she listened to the water slapping the boat sides, felt the motion of the boat slicing the water and took deep breaths, tasting the lake-moist air.

Just as her mind and emotions began to quiet, Alex felt a hand taking hers. She opened her eyes and saw Matt looking down at her with concern. She hadn't even noticed that they'd moored. She looked gratefully up at him. The flare of confusion and anger was gone for now, but she knew she'd have to deal with those feelings soon.

She saw Kathy still giggling at Daniel's last joke, but holding one palm to her forehead as she rose to disembark. She leaned against Daniel's stabilizing arm as everyone climbed out on the dock.

As they walked down the gangway toward the beach, Mrs. Lauren looked casually up at the returning sailors. Her welcoming smile faded as soon as Kathy's bandaged head registered. She gasped, dropped her paperback and knocked over her beach chair as she hurried toward the teenagers. She and Mr. Lauren arrived at Kathy's side at the same time. The younger kids ran over, too, crowding around to see what had happened while exclaiming and blurting questions.

Mr. Lauren quieted everyone and steered Kathy to a beach lounger. With parental concern, he reviewed what had happened, looked over her wound and asked her all the same questions the teenagers had initially asked. Finally, he sat back with a relieved and appreciative look at the young men and announced, "You are one lucky girl to have friends who take such expert care of you." He patted Kathy's shoulder, reassuringly. "Just let us know if you start feeling odd in the next few hours, OK?"

❖❖❖

Mrs. Lauren emitted a motherly sound of relief and said, "We have just the thing to soothe you all after this. Come on up and enjoy the surprise delivered while you were out on the boat." Davey bounced up and down and Jake grinned widely, but Mrs. Lauren shot them both a friendly warning look. "It's a surprise now, boys, don't be ruining it."

The teenagers shared expectant looks and followed Mrs. Lauren up the path to the deck. "Sit down everyone," she said, motioning to the picnic table, decorated with bright party ware and a festive paper table drape. She disappeared into the cabin while the rest sat down at the colorful table.

She reappeared in a short time, the screen door clapping closed loudly behind her. On a large tray, she balanced a frosty cardboard gallon of ice cream surrounded with containers of warm chocolate syrup, marshmallow cream, Maraschino cherries, bananas and whipped cream.

"Mom and Dad sent us an ice cream social!" Becka said, her eyes glowing with joy.

"A delivery guy brought it right to our dock on a really big boat," Davey said, bouncing again. "And when we opened the cooler it steamed. Dry ice is so boss!"

Mrs. Lauren smiled at his enthusiasm. "Since they couldn't be here themselves, your parents sent us a party, right down to the decorations." She nodded at the cheerful table. "They wanted you to know how proud they are of you for completing the recording of your song. Wasn't that thoughtful?"

Matt smiled at her and at his siblings, but joy did not touch his eyes. Alex knew he was thinking his parents should have been here themselves, not just their ice cream party. She saw him give an almost imperceptible shrug and gently direct Jake to the head of the sundae assembly line.

Mr. Lauren scooped the frozen cream and each person created a mouth-watering masterpiece. Not too many bites had been consumed before Brett began circling the table, balancing his banana split while trying to steal spoonfuls from everyone else's bowls. This resulted in gales of laughter and one big brain freeze caused by Davey's very fast gobbling. Even without Brett's influence, it didn't take long for everyone to scarf the cool treats.

Once everyone had helped clean up, they moved back down to the beach. Becka and Davey immediately pulled Matt and Brett out into the cove for some beach ball "keep away."

While their guys were occupied, Alex and Suzanne walked out to the far end of the dock and settled down on beach towels to sunbathe. Suzanne smiled at Brett's wave and turned her gaze back to the beach where Daniel was leading Kathy to a pair of shaded beach loungers. "What's with Daniel? He hasn't let Kathy out of his sight since her head bonk," she asked.

Alex watched Daniel place his hand over Kathy's bandaged forehead, and willfully crushed unexpected pangs of envy. She couldn't quite keep the sting from her voice. "I have no idea."

Suzanne gave her a sidelong glance. "Maybe he just feels responsible for her. She is living with his family while her father's in Europe, after all." She continued almost to herself, "He didn't have anything but you on his mind before that. I saw him making the moves on you back on the boat."

"He's a scuz bucket," Alex said more vehemently than intended.

Suzanne looked full at Alex and pursed her lips. "Hmmm, I see."

"What do you think you see?" Alex asked, for the first time uncomfortable that her friend always knew what she was thinking.

Suzanne looked across the cove at Daniel, who lay in repose in the lounger. Sun glinted off his blonde hair and summer sweat shimmered on his mostly bare athletic form. "He *is* a stone fox," she said shaking her head slowly. "Hard for anyone to resist."

Alex tried to keep from blushing. "I'm in love with *Matt*."

"Uh-huh. But there are certain distractions, aren't there?"

"That distraction is apparently Kathy's territory," Alex said, glaring as she saw Kathy reach over and take Daniel's hand with a comfortably contented smile. "It seems her role is to try to steal anyone I'm attracted to." Alex immediately regretted saying it.

Suzanne gave her a sympathetic glance, followed by a wry smile. "Love is confusing." She paused, looking back toward the couple on the beach. "Daniel's apparently Kathy's savior at the moment, so she's gravitated toward him for now. Anyway, she's not getting what she needs from Matt. Maybe she's trying to make him jealous."

A burst of anger flared again in Alex. "And what about Matt? He's just backed off and let Daniel do everything for Kathy. You'd think he didn't even know her."

"Matt's in his adult role today."

"What does that mean?"

"You haven't noticed how he's acted like the parent of all of us today? Giving us direction. Keeping us safe."

Alex *had* noticed. She turned to watch Matt. At the moment, he held the beach ball high above the water, animatedly shouting directions to the boys on how to keep-away his pending toss from Brett. Lake water glistened against his lean, well-formed chest and arms. The muscles rippled as he moved the ball above his head and Alex unintentionally leaned toward him, a warmth spreading through her. A toss of his sopped hair caused a flat arc of spray to fly through the air in Alex's direction. Its disk-like shape jogged a memory and Alex jerked her head back as if to avoid it.

She remembered Daniel and Kathy dropping by to ask Matt to play Frisbee, interrupting her Fall Concert practice in Matt's music room. On the surface, it had seemed just a request to share some fun, but Alex remembered now they hadn't gone on their own once he'd said no. Their decision centered around him, whether or not he went. She hadn't seen before how much his childhood friendships pivoted around him. Even with his quiet presence Matt had an underlying strength and always seemed to control the situation. He took care of his friends just like his siblings.

She suddenly understood her sudden anger at his nonverbal reassurances following Kathy's accident earlier. "Matt doesn't really need me," she said in a flat, quiet tone, realizing that the guy she thought she was cosmically attached to her wasn't the dreamy musician she held in her heart. He was strong. Stronger than her. She realized how much she wanted to be the one to help him use his talent to become famous. But now, she could see he didn't need her for that. He could stand alone and really needed no one's support. And now it became clear why he had broken up with her in Moscow.

Suzanne bit her lip with a slight nod. "He's had a lot to take care of in his life. Lovesick Kathy to placate and care for, troublesome Daniel to manage, two innocent siblings to raise…he's gotten self sufficient."

"All I have to care for is some laundry and household chores mom expects me to do every week," Alex said, imagining what it would be like to have to care for her only sibling almost full time.

She could barely care for herself, let alone Jake, or any of her friends. She suddenly realized she hadn't taken any action at all to help during Kathy's accident earlier. Alex's hands clenched against her stomach. She hadn't done anything, just sat and watched. What did that say about her?

"I didn't even think about trying to help during the accident earlier, Suzanne," she said. "I'm the only one who didn't do anything." Her stomach suddenly felt sick.

"Yeah, well, the situation was out of your control. It was a new experience for you."

Alex felt her world tumbling in new directions. Everything she'd thought about herself and her role in these relationships was twisting. She realized she could have more forcefully discouraged Daniel's advances earlier that day as well.

"I can't even get Matt's best friend to back off where he isn't welcome," she said.

"He's not that easy to get rid of, I've noticed," Suzanne said. "Especially when you're crazy attracted to him." She looked at her friend knowingly.

Alex hung her head and shook it.

"I'm trying not to be."

"I know."

"I'm supposed to be with Matt."

"I know."

Alex stopped and examined her friend's face. It was not judgmental or pitying, just matter-of-fact.

Suzanne looked up into the sky and said, "It's the way it's supposed to happen, you know."

"I know..." She quoted Suzanne's guiding philosophy, "I am 'a child of the universe...'"

"Yup. '...no less than the trees and the stars.' Suzanne smiled and nodded. "You're part of the mix, in the right place, right now."

Something in the fact that her wise friend Suzanne truly believed that statement was comforting. Alex smoothed her hands down each side of her neck and felt her stomach relax. She pulled a ponytail over her shoulder, holding onto it as she turned her gaze to Matt. She blew out a long breath, squared her shoulders and said to her friend, "I don't know, Suz. You may be right. The universe may unfold in a way that's testing me. But I'll tell you one thing..." She nodded in Matt's direction. "That guy may think he can go it alone, but he's going to realize eventually that he needs me. I'm stickin' with him. I just *know* it's right."

"It may be, but what about Daniel?"

"I'm not meant for Daniel. I just have to find some way to deal with him."

"We'll see, won't we? A sensual battle between the King of Cunning and the Queen of Control, that'll be interesting to watch."

Alex snapped her head toward her friend and held her mouth open in disbelief. "I can't believe you said that."

"You're denying that I've got you both pegged?" Suzanne's eyes twinkled with self-assurance.

Alex shook her head at her insightful friend and smiled. But, when her eyes rested on Matt again, she set her jaw. He may already love her, but she would make him *need* her, no matter how strong he was.

The rest of the day, while Daniel and Kathy continued to relax on the beach, the rest of the group went out on the lake, taking turns waterskiing in and out of secluded coves. Alex took the last run as they boated back the half-hour distance to the Roberts' cabin. This late in the day, the wind had died, leaving the lake surface unruffled and reflective. Alex took full advantage of the smooth ride.

As she slalomed, Alex closed her mind to everything but the feel of moving across that silky water. Time after time she leaned against the powerful pull of the boat, laying her body almost parallel to the lake surface and using the increased speed to take her wide out to one side of the boat. She deftly cut the tip of her ski back to the inside to decrease her speed, leaning back to take up the resulting sag in the ski rope. She glided along until the speed of the boat took up the slack. As the rope snapped taut against her grip again she abruptly increased speed. The momentum allowed her to jump the closest crest of the boat's white wake and catch enough air to clear the far crest. She felt pure exhilaration with every controlled landing.

The emotions of the day slipped away as the glass-like water slid under her ski. Alex felt fully relaxed and happy as they approached their destination, even as she caught sight of Daniel and Kathy waving from the beach.

Judging the distance to the dock as the boat approached, Alex let go of the rope. Using her momentum to glide atop the water, she slowly submerged until she stopped, floating right next to the dock. Alex pulled off her ski, slid it up on the dock and climbed up after it. She stood, checking her balance as the boat's dual wake rocked the dock. She unfastened the ski vest and worked to catch her breath as Matt circled the boat back around and nudged it into its slip.

Brett hopped out of the boat and hugged her. "Gnarly run, girl!" "How can you ski for that long?" he asked. "I was dead tired after five minutes." He grabbed Suzanne around the waist as she walked up.

Alex just smiled at him and blew out a long breath.

"You're sure living up to your crab Zodiac, water girl," Suzanne said over her shoulder to her drenched friend.

Alex laughed. She threw her life jacket into the cockpit and caught the towel Matt threw to her. As she finished rubbing down and tucked the towel around her, Matt finished tying off the boat and grabbed her hand. "So, music isn't the only thing that flows from you, is it?"

Alex looked at him questioningly.

"'Water girl…'" he mimicked Suzanne.

Alex shook her hair back and looked out over the water. "I just love it, that's all."

He looked around to make sure her parents weren't watching. He whispered, "I love you," and pecked her on the lips.

❖❖❖

In the late afternoon, everyone gathered around a beach campfire to roast hotdogs and marshmallows for s'mores, and to await dark and the fireworks. With all their reminiscing, laughing and singing of folk songs, Alex barely remembered her awkwardness with Daniel and Kathy. Those feelings had completely dissipated in the glory of the afternoon's skiing and the warmth of the campfire.

As darkness began to fall, Matt directed everyone to pull the lawn and lounge chairs out on the dock while he gathered sweatshirts and flashlights from the sailboat.

Alex couldn't wait to see the fireworks. She imagined the spectacular sight of the colorful plumes reflecting against the lake waters. "Shoot! I forgot my camera," Alex said. "I need to run up to the cabin."

"I'll go with you," Matt said. He picked up an ax near the smoldering fire.

"You gonna chop wood while we're up there, SuperMatt?" Alex teased him.

"I'll just feel better if I have it along," he said. "We don't often see them, but cougars come down from the hills sometimes on this side of the lake."

Alex pulled her hands back under her sweatshirt sleeves, folded her arms and looked warily around as she followed Matt up the path. The trek to the cabin somehow seemed longer in the dark, but they soon reached it without incident. Alex popped into the cabin and retrieved her camera. Matt was standing at the edge of the deck looking out over the twilight lake and the distant city lights popping on. "Our little city is so beautiful," he said. "Someone should write a song about it."

"You're just the right person to do it," Alex said, snuggling in by his side.

Matt looked down at her in silence, pulling her chin upward with his forefinger. "I'd rather write music about you." He looked down into her eyes until Alex felt a little tremble in her legs. Matt bent down and moved his lips against hers. The kiss lingered and Alex felt Matt's arms tighten around her.

She lost consciousness of anything but his increasing need for her, until a wild cry startled them apart. Distant but clear, from behind the cabin, it came again. Part snarl, part scream. Matt slowly put his hand on the ax handle where it leaned against the deck railing and stared into the near darkness. "Big cat, but not too close. Probably just missed pouncing on his dinner." He turned a regretful look on Alex. "We'd better go back down or we'll miss the fireworks."

Alex nodded and took one step before he pulled her back to him. "We may not have another moment alone and I have to…" He stopped and put his head back as if to see the bright stars forming above him.

"What is it, Matt?" Alex got the feeling he was debating whether to share something with her.

He sighed and dropped his head to look into her eyes. "I love you, Princess. I really do," was all he said, lightly kissing her. He picked up the ax and flashlight and turned to go.

Alex stood still for a moment wondering if she'd just imagined his hesitance. "Was there something else?" she asked, hurrying after him.

He hesitated again and sighed heavily. "Just trying to figure stuff out, I guess."

"Should I worry?"

"You never need to worry, Princess. You always know what to do and think."

"What does that mean?"

"Nothing. It's just that I'm not always as clear about things as you usually are."

"I can help you, Matt."

"I know. But you can't help until I get my thoughts together."

Alex pondered that comment until they arrived back at the dock with a small weight in her stomach.

The kids had sprawled out on beach towels along the dock while her parents and the young adults had settled into the available chairs. Just as the first fiery blossom bloomed in the sky, Matt took a seat in the remaining lounger and patted the few square inches on the seat in front of him. He looked at Alex expectantly. Her parents' warnings about public displays of affection rang in her head and she looked over at them. The Laurens sat at the forward end of the dock with their backs toward the group.

Alex mentally shrugged, snuggled down in front of Matt and lay back against his chest. She rationalized that it was dark and everyone's attentions would be on the fireworks. Besides the warmth of his body felt incredible against hers. The heaviness in her stomach lifted and she turned her head to look up into his eyes. "Thank you for arranging this weekend for me, Matt," she whispered. "I love you."

He snuck a peek at her parents' backs and quickly kissed her. She glimpsed reciprocated feelings shining through his eyes as a series of colorful explosions lit up the sky.

As they watched the florets burning the darkness, she thought, "For the first time in my life, I am really happy." But as soon as she thought it, an inkling of fear moved into her heart. She knew Matt really loved her, but he didn't really need her. That could change everything... But this beautiful moment wasn't the time to worry about that. Alex pushed her fears aside and snuggled closer to Matt.

❖❖❖

After the fireworks, everybody chattered as they walked back up the hill, wondering if the barge actually did catch fire this year and making plans for tomorrow. As soon as they reached the cabin, Mrs. Lauren corralled the girls inside to get ready for bed.

Alex was relieved when Kathy took Becka under her wing. The light duty of answering the girl's constant chatter and overseeing her bedtime routine kept Kathy preoccupied with something besides her injured head. This left Alex and Suzanne to themselves during their lengthy nighttime rituals.

They gossiped quietly to each other in the bathroom as they removed makeup, moisturized skin, brushed teeth and hair. When they finished and came back out to shake their sleeping bags into line along the floor, Alex snuck a peek out the window at the guys on the deck. "They're already in their sleeping bags?"

"No Noxema to wash off," Suzanne snickered.

"They spit their toothpaste over the deck rail," Mrs. Lauren said in disgust, shaking her bag out on the cot by the door.

Becka made a face. "Gross me out!"

"They actually brushed their teeth?" Kathy asked, putting the last hair band around Becka's nighttime braid.

"Let's say a proper goodnight to those raunchy ol' boys, shall we?" Mrs. Lauren asked. She directed the girls to line up from smallest to tallest beside the door and whispered, "Now, on three, everyone yell 'Goodnight, boys!' when I open the door." She quietly counted and on "three" she pushed the door open. The girls shouted and every guy on the moonlit deck flinched. Brett nearly jumped out of his bag and the girls collapsed into fits of laughter.

"Freak out! I'm nervous enough out here with the big cats, without you guys screaming up behind me," Brett exclaimed, running a hand through his red hair.

"Don't worry, Brett," Mr. Lauren assured him. "The cougars have much more easy prey in these mountains than us. They'd have to be really starving to come down this far." He rearranged his sleeping bag underneath him and lay back down with a grin at his wife.

Davey's eyes were as big as saucers. He flicked his gaze up to his big brother, who nodded and patted his sibling's shoulder reassuringly. "You're too scrawny and tough for any ol' cat to want for dinner anyway, chump," he said.

Davey laughed and his face relaxed.

"Besides," Kathy chimed in from the doorway, "Given a choice, that cat's gonna want the biggest meal. She's gonna make a bee-line for Daniel's well-fed muscles."

Alex saw Daniel's gaze connect with Kathy's. He smiled a cheesy smile, flexed his biceps and repeatedly raised his eyebrows at her as everyone laughed.

"It's been an exciting, tiring day, everyone. Time to sleep now," Mrs. Lauren said, opening the inner door wide to let in the cool air through the screen door.

Alex caught Matt's good night wink meant just for her. But, as she turned away, she also caught Daniel's gaze. Its penetrating power startled her. She'd become so used to his preoccupation with Kathy today, his look took her off guard. Heart pounding, Alex crawled into her sleeping bag as her mom secured the window screens and shut out the lights.

It didn't take long for the deep breathing to start both inside and out of the cabin. Alex lay awake enjoying the moonlight and cool breaths of mountain air wafting in. She re-created the feeling of Matt's arms around her as the fireworks exploded above them just an hour before. She lifted her head up onto one hand to see if she could catch a glimpse of him through the door before she fell asleep.

The moonlight revealed Matt's silhouette, also propped on his elbow and looking toward her.

She saw his shadowy arm move to his mouth and blow her a kiss. She returned the gesture. For nearly a minute, they remained motionless, looking at each other's form in the darkness. Without words, Alex knew exactly his feelings and that he felt hers. She fell asleep with a small smile on her face.

❖❖❖

They walked above the icy river falls along a snowy, unstable footbridge. Cold spray hit Alex's face and she snuggled into Matt's warm embrace. Unexpectedly, the bridge trembled beneath them and Matt stumbled and fell away. Scrambling to catch him, Alex lost her footing and fell along the railing, nearly toppling into the rushing water below, too. But, something caught her leg. She tried to shake it off, but the grip was tight. She turned to look at what had gripped her.

❖❖❖

Emerging from her sleepy stupor, Alex realized her mother was gently shaking her leg, which had strayed out of her sleeping bag.

"Can you get up and help me with breakfast?" her mom asked quietly, patting her calf.

Alex pushed away thoughts of the dream and nodded sleepily. She shivered as she sat up, rubbed her eyes and looked outside to see if Matt was yet awake.

The guys were all still in their sleeping bags on the porch, but beginning to stir. The screen door framed a very stormy daylight beyond the guys. Alex frowned and squared her shoulders. *Bad weather is not going to ruin my weeken*d. She rose to grab her swimming suit and sweats.

The other girls were beginning to rouse, except Kathy, whose bandaged head lay motionless on her pillow. She was still, except for a slight movement of her lips as she exhaled. Careful that no one else in the room noticed, Alex stuck her tongue out at the sleeping girl.

A quiet giggle escaped from the direction of the bathroom and she turned to see Suzanne motioning to her from behind the cracked door.

"She deserved that," Suzanne said, as Alex closed the door. Hanging up a towel, Suzanne asked, "I slept like a rock. You?"

"All except for the part where I almost fell into the freezing river in my dream."

Suzanne cocked her head to one side. "Dreamed it again, hmmm?" Alex just nodded. Suzanne looked at Alex expectantly, as if waiting for additional details. When none came, she turned to smooth her black hair in the mirror. "Looks like the weather may make this kind of a short day."

Alex glowered at her. "Unless there's lightning, we can still ski and sail today."

Suzanne pressed her lips together in a tight smile. "I know you think if you put enough energy behind your words, you can make it so. But, you know, you just can't control the weather, Lex."

Alex just had time to give Suzanne an exasperated look before her friend slipped out of the bathroom. Just as the door was about to close, Suzanne yanked it back open just far enough to peek in and stick her tongue out. Smiling, she quickly disappeared. Alex couldn't help grinning into the mirror as she ran her brush through unruly curls.

When Alex came back out into the main room, Mrs. Lauren was pulling out eggs, cheese, bacon and bread, and asking Becka to find needed cooking utensils. She assigned table-setting duties to Suzanne and cooking to her daughter.

One by one, the sleepy, tousle-headed guys trooped inside to clean up and get dressed, and Mrs. Lauren enlisted them to roll up sleeping bags before eating.

The meal went quickly with all the kids pitching in except Kathy. Daniel had awakened his friend from her recuperative rest, and she now was sitting up in her sleeping bag taking bites of toast he'd spread with butter and jam for her. She kept putting a hand to her aching forehead, but smiled up gratefully at him with puffy, strained eyes.

Alex noticed Kathy's eyes occasionally darted to Alex, as if she was embarrassed by her infirmity; uncomfortable with not being up-to-snuff with her "competition."

As everyone finished breakfast, Mr. Lauren came into the cabin. "Looks like we'll need to get back to town within the next couple of hours," he said with an apologetic look at Alex. As if to emphasize his words, thunder rumbled in the distant horizon.

"OK, let's clean up breakfast and pack up our gear. If we do it quickly, maybe you'll still have time to do some skiing as we cross the bay to town," Mrs. Lauren said.

Alex looked at her mom appreciatively.

"We still have to get the sailboat back across," Matt said.

Alex perked up. "Will we have time for Matt to give me a quick sailing lesson before we go?" she asked her parents.

"Well, the storm's a ways off," her dad said slowly. "But, didn't you get a sailing lesson yesterday?"

"We'd just gotten going when Kathy had her accident," Matt replied. "I didn't have a chance to show anyone the ropes." His eyes moved regretfully to Alex.

"I really need to learn, Dad. That way, if something happens again, I actually might be able help." Suzanne put an understanding hand on Alex's shoulder and Alex glanced appreciatively at her friend. But Alex's face fell as she caught Kathy's contemptuous sniff and knowing nod. Moving her head must have hurt because Kathy immediately raised both hands to her bandaged forehead.

Daniel stood up and made his way to the sink with Kathy's breakfast plate. "Matt had the boat under control all by himself, didn't you, Matt?"

Picking up the derisive undertone in Daniel's comment, Matt gave Daniel a glance. "As you had control of Kathy's situation," he responded in a tolerant tone. "We all did what we know to do."

Except me. Alex turned quickly to Matt before anyone saw her unease and asked, "But what if you'd been the one to get hurt, Matt? How would we have gotten the boat back?" He didn't answer immediately and Alex raised her eyebrows at her dad. "I need to know what to do," Alex reiterated.

"You make a good point, Alex," said Mr. Lauren. Looking at his wife, he asked, "How about if you and I and the younger kids have a quick skiing run, while the teenagers go out for a fast sailing lesson?"

Mrs. Lauren nodded assent to her husband and turned her gaze to Alex. "As long as you watch the sky and come immediately back to town if you see even one bolt of lightning."

Alex shot a questioning expression at Matt.

"You got it," Matt agreed.

"Mrs. Lauren, would it be OK if I went back on the motorboat with you?" Kathy asked. "My head is splitting."

"Oh, my dear, of course," Mrs. Lauren replied, placing a hand gently on the girl's back. "We'll do all of your packing. You just rest."

Alex caught a shadow of irritation passing across Daniel's face as he looked away from Kathy to glance at her. She realized, despite his caring for Kathy, he really didn't want to go back yet. But he quickly turned back to his long-time friend. "I'll get you home, Kath."

Kathy smiled up at him appreciatively and immediately winced at even that small effort.

Everyone bundled up their belongings and traipsed down to the docks to ready the boats. With the transistor radio blaring James Taylor's "Carolina on My Mind," they placed gear and flipped bumpers inside the boats. Daniel propped Kathy comfortably against a stack of sleeping bags and pillows in the motorboat.

"Kathy, will you be alright if we take turns skiing back to town?" Mr. Lauren asked.

"Sure. I'll be fine as long as I don't have to move much," she said.

"We won't bounce you around too much, it doesn't look too choppy yet," Mr. Lauren said, looking out across the water. "OK, who's going first?"

Davey jumped up and down waving his hand in the air, shouting, "Me, me! I'm already in a life jacket!"

"I'm next then!" Jake added, quickly climbing into the motorboat.

The rest of the group stood looking back and forth at one another. "Well, if there's no one else, I'll take the last spin," Mrs. Lauren said with a grin. She turned to Matt and Alex. "So, you're all set? We'll expect you back at the city docks by…" A loud shriek cut short her comment and everyone turned to stare at Becka's bounding form as she grabbed the transistor radio and cranked the volume even higher.

From the radio flowed clear vocal tones that Alex had only recently begun to recognize…her recorded voice. She clapped her hands to her mouth, muffling a small scream and turned wide eyes on Matt. She watched as it hit him that it was *his* song playing on the radio. Matt bit his lip and folded his fingers together on top of his head. He stared back at her, a twinkle of pleasure blended with disbelief sparkling in his hazel eyes.

For the next couple of minutes, "Like the Moon Pulls The Tide" played on. Everyone stared, mesmerized, at the radio, or grinned astonished smiles at one another. During the closing notes, the DJ came back on, announcing that only this Coeur d'Alene station had been given the exclusive right to play the single's rough recording before its nationwide release. He reported the tune had been partially recorded at Frankie B. Crosby's home studio in nearby Hayden Lake and asked for listener feedback on "this beautiful new tune from Coeur d'Alene high-school grad's Matt Roberts and Alex Lauren."

Everyone began talking at once. Suzanne screamed, grabbing her best friend in a bear hug and dancing in circles. Brett nearly knocked them over as he joined their pirouette.

As they spun in an extended hug, Alex's mind took snapshots of her friends' and family's reactions. Daniel walked over to Matt and shook his hand. Davey cannonballed into the water with a giant yell and a splash. Jake sat up abruptly in one of the boat seats, staring at the waves Davey's leap had created and whispered, "…My sister is famous." Mrs. Lauren, mouth gaping in wonderment, looked up at Mr. Lauren, who put his arm around his wife's shoulder and grinned proudly first at Alex, then Matt, and back again. Becka stared with awe, alternately at the radio and her big brother. Alex was astonished to see respect in Kathy's expression as she stared up at her nemesis. But the look abruptly changed when the brunette realized she was showing her genuine feelings. She immediately dropped her head.

"Yahoo!" Brett yelled to the sky, both arms in the air.

Everyone laughed and all the kids mimicked Brett's cry.

"Boss!" Suzanne said, pushing Alex back to arm's length.

As the group quieted, they turned to look at Matt and Alex, who stood facing each other, speechless. Daniel smirked and said, "Good thing someone let the world know how talented you are."

Presently, Matt shook his head as if to clear it and looked around. "Unbelievable, Dan. It never would have happened without you."

Impulsively, Alex ran over to him and gave Daniel a tight hug. "Thank you," she said. Daniel was slow to release her and she read a fleeting expression of determination in his face as she pulled away.

Alex was just about to run over to hug her parents, too, when she realized she was ignoring Matt, the real mastermind behind all of this. His song. His success. She'd simply sung what *he'd* created. Matt stood there with his hands back on his head, looking out across the bay. "Matt," she said, moving beside him. "You did it! People are hearing your song."

He nodded at her and placed his chin on her head as she wrapped her arms around him.

"I wonder what this means."

"What it means?" She pulled away and stared into his face. "It means you're going to be famous."

"Hmmm," he said, his eyes clouding.

"Well, maybe," she said quickly, responding to his expression.

Daniel shook his head in disbelief at his buddy and took Alex's arm, rotating her. "And what about you, Alex?" His hands on her shoulders directed her gaze to his face. She searched it questioningly. "It may be Matt's song," he said, "but it wouldn't be complete without your amazing voice, Foxy Lady."

The icy blue light from his eyes penetrated into the depths of her. Alex suddenly dropped her eyes to the ground, not trusting herself to mask the emotions bubbling inside.

"You *are* going to be famous," Daniel said, emphatically.

Alex felt her stomach flip. *That might actually be a possibility, thanks to him.* She looked back up into Daniel's dilated pupils. Her heart squeezed hungrily as a wave of longing washed over her. She wanted Matt to be this excited, this sure about her future. *Why wasn't he?* Suddenly, her lips itched to kiss Daniel, to show him how grateful she really was. The inclination was immediately followed with the realization that she was thinking these thoughts inches away from her true love, while everyone was watching her. She turned abruptly from Daniel and put one arm around Matt's waist. "Yeah, right. Famous." She hoped they'd take the tremble in her voice for excitement.

Daniel's eyes widened as if he'd forgotten something. He suddenly turned and climbed into the motorboat and sat next to Kathy. She glared up at him.

Even from where she stood, Alex could see unmistakable jealousy and pain in her expression. Mrs. Lauren must have noticed the same thing; she stared quizzically at Kathy and Daniel, and turned a perplexed eye on Alex and Matt. Clearing her expression, she walked over to surround Matt and Alex with a loose squeeze.

"Congratulations, you two. You're on your way to… well, to wherever this is going to take you." Her gaze was filled with pride and expectation, and a smidgeon of concern.

"Thanks, Mom," Alex said, dropping her arm from Matt's waist and giving her mom a long hug.

A low growl of thunder on the horizon of dark billowy clouds refocused everyone's attention.

"OK, enough excitement," Mr. Lauren said. "We'd better get out on the water before we run out of time." The comment immediately put Mrs. Lauren in motion, herding everyone into boats.

Mrs. Lauren paused to check her watch. "As I was saying before I was so pleasantly interrupted by your beautiful music…" she said with a grin, "we'll expect to see you sailors back at the city docks in two hours. Sooner, if the weather gets worse. OK?"

"OK, Mom." Alex said, pulling up Matt's arm to look at his watch.

"Be smart now. You know how quickly a summer storm can move across a lake," Mr. Lauren reminded them.

"We'll be extra careful, Dad," she said, noticing Becka sliding a second water ski down to Davey. Alex leaned out sideways around Matt for a better view of Davey who was still floating in the water after his celebratory cannonball. Alex told him, "I expect to hear that you've learned to drop a ski and got a good slalom run in today."

Davey nodded vigorously and grinned widely with a thumbs-up.

Matt moved over to the motorboat, received a hug from his sister and helped her into the boat. As he held out a hand to help Mrs.

Lauren in, he said, "Thank you so much for keeping an eye on Becka and Davey today. And for this weekend... It means a lot."

"Anytime. We loved the opportunity. Please thank your parents for allowing us to use the cabin," Mrs. Lauren said.

"Sure," he said.

She took his hand as he stabilized her step down into the boat. "You all have fun and be safe now! See you in a couple of hours."

During this exchange, Kathy watched Matt with more hurt in her expression than was warranted by her head injury. As he turned from the boat, she averted her gaze to Daniel. Alex wondered at the way Kathy's expression turned to gratitude and comfort as she looked up into Daniel's face.

As Mr. Lauren started the outboard motor, Brett pulled Suzanne toward the sailboat. He yelled above the engine's roar, "C'mon, doll, let's get this tug a'movin'."

"Tug!" Matt exclaimed in mock irritation as he threw the last securing rope into the motorboat. "You have a lot to learn about boats, Texan." Brett helped Suzanne into the cockpit and awkwardly climbed in after her. Matt motioned to Alex to help him loosen the sailboat lines. Once she had boarded, he gave the side of the boat a shove and leapt in himself.

Matt trimmed the sails to catch the wind and, as the sailboat picked up slow momentum, Alex looked over to see Davey catch the ski-rope handle and position the rope between the tips of his skis. He yelled, "Hit it!" The motor revved and the bow of the boat rose high. The teenagers all waved farewell to the occupants of the other boat as its bow slowly leveled off and Davey popped up onto his skis with a hoot.

June 2003: Matt

*M*att's gaze moved across the art gallery to Daniel, who had just recognized Alex. He sighed heavily. Even from this viewpoint, Matt could see Daniel's eyes narrow in anticipation. The lawyer immediately excused himself from the young *Smallville* star, made a quick comment to his wife, and moved toward Alex eagerly.

For the moment, Mad Bo held Alex's attention with a few last comments. Before Daniel was within speaking distance, she winked at Alex, fluffed her hair and retreated in a shimmering blur.

Dan's lips touched Alex's cheek just as she turned back to see him. Her eyes flew open as Dan rubbed his hands along her arms, which made Matt seethe. Within mere minutes Daniel was leaning in close, an exaggerated look of sympathy on his face, obviously trying to convince her to do something. Old feelings of jealousy and anger wrenched Matt. His only saving grace was to see Alex's careful response. Warm enough to seem friendly, but wary. *Interesting!*

Kathy joined them and the three former friends shared a short, what looked to be amicable, conversation. After Kathy shook Alex's hand and walked away, she fixed a wayward sprig on a table bouquet and spoke to a waiter who quickly tucked in a loose shirttail. She'd obviously noticed these details while talking with Alex, and her eyes continued to sweep the room for other items needing her attention. Before Matt remembered to duck back behind the column, she spotted him. Surprise registered in her expression.

He turned, pulled his hat down further over his eyes and walked quickly down the corridor toward the exit. Unfortunately, just before reaching the museum foyer, he felt a firm hand on his arm. "Matt!"

Damn! She must have run! He stopped, removed his hat and glasses, and turned around to her. "Hello, Kathy," he said, hoping his voice didn't betray his racing heart. Acid washed his stomach. The feeling took him right back to their sailing excursion just after hearing "Like The Moon Pulls The Tide" at the cabin that long-ago day.

July 1978: Matt

The sailboat caught the breeze and briskly moved away from the shore. Matt began sailing instructions at once. He was glad for the distraction, which kept his mind off the fear gnawing at his insides.

He threw out instructions and explanations, keeping everyone busy. They learned safe tacking maneuvers, zigzagging the boat so the sails caught the best wind to carry them where they wanted. On each straight reach between tacks, when he had time to think about anything but sails, lines and wind direction, Matt pondered the future.

Cig Gary was obviously starting in on the PR early, giving a rough cut to the local DJ. That seemed unprecedented, sort of like what Matt was feeling right now. He just hadn't considered what it would be like to hear his music on the airwaves. It was exciting on one hand, but Alex's words kept resounding in his head. "It means you're going to be famous." He remembered the light in her eyes as she said it. *That's obviously what she wants.*

Fame always sounded so glamorous. But he had a strong inkling of what really went on inside the lives of people who were in the public eye like his parents. Under the glitz lay sick priorities where money makes up for everything. Everything that really counts anyway. Like parents who are there for you, who gladly share your successes and even your failures because they truly love you, or even care to spend a weekend at the lake with you.

Matt wanted to get away from the shallow people in that world, not delve deeper into it. He had no desire to be trapped in a familiar gilded cage…or a worse one.

He shuddered as a glint of sun on the lake water reminded him of a photographer's flash. His fists tightened on the boat lines as he imagined having every activity in his life documented by the media. His freedom completely restricted. "No way!" he growled through gritted teeth.

Surprised he'd said it aloud, he looked around and realized gratefully the comment had been lost in the wind. As he scanned for other boats along their current course, he shook out each hand to relax it. He pulled the main sail line tight and felt the boat moving like a living being beneath him. His ability to control its destiny reconfirmed Matt's love of sailing. It represented total power and freedom. Freedom he'd have to give up if he were to become famous. *Why didn't I think this through before I agreed to record my song?* He'd always wanted to share his music with the world and gain an audience to believe in his music. But, he'd been too quick to sign on with a record company, seduced by the potential money and the opportunity to spend time with Alex.

His girlfriend just seemed so sure fame was what she wanted. Didn't she realize how tough fame could make her life? He watched her face into the wind, curls blowing backward like blonde whips struggling to free themselves from her head. She didn't even know it, but her demeanor oozed control…of herself, her environment. He could almost envision the wind changing direction at her whim. All it would take is her winning smile and a wiggle of her nose.

She must have felt his eyes on her because she turned and smiled back at him briefly. The sheer power of her presence made his heart leap and mental music start. *How can she do that to me?*

A heavy spray of water whipped up by a gust of wind splashed across Matt's face and he wiped the cold water away with his arm. He suddenly realized how much stronger the wind had become. Even though the storm was still not imminently threatening, the clouds had become darker and more menacing and were moving toward them. *We'd better head back.*

"Prepare to tack," he said loudly to his novice crew. He instructed Alex to loosen the foresail line so Brett could be ready to pull it tight on the other side once they'd tacked again. "Suzanne, watch the boom coming across," he warned.

When everyone was looking at him, waiting for instructions, he yelled, "Tacking now!" and whipped the main sail line out of its cleat. He pulled the tiller to him until the boat pivoted and the main sail caught wind again. He quickly pulled the length of main sail line back in from the other side until it lay tight to the wind and he felt the boat moving forward in its new direction. He checked the position of the foresail to make sure Brett had it positioned to spill just the right amount of wind. Assured all was right, Matt set a straight course toward the town of Coeur d'Alene.

In the new calm, his lyrics from "Like the Moon Pulls The Tide" innocently played into his head. Fear began to settle back into his stomach. Before it could fully take hold, an intense expression from Alex floored him. She stared at him with unmasked admiration, love and powerfully eager anticipation. *Had she read his mind? Were the lyrics playing in her head, too?* Immediately, his heart began to flood with yearning. He felt like lunging across the cockpit to clasp her to him, but found instead he couldn't move. He couldn't even tear his eyes from hers as her soul pulled him in.

At that moment, the boat pitched over a rogue wake and the rising wind blew a large shower of cold lake water over everyone. Suzanne hunched and turned against its force. Brett actually screamed. The dousing acted on Matt like a mental wake-up call. He loosened the main sail to spill wind and slow the boat. He returned his gaze to Alex, who was suddenly dripping and frozen in shock with her mouth wide. He had to laugh. A grin spread over Alex's face and she reached into the still-dry cockpit for a towel. After blotting her own face, she threw it over to her soaked girlfriend.

Suzanne stopped wiping down her arms and punched Brett. "You scream like a girl," she ribbed. Brett ventured a sheepish peek at Matt and Alex, but recovered with a glared challenge at his girlfriend. He set his shoulders and lifted his chin. "Yeah. Well, bet you can't do it better." Everyone laughed.

Suddenly, Matt's fears seemed imagined. *This is what is real. Why am I worried about becoming famous? Is one song on the radio really gonna take me there? Not likely.*

He met Alex's gaze with as much love as he could communicate. The moment was fleeting, as another powerful gust of wind hit the boat and caused it to heel swiftly to port. Immediately, three sets of scared eyes under dripping hair turned to him for guidance. "Loosen the foresail, Brett!" he yelled, simultaneously snapping his own ropes loose. As the boat righted itself, he quickly assessed the situation.

They lay on the perimeter of the approaching storm and its fore-winds were just beginning to buffet them. Judging from the whitecaps nearer to the city shoreline, the storm was concentrated more over the town. He saw a bolt of lightning in the dark clouds approaching Coeur d'Alene. Luckily, toward the cabin, the water was choppy, but Matt saw no whitecaps and no lightning.

"We're heading back to the cabin," he said loudly, with thunder punctuating his words. "The storm's not as bad back there."

"But, we're supposed to meet my folks," Alex said quickly.

"I know, but I'm sure they'd rather have us safe at the cabin rather than try to make it back in a thunderstorm."

She nodded assent, but worry settled on her face.

Within 20 minutes, using the heightened wind, the group had moored at the cabin docks again, lowered sails and tied everything down against the wind.

"You guys sure are quick learners," Matt said loudly, his hair whipping across his face. "Good thing. You made the trip back easy, even in this wind."

He looked up at the dark, blustering sky. Still no lightning here at least, so they'd be safe staying in the sailboat. "Why don't you guys stay here inside the galley in case the rain hits? I'll just run up to the cabin and make sure its completely closed up against the storm. We shouldn't have to stay here more than an hour, I would think."

"I'll come up with you," Alex said.

"Yeah, you guys go on up," Brett shooed them along by waving his fingertips. "Suzanne and I will be perfectly snug here in the galley." He smiled at his girlfriend, licked his lips pointedly and grabbed a hand to pull her to him. "I'm sure we'll 'make out' by ourselves while you're gone."

Suzanne cocked an eyebrow at him and turned to shrug sheepishly at her friends.

"We won't be very long," Alex said with mock disapproval.

Matt took Alex's hand. "Try to be good," he said to the couple.

"Suzie will be *very* good, won't you?" Brett drawled, raising his eyebrows twice.

Alex smiled and squeezed Matt's hand as he led her up the hill. Once in the cabin, they moved through the rooms, double-checking all the windows and doors. As Matt leaned over to check the stove flue, Alex interrupted him.

"Our song was on the radio!" she said, pulling him upright.

"It was," he said, placing his hands on both sides of her face. He gave her a light kiss to cover the uneasiness vibrating his core. "You sound amazing on the radio waves."

"Thanks, but you're the one who sounds so *decent*. It's your music. Aren't you happy?" she whispered expectantly.

Matt exhaled heavily, quashing the shaft of fear shooting through his heart. He saw the light shining in her eyes, knowing he walked a fine line here.

"It's hard to say." He fought his internal doubts and ventured slowly, "It does have a catchy melody…"

"*Your* beautiful melody." She started humming the tune through a tiny smile and cocked her head, watching him.

Matt's heart began thumping in his chest. He couldn't decide if it was her rich tonal quality, or the fear of how lovely she'd made his song sound to the world, that aroused his senses so.

He kissed her and her humming was replaced by a small moan. When he pulled away, Alex's eyes shone up at him, with love and excitement for their future together he guessed. He just couldn't let her focus too much on future fame; that wouldn't be good for either of them. He lightly rubbed her cheek with his thumb as he spoke quietly. "It is a pretty song. Still, I wouldn't get your hopes up, Princess. A lot of people will think it's just a cheesy ballad from some little high-school kids. It's not like a hot rock n' roll number or anything."

"But it's so beautiful. It interested BJ Starr enough to…"

"I know,' he interrupted her. "But don't place too much stock in our little number, OK? We'll just have to wait and see what happens."

"You're right, I can't get my hopes up too high." Alex's expression hardened slightly and she shivered against him.

"You cold, Princess?" Matt asked, knowing there was probably more emotion behind her trembling rather than just still-damp clothes.

"A bit chilly."

He pulled her to him in a long, close hug and glanced out the window at the rain, now falling heavily. "We have time yet, I'll stoke up a fire in the wood stove."

Alex curled up in the wooden rocking chair, watching him open the flue and prepare and light the pine logs in the black potbellied stove. Within a few minutes, a blazing fire radiated heat through the cabin. He stood and briefly admired his handiwork, but couldn't resist the pull of attraction from the beautiful woman sitting behind him. In one deft movement, he raised Alex up and pulled her back down onto his lap in the rocking chair. He wrapped his arms around her as her head fell lightly on his shoulder. They sat watching the flames for several minutes, listening to the crackling and popping of pine burning, and the rhythm of new raindrops on the roof.

He wondered again at the strange control she had over him, without trying to control him at all. He serenely traced his fingers up and down her arm, but his mind was anything but calm. He felt the heat of the fire against his legs and the warmth of Alex's body along his chest, but it was his mind that burned.

This was the perfect time to explain to her what he couldn't say yesterday on the porch before the fireworks. But, how could he ruin this romantic moment with an apology?

He said, "Alex. I... I've never felt about anyone the way I feel about you."

She put one hand on his cheek and raised her head to meet his eyes. "Me neither."

"I mean, I don't think I will *ever* feel about anyone the way I feel about you."

She looked him full in the face. "I hope that never changes. For either of us."

Alex rested her head back on his shoulder. Matt rubbed his hand slowly up Alex's back and pulled the neck of her blouse down over her shoulder to lightly nuzzle her skin with his lips. She squirmed with the tickling sensation. He kissed the base of her neck and slowly nibbled along her jaw until his mouth enveloped hers.

After a long while, he broke away. "Alex," he whispered. "I just have to say I'm sorry."

"Sorry?" she pulled away and gave him a quizzical look.

"For what happened in Moscow."

Alex tensed visibly and dropped her eyes.

"I...well, I guess I was scared."

She sniffed. "Scared? Of what?"

"Of not being able to reach my dream."

"You mean your kids' music school?"

He nodded. "Every time I've had a goal, life has put an obstacle in my way. More responsibility. More distractions."

Alex nodded with understanding. "Your parents expect a lot of you, I know."

"Yeah, well, sometimes it's just me. Not believing in myself. Allowing myself to be distracted by my responsibilities…or people…"

"Sometimes it's just not possible to 'make it happen,' you know."

"I know. That's why…" Matt sighed, steeling himself, "…why I pushed you away." He hesitated. "But, I was fighting destiny."

Alex furrowed her brow and clasped her hands in her lap. "What does that mean?"

"It means I couldn't face your power over me."

Alex pulled back.

"Not really you. Us. Your dreams about us scared me." He went on tentatively, trying to find the right words. "What if we aren't really in control? What if destiny really sets our course? What if your destiny is to be famous and mine is tied to yours?" He hesitated. "I don't really want to be famous." His eyes searched her face for a reaction.

The light in her eyes flickered into a dull intensity. "Do you think we're going to be famous, SuperMatt?" she asked quietly.

A familiar wrinkle of fear unfolded into his mind, but he smoothed it. "It's not likely." He stopped and absently ran his thumb over her lips. "Have you had dreams about us being famous?"

"Not sleeping dreams," she said looking askance at him.

He let out a long breath he hadn't realized he'd been holding. "That's good. I guess Suzanne spooked me with her talk of the importance of your dreams…how they're really guiding your life."

"My dreams are nothing!" Alex said vehemently, shifting on his lap to face him. "Dreams. Not reality. Just dreams." Her eyes bored into his.

Matt pressed his cheek against hers, suddenly aware of the fresh scent of her skin. "But you're so strong, Alex. You're in control of everything. If our destinies are tied together, I was afraid I'd get swept away by you and your goals, and that I'd never fulfill mine. Especially if your dreams really are directing you…us."

Alex pulled her head back from his and laid her warm palms against his cheeks. "SuperMatt, I'm 18, just like you. Trying to figure out what I want to do. I can't even decide which college to attend. I'm not getting any special guidance from the gods here."

"I guess I finally realized that. That's why I'm sorry."

She gazed at him with grateful understanding and then quickly batted long lashes over two small green fires. "You sure it wasn't just my lovely eyes that lured you back?"

"I have to admit that was part of it," he said very seriously, leaning down to kiss each eyelid. "I just can't seem to fight my deep feelings for you."

"We are tied to each other, but it isn't my dreams causing it, Matt. It's just chemistry."

"And, oh, what chemistry that is," he said, kissing her slowly, faintly aware of a melody wafting through his thoughts.

She smiled and wriggled deeper into his embrace.

They snuggled there in the rocking chair for what he wanted to be an eternity. They kissed, watched the fire burn and listened to the rain on the roof until it slowed and stopped.

Matt sighed and whispered into their comfortable silence, "I haven't heard thunder in a long time. We probably ought to boogie."

Alex looked up into his eyes and gave a brief nod. She hugged him tightly. "I love you, you know, SuperMatt."

"Princess, I am going to love you for a very long time."

June 2003: Alex

*A*lex watched Kathy's teal gown flowing behind her as she retreated across the museum lobby. Her thoughts jumped to a long-forgotten memory of an injured, jealous girl returning home with Daniel in the motorboat as the other teenagers left to go sailing. *How did that jealous high school girl become this sophisticated woman?* Even hurrying, Kathy looked graceful and in control. "Who is that woman, Daniel?" she asked the lawyer, whose eyes also followed his wife. "She's not the girl I used to know."

Daniel looked thoughtful. "Actually, she started changing shortly after that sailboat accident she had the summer after graduation."

Alex shot him a surprised look, wondering at him bringing up the scene just in her mind.

Daniel laughed. "Are you surprised? All Kathy ever wanted was someone to nurture and appreciate her. I guess my care and attention to her that day shadowed Matt's brotherly interest."

"Really?"

"Yeah, I started noticing it then, even though my true attention was elsewhere at the time." Unexpectedly, he reached up and ran a finger lightly along her jaw line.

A small thrill ran up Alex's spine, but she shied away from his tender touch.

He continued, "Shortly after we started at USC, Kathy's attentions started shifting away from Matt and toward me."

"That was while you and I were working together on the 'Like The Moon' publicity together," Alex said absently.

"Yeah. Having some time away from Matt while he was preoccupied with college and then, well…his parents' tragedy… That helped her see her own worth."

"But, then she went to live and work at Matt's music camp."

"Yeah. He should credit her for almost single-handedly getting parents to sign up their children at the school those first years. She was a dynamo sales woman, luring potential customers through irresistible kid activities and family parties held at the school. She'd already started to transform herself."

"Certainly with your encouragement."

Daniel smiled crookedly. "I gave her a lot of advice and spent as much time with her as I could."

Alex had once wondered how Matt had ever managed to gain visibility for his camp when he was so loathe to face the public. It was obviously Kathy's doing. "But that meant you were indirectly helping Matt, Daniel."

The lawyer pushed his hands deep into his pockets. "Well, he wasn't a threat to me any longer.

Alex swallowed. "He was away from me."

"Yeah." Daniel nodded with a wry smile. "But, you were distant, to say the least, not to mention solely focused on rocketing your career." He waited for her reaction, but Alex only nodded.

Daniel stared at her as if weighing a comment. "To be honest, I had to switch my strategy. I distracted myself for years with law school and starting my practice, until one day I really *saw* Kathy. She always had great potential, so I decided to just create the 'someone' I wanted by supporting her training. He shrugged. "I capitalized on her increasing interest in me and wooed her away."

Still feeling the tingle of his finger along her jaw, Alex asked sarcastically, "So, you gave up on me because you didn't think you could change me?"

He lowered his voice to a near whisper. "I never wanted to. You were perfect from the start. Sometimes you just have to cut your losses and go to 'Plan B.'" He moved closer until his arm brushed hers. "But, one should never totally give up hope on Plan A."

Something in his penetrating look bubbled up the old, but familiar, chemistry. *How could he raise feelings like that in her so easily?* Alex mentally stamped out the fire and steered the conversation elsewhere. "What did Matt think of you taking Kathy away from him?"

Daniel scrubbed his hands together and stared out across the lobby. "That was pretty much the last straw. He hasn't really spoken to me since then. Not that he talked with me much anytime after finding out about the music rights thing." He folded his arms and pursed his lips.

Is that a tiny bit of regret I see on his face?

Daniel's expression cleared. "I worked with Kathy on fashion, grooming, etiquette, languages, poise, knowledge... She is really *something*." He turned to nod at Alex, "Even if she isn't you."

Suddenly Daniel's continuing infatuation seemed completely ludicrous and Alex put one hand over her mouth, hiding an incredulous smile. "Daniel, what planet are you from? I never got training in any of those things. I am just the product of a caring family and a lucky career break, thanks to you."

With a deeply serious expression, Daniel admired every inch of Alex in one slow sweep of his eyes. She felt his gaze, like hands, caressing her form. "Still, the perfect package," he said.

Color rose in her cheeks.

"Mmmm, I see I can still get to you," he said, rubbing his knuckles against her forearm.

She was saved from the feelings rushing through her as Mad Bo popped in, grabbed Daniel's hand and shook it. "Great to see you, Daniel! Another amazing Katherine Post party tonight! Where is the woman of the day?" she asked, sweeping her head to take in the entire room in one glance. Alex acknowledged a knowing smile in Mad Bo's eyes as they met hers on the way back to Daniel.

Still holding Daniel's hand, Mad Bo pulled his arm through hers. "Take me to your fearless leader, I have to congratulate her," she said, as she turned to march him away. "Say bye-bye to your friend, Danny-boy, Alex has schmoozing to do." Mad Bo nodded over her shoulder toward a radio personality cracking jokes in a nearby group.

Alex smiled at her manager and nodded farewell to Daniel. She made her way over to the disk jockey's group, wondering how in the world Mad Bo had known she'd finished her business with the man and needed an escape. *That woman had to be clairvoyant! Thank goodness she's on my side.*

June 2003: Matt

*T*he foyer of the art museum blurred and slowed as Matt's senses zeroed in. His world narrowed to Kathy's tight grip on his arm, her brown eyes peering into his face, her floral perfume wafting around him, and the beseeching timber of her voice. He heard her say, as if muted and in slow motion, "You mustn't leave!"

Suddenly, the museum bustle all around him snapped back into full action and his mind raced for an excuse to even be here. He nodded toward the donation box just up the aisle and managed, "I've already deposited my check. And, I don't really have time to stay." All he could think about was escaping as soon as possible.

"Not even going to say hi to your old friends, Matt? It's been so many years...!"

"You know they're not my friends, Kathy."

"But they want to be."

"That's *their* problem."

She knit her eyebrows. "You saw Dan?"

"From across the room."

She paused. A shadow eclipsed her face and she said quietly. "And Alex, of course?"

It was his turn to pause. He simply nodded and patted her hand, which still rested on his arm. Struggling to add just the right tinge of cheer to his voice, he said, "It's a beautiful party, Kath. You've really outdone yourself."

"Thank you. Just wait to see what I cook up for our Cd'A High reunion and..." She looked at him from the corners of her eyes. "A benefit concert sponsored by our famous classmate Alexandra Roberts.

Matt blanched. "At the reunion?"

"Yes, the main event. She's just committed to it, so we don't have any firm plans yet. But," Kathy paused for emphasis. "She did mention she'd like to honor you by bringing in performers who've recorded your tunes."

"What!" Had he heard her right? "Why would Alex do that?"

Kathy shrugged. "Maybe to make amends and honor your talent."

Matt's heart pounded and sweat prickled his forehead. "Guess I'll plan to be out of town that weekend."

"Matt!" She looked at him suspiciously. "You should be there. She's adopted kids' music charities to support, just like you."

"Yeah, so I hear. What's she up to? She's probably just using me again to get what she wants. Tax write-offs or something."

"It didn't sound like that when I spoke with her just now," Kathy said, admonishingly. "She wants the event focus to remain on the children's programs. But, she did say gaining your friendship back might be a 'silver lining.'"

Matt couldn't stop a small rush of pleasure in spite of his misgivings. Alex might still think of his friendship as something good? Would she even *consider* being friends with him again? Excitement must have registered on his face during the subsequent seconds of silence, because Kathy's broad smile slowly faltered and doubt crept into her eyes.

What are you thinking, Matt? You're the one who doesn't want anything to do with Alex, remember? He forced his thoughts away from his former partner, cocking his head to study Kathy purposefully. As his eyes lingered searchingly on hers, Kathy's color rose. The previously kind expression and keen interest on her beautiful face was replaced by a deep longing stare he recognized all too well. He hadn't seen that look in years. *She can't possibly...* Matt sucked in a quick breath and involuntarily stepped back half a step. He looked around to make sure they weren't in view of their other friends. "Look, Kath, I'm not here to dredge up old feelings. Staying here any longer is unnecessary and possibly distracting to the cause."

Her eyes glittered with anger as the pink rose in her face. "So, why come here at all, Matt?"

He paused, his own color heightening as he realized she had obviously been counting on him being completely over Alex. "I just came to make a donation to the cause," he said lamely.

She obviously saw through that, which gave her an opening to regain her poise. Kathy lifted her chin and stared levelly at him. But, despite her regal demeanor, he watched hurt grow in her eyes as she spoke. "My guess is you're here because of simple curiosity. You wanted to see her in person, didn't you? How long has it been?"

Matt immediately fought the inclination to turn and leave so he could avoid the topic. Instead, he stood his ground. "You think our old impossible relationships are still in place, Kath, but they're long gone. Water under the bridge."

Matt turned at that moment to see Mad Bo steering Daniel toward them, a bemused expression on her face. His heart quelled and he gave a quick glance back to where he'd seen them last. Thank goodness Alex was still across the room. She had her back to them now, busily talking with other guests.

Matt moved forward to greet his old schoolmates, while mindfully positioning himself out of Alex's line of sight. He was pulled into an impetuous hug by Mad Bo and couldn't help laughing as he hugged her back. She held him at arms length, beaming, and nudged him toward Dan. Matt held out his hand and Daniel took it in a firm grip.

"It's been a while, Dan. You're looking good."

"Too long, Matt, my man."

He nodded and turned to Mad Bo. "I was just telling Kathy here what a beautiful job she's done on the party tonight. I take it you had a hand in it, too, Madeleine?"

"Kathy's the star," Mad Bo said, fluttering her red lacquered fingernails in Kathy's direction. "I'm simply here in a supporting role. Just like I was for you in college."

Matt acknowledged her comment with a nod. "Well, I'm sure you'll attract a significant number of sponsors tonight. Nobody wants to miss a Kathy Post shindig these days," Matt said.

"Even you," Mad Bo said with twinkling eyes.

"It's my cause, you know. I'd be remiss not to contribute."

"You actually came down to LA in person to support the cause?" Dan asked. "You might have sent one of your siblings, no?"

Matt turned a guarded look on Daniel. "I was here anyway meeting with some folk about supporting my Coeur d'Musique camp. Quite a few people down here were intrigued by an article on the camp last month in the *Times*."

"That was one heartwarming feature article," chimed in Mad Bo. "I'm not surprised it got you some solid interest."

"Indeed." Matt smiled at her.

Kathy interrupted. "I was just telling Matt about the upcoming reunion activities."

"Ah, yes, our famous Alex will certainly be a big draw," Dan said.

Matt suppressed a flinch at the mention of her name and redirected the topic. "Sounds like a big endeavor in a short amount of time. I hope it goes well."

"You're not planning to attend your own reunion events, Matt?" Mad Bo asked.

"And, have your work honored?" Dan added, his eyes glinting with mischief. That earned him a glare from Kathy.

Matt ignored the bait. "Probably not. That's a busy time of year for the camp."

Mad Bo gave him a skeptical look. "We hear your students will be performing in Washington this fall."

"Yes, Matt, you should think about doing some fundraising while your talented kids are out there making an impression," Kathy said, subtly elbowing Daniel.

"I have some contacts there and maybe we could drum up some support together," Dan said.

Matt stared at Daniel. Did this schemer actually think they could do any kind of business together, ever again? After…everything?

An uncomfortable silence stretched until Matt said, "That's something I'd really have to think over, Dan." He donned his fedora. "Well, I'm sorry I can't stay longer. I have another engagement tonight." He reached out and shook hands with Daniel, who gave Matt a potently appraising look.

Mad Bo hugged him and looked long into his face with a somewhat sad expression. "Take care of yourself, mon cher," she said.

Kathy took his arm. "I'll walk with you." Matt didn't miss Dan's wary expression as his wife walked away with his former nemesis.

Kathy clung tight to Matt as they walked in silence through the marbled foyer and out the front entrance. She didn't let go even as Matt handed his parking receipt to the valet. They stood on the museum sidewalk, the setting sun throwing its last rays across the museum's glass windows above them. After a moment, Kathy looked up into Matt's face. "Think about what Dan's offering you, Matt.

Working together with him to get federal funding for your programs could really make a difference in the lives of many talented children."

Matt nodded. "Of course, you're right. But, you know, Dan has never given me a reason to trust him. He's made little effort…"

"It's been a long time, Matt. People change. Just look at me. It would mean the world to me if we could be friends again."

"And that won't happen unless I make amends with Dan."

"Exactly."

"And, how does Alex fit into this picture?" he asked. Kathy's eyes dropped momentarily and she fell silent.

"Say we all actually reconciled, working together through Alex's reunion fundraiser concert plans. You'd be fine if I became friends with Alex again? Even close friends?" he asked. The thought sent an involuntary shudder through him, which he was sure Kathy felt.

He watched the muscles in his friend's jaw tighten and pain darken her eyes. But, quickly recovering, she smiled and leaned to whisper, "If it means I can be close to you again, it would be worth it."

At that moment the valet drove up with Matt's car. Matt drew back slightly and looked questioningly down at Kathy. "I obviously have a lot to think about."

"If you need to discuss it any more just call me. Please, Matt?"

He nodded and turned to tip the valet. As he thanked the young man, he noticed Daniel standing at the top of the museum steps watching them. Just as he turned back, Kathy pressed a lingering, sensual kiss against his lips. Matt withdrew quickly and noticed Daniel immediately starting down the steps toward them.

Matt gently pressed one palm against Kathy's cheek and nodded farewell to her. He climbed into his car and pulled away just as Daniel reached Kathy and firmly spun her toward him.

How had everything gone so wrong when they all used to be so close? As he turned a corner out of sight, Matt flashed back to Daniel's one unselfish act of friendship offered during Matt's first chaotic and uncomfortable weeks of fame.

August 1978: Matt

With the national release of "Like The Moon Pulls The Tide" that August, the single started receiving significant airplay. Disc jockeys shared the teenagers' story with America and people began to recognize Matt and Alex. Even friends stopped them on the street to ask for their autographs. The students' plans to share a quiet, romantic summer quickly turned into a whirlwind of activity. They were asked to appear on the local TV morning shows, interviewed by national music magazines, and sang their song at local charity and civic events. They were barraged by constant phone calls.

Matt watched Alex bask in her element. She talked and joked with the talk-show hosts, hugged people who recognized her whether she knew them or not, and grinned incessantly.

Matt participated in his reserved manner, although he would have done almost anything to avoid the attention. But his contract said he must play a role in the single's publicity. So, since the work brought him one step closer to creating his music camp, he walked through the motions with a grateful, if somewhat tight, smile. He answered media questions intelligently and even sometimes with a touch of humor.

Each day started with the phone ringing and today was no exception. Matt was startled again from his sleep by its sharp tones at 7 a.m. He pulled a pillow over his head, wondering whether it would be their pesky record producer Cig Gary, like it had been for the past several mornings. More praise. More excitement. More ways to have a camera shoved in his face. More pressure to record more music. More incentives to sign another contract.

He groggily picked up the receiver and droned into it, "Hullo."

"Matt, my man. It's Daniel. Geez, you're hard to reach. I called all afternoon yesterday. Busy signals. No answer. Sorry, but I had to call this early to get you."

"Good morning to you, too, Dan." He yawned.

"Man, you sound beat. You've gotta be a busy rock star. But, life is great, yeah?"

"Yeah, it's good."

Daniel snorted. "Well, there's a boatload of enthusiasm."

"Seriously, Dan, it's only seven in the morning."

"Yeah, I know. Sorry. Just wanted to catch you and see how you're doin'; if you need anything."

Matt paused, warily. "What? If I need anything...? What do you really want?"

"Hey, I don't *always* want something when I call."

"Oh, yeah, I forgot. For sure."

"C'mon, I know everything's changing for you and well..." His voice tinged with genuine concern. "Sometimes you just gotta make sure things are solid with your pals."

Matt weighed the tone in Daniel's voice and said, "I hear that." Stretching and leaning back on the bed with one hand behind his head, he admitted, "It is pretty heavy. But, I'm all right, Dan. Thanks."

"Ace!" Daniel said. "Getting rich makes up for a lot, doesn't it?"

Matt scoffed. "Rich. Yeah."

"What? You should have gotten your first check already."

Matt laughed. "Yeah, came in the mail yesterday."

"So, that should be the start of your riches, eh?"

"Not unless the checks get larger."

"No doubt they will. Alex seems over-the-moon about getting hers," Daniel said. "Why's she so excited if it's such a small amount?"

"No idea. We've been so busy with interviews and everything, I haven't had a chance to talk with her."

"Sounds like you need some time to get casual. How about if I plan a quiet friends get-together?"

"A breather from all this would be great. But, I'm not sure we can fit in something like that right now."

"Man, you're stars. You can call the shots when it comes to your personal needs."

"You think so? Doesn't seem like that so far." An image flashed through Matt's mind of relaxing with his friends in the Post's backyard Jacuzzi. "But, it really would be great."

"I'll see what I can manage. Maybe a barbeque. Should we shoot for Thursday night?"

"Talk with Alex. She knows the schedule better than I. If anyone can set up some down time for us, you guys can." *Mr. Schemer and Ms. Organization, have at it.*

"Yeah, we'll come up with somethin'." He paused, "OK, man, you just keep on keepin' on."

"For sure. I'll just flash my charming smile and all the young girls will buy our music."

Daniel gave a begrudging snort, "You could have worse stuff to do, you know," Daniel said.

"I know. All this fake publicity is just…"

"No pain, no gain, man."

"I know. I'll just have to hang in there."

Daniel signed off with a promise to keep everyone posted about Thursday's plan. After hanging up, Matt fisted the bed quilt to minimize the tightening in his stomach. Every morning the feeling had come on more quickly and a little more powerfully. Forcing away thoughts of today's schedule and the demands on his time, he focused on his end goal. The reason he decided to participate in the recording of this song in the first place. His music camp.

His first check for record sales was already socked away in a special account set aside for a future down payment on some unknown location for his camp. It was a good sum of money. Not as much as he'd expected, but it was a good start. He wasn't "over-the-moon" about it, though.

How had Daniel known about Alex's reaction to her check anyway? Matt's heart constricted. *Dan and Alex got together originally because of my own stupidity. You can't blame Dan for staying in touch with her.*

Matt reminded himself that he was the one who held her heart, not Daniel. He envisioned the sway of her hair and how her eyes flashed when she was excited. He heard her warm vocals in his head as if she were in the room, transporting him to another world where all was fine and in control. He let the powerful feeling of her touch envelop him and he hummed the quiet melody that sprang into his head.

Alex now had become a part of him. She'd pulled his soul into hers and entwined it with her own. He couldn't pull away now even if he tried. Suddenly, he needed to hear her voice. He reached for the phone and dialed her number.

August 1978: Alex

A lex was on a snowy bridge, watching the water run beneath her. *A stump of a tree crashed into a large rock in the rapids and rang out loudly. It bounced away into an eddy and struck the rock again, creating another loud ringing noise. Busy trying to read the writing carved into the stump, the thought barely registered that stumps usually didn't ring when they hit stone.*

In half sleep, she realized the persistent noise was actually the phone. Groggily, she opened one eye and reached for the receiver on her bed stand.

"Hello," she croaked into the mouthpiece.

A low voice sang, "The first time…ever I saw your face…"

"SuperMatt." She closed her eyes, rolled over on her back and smiled. Clearing her throat, she said, "Mornin'."

"Good morning, Princess."

"You're up already?"

"Daniel called."

"He did? What did he want at seven in the morning?"

"To make sure his friend was OK with all the pressure."

She paused. "He did not. What did he really want?"

"I'm pretty sure that was it."

"Really? Decent! But weird."

"Yeah, he wants us all to get together Thursday night. I'm sure he'll be calling you about it. A barbeque or something."

The week's publicity schedule went through her mind. "Are you sure we'll have time?"

"I say we'd better make time, or we'll end up burning out like shooting stars." Alex heard the bite of frustration in his tone.

"*Are* you doing alright?"

"This isn't what I love doing with my life, you know. But, I keep on truckin'."

"OK. Well, you know I'm here for you, right?"

"I know. It's just been hard to manage everything at home while we've been out running around for Cig Gary every hour of every day."

"It's not for Cig Gary, SuperMatt. It's for us."

"Doesn't feel like it."

Alex crumpled the edge of her sheets, mirroring the fingers of dismay gripping her heart. She knew he really didn't want to do the publicity. "I can take on most of the work. You know I'd be glad to."

He chuckled. "You are really good at it. I've seen you in action."

Alex's laugh slightly eased her heartache. "You aren't going to quit on me, are you?"

"Quit?" he said incredulously. A long silence filled the line between them. Was he thinking how to break it to her? Was he shocked? Had she given him the idea? She held her breath until he said, forcefully, "Princess, I couldn't do that to you."

But will you hate every moment of it? Will you resent it...and then me? The claws around her heart tightened. She had to think of a way to make it worthwhile. "SuperMatt, just think of every event we do as a means to get what you want. One step closer to creating a children's music camp."

"That's exactly what I'm doing."

"Every interview, every photo shoot, every phone call gets us and the music in front of more people."

"That's it."

"Especially if they ask us to go on a concert tour. That would be the best visibility ever. A quicker end to the goal."

She heard his intake of breath as if he hadn't thought of that idea. "How could I tour? I'm already maxing Kathy's generosity in watching Becka and Davey so much now."

"SuperMatt, the record company has invested a lot in us. They're not going to let family issues get in the way of a tour. They'll certainly have influence with your parents. They might even figure out a way to pitch in for a professional baby-sitter."

He didn't respond right away. "That may not be the best thing for my family."

Alex lowered her voice into an understanding tone, wondering as she spoke if she should really say this. "Well, if you don't get professional help, your parents may just have to figure out an alternative to you. It's your life, Matt and it's time your parents realized they can't continue taking advantage of you."

"If only it was *that* easy," he responded.

"It is easy, actually."

Matt sniggered. "You have no idea how they think."

"I guess not. But you've got to be available, Matt. The more people who know us, the more money we'll have to do what we want."

She heard his bed covers rustling as he climbed out of bed. He sighed loudly. "Yeah, I know," he said. "I just wish getting the money didn't have to compromise who you are."

From a light rhythmic vibration as he spoke, she knew he'd begun pacing. She could almost see him running his hand through his hair. "Especially, when the checks aren't what you thought they would be."

Alex was taken aback. She'd been amazed at how much money they'd earned in just their first check. "You didn't think the check was big enough?"

"Well, it was a good amount. I just thought it would be more."

What *was* his idea of a large check? She'd been thrilled.

"Hmmm. Well, at least it means you can eventually build your camp, which is more than you had a month ago."

Matt sighed again. "Yep. You're right. I just have to stay focused on that. But…touring. Ouch."

"We'll be together, " she said.

She heard Matt's smile, "Yes. Now, that's worth focusing on."

August 1978: Matt

*T*hursday night, Matt found himself walking with Alex into the Clinkerdagger, Bickerstaff and Petts restaurant in Spokane. He glanced around at the wood-paneled walls and heavy timber beams in the ceiling. From within the dim interior, accented by Olde English pottery and pitted pewter pitchers and mugs on heavy wooden shelving, Daniel suddenly appeared.

He walked directly to Alex and lightly kissed her cheek, then moved to place an arm over Matt's shoulders, although his blue eyes never left Alex. "Now isn't this better than a barbeque? I've arranged for everything. We have a reserved corner table." Daniel nodded to one side of the restaurant. "I've requested the best staff to serve us. You won't have to lift a finger. You can just sit back and let them take care of you like the rock stars you are."

Matt gave his friend a half-hearted smile and moved away to place his arm around Alex. *I'd rather have had burgers in a private* backyard, *acting like the nobody I'd prefer to be.*

"Oh!" Alex said, squinting into the muted depths of the restaurant. "Suzanne and Brett are here, too?" She turned grateful eyes on Daniel. Matt saw Kathy waving at him, too, from deep inside the room.

"It's a celebration!" Daniel exclaimed, still keeping his attention on Alex.

Matt pulled Alex closer. He'd been torn about whether or not to say something to Daniel about his power flirting with Alex, especially since graduation. Deciding not to ruin this relaxed evening with any conflict, Matt darted a perturbed glance at Daniel and quickly moved with Alex toward their friends.

Walking by other tables, Matt watched recognition dawn on several patrons' faces and felt their eyes boring into his back as they walked on. He saw Alex wink at one family and he steered her along even more quickly. It would be just like her to stop and chat with everyone and they'd never get their quiet evening.

As they arrived at the table, Brett gave them an enthusiastic, "Hello, ya'll!" and Suzanne rose to greet them. "I'm so glad to see you!" she said, pulling Alex into a tight hug. She peered into her friend's face. "You don't look as tired as you've sounded on the phone over the past two weeks. I'm so glad!" Her sympathetic eyes took in Matt over her friend's shoulder. He smiled back with genuine gratitude for her concern.

Matt held a chair for Alex. But, before he could pull his own chair, Kathy flung her arms around him. With a quick glance at Alex, she focused her attention on Matt's face. "I'm so proud of you, Matt!"

He snorted lightly and gave her a dubious look. "Yeah, you want my autograph?"

She slapped his arm playfully and took her seat. "Always so humble. What are we going to do with him?" she asked Daniel as she slid back into her seat.

"So, what's it been like, you two?" Suzanne asked.

"Crazy, but bitchin!" Alex replied.

"Tiring," Matt said. "Everyone wants a piece of us."

As if to punctuate his comment, a woman and her pre-teen daughter, whose table they had just walked by, shyly approached the table. "We saw you two interviewed on TV," the woman said. "My daughter loves your beautiful song. You're so talented…"

"Could you sign this for me?" the girl blurted, holding out a napkin at Alex.

"Sure," Alex said, glowing. She signed it and handed it to Matt.

With a kindly outward smile at the young girl, who blushed, Matt struggled to sign his name clearly on the fragile napkin.

"Are you interested in music?" Alex asked her.

"Oh yes!" the girl blushed. "I just started vocal lessons at my junior high school."

"Well, in a few years, if our music keeps selling…" Alex turned a sly smile on Matt. "…you'll be able to study under Mr. Roberts, here. He's going to start a music school for kids, you know."

What was she bringing that up for? Let's just get the autographs done and get on with our dinner. He frowned.

"We heard that on the interview," the mother said. "What a great thing to do!"

Matt's heart melted and, despite his frustration at their intrusion, he couldn't stop a thankful grin. "Music brings a lot of joy to me and I want to share it with young people who love it, too."

"Don't worry, you'll hear about it in the newspaper when he's got the camp up and running," Alex said, putting her hand on the young girl's arm.

Before the woman could ask another question, Daniel interrupted. "I know you understand these two would appreciate a quiet dinner with their friends." He leaned over to the daughter. "Take this record with their compliments, young lady?" He pulled a single 45RPM record from his pocket and handed it to the girl with a charming smile. The girl's eyes widened and the mother colored slightly. "We're sorry to have interrupted your dinner. That is lovely of you, Mr...." She paused in embarrassment, not know exactly how to continue.

"Daniel Post," he said, shaking her hand with deep blue eyes sparkling charismatically. "I'm one of their legal representatives."

The mom gazed in surprise at his young face and swept her eyes across the other table occupants. She placed a hand on her daughter's shoulder, nodded her head with a "thank you so much!" to Daniel and directed her daughter back to their table.

"So," Brett drawled, eyeing Daniel's pockets, "How many more records ya got up your sleeve?

Daniel grinned at him. "A couple."

"Always prepared," Kathy said, shaking her head. "All those years of Boy Scouts apparently trained you well."

"I just thought through what might happen when we were out with the superstars." He smiled knowingly at Alex.

She smiled back at him, but commented, "Maybe from now on you could give away our promotional photos instead of our money-making vinyl, big spender?"

"You're right, of course. Have some made and we can all pass them out."

Everyone nodded agreement.

Matt picked up a menu. Somehow, whenever Matt was most frustrated with Daniel's tricks, he came through and recaptured his friends in his web of charm. *He may be a flirt, but he's a good friend and thinks of every angle. He's bound to be a great lawyer.*

"That way, you won't have to autograph table napkins, Matt. You'll actually have something neat to give to all your fans at WSU," Kathy said.

"You're both going to Washington State?" Suzanne asked, sneaking a glance at Alex, but bringing her gaze to rest on Kathy.

"That's the last I heard," Kathy replied, turning large, puppy dog eyes on Matt.

Matt glanced at Alex. "We'll have to see how many demands the record company puts on us for publicity. That will determine whether I go or not. But, I have been accepted there."

Alex sat up straighter and shot him a you-know-we-still-need-to-discuss-that glance.

Matt suddenly pretended an inordinate interest in the napkin on his lap. He'd meant to talk through college plans with Alex, but the recent weeks hadn't allowed for many quiet, let alone private, conversations. All he'd told her was he couldn't afford to attend the University of Southern California where she'd been accepted.

Suzanne piped up into the awkward silence. "Looks like most of us will be going our separate ways in a couple of weeks."

Brett reached out his hand to Suzanne. "'Cept Suz and I are off to the University of Idaho together."

"Not separate then, in pairs," Kathy said, giving Alex a self-satisfied smile. "I'll be at WSU with Matt, and Dan with you at USC."

Whether Alex's or his own head swiveled faster in Daniel's direction, Matt couldn't tell. They both stared at him.

"Re-e-eally?" Matt said.

"Yeah, man, the University of Southern California. LA's most awesome law school. Not a bad music school, either," he added, smiling broadly at Alex.

"What a coincidence," Alex added, glaring at Daniel.

Matt felt a knot in the pit of his stomach. Daniel let loose at the same university as Alex? That did not make him one bit comfortable. *Conniving sneak. He's gonna try to get her any way he can.* Alex squeezed Matt's hand reassuringly under the table. He looked over, but she was intently staring at Daniel, green eyes flashing. Matt's pulse quickened looking at her. *Can I blame Dan for trying?* Matt realized he would have to deal with the situation head on sometime soon, but not tonight. It would require some creative thinking. Right now, he needed to mellow out and enjoy this rare time with his friends.

The rest of their meal progressed uninterrupted except for consistent stares from neighboring tables. Matt ate prime rib, held Alex's hand under the table, and enjoyed a conversation heavy with Suzanne's common-sense suggestions for dealing with fame and Brett's humorous commentary about those suggestions.

Throughout the evening, Matt noticed Kathy's silent gaze moving between him, her plate and Daniel. At one point, when Suzanne tried to engage her in the conversation by asking her opinions on whether Matt should talk with the media, Kathy just shrugged and turned to Matt, "You should listen to your gut reaction, Matt." He watched a disparaging look pass between Suzanne and Alex while Kathy's eyes returned to her plate. A faint pang of sadness stabbed his heart. He knew this was hard for Kathy and made a mental note to try to find some one-on-one friend time for her. Unfortunately, he had no clue when he was going to find that time.

The delicious meal neared completion all too soon. As he and Alex finished up their shared dish of crème brûlée, Daniel attempted to set up after-dinner plans. "I thought maybe we could all go down to the ice rink after dinner."

"The one at the old World's Fair grounds?" Alex asked.

"Yeah. That sounds fun," Suzanne said, looking at Brett hopefully.

"I'll be on my sore, icy buttocks all night, but I'm in anyway," Brett laughed.

Kathy looked doubtfully at Daniel. "Well, if everyone else is going," she said tentatively.

Matt turned to Alex for her reaction.

She studied his face as if weighing an idea and finally made a decisive nod. "That is a great idea," she said, speaking to Daniel. "But, I think Matt and I need to take a quiet walk."

A flash of anger flittered across Daniel's face but he quickly calmed his features. "Like you two aren't spending enough time together," he said.

"Not enough *quiet* time recently," Matt said.

"You prepared to meet your fans out there?" Daniel asked.

Alex nodded. "Sure, if you give us a couple of those 45s from your pocket, we'll be fine," she said.

Daniel tightened his mouth and hesitated. But, he reached into his pocket, pulled out the records and handed them to her.

"I know just the spot for us to go to be unnoticed," Matt said, with a sly grin.

Brett got up from his chair and held out one hand to Suzanne and one to Kathy. "Come on, ladies, looks like it's going to be up to one of you to warm up my icy derriere." Both laughed and took a hand, Kathy somewhat hesitantly. He pulled the ladies up and tweaked his head toward the front door. "Oh, yeah. You, too, Daniel. C'mon!"

Daniel got up and paused to look down at Matt. "You sure this is a good idea?" Daniel asked, eyes tight.

Matt didn't know whether to read concern or anger in his friend's expression. "Thank you, Dan, for putting this dinner together for us." He clasped his friend's shoulder tightly. "It hit the mark. Meant a lot."

Daniel nodded. "I intended it to last longer." He held Matt's gaze and then bent to give Alex a kiss on the cheek. "Make sure he takes care of you, m'lady," he said with a glint in his eye, and walked away.

"You guys have fun," Suzanne said as they followed Daniel. Alex waved at her. "Don't let the avid fans get you."

Kathy added, "If you want some safety in numbers you'll know where to find us." Matt hugged Kathy. She took Daniel's hand as she walked away and blew Matt a kiss over her shoulder. Alex narrowed her eyes at Kathy's retreating back and pulled Matt's arm securely through hers.

June 2003: Alex

*A*lex's potential sponsors had filled the art gallery with laughter for several minutes. She and the DJ in the group were trading behind-the-scenes radio stories and her own tales of celebrity stage mishaps. As another burst of friendly laughter from the group dissipated, they all heard a loud, angry hiss and turned toward the gallery entrance. Alex was shocked to see Kathy, teeth gritted, storming into the room. A slit-eyed Daniel followed close on her heels. Kathy had taken only a few steps into the gallery when Daniel caught her arm and spun her back toward him, fiercely whispering.

Alex gave her group an apologetic smile, excused herself from their company and headed quickly toward the couple. *Those two are not going to spoil my plan with a public spat!*

She strode toward them. Reg fell in behind her, poised for action. She noticed that all eyes in the room were on the couple, including a handful of fascinated magazine photo editors. *Damn!* Thankfully, Mad Bo was already headed toward the paparazzi, no doubt speedily formulating a distraction plan to diffuse the situation.

Kathy and Daniel still glared at each other, exchanging short heated whispers. In mid-sentence, Kathy made a grand gesture toward Alex. Daniel's gaze followed the movement and caught Alex's eye. He glanced back at Kathy, turned immediately and started moving in Alex's direction.

Alex pulled up short, but he quickly moved within speaking range. She whispered tightly, "Daniel, what…" But, he cut her sentence short, grabbing her brusquely and lowering his mouth onto hers. Alex was so shocked by his passion, she couldn't even resist. She just clung to him, dully registering gasps and slow-motion flashes going off in her peripheral vision.

Daniel pulled away slightly, his eyes burning into Alex's. The world had stopped. Another flash brought time back into sync and she watched Reg grab Daniel from behind and pin his arms behind his back. Daniel didn't react. He just cocked his head sideways and shot a look of triumph at his wife. Kathy, pain wrenching her face, set trembling fingers against her lips and ran for the back room.

Anger welled up inside Alex and, before she could stop it, her hand cracked against Daniel's cheek, shattering the dead silence in the room. It also drew his gaze away from the door through which his wife had just disappeared. Alex expected to see conquest in his expression, but she was shocked to see him fighting tears instead.

He did it to make Kathy jealous! What the h...? The answer to that, she realized, must wait until later, when they were out of the public eye. Right now, she was in serious jeopardy of becoming tomorrow's tabloid headline. Madeleine was already talking to the photographers, spinning her magic.

Alex signaled Reg to bring Daniel with her out of the public eye and they left the gallery through the same side door behind which Kathy had disappeared. There she was in the service hallway leaning against the wall, mascara smearing her lovely face. She ran, fists up toward Daniel.

"How could you, Dan?"

Alex quickly told Reg to release Daniel. He wrenched away from the bodyguard and enfolded his fiery wife in his arms. He planted kisses in her hair as she struggled against him. "Honey, I'm so sorry."

"You creep."

"I'm not, I'm just a fool. Just so in love with you that I couldn't stand seeing you with him."

Alex had no idea what was going on, or who Kathy had been with, but she knew this was no time to step into the couple's conversation.

Kathy pulled back and glared at her husband. "He's my friend, Dan. He's always been my friend."

"I saw how you are around him, how you feel about him."

His wife looked sheepish. "Well, I might have had a twinge of old feelings, but they left as soon as you...as you..." She looked over, embarrassed, at Alex.

Daniel put his hands on either side of her face and made her look at him. "It didn't mean anything!"

"It looked like it did." Kathy stifled a sob.

It was Daniel's turn to look sheepish. "Yeah, well, maybe I had a twinge of old feelings, too." He paused and looked into her eyes. "But," he said with a hint of amazement in his tone, "it didn't feel like I thought it would… Like it used to."

Alex felt decidedly uncomfortable and looked nervously back at Reg. He just shook his head and shrugged. He obviously, was as in the dark as she.

Kathy peeked at Alex, but addressed her husband. "I guess that makes us even." She kissed him fully and touched her cheek to his.

Daniel looked across at Alex. "I'm sorry, Alex. But, old habits do die hard."

Old habits? Could they be talking about…?! Alex shook her head and began to formulate a question, the answer to which she was pretty sure she did not want to know.

At that moment Madeleine burst into the hallway and strode toward the clinched couple. "Time for you to make a statement, Mr. Post," she said. Taking Daniel and Kathy each by an elbow, she spun them back toward the gallery door. "Kathy, the role you'll be playing is that of the loving wife."

Kathy nodded meekly and blushed deeper as Madeleine marched them back through the door. Alex caught Daniel's comment. "You think they'll buy me as a publicity hound?"

"Exactly what I was considering. Let's go find out," she retorted with an arched eyebrow.

Alex and Reg followed them back into the gallery. Groups of people were bunched together speaking in hushed whispers as Daniel took the PA system microphone, one arm around his wife.

He cleared his throat. Not that he needed to get anyone's attention. Every eye was on him. "Sorry for the disruption, folks. I suppose I owe our host Alex Lauren a public apology. For a brief moment there I thought it was a good idea to use her lips to put this event on the map."

That broke the tension with some snickers, and he added, "I was just trying to drum up broader interest in what we're doing here for kids music programs. But, if I'd thought it through, the event speaks for itself. Thanks to my talented wife, Kathy."

That brought scattered clapping. "Let's hear it for this beautiful fundraiser, shall we? A round of applause?"

A sincere ovation followed, partly appreciative, partly in emotional relief. "Yeah, well, that's more like it," Daniel said. "Still, we all know who is the real star of the evening. He kept his arm tight around Kathy, but gestured Alex to join them. Let's hear it for the lady of the hour, shall we? Alex?"

Alex nodded and smiled, playing her role, and approached the couple in the spotlight. She backhanded a thumb at Daniel. "My long-time friend Daniel. Always the schemer. If you knew him like Kathy and I do, you'd totally understand. And, you'd also know why we're nipping his big idea in the bud right now."

Daniel nodded depreciatingly and leaned into the mic. "How about a group hug, then, among old friends?" He put his free arm around Alex and they all smiled while camera flashes blinded them for several seconds.

"Now, do make sure you get both pictures in your publications," Daniel suggested to the photographers. "And don't forget to mention where people can send their financial support."

The reporters shook their heads, some even rolled their eyes, but they stepped down with smiles on their faces.

Alex took the mic again to thank everyone for being there and to thank Kathy for her beautiful party. She encouraged everyone to stay and enjoy the refreshments and art, and turned the party back over to Kathy's management.

"Well, hopefully that will diffuse the worst of it," Madeleine said. "You can bet there's going to be fall-out, though. I'd better call Cig Gary to tell him what's happening." She turned to leave, but Alex stopped her.

"What just happened, Mad'?"

"Then you didn't see him."

"Him? Who?"

"Matt."

Alex blinked twice.

"Your former music partner. Matt Roberts. Yes."

"Matt was here?" Alex said dumbly.

"He made an appearance. He had to have known you were going to be here. He probably just wanted to check you out in person, Sweetie."

Alex snorted a breath. "What would make you think that?"

"The way he lurked behind a pillar for a good 20 minutes watching you before Kathy saw him and forced his hand," Mad Bo said, gathering her skirt train in one hand and moving off with a smile.

Suddenly, Alex's throat felt uncomfortably dry. She chased down a waiter for some water and headed directly for the women's room. *Matt had been here? He came to see me?* She dropped onto a soft lounger, took a sip of water and stared at herself in a wall-sized mirror across the small entryway. She pictured Matt studying her. What expression would his face have held gazing across the gallery at her? A random image popped into her mind: his intense expression just before she proposed to him on the Spokane River bridge that fateful night back in that other life they'd shared.

August 1978: Alex

"This was a great idea," Matt said as he led Alex along a narrow unimproved path skirting the Spokane River. They'd just parked their car in an industrial area still within view of the restaurant.

Alex stopped to get her bearings. From their slightly elevated position and across the spray from the Spokane River Falls, Alex could see all the way to the east end of Riverfront Park. Lit like beacons in the darkness, she saw the Great Northern Clock Tower and the 1974 World's Fair's U.S. Pavilion rink where her other friends would soon be ice skating. People strolled and played all along the great park's verdant grass lawn. Its earthy smell wafted up to them, mingled with the fresh scent of spray from the falls. Alex could hear the tinkling music from the historic Looff Carrousel carried to them on the wind.

Lit by tall lamps, an improved path snaked through the length of the park. It ended here in a pair of metal footbridges connecting each riverbank to an island around which the main falls roared. The northern bridge connected the island to the path not many yards ahead of where she and Matt stood.

Alex felt safe here on this secluded trail and the view of the park was impressive, especially with the falls just a few hundred feet away.

"My mom used to pay our utility bills over there." He nodded at the Washington Water Power building on the other side of the falls. "She'd combine the trip with a visit to one of her glass suppliers in that office park over there. While she was busy doing her errands, I used to bring Davey and Becka outside here to play."

"Well, aren't you just the expert finder of secret places." Alex looked up into his face, thinking of his secret meadow near the cabin. He pecked her on the lips.

"Come check this out," he said, leading her up the path. As they approached the bridge, the roar of the falls grew louder. As they stepped out onto the metal structure, Alex felt spray from the rushing water swirling up through open grating underfoot and around her legs. The sensation made her head reel and she pulled closer to Matt.

He steered her to the center of the bridge and stopped, pulling her back against his chest so they could both look out at the thundering falls almost beneath them. The powerful rushing rapids, illuminated by floodlights from the park, glowed and writhed like scores of white, billowing sheets in the moonlight.

Alex watched a distant group of young boys on the far side of the river throwing rocks into the falls. One athletic-looking young man lifted a large river rock over his head and tossed it into the splashing water. It landed with a loud cracking noise against a boulder in the rapids. His motion and the sound hit Alex like a physical blow. She'd seen something so similar in her cabin dream and the memory quickly threaded through her mind.

Blinking against the river's watery spray in her dream, she'd seen Matt carving something in the tree trunk. He smiled at her sadly, lifted the wide stump with great effort and heaved it through the misty spray. The stump splashed with a loud kerplunk into a deep pool just below the river's rapids. It quickly surfaced with a watery pop and bobbed erratically against the river rocks until it caught in the current. As it flowed away, she glimpsed a message carved in the flat top of the stump, but couldn't quite make it out for the thick snowflakes and speed of the water.

Her body went rigid.

"Everything OK?" Matt asked turning her to face him.

Alex didn't dare tell him. She managed to make her voice light and steady as she looked up in his face, hoping the fear she felt wouldn't show in her eyes. "Oh, it's just the rushing water down there making me dizzy."

"Don't look down," he said pulling her face toward him with both hands. As his lips warmed hers, any thought of dreams spiraled away and mingled with the river mists around them. Matt's arms enclosed her in a tiny world where nothing existed beyond the scent of his skin, the quick rise and fall of his chest against hers, and the softness of his breath tickling her cheek. He deepened his kiss, tilting her head back and leaning her against the bridge railing. She registered only a faint sensation of the cold metal against her back as she ran her hands up into his hair and pulled his mouth harder against hers.

The booming of the falls echoed the drumbeat of her heart and she felt their world pressing into a smaller and smaller space. His hands against her lower back pulled her against him and she felt a sudden tremble spasm through his thighs. Passion constricted her breath. She couldn't open her eyes. Drowning in a river of emotion, Alex was carried along, unaware of any past or future. Images flashed through her mind.

The tune "Killing Me Softy" filled her consciousness and she was dancing with Matt again for the first time. She pictured his face after hearing their song on the radio. Matt was kissing her in the secret meadow. She was walking with him in the snow. A stump was bobbing along rushing water. An icy wedding dress fell from her shoulders. Matt disappeared behind a tree and… a devastating sense of loss overwhelmed Alex.

She dropped her head and pushed Matt away with both hands. Turning, she gripped the railing, heaving with the effort to get enough air. A crushing sense of dread filled her.

"Alex?" Matt snuggled up behind her, leaning around to try to see her face.

"No!" was all she could get out between gasps.

"It's OK. We just got a little carried away. I'm sorry."

Alex fought for breath. "No!" she repeated, her mind struggling to reconcile the images that had just ripped through her consciousness and the feeling of panic she now felt. "No! This has to stop!"

"Stop?" He turned her to him. "I wasn't trying anything."

The full cabin dream came rushing in upon her. What was happening to her? Why were these images in her dream showing up in real life? Why did she suddenly feel like she was going to lose Matt? She had to stop it.

"No, no. Not you," she managed to pant. "It's me." She grabbed Matt's arms and stared up into his face. "I love you."

His gaze relaxed but concern still burnished his eyes.

"We're meant to be together," she said, more vehemently. "Nothing in this world is going to keep you from me."

Matt pulled away slightly and examined her face. "OK," he said hesitatingly. "I don't understand what's going on, Alex. Is someone or something trying to keep us apart? He hesitated. "Is it you? Does it have something to do with your dreams?"

Alex's eyes widened in fear. "No!" she said, a little too quickly. She leaned toward him. "I'm just so afraid to lose you," she said, dropping her head onto his chest.

"I'm right here, Princess."

Alex suddenly felt the need to deny her dreams, to banish them completely from her thinking. They couldn't possibly mean anything. These weird thoughts were just coincidence. She was meant to be with Matt. She knew it. She pulled his head to hers and kissed him. He moved into the kiss and, when several hours had lapsed within a few seconds, she pulled away. His eyes gleamed with love and desire.

She had an urgent need to connect him to her so he could never leave her. A sudden impulse came upon her. "Matt, let's get married."

"What?" The intense emotion in his eyes turned to bright surprise.

"I know we're young, but don't you feel how right it is for us to be together forever?"

Matt's mouth opened and his eyes darkened.

Alex couldn't stop the floodgates. She cupped his face with her hands and forced him to look at her. "We love each other so much. All we did was think about each other when we were apart. We're off to such a great start with our music and we have so much more we can create together. I know we have an amazing future. We can support each other through the craziness and fame." Matt took a step back. She continued, "You know we're going to be famous. You know we need each other to get through it."

Matt held her at arms length. "You know I am not really comfortable with becoming famous."

"I know. But I'll be there with you. I can help you. It's your destiny, Matt. Just like it's your destiny to be with me." Matt's penetrating gaze took her aback and a sharp icicle of fear froze immediately in her chest. Of course he had to accept his destiny. "But, how can you avoid fame now? It's already started."

"I can stop it any time. All I have to do is quit." He added almost inaudibly, "Don't think I haven't thought about it already."

Another droplet of fear dripped and froze on the frosty spike growing inside her. "But, if you are ever going to have enough money to build your music camp, you have to pay the dues to get there."

"There are other ways to get money."

"What else would you do?" she pleaded.

"I don't have to be a performer, you know, I can just be a songwriter or studio musician."

"But, what about…?" She suddenly realized he was avoiding the topic of marriage and more ice froze her chest. "That leaves me out."

"Not necessarily," he took her hands. "You can be the performer."

"But that won't allow us to work side-by-side. Always together."

He just looked down at her regretfully and ran one hand through his hair. "I'm sorry, Alex. I'm just not ready for…forever."

The sharp, icy emotion forming inside broke loose and stabbed its cold point into her heart. Pain exploded in her chest and she clenched her arms tightly against her torso. Matt tried to lift her chin, but she resisted, turning away to the falls again.

"Too much is happening right now, Alex," he said. "I'm barely surviving the pressure now. I can't add a wife to the mix."

The icy stab to her heart stung and a smothering ache spread around it and filled her entirely. "Not even if I'm here to support you?" she whispered.

"Alex, fame is what *you* want. Not me. I'm sorry that's the way it is. But, it is." Alex could sense him pacing short steps behind her. Back and forth like a caged animal.

Alex watched the falls crashing over rocks below her. The future she'd envisioned for them was washing violently down the rapids along with the white water, just like the stump. Lightheaded, her thoughts misted as if spray from the falls was drifting inside her head. Trying to clear her mind, she pressed her hands to her head. She swayed and almost fell before grasping the bridge railing. The cold of the metal on her hands brought her back to her senses. *She had to think of a way to fix this.*

Ignoring the internal heartache still punishing her, Alex wrapped her arms around herself again and faced Matt. "OK, then. We have a lot to figure out before we take off for school."

Matt tried to take hold of Alex's arms, but she tightened her arms to her body and twisted away.

"This doesn't have to change our relationship, Alex. I'm just not ready for all these obligations."

A lump filled Alex's throat and she had to pause to let it subside before she could speak again. "I expected you to be committed…at least to our work. I expected too much, that's all. Let's just move forward from here."

"Alex, come on. Don't shut me out. Let's talk this through. You know how much I love you."

"Enough to finish what we've started here? It doesn't really sound like it."

"But, this is a huge adjustment for me. I can't just change the way I do everything in my life all of a sudden."

"I know. But I can."

"Yeah, that's because it's what you want. For me, it's a struggle. I have more family responsibilities, and other goals."

"I know." She forced herself to look at the situation logically, to ignore the pain and to hold an expressionless face. "Well then, let's just see how we can make it easier for you," she said matter-of-factly. Her mind grasped for ideas. *Other songwriting teams work together so only one falls into the spotlight. What about The Carpenters, or Captain and Tennille?* She had to make their relationship work now, so Matt would become more comfortable later, maybe even with the "M" word. *Barbra Streisand had all kinds of songwriters behind her, many of whom the public hardly ever heard about. All she did was sing and give infrequent interviews. She had other people doing everything else for her.* "OK," Alex ventured, "How about if I take on all the interviews and meetings from now on?"

Matt stared intently at her. "Well, aren't you just all business, all of a sudden."

"It is business, Matt. Our business. Our future. We have to deal with it that way." She said it as much to convince herself as to convince him.

"How can you just turn off your emotions like that?"

Little did he know the turmoil surging through her system, how much this hurt, how she had to hold onto the threads of her pain so she didn't have a total freak out right here, right now.

"What about talking through our feelings so everyone's comfortable?" he asked implacably.

"That's what I'm doing, Matt." Her ribs throbbed from battling the ache inside her.

"I don't feel comfortable. And, Alex, you're not talking feelings."

"You'll *feel* more at ease if you don't have to be so visible. Right?" She stared up at him.

"And, you're good with handling all the media? Everything the record company and the public demands of us, you're comfortable handling it all yourself?!" he demanded.

Her mind screamed, *NO! I want you, Matt. I need you, to do it with me.* But that just wasn't going to happen. One of them had to be the realist. "You know I'm up for it. It's what I love and want, as you said. It only makes sense for me to handle the publicity."

Matt's hands trembled visibly. "So, I should just go home and sit in my music library?"

"You'll be with your brother and sister, and it will give you the opportunity to focus on the music you love. That way we both get what we want."

"What if I want to go to college?"

"You can write music at college, too, you, know."

He set his jaw. "So, I should spend my time creating more songs for you to get famous on? That's what you want? You're just going to use me – my music – to get the fame you crave?"

Pressure from the unbearable internal ache expanded until she thought she might explode. She took two, slow, deep breaths. "You'd be doing the part you're best suited to, Matt. And, I'd be doing mine."

Matt splayed his long fingers. He studied them, stretched them rigidly and clenched them into fists. With a deep breath, he looked up at Alex, eyes smoldering. He lowered his voice almost to a whisper, "This is exactly what I feared back in Moscow. Relationships always make things so complicated."

The emotional ice gouged viciously deeper into Alex's heart. She worked to control her knee-jerk desire to drop to the bridge floor and clutch her knees to her chest. Instead, she involuntarily reeled and staggered backward.

Matt was there in an instant, catching her and crushing her to him. "Why does this have to be so hard? Why do I have to love you so much? Why do we have to bring the world in to share what we create? Why can't it just be you and me and the music?" he asked fiercely. Alex felt his whole body shaking against her.

Barely able to breathe against his shoulder, Alex struggled to manage the fear and love and need for control waging war in her heart and mind.

"I want to focus on *you*. It's you I love, my Princess," Matt said thickly. "I can barely stand the thought of you going away to college without me, let alone having the entire world take you away from me interview by interview, song by song." He enveloped her mouth with his, possessing her.

Every beat of Alex's heart heightened her pain. She wanted nothing more than to stay here in his embrace forever, letting emotions flood over and into her to heal her suffering. She loved him so much, but could she sacrifice their future for their chemistry? Love wasn't going to smooth over the real issues they were facing. It took every ounce of fortitude she had to push him away.

"Look, Matt..." She searched for the right words, struggling against tears welling up from the ache constricting her throat. "I love you, too. You know how much, or I wouldn't have asked you to..." She gave a tight laugh. "But all this needs to be addressed. Better now than later."

Matt pressed his lips together and nodded slowly.

"We've got to set some parameters so we can each be happy and not wreck our relationship along the way," Alex said, raising her hand in an attempt to wipe away leaking tears. Matt stopped her arm and gently fingered away the rivulets on her cheeks. He nodded again.

She swallowed hard, trying to ease the lump in her throat. "This isn't going to be easy. We have contract commitments and, it appears, we're going to be separated for college. "It sounds like you've decided to go to WSU."

"I need to at least give college a try."

Alex looked down at the bridge floor. "So, are you willing to work something out for our music, even though we'll be apart?"

"I'll try." He dropped his eyes and tightened his grip on her arm. "I'm sorry for getting mad. I just feel so…trapped."

She dropped her gaze and looked over his shoulder out at the green lamp-lit park, active with people having fun. "I wish you could see it like I do. Like a door opening wide on a world of opportunities."

He closed his eyes as if trying to see what she saw. "All I see is walls closing in."

"OK, then. We'll just make sure you do the minimum public relations required in your contract and I'll handle anything else that comes up. That work?"

Matt inhaled deeply and looked up into the dark sky. He nodded and let out a long sigh. "If the record company will let me out of my PR duties…"

"I hope they will if I take it on and all the work gets done."

"That will feel better. Thank you, Alex."

Unanswered questions swirled through Alex's mind, but she didn't have the fortitude tonight to pursue all the details. The sharp pain in her heart was ebbing, but it was leaving a throbbing ache and exhaustion. She put her head on Matt's chest and held him close, listening to his uneven breathing.

As the minutes passed, images from her recurring cabin dream flowed, unstoppable, into her mind again…

She stood on the icy bridge searching for any sign of Matt behind the falls' white misty spray. Pricks of cold crystal began to hit her face. The snowflakes fell faster and heavier, collecting in folds around her. Within minutes, snow had drifted around her, covering her form in the shape of a long, flowing white dress. Larger snowflakes clung to the bodice and shoulders like lace. The lengths were dotted with shining ice crystal rhinestones. Down her back, gauzy snow lightly dusted her long hair in a veil.

She looked up and saw a shadowed stretch of winding pathway ahead. It appeared long, steep, lonely and cold. But, she knew at the end lay the warmth and safety of the cabin. She felt so alone, all that was left was the allure of the cabin and her heart yearned to reach its safety. She quickly hastened up the icy path toward it.

As she moved forward, the snow dress fell from her in one swift avalanche of powder. Leaving the frosty pile behind her, she moved up the path. She found the going steep and slid back one step for every two she took.

❖❖❖

Alex became aware of a real chill overtaking her, not only from her mist-dampened clothes, but also from the raw frost of emotion still within her. Her legs started to tremble, then her arms. In moments, her whole body was quaking.

Matt pulled her closer. "Are you cold, Princess?"

She couldn't even answer for the sudden mind-numbing quivering. She pulled at reality drifting somewhere in the distance and her mind dully registered the shaking as some kind of stress reaction.

Matt pushed her to arms length. "Alex?" he asked, worry overtaking his expression.

She looked up at him and, shaking from the innermost fibers of her being, said in a forced voice, "Please take me home."

She probably could have walked, but she allowed Matt to pick her up and carry her to the car.

August 1978: Matt

On their drive back to Coeur d'Alene Matt kept glancing at Alex shivering uncontrollably in the passenger seat. Hands clenched and face set in determination, she insisted he turn off the car radio and hold a halting planning session with her. As the miles clicked by and they discussed action steps she could take, her trembling began to subside. They came up with a plan to assure the record company. Though Matt would back away from his publicity duties, he'd actively work on composing. Surely, the record company would agree that an album of tunes would make more money than just publicizing a single.

This decision salved Matt's uneasiness. He literally felt as if the large knife pressed to his chest for the past few weeks had withdrawn. By the time they pulled into the driveway of Alex's home 45 minutes later, Alex seemed her old self and he felt more optimistic than he had in weeks.

Alex put one hand on the car door handle as if to get out, but Matt caught her other hand and drew her to him. He smoothed hair from her temple and gazed at her beautiful face. Unbidden lyrics flowed into his head and he started humming Barbra Streisand's "Evergreen."

Alex rewarded him with a knowing smile.

"Thank you, Princess," he whispered.

She cocked her head to one side.

He pulled her to him and whispered, "I know this would be a lot easier for you if I could just walk at your side."

A brief shadow of disappointment moved across her eyes, but she said, "We'll figure it out. That's what lovers do."

Lovers? He liked the sound of that. "I promise to write the best songs I can for you."

She kissed him lightly. "You won't be able to help it, since it comes so naturally."

He pressed his lips against her neck, relishing a lingering scent of "Charlie" perfume radiating from her soft skin and whispered, "I love you, Alex."

Hesitating just a trice, she replied, "I love you, too," Matt." Did he detect regret tingeing her tone? Or was it just fatigue? His heart skipped and, with more force than he intended, pulled her across the seat and kissed her possessively. She immediately melted into his embrace and he chalked up her regretful tone to the evening's chaotic, raw emotions. Ten minutes later Matt opened the car door for Alex and walked her to the door for a last, tender goodnight kiss.

August 1978: Matt

*T*he record company agreed, on a trial basis, to allow Matt to focus more on creating music while Alex handled the PR separately. But, to Matt's annoyance, Cig Gary assured the students remained focused by assigning them a personal assistant and manager. Madeleine Beauchamp's job was to make sure the students each got settled in their respective colleges while remaining focused on their music and contractual duties.

During his move to Washington State University that last week of August, Matt quickly came to understand why business associates called her "Mad Bo." Her constant flourishing of overly long, overly bright, polished fingernails drove him crazy. Not to mention how she nervously and repeatedly fluffed her thick, feathered-shag hairdo, and cuddled herself in luxurious mink coats no matter the weather or public sentiment about wearing fur.

Madeleine focused mainly on helping Matt with his move to WSU, since Alex's parents were actively helping their daughter. They'd already helped Alex pack her belongings, select her music performance and other courses at USC, and arrange for housing. With no parental support, Matt reluctantly relied on Madeleine. Even if she was embarrassing to have around, he had to admit she was very efficient and thorough with details.

She'd discovered a comfortable furnished apartment right on the edge of campus, with a piano no less, and had his few personal effects moved in for him. She bought his textbooks, arranged daily music practice times in the music building for his composing, and handled everything that could possibly make his life easier. She'd even helped his parents hire a young English au pair named Buffy Magnolia to care for his siblings. Mad Bo's frenetic help had driven him crazy while it was going on, but she'd completely freed him from responsibility. He immediately immersed himself in his composition classes and was writing music to his heart's content.

One evening at the end of his second week of school, Matt plunked down on his brown corduroy couch with a sigh and placed his TV dinner atop a pile of lyric notes next to the couch. He took a sip of milk, wishing Alex were there to enjoy his new apartment with him. He relived holding her that last tear-filled afternoon in Coeur d'Alene and how hard it had been to leave. Thankfully, they had made plans to phone every few days and to rendezvous somewhere convenient during the first available school break. He resolved to call her again tonight once he was done with dinner and ask if she'd received the bouquet of flowers he'd sent.

His farewell with Alex contrasted sharply with the uncomfortable goodbye he'd shared with Daniel. His buddy had punctuated that experience with gratuitous comments about how "Like The Moon Pulls The Tide" would be hitting number one on the charts any week now. He also made pointed promises about taking care of Alex.

Matt shook his head. He was grateful for Alex's strength and capacity to take care of herself. He'd seen her actively keep Daniel at bay, like that afternoon on the bow of the sailboat when Daniel was making moves on her. Matt also was counting on Alex being so busy with schoolwork and their record publicity that she wouldn't have time for Daniel anyway.

As he chewed his warmed-up turkey and gravy, his thoughts drifted to Kathy, who had driven down to WSU with him. She was busy trying to settle herself into college life. Matt had barely seen her.

I can hardly believe I'm here in Pullman, Washington, on my own for the first time in my life! He set his aluminum tray aside and, throwing both fists in the air, smiled at the ceiling of his own apartment. He admired the growing pile of lyrics beside him and reached for the phone to share his joy with his wondrous woman.

August 1978: Alex

*A*lex was a big-city girl who had lived in the relatively slow velocity of a small town for only one school year. So, during her first weeks at USC she glided right back into a fast pace and its pressures with very little adjustment. She delved immediately into balancing school requirements with additional song publicity. Besides, a full plate kept her from pining too much for Matt.

The thousand-mile distance between her and the man she loved continually aggravated the inner ache first formed on the Riverfront Park bridge. Whenever she stopped long enough to think, its icy fingers gripped her heart and coated her insides in permafrost. Still, she actively worked to subjugate the pain and dread with thoughts of what great progress they were making toward a future together. During evening phone calls with Matt every few days, he shared the musical progress he was making. She was grateful and proud he was accomplishing exactly what they had planned when he decided to become less visible to the public.

So many times on their phone calls she had almost slipped and told Matt about what she'd been working on. Even Mad Bo and Cig Gary were surprised by the publicity ideas Daniel helped her cook up, so she knew Matt would be amazed when she could finally reveal everything.

Yeah, that Daniel. She really tried to ignore his presence at USC, purposefully not giving him her housing information or phone number. She hoped they'd never cross paths since the university was so big and surely he'd be too busy with legal classes to pursue her. But, she had, once again, underestimated his resourcefulness.

The second day of classes, he showed up after Marketing 101, nonchalantly waiting to walk her back to her dorm. She'd warily agreed to dinner after that, and had successfully warded off his exploratory advances. She was proud of how she'd controlled her feelings of attraction to him. Apparently realizing he wasn't going to get anywhere with her, he'd behaved quite civilly since then. Still,

Alex sensed an anticipatory patience in him, which she couldn't quite explain. She remained watchful for any romantic maneuvers, but instead was rewarded only with generous ideas for "Like The Moon's" publicity. He helped her whenever his legal coursework allowed.

He had made it obvious to her that since she and Matt owned the music rights, they could use the lyrics and music in any way they could dream up. Daniel had suggested some amazingly fun and extraordinary marketing techniques to publicize the single. His coup de grâce was pulling in a favor from his dad's brother, a mover in the music scene. When an act cancelled its appearance on *American Bandstand*, he was able to sneak Alex into the upcoming slot. Daniel had even convinced Cig Gary and Mad Bo that Alex should do it all secretly so as not to put any additional pressure on Matt.

Alex really appreciated the idea of managing the increased publicity work, especially the music show, without burdening Matt at all. They all agreed Matt wouldn't want to be on the show anyway, as it would make him too widely recognized. She, of course, would love the notoriety. And, it was also a way to make herself invaluable to Matt, without distracting him from what he loved doing.

As the weeks went on, her hard work started to pay off. Fellow students, even teachers, recognized her and stopped her all over campus to say how much they loved her song. She always carried a supply of publicity photos with her and autographed one for whoever asked.

Cig Gary attributed a surge in sales to Alex's publicity efforts, resulting in the song being heard on the radio constantly, especially in Southern California. Her work involved TV and radio interviews, and performances in regional lounges, at poetry slams, even in classrooms. She sang the popular single, but also added in jingles, poems and parodies she'd based on the song.

Madeleine helped her arrange the gigs, licenses, permissions and research required. She had been at Alex's beck and call ever since Matt had been settled at WSU. Alex loved the energetic woman, no matter her eccentricities. Her work taking care of all the miscellaneous details allowed Alex to concentrate solely on school and music PR. Alex was busy and happy, with the exception of being separated from Matt. But that's why she was working so hard, so they could move forward and be together sooner than later. She could hardly wait.

September 1978: Matt

*E*ven as he enjoyed his new life, Matt had pangs about shirking his responsibilities at home. He worried about Becka and Davey who were now in the permanent care of Buffy Magnolia. He wouldn't have worried as much about his siblings if the au pair hadn't been a junior clone of Mad Bo, who had found, interviewed and hired the young English woman. His parents and siblings seemed to love the flashy new European addition to the family. Buffy did offer good credentials, even if she was just out of college.

He reminded himself he must learn to let go of responsibility for his siblings now, so he could follow his own dream. It didn't make sense to distract himself from his music by trying to make new friends, either, so he kept to himself. That didn't stop classmates' stares, or pre-and post-class interruptions from co-eds who recognized him from previous TV interviews and the 45's cover slip. A number of girls from his music classes hung around the practice rooms he used and peeked in the windows when they thought he wouldn't notice. He was outwardly friendly with them and signed the publicity photos he begrudgingly carried around, but mostly he tried to ignore their antics. Not to mention Kathy's, now that she had settled in.

She would have spent all day long hanging on his arm if he made himself available. She kept trying to get him to do college things with her: going to concerts, studying at local coffee shops or hiking in the nearby mountains. Her ideas were somewhat tempting, but he had to disappoint her time and again. His concession was eating at least one meal a day with her. After all, who wanted to eat alone? Still, he had become almost manic about his music studies and composing. For the first time in his life he was experiencing the freedom to manage his own time and he wanted to fill every moment with music. After only a month, he already had several melodic tunes in the arrangement stage and his progress, related to Mad Bo by phone three times a week, elated both her and Cig Gary.

He was glad they were happy, but their enthusiastic reactions often made Matt flinch. It brought home what recording these new songs – an entire album – might mean to his future. But, he was determined to be smarter about protecting his time and privacy rights with a new contract covering the album.

One afternoon in late September Matt was walking across the campus after a full afternoon of composing. Mentally running through a troublesome chord progression, he absently admired the changing leaf colors shimmering on the campus trees in a cool breeze. Their vibrant yellows, browns and a few dusty reds set off by the verdant backdrop of evergreens signified the approaching turn to winter. He sucked in a deep breath of the pungently fresh fall air and walked up a shadowed sidewalk to his dorm.

In the lobby, he was surprised to be greeted by Mad Bo. She pulled her fur coat around her with one arm, reaching out to embrace him with the other.

"Madeleine! What are you doing here?" he asked. That she had actually come here to WSU was bad news enough. But, the fact that she was here probably meant the record company wasn't happy.

She steered him back outside to a shady secluded bench around the corner. "Sit here, mon cher," she said. "You haven't had any official phone calls today, have you?"

"Is our single losing momentum?" he asked, running a hand through his hair.

"No, no. Nothing like that, bébé… I'm afraid I have some very bad news for you." She sat next to him and put a hand on his arm.

Unnerved by her use of French endearments in almost every sentence, he hastily said, "Am I not writing music fast enough? I thought I was doing really well. I can work…"

She laid two fingers over his lips. "No, it's not that at all, dear." She paused. "Have you seen a newscast today?"

He shook his head slightly. "No. I've been in a rehearsal room almost all day. I did hear some guys at lunch talking about a big plane crash on the news, though."

"Yes. A plane crash. In San Diego…" she stared compassionately at him.

He shook his head trying to understand where this was going. "In San Diego…" he prompted her.

"Petit l'un, your mother and father went there for an art and architectural show this week."

"I know." He frowned at her as the familiar frustration and anger at his parents' continual absence flared inside him. Madeleine blinked back at him with concern and bit her lip, and suddenly Matt got the connection. "My parents were in that plane crash."

"Pacific Southwest Airlines flight #182," she said, waiting to see if this registered at all. Getting nothing but his questioning expression, she dropped her eyes to her shiny crimson nails and rubbed them together distractedly. "Well… I'm so sorry, Matthew, but… mon dieu, this is hard to say."

He suddenly sat perfectly still and whispered, "They said everyone died in that plane crash."

She peeked at him from the corner of her eye. "Yes, Matthew, I'm afraid your parents are gone."

Matt stared at her, numbness overtaking him. "My parents died."

"I'm so sorry, Matthew," she whispered. "The police called your home this morning looking for you. Buffy had seen the newscasts, put two and two together and called me. I got right on a plane."

Matt's mind registered dully that Buffy and Mad Bo knew before he did, and he wondered why that would be his first thought. Perhaps it was because his subconscious didn't want to deal with the most obvious facts. "Becka and Davey!" Suddenly panicked, Matt stood up. "I've got to get home!"

"I knew you'd want to be the one to tell the children what's happened, so I've already made your flight arrangements." She zipped open her black patent-leather purse and pulled out an airline ticket. "I have a car scheduled to pick you up here in half an hour. The children are in good hands until you get there."

Not for the first time, Matt actually felt genuine gratitude for Mad Bo. "Thank you, Madeleine." He hugged her stiffly and quickly turned to go.

"Don't worry about things here," she called after his retreating form. "I'll make sure Kathy and your teachers know what's going on."

Matt waved a hand in recognition of her comment without missing a step. He thought he should be sad, but what filled his mind was how the death of his parents could kill his dream. He leaped up the stairs two at a time. *Why did they have to go get themselves killed? Stupid, selfish people. Always leaving us to fend for ourselves, and now it's permanent. How true to form.*

September 1978: Alex

*T*he following week, Alex's apartment phone rang. Her head jerked up off of her Music Business textbook and she rubbed her eyes, trying to clear the impression of loneliness and cold lingering in her mind. She'd been dreaming again about the cabin. This time, after the frosty wedding dress had fallen from her shoulders and she had begun to move up the path toward the cabin. On the steep incline of the hill, she'd slid back almost as much as she moved forward. "Matt!" she had called into the stillness. Matt was nowhere to be seen and she'd felt desperate to find him, or at least to reach the safety of the cabin.

The phone rang again. She blinked rapidly and, in her stupor, bobbled the handset before answering. As soon as she heard the voice at the other end, Alex cradled the phone with both hands and whispered forcefully into it, "Oh, Matt, hi. How are you holding up?"

"I've been better."

"Oh, SuperMatt, I've been thinking about you every minute. How was the memorial service yesterday?"

"About what I expected. A ton of business associates showed up who'll miss my parents' work and connections. No one who really cared, though."

"How did Becka and Davey do?" she asked, rubbing her eyes with her free hand.

"They're pretty good. They love Buffy and are actually excited we pulled them out of school to hang with us. I'm not sure the kids even miss my folks."

"Oh," she said, quietly. "Well, I imagine it's hard to miss someone you hardly ever saw."

Matt sniffed. "That's for sure."

She heard exhaustion, deep pain and a touch of anger in his voice, which she attributed to his grief. A pang of guilt stung her. *And I'm not there to help him.* "Matt, you know if I possibly could have gotten out of our scheduled publicity gigs I would have. I'm so upset I couldn't be there."

"Yeah, well...I know you and Daniel had other commitments. Daniel said his coursework was too heavy to leave right now." He exhaled.

Alex couldn't tell Matt the real reason neither she nor Daniel could come. They'd been filming *American Bandstand* in Philadelphia. The show's last-minute cancellation left only two weeks of lead time. So, Mad Bo, Daniel and Alex became the critical focal points in pulling everything together. Mad Bo had the students continuously on the phone whenever they didn't have their noses in textbooks. Alex couldn't believe the speed with which she and Daniel had discovered and hired back-up musicians, a costumer, a stylist, prepped Alex for filming and handled so many other details. What a whirlwind it had been! Her heart expanded with excitement thinking about it, but shriveled as she realized she couldn't share one sliver of it with the man she loved.

Matt continued, "At least Kathy is here, so I wasn't completely alone. You know, she actually quit college for a semester to be here for me."

Alex hesitated. That was an unmistakable dig, which from his perspective, she supposed she deserved. "That's good," she said guiltily but quickly changed the subject. "SuperMatt, you sound tired."

"Yeah. You wouldn't believe how many decisions and calls there are to make, not to mention the paperwork in an estate."

"I can't imagine. Do you have help?"

"Well, I've retained Daniel's dad to help me sift through some of the tougher papers."

"Mr. Post?" It came out more forcefully than Alex had wanted, as a stone dropped in her stomach. She prayed Daniel had warned his dad not mention anything about *American Bandstand* to Matt.

"You have something against Mr. Post?" Matt asked.

"No, no, that's great," she said, hurriedly. "I'm sure he'll be a great help." She pulled her hair over her shoulder.

Matt sucked in a long breath and let it out slowly. "Yeah, like I'm sure Dan has been to you."

What did that mean? What did he know? "Uh, what?" Alex's heart began to drum.

Matt continued in a tired voice. "I know Dan pretty well and I don't think he stayed there in California just to do schoolwork, Alex. He's smart enough to do class make-up work. He had another reason not to come up here for the memorial service." He paused. "I think that reason is you."

Alex couldn't stop her quick intake of breath. "Matt…" She had no idea how to respond, and silence deafened the phone line.

"Daniel usually gets what he wants…eventually. He finally got to you, didn't he?" Matt's voice was resigned.

"You can't possibly think that!"

"I know Dan. Unfortunately, I thought I knew you, too."

"You do! There's nothing…" She started to say "nothing going on between Daniel and I," but that wasn't technically accurate. She quickly shifted gears. Her voice felt tight. "There's nothing romantic going on between Daniel and I."

"Yeah, that really sounds convincing."

Still at a loss for words, Alex nervously straightened the books and papers on her desk.

"Let's just say the signs don't point toward honesty here, Alex. I know Dan's in love with you."

Alex snorted and threw down the pencil she was about to place in its pencil cup. "He just wants something he can't have."

"I tried overlooking the way he watches you. And I've tried overlooking the way you react to him. But I can't overlook chemistry when it hits me in the face."

Alex put a shaking hand to her head. "Matt, name me a girl who isn't attracted to Daniel. But just because you're attracted to someone doesn't mean the relationship works, or even that you choose to give in to the emotion. Just because you're attracted to someone doesn't make it a romance."

"Yeah, well, his loyalty is obviously with you, not me. Where's yours, Alex?"

Alex could feel panic rising up inside her. "With you! Matt, I'm not meant for him."

"Really? Is that why you two are there and I'm here at this time in my life?"

Alex's mind spun. *How to get him to see without betraying the surprise she and Daniel had planned just for him?* "You have to trust that what Daniel and I are doing here is in your best interest."

"*My* best interest?" Matt laughed.

"Yes."

"You know when someone dies you think you're going to have your friends around you to support you. Especially the ones who say they love you."

"But I do love you!"

"I'm sure you do in your own way."

"Are you kidding? Everything I've done is for you. All this publicity is for us. For our future."

"Don't you mean *your* future?"

Alex's face flushed hot. "Look, Matt, everything is about you. I'm not having prophetic dreams about Daniel." She pressed a hand over her mouth and squeezed her eyes shut. *Why had she said that?* She had said the exact same thing to Daniel at the graduation party. What was wrong with her? Her dreams, stupid and worthless as they were, were exactly why Matt left her before.

After a long moment of silence, Matt answered in an almost inaudible voice. "So, now your meaningless dreams are prophetic?"

"I just blurted something I don't even believe! I hear it from Suzanne so often, it just popped into my head," she said desperately.

"Cho-o-oice."

"Matt, look. Don't flip your wig here. You can just forget the whole dream thing. If I don't believe my dreams mean anything, you shouldn't either. I was just drawing at straws to make you understand. You are my one and only. You know you are. You have to be." She hesitated momentarily, considering whether she should continue. But their relationship hung in the balance and she had to say everything. "You are the one I want to spend the rest of my life with. I'm the one who asked you to marry me, remember? You are the man of my dreams. I can't stand to lose you again."

"The man of your *dreams*, eh?" The comment was sarcastic, but Alex heard diminished emotion, maybe even a small smile, in his voice. Her pounding heart slowed a bit.

"Matt, listen to me, we need to just mellow out here. I know this is a very difficult time for you. It's tough for me, too. We're both going through huge change. Some of the biggest changes we'll ever have."

"Yeah."

"You have to believe me when I tell you I can barely stand having to be here when you need me there. But the timing just stinks. If you'll just hang in with me for one more week, I have a surprise for you that will make everything clear."

"A surprise? What surprise can be so important that you can't tell me about it right now?"

Alex could just tell him now, but it would *totally* ruin the plan. They'd specifically scripted into the show a dedication to Matt and an explanation that he couldn't perform on the show with her because of the deaths of his parents.

"Matt, I've been planning this surprise for awhile and it's geared especially for you. Won't you trust me for one more week?"

"I assume Dan is in on this."

"Yes. Actually, it was his idea."

Matt thought for several moments and growled in resignation. "Unless I tell you I never want to see you again, which I'm not really up to right now, I don't really have much choice."

"I really want to tell you, but it would just blow everything. And, you *are* going to think this is outta sight. I know it! Trust me."

He sighed deeply. "We'll see."

October 1978: Matt

*M*att picked up the phone after the first ring. Before he could even say hello, he heard Alex's excited voice. "So, are you ready for the surprise?"

Much calmer since last week's call, he was glad to hear her voice. Last week's verbal attack on her wasn't the only example of the effects of stress he'd seen in himself since his parents' deaths. "Hello to you, too, Alex. Yeah, I'm here in front of the TV, as promised. So what's this about?"

She took a long breath. "OK, go ahead and turn on *American Bandstand*."

He didn't answer immediately. "*American Bandstand*?"

"Yes."

"Like with the top hits in America?"

"Yes. Like ours."

Could she mean...? He shook his head to clear it as he turned the television dial from *Happy Days*. "OK. Who's on?"

"Just watch. I'll stay here on the line."

"So, this is going to be like watching the same moon from different cities so we feel closer together?"

"Kinda. Only I hope seeing this will make you happier than seeing the man in the moon."

Matt leaned back into the soft corduroy couch, his eyes glued to the TV and ear to the phone as the show progressed. "Here we go!" Alex exclaimed as the show's recognizable host introduced "Like The Moon Pulls The Tide," and her image came on the screen.

"You're on *American Bandstand*?" Matt exclaimed.

"Yowsers, yes! Shhhhh...listen."

He watched Alex's dedication of the song to him and her explanation of the personal reasons he was unable to perform with him. She looked so beautiful and self-assured, and her eloquent words made his absence seem so natural and necessary. Relief flooded him and he actually felt tears pricking his eyes. "That was sweet of you to let me off the hook like that," he said.

She blew him a kiss through the phone line.

Matt watched in silence as an unknown accompanist sat down at the piano. Immediately, queasiness started churning his stomach. Alex began to sing and the tune played out as the camera captured the dancers in the room. *They are dancing to my music. My song is on* American Bandstand*!* The thought made him proud and amazed on one level but, on another, he couldn't quell a rising panic. The confusion kept him silent and unable to formulate a comment throughout the remainder of the song. Even after the melodic tune ended, he sat mute, his hands sweating and his mind roiling.

"Matt?" Alex's voice in his ear startled him. "What did you think? Are you surprised?"

He cleared his throat. "Surprised? I'm pretty sure that doesn't cover it."

Her voice grew quick and high with excitement. "You see, this is what Daniel and I have been working so hard on. We needed every available moment to make this happen on the short notice we got from the show. We actually contacted them a couple of months ago, but a cancellation came through unexpectedly two weeks ago. Can you believe it? Us! On *American Bandstand*."

"Yeah, just think of the exposure," he said unevenly as an uncomfortable burn ate his insides.

"No kidding!" she said. "Mr. Post's brother told us about the cancellation. He's a lawyer for WFIL-TV in Philly. Mr. Post didn't say anything to you about the show and spoil the surprise, did he?"

"Not a word."

"Whew! He apparently heard through Daniel that you didn't want any TV exposure. That's why we decided to surprise you."

"Ah. Who's we?"

"Well, you know it was Daniel's idea. And, of course, Mad Bo and Cig Gary were involved."

"Who was the accompanist you hired?" His voice came out flat even to himself.

"Some studio musician Cig Gary knows. That was OK with you, wasn't it? He's nowhere as good as you, SuperMatt. But he did pretty well in a pinch, don't you think?"

Matt swallowed hard and answered in a tight voice, "The performance was very good."

"You don't sound very enthusiastic for someone whose song just got played on one of the hottest shows in America."

He struggled to control the range of emotions washing through him. "I can't believe you guys pulled this off. I feel like I'm sitting inside a Dali painting with clocks dripping around me."

"Was it a nice surprise anyway?" She sounded worried.

He rubbed his hand along the corduroy surface of the couch and answered slowly. "Well, you sounded great. I guess I just wasn't ready to see someone else sitting at the piano playing my song."

"Oh, Matt! I didn't really even think of that. It seemed like such an amazing surprise to have your song on the show. And I just thought you'd love not being distracted from your composing. That *is* what we agreed to. I was just doing what I thought...what would help *us*."

"I know. It's what I asked for. But..." He laughed. "I guess I'm feeling left out." He got up to click off the TV.

"Oh, SuperMatt." Tears thickened her voice. "I didn't think you'd feel that way. I really thought you didn't want to be involved."

"I didn't." *I don't know what I think.* "I'm confused. It has something to do with not wanting to be involved, but not wanting anyone else to do my performing, and also something to do with Daniel..." He stopped. "What other surprises do you and Daniel have in store for me?"

"Are you still worried I'm more interested in him than you, SuperMatt?"

"Not as much. But, I still don't trust him."

"I've been watching for anything out of line, but he just seems to want us to succeed."

Matt weighed that comment quickly and rejected it. *He's got to have a motive. Daniel wanted something and, most likely, it had something to do with winning Alex.* Matt absently ran his hand through his hair as he paced his living room as far back and forth as the phone cord allowed. He suddenly saw the need to protect his own interests, both musically and personally. Obviously, his desire to avoid cameras and microphones had blurred his clear vision about his role. He'd completely lost his place in the mix by stepping backstage. But, one thought heartened him. With the loss of his parents, he could completely control what happened now. Nodding to himself, he said in a much stronger voice. "I get it now. Alex, I was wrong to totally step away from the process. I would like to have more say in what we do with the tune from now on, even if I'm not on-camera."

"OK," Alex said, getting her feet back under her. "Let me tell you about what else we've been working on." She told him about the interviews, jingles, regional performances at campuses and poetry slams, and their obvious result on record sales. "There are so many opportunities, especially since we retain the music rights. We can do whatever we feel is best."

Matt didn't remember anything about owning music rights from his contract. He thought those had gone to the record company. "You have music rights?" he asked her.

Alex paused and said very quickly, "Of *course* we do."

He didn't know exactly how to read her response. *Did her emphasis imply wonder at his not knowing she had music rights, or was she questioning him?* A niggling concern itched his mind and he made a mental note to reread his contract. "So, what's next?" he asked.

"Probably not another *American Bandstand*!" She laughed. "I'm not sure we can come up with something like that again very soon."

"Well, the next time Dan comes up with a great idea, please don't assume I want to be surprised. I'd rather know before the fact, OK?"

Alex barely let him finish his thought before saying, "I'll keep you informed about everything." She sniffed. "Be prepared though. We're on a roll now…assuming we get a good reaction to the performance.

"*You* will."

"Me? What about you?"

"Well, you were the only one that appeared on the show. And, it probably ought to stay that way, even if someone else does sit at the piano. You were right, Alex. I'm not comfortable in the spotlight. I'll stay in the background as the songwriter. You can be the star."

Alex sighed. "A Carole King move. Create one smash album for yourself, only to disappear behind the piano to make hit songs for everyone else in the industry. That the plan?"

"Something like that." He laughed ruefully. "Is that going to work for you?"

"I can't say I haven't been expecting this. All I can say is, if it works for you, Matt, I'll make it work for me." Alex hesitated, inhaling deeply. "Matt, are you OK? Are we OK?"

"It's all fine." *I just need to find out what my scheming best friend is up to.* "Dan will stay involved, won't he?"

"It would make sense to keep him involved as long as he keeps coming up with good ideas."

"Probably. But we should keep an eye on him."

August 2003: Matt

The last time Matt had snuck into one of Alex's big events, it hadn't gone so well. But, tonight, he'd successfully made his way into Spokane's INB Performing Arts Center without anyone seeing him. He congratulated himself for timing his arrival just minutes before Alex's reunion concert curtain when most everyone would already be seated. He now climbed the back stairs to the control booth where Pablo, his lighting-technician buddy, had promised him a bird's-eye view of tonight's concert.

When he entered the lighting booth, Matt's headphone-clad friend, busy at the control board, signaled a thumbs-up and waved Matt to a seat in the shadows near the viewing window. Matt picked up the playbill Pablo had left for him and peered out over the audience. *A sold-out crowd from the looks of it.* He recognized several high school friends' faces in the crowd. Tiny lead weights immediately filled his stomach and started lurching nervously around on the backs of sizeable butterflies. His head was telling him to get the heck out of here. But his soul wouldn't leave. The pull to see a live glimpse of Alex again was just too alluring.

Within moments, Pablo dimmed the house lights halfway and a prerecorded announcement filled the auditorium. "Ladies and gentlemen, you are about to experience an unequaled night of entertainment. Ten select artists have traveled here to the INB Performing Arts Center tonight from all over the world to sing for you. All of these artists have contributed their time so the price of tickets can be donated to music and arts programs all over the Pacific Northwest. The mastermind behind this event is a Grammy-award winning vocalist. She is known all over the world, but got her start just across the Washington State border as a graduate of Coeur d'Alene High School. She is back this weekend with more than a hundred of her classmates celebrating their 25th high school reunion. We're sure all of you who know her, and all who are about to meet her, will want to give our hostess a warm Spokane welcome. We welcome you, Class of 1978, and your benevolent hostess... Ladies and gentlemen, Alexandra Lauren."

Pablo spotlighted Alex as she walked out on stage to thunderous applause. Strains of Matt and Alex's original single "Like The Moon Pulls the Tide" played as she strode to center stage and bowed. A glittering emerald green gown flowed around her lithe form and her long curly hair bounced and glistened like riotous polished gold in the spotlights. She hugged her hands to her chest, lifting them once or twice into a steeple-palmed gesture of thanks as the applause continued. Matt couldn't stop a quick intake of breath when she parted her lips into a brilliant smile. *Damn, she was lovely.* Matt couldn't take his eyes off her. All the emotion he'd felt when he'd penned that first song for her flooded his soul. As the thunderous applause in the auditorium pounded in his ears, he thought his chest might burst from the pressure and the pain of loss.

The ovation for Alex died down some when she pushed her palms repeatedly toward the floor, asking the enthusiastic audience for permission to speak. But it kept on.

Matt took several long, quiet breaths to gain control, even as music started in his head. As if the sight of her wasn't enough to get his musical juices flowing, all he had to do was hear her crisp tonal clarity and the musical arrangements would carpet his mind like stop-action daisies growing in a field.

Almost as if she'd heard this thought, she started singing a cappella. The fans and classmates quickly hushed to hear her. Matt's heart quelled at the sound and didn't restart until she stopped her singing shortly after the auditorium went quiet. In the ensuing momentary silence, she looked around the auditorium with what Matt could only categorize as amazement. Was she surprised at the response? Hadn't she ever experienced that kind of gratitude before for doing something selfless?

Alex sighed with a smile and said, "Oh, my friends, we thank you so very much for being here to support this worthwhile cause. I cannot tell you how full my heart is, seeing this auditorium bursting with friends, colleagues and music-program supporters. You are the ones allowing our children to remain active in this universal world language of music. Sharing this commonality makes our world smaller and our differences less important."

As she spoke, she scanned the audience and nodded briefly to several people with whom she shared eye contact. Matt noted her small expression of disappointment as she finished her visual sweep of the auditorium. At that point she dropped her head for a moment. Matt's heart leapt. *Was she looking for me?*

"First, I need to thank my long-time friends, Daniel and Kathy Post for helping me make this evening happen." She grinned apologetically at her audience. "Yes, we're all just *friends*… Despite the photos appearing all over the Internet and tabloids recently." This brought a huge laugh from the audience.

"So, let me bring Daniel and Kathy out here on stage so you can show them our gratitude for their hard work on this reunion weekend," Alex continued. She waved the couple onstage and they entered arm-in-arm from the wings into the spotlight, Kathy carrying a honey-toned violin and Daniel a matching bow. Matt's stomach contracted as Alex introduced them and hugged them each in turn.

Matt had seen the tabloid photos. He wouldn't put it past Dan to pull a stunt like that just for the publicity. But, it might have been witnessing Kathy's impromptu kiss outside the art museum that incited Dan's actions. Or maybe, he just still wanted Alex. No matter the motive, Daniel hadn't changed one bit. Matt could barely bring himself to look at the crafty lawyer.

How could Dan possibly think he could appear out of the blue and expect me to lobby with him for music funds in Washington D.C.? And, then there was Kathy. She had changed so much, she'd obviously moved completely into Daniel's camp. Daniel manipulated everyone. *Didn't they see through him?* With his whole being, Matt wanted Alex to have nothing to do with them. But then, did he really want to have anything to do with Alex himself?

Matt's internal struggle burrowed below consciousness again when Alex called two formally clad students onto the stage. Neither could hide their excitement as they approached her. The high-school-aged boy, whom Alex greeted with a handshake, couldn't stop beaming and his face reflected the color of his red hair. The diminutive girl with the short black braids barely stopped bouncing long enough to allow

Alex's hug. After responding to the girl's white spotlight of a smile, Alex turned back to the audience.

"Because of your financial support tonight," she linked her elbow through the young man's arm, "Jordan's high school is able to continue his orchestra program this year. Thanks to your help, he will be able to move forward pursuing all available opportunities for an orchestral scholarship next fall."

"And little Caprice here," she captured the grinning, bouncing girl's hand and smiled down at her. "Without you, Caprice wouldn't be getting her own instrument to pursue her genius through junior high and high school. At that cue, Kathy handed the girl the shiny violin and Daniel gave her the bow. As the couple moved upstage out of the spotlights, Caprice took the instrument and immediately stilled, her eyes sweeping the length of the prize in her hand. The girl grinned the width of Alaska and gazed up at Alex as if she were The Supreme Goddess herself.

"These two aspiring young musicians have written a piece they'd like to perform for you tonight, which they've entitled 'Music Rocks.' Won't you help me encourage their work with a round of applause?"

As the audience clapped and Alex nodded for Daniel and Kathy to stand aside with her, Jordan took a seat at the grand piano center stage and Caprice placed herself in front of it. Jordan began the piece with slow, classical piano, joined shortly by Caprice's sweet violin phrasing. The instruments crescendoed quickly into a catchy, rollicking rock melody, and soon the audience was clapping and tapping feet along to the beat.

Matt watched the blur of the students' fingers on their instruments in as much amazement as the rest of the audience and couldn't stop himself from slapping his hand against his thigh in time to the music. These were kids who could change the music world. He obviously would never have seen them at his music school because of their financial considerations. But now, they'd gotten what they needed through Alex's generous efforts.

Matt suddenly stilled and dropped his head into his hands. This is why Kathy had wanted him to work with Alex and Dan to help these deserving kids. This feeling of joy in helping young musicians. Kathy had said Alex was looking for fulfillment and had found it in the same place Matt had. He saw now what his three friends were trying to do. How much more powerful their influence could be if they all worked together, each contributing their individual skills.

But, was it worth getting involved with Alex and Dan again for this great cause? He still didn't trust them. Matt lifted his head as the music stopped and the crowd erupted in response to the young talent.

The students took their bows, twice, and walked offstage flushed and grinning at one another. As their ovation died down, Alex took center stage again. "Can you believe them?" she asked, shaking her head. "*You* have made it possible for these young talents to fine-tune their musical expression. Expect to hear more about those two as the years go by," she said, clasping her hands and looking down at the floor. After an almost too long moment of silence, she looked earnestly back up into the crowd.

"Friends," she said, "I have to tell you that in the midst of all the light we're creating tonight, there is one small dark spot for me. I had hoped to share this success with a classmate of ours, my one-time friend who helped me get started in this business. Many of you know him only as the songwriter for our hit single back in the 1970s, 'Like The Moon Pulls The Tide.' But, all of the songs you will hear performed by our generous and amazing artists tonight were written by our fellow 1978 Cd'A High School graduate Matt Roberts." The crowd applauded loudly and expectantly.

He'd know this was coming. But the impact of its reality hit him squarely in the gut. Matt sat back deeper in the shadows of the control box. No one but Pablo knew he was here, of course, but the action was involuntary. He felt Pablo's eyes on his back, but didn't dare turn around. Matt's immediate inclination was to bolt, but again he found he couldn't move. He had to know what she was going to say.

Alex continued, "I so regret Matt cannot be here with us tonight." There was an audible sigh of agreement from the audience. "As you may know, in addition to his songwriting, Matt is a behind-the-scenes force in educating and shaping the careers of the world's best and brightest young musicians. His Coeur d'Musique camp on Lake Coeur d'Alene has become a coveted destination for young virtuosos everywhere. As a matter of fact, later this year, his students will perform at the White House and he will take that opportunity to lobby the government for additional music-program support."

Matt felt his face flush hot. He hadn't asked for this notoriety, this much detail about his work. His heart began to race. She was back again, pushing him into the limelight where he didn't want to be. Only, he couldn't figure out why she was doing it. *What's is her real motive?*

Daniel asked Alex for the microphone and she handed it to him. He cleared his throat. "I just wanted to say to our mutual friend, Matt Roberts, should he be listening in somewhere, that his three best childhood friends are here to support him in his lobbying efforts." He looked at Kathy, who nodded encouragement. Dan returned his attention to the crowd. "We all need to work together for the greater good on this. We sincerely thank everyone here for their support of this amazing cause and hope you'll get behind Matt Roberts' efforts in Washington, too, at the Web site listed on your programs."

A public declaration of support for my charitable work? And a Web site to support me? Those three are working incredibly hard to entangle me in some scheme of theirs through this concert. A trickle of sweat slipped from his temple. *But, why? What did they want?*

The Posts bowed and left the stage. Once they had exited, Alex clasped her hands together and addressed the audience in a hushed tone, as if she was talking to her dearest chums. "Honestly, folks, I was hoping that, for this great cause, my long-ago friend would be here on stage with me. But, he is an extremely private person. He turned down fame long ago to become the underlying musical force that he is today. I won't go on, as I know he wouldn't like the attention. But, following Dan's example, let me just conclude with a personal plea." She smiled around the audience, alertly eyeing the crowd as if looking for him again. *Was it the stage lights, or were her eyes shining because they were full of tears?* "If you're out there, Matt, hearing any of this... I want you to know..." Her voice faltered, "I miss you. I'm looking for a bridge to walk over, if you're willing to meet me halfway."

Matt half rose out of his chair, ready to go to her, before he caught himself and sat down hard. He stared at the stage for a moment, digesting her words. His breaths became shallow and labored as his chest constricted.

A sympathetic hush fell over the audience. Alex straightened her back, pulled her hair over one shoulder, and said with a small laugh, "Let's just all hope he's actually listening to us out there somewhere, shall we?"

As audience laughed sympathetically, Alex almost imperceptibly dashed a tear from her cheek and turned to gesture toward the center of the stage. Resuming her stage voice, she said, "With that humble entreaty to my friend, I invite each of you to enjoy an evening of outstanding musical artistry. And I thank each of you from the bottom of my heart for your willingness to participate in supporting our world's talented musical youth." She curtsied, flung her hair back with one hand and glided into the wings of the stage. Applause thundered in waves throughout the auditorium as the curtain opened and the opening notes of BJ Starr's "Mind & Time" wafted forth.

"Ladies and gentlemen," boomed through the public address system, "The man who introduced Alexandra Lauren to the music community. *The* Entertainer…BJ Starr!"

Barely noticing the rock icon singing as he took the stage, Matt sat on the edge of his seat listening to the chorus lyrics he'd penned so many years ago for the rock balladeer's fourth album.

Time…made us cry.
Time, time…makes love die.
Time, time, time… I ask you why?
Time…passed us by.

Matt slowly rubbed the back of his neck. Only he knew the words were really written about Alex shortly after he broke up with her. He thought about what she'd just said and he felt her drawing him in again. *How can I possibly still have these strong feelings for Alex? Surely, she has moved on. She couldn't possibly have just said… There was no chance in h…* His heart raced and a new bead of sweat chased others down his cheek. He needed to get out of here.

Leaping up, Matt hurried to the door, only turning back from the control room door to quickly thank Pablo. The lighting tech raised his eyebrows twice, licked his finger and touched his knee voicing a sizzling sound. "She thinks you're hot and you're deranged if you don't immediately go backstage looking for her, dude," he said.

Matt shrugged and quickly closed the control room door behind him before Pablo could see the color rising in his cheeks. He momentarily leaned against the wall in the back stairwell. Once he'd collected himself, he hurried downstairs, eager to gain the lobby's side hallway where he'd entered just minutes before. Matt incautiously flung back the curtain shielding the stairway from the hall and bumped right into Daniel Post.

Daniel didn't appear to be surprised at all to see Matt. It was almost as if he'd been waiting for him. "Just the person I was hoping to bump into," Daniel said, taking his friend's arm and leading him just a few paces into a semi-secluded alcove.

"I don't have anything to say to you, Dan." Matt tried to shake Daniel's hand off his arm, but his former friend's grip was firm. "Ah, but if you ever loved Alex, you're going to want to listen to me."

Matt stopped struggling and Daniel let go of his arm. "How'd you know I was here?"

"The ever wise and intuitive Suzanne Thompkins thought you just might try to sneak in here tonight. The back stairs is a logical bet when someone doesn't want to be seen."

Well, didn't that just make perfect sense that Suzanne would be involved, too. "I'm not sure it's in my best interest to listen to anything you have to say, Dan."

"It is when there's something in it for me, too."

"That's the first truly honest thing I think I've ever heard you say," Matt said. "Make it quick. I need to get out of here."

"OK. First, I have to apologize to you for the whole music rights plan I made to break up you and Alex."

Matt stared at his friend. *The plan had been to break him up with Alex? Not to take his music rights?*

"You know, she really didn't have anything to do with it. But I know you'd think she did. I really thought I needed her then…"

"And *I* didn't?"

"OK, I was a stupid jerk. Totally infatuated with the girl. I wanted her." He shrugged. "I *was* just a kid."

Matt's mind spun. If Daniel didn't put Alex up to stealing his music rights, had he thrown away his relationship with her for nothing? In his anger he hadn't listened. In his fear of losing control of his life any further, he'd shut everybody out. He ran a hand through his hair. His heart drummed against his ribs, but he calmly said, "You are ultimately more clever than I ever expected, Dan."

Matt could see his comment pleased Daniel. But, there was also a look of unfinished business in his former friend's expression. Daniel's eyes flashed an alert wariness, and he wove his fingers together and stretched his palms. "I have something else to tell you," he said, meeting Matt's eyes. "Shortly after your break-up, I promised Alex I would take half of her royalties from your first single and send it to you every quarter."

Matt scoffed. "She trusted you to do that?"

"Well...yeah," Daniel said, looking almost shamefaced. "She wanted it as a show of good faith on my part. And, she didn't want you to know she was the one sending you the money."

Matt glared at his former friend. "And where is the money, since I haven't seen one dime of it?"

"I brought you a check." Daniel reached into his coat pocket and pulled out an envelope.

Matt ripped open the envelope. His legs nearly buckled when he saw the amount. "You've been sitting on more than two million dollars of mine?"

"Uhhhh...yeah." The lawyer frowned down at his hands.

Matt stared at Daniel. His mind raced. "Alex thought you'd been sending this along to me in installments?"

"Yeah. She thought having me manage your account would always remind me to be a better person." He scarcely suppressed a smile.

"Didn't she realize you weren't doing it?"

Daniel chewed his lips as if not wanting to give up a secret. He hesitantly explained, "Actually, she got statements showing transfers to an account with your company name on it, but the account was actually mine. She didn't know I never gave you access to it." He shrugged. "Anyway... all that stuff. It happened so long ago. So many things have changed. It's yours now."

The dubious look Matt shot at his former friend didn't even touch the doubt and suspicion warring inside his battered soul. He spoke slowly. "It does say something...that you actually haven't spent this money of mine. But...Daniel Post admitting guilt? What's your real reason, Dan?"

Daniel dropped his head back and laughed. "You always did understand me, Matt." He pursed his lips and became pensive for a few seconds. "OK, you probably won't believe me, but how about some total up-front honesty? Let's say it's just for old times' sake."

Matt waited.

"I want to make some contacts in Washington D.C. and you're my ticket in. I can help me, while I'm helping you. Didn't seem right for me to hold on to your money when both you and Alex are actually helping me get what I want."

"What makes you think I'm going to let you come with me to Washington to lobby and make contacts with all the people holding power and money there?"

Daniel smiled knowingly. "Because I'm going to give you Alex."

Matt stared at his blue-eyed nemesis. "You don't own Alex, Dan. You're not even close to her any more, according to Kathy. And, may I remind you that you have a wife?"

"Yes, exactly. Kathy, my wife." Daniel actually looked wistful. "I suppose I owe you another apology for taking Kathy from your music camp to plan my client entertainment. She's just so blessed good at her work." A note of reverence touched his tone.

Matt waved his hand. *Since they were being honest with one another...* "You actually did both of us a favor, Dan. Her leaving opened up the opportunity for Becka and Davey to come to work for me. Plus, she needed to get away from me to fulfill her potential."

Daniel nodded. "She is everything I could have dreamed of."

"Except no curly blonde hair?"

Daniel's eyes got a far-off look. "Alex? I loved chasing that woman. But, you know, at the fundraiser... I watched her that night. The life had gone out of her. She obviously felt like she was in a cage. Eyeing her bodyguard. Nervous. Digging for information about you. It dawned on me she was still in love with you."

Matt's eyes snapped onto Daniel's.

"And, when I saw Kathy…uh…with you…" He paused. "Well, it made me plant that wet one on Alex in front of God and everyone…" He laughed lightly. "That experience flipped a switch inside me. I suddenly knew I was never going to win Alex's heart. I didn't even want to anymore. She has wanted you from the day she set eyes on you. And, I'd created the woman I was meant to be with from the beginning, too."

"You're telling me that you're actually in love with your wife?"

"Yeah." Daniel laughed and shook his head. "I am."

His honest expression left Matt speechless.

"So, I am in love with my wife. She wanted me to give you the money I'd been keeping from you. So, I'm making her happy. I can also make you happy by helping you get the funding you need in Washington, my friend. What do you say?"

Matt pulled taut the check in his hands. "I already have two million dollars to work with now. Do I really need you?"

Daniel scoffed. "You know how fast two mil' is going to go. Besides, Washington money will benefit other programs besides yours. If I work existing contacts and new ones from Alex…"

Matt interrupted. "Alex promised you contacts in Washington?"

Daniel smiled. "Offering intros to her entertainer-loving politicos was obviously part of her plan to entice me to nudge you back into her life. You know, she'd provide me with what I want. Then, I'd befriend you and help her get what she wants."

Matt looked at Daniel incredulously. "She's actually gone to all this trouble?"

"Yep. Win, win, win. I get to pursue political aspirations. You raise influence and more money than your music and art people ever thought possible. Plus, you get the girl."

Matt didn't want to admit it, but Daniel was right. He opened his mouth and closed it again. His temptation was to say yes, and go for all the things he wanted in life. But doubts about Daniel remained. "What guarantee do I have that you aren't offering this for some other hidden reason, Dan?"

"I hand you millions of dollars, offer you the girl of your dreams, and promise to help your career and industry. I even admit what's in it for me. Hell, what more can I do? Still, if it will make you feel more comfortable, we'll have an objective lawyer draw up an agreement. You pick the lawyer."

Matt ran his hand through his hair and considered the evening's events. Suddenly the pieces began falling into place. Alex hadn't purposefully stolen his music. And she was still in love with him! She had concocted this complex plan, involving old friends, and heavyweights in the music industry, not to mention Washington, just to get back in Matt's good graces. *Wasn't the leap at least worth exploring?* It did seem to be a win for everyone, even him.

Matt couldn't think of a reason to say no. Still, he was extremely wary. "That will make me almost comfortable, Dan. We can talk more at my office on Monday," he said, shaking his friend's hand. "Now, I need to get out of here."

October 1978: Alex

*I*n her college apartment one mid-October afternoon, Alex answered her phone to hear Suzanne's voice.

"Hey, Lex, I have great news!"

"You mean, the King of Rock and Roll really does live?"

Suzanne laughed. "No. I've patched things up with Kathy."

Alex stopped short. Kathy had been civil to Suzanne whenever they were brought together by circumstance, but Alex thought she had been too wrapped up in Matt to have any interest in wanting to be close friends with Suzanne again. "What?!"

"Yeah, she called just a little while ago and apologized for dumping her girlfriends after her mom died."

"Whoa! Really?"

"Jinkies, yes! She actually said she realized she missed us and had become too focused on Matt."

Alex's jaw dropped. "What in the world brought this on?"

"Something to do with growing up, I'd say. She's mostly had to fend for herself at college while Matt worked incessantly on his music. And, with him leaving after his parents' accident to deal with estate issues and make plans for his music school, Kathy's had time to think and talk over everything with Daniel."

Alex made a noncommittal noise and Suzanne continued, "Matt's actually asked her to come back to town to help him drum up business for his music school. But she said she doesn't know if it would be the best thing for her. Well, she's going to take at least the rest of the semester to think about it. Can you imagine Kathy turning down an opportunity to be with Matt?"

"No, I really can't," Alex said, a chill slipping up her spine and plunging its cold fingers deep into her shoulders. *I wonder what this is going to mean?*

As if in answer, Suzanne continued, "Minus Kathy's jealousy and attitude, maybe we can all be better friends. She actually said she wanted to get to know you better, Lex."

Alex blew out a quick disbelieving breath.

"One thing I'm really happy about is that she offered to help me plan my wedding next summer," Suzanne added.

Alex had to stop to think if she'd heard that right. "Your *wedding*?!"

"Absolutely!" Suzanne giggled. "Brett is so outta sight. He popped the question last night while we were on a rollercoaster at the funfair."

Alex laughed. "Why would anyone expect Brett to pop the question in a civilized place? Were you surprised?"

"Flabbergasted. But, oh, so happy. And you, girlfriend… You've just gotta be my maid of honor. Even if you're scheduled to sing for the president! You'd pick my wedding over ol' Jimmy Carter, wouldn't you?"

Alex gave a little squeak of excitement. "Decent! Of course I'll be there. When? Where?"

"The first weekend in June. Kathy suggested we try the Hitching Post wedding chapel in downtown Coeur d'Alene."

"Suz, this is so neat!" Alex's mind abruptly focused on her friend's comment about Kathy helping plan the wedding. *She'd told Kathy about her wedding first?* Alex swallowed her pride and tried to keep her voice level. "How exactly is Kathy going to help you?"

"I hear that disappointment in your voice, Lex. Please don't be upset I accidentally spilled the beans to Kathy first. She was apologizing. And, I was going all funkadelic about my news. I just blurted out that I needed her help."

Alex couldn't help but laugh. "Okay, Suz. I forgive you."

"One thing about that girl, Alex, she knows how to plan stuff. Why do you think she was so great with Becka and Davey Roberts? And remember that delicious spread at the recording session at Frankie B. Crosby's house?"

"Oh yeah. Faintly. I had no idea she was so good at planning events and parties."

"Yeah, well you haven't exactly seen the best side of Kathy for the past two years. She really does have some redeeming qualities when she isn't being controlled by…"

Alex spoke up as Suzanne continued, and they both said, "…the green-eyed monster."

"Groovy!" Suzanne said as they both giggled. "We've still got it!"

"Will Kathy be in the wedding party, too?" Alex asked.

"Naw, I want to keep it small. Just you standing up with me and Brett's brother with him."

Being the only one in the wedding party made up for her being told about the wedding *after* Kathy. The tightness in Alex's shoulders loosened and relaxed. At least they weren't going to be forced together in that intimate setting right away.

"My parents are throwing an engagement party three weeks from now, if you can get back up to Coeur d'Alene," Suzanne said. "For some reason, they want to hold it on a quiet Thursday night. So, maybe you can come up for a long weekend."

"I'm sure I can work that out somehow, unless another *American Bandstand* opportunity comes up, but that's not likely."

"We can't do it without you, Lex. Make Mad Bo arrange your schedule so you can come. Ple-e-ease? Oh, there are so many things to take care of now!" She launched into a monologue covering every detail: she shared ideas brainstormed with Kathy, described Brett's take on all of them, and expressed her doubts that she'd actually be able to wait 'til next summer to be married to her Brettman.

Alex listened, suggested and consoled, but her mind churned. She couldn't help but feel significant winds of change blowing into all their lives with Kathy's change of heart.

August 2003: Alex

*A*lex stood unsteadily at the helm of a self-chartered boat leaping the early morning waves on Coeur d'Alene Lake. She looked back over her shoulder at the shrinking activity on the Coeur d'Alene Resort boardwalk. Reg and the resort security had successfully waylaid a couple of photographers back there while Alex escaped in the boat.

She felt her hair stinging her neck, the curls whipped by the cool wind, as she and the boat pummeled toward her destiny, whatever that was. With nostalgia and a familiar longing in her heart, she watched the hilly horizon banking the gray lake. The hills seemed to move in slow motion because of their distance from the boat, with the tips of dense, dark, pine trees slowly sliding against the late August sky. A thick, gray Northwestern cloud mass hovered threateningly overhead and cast its pewter hue onto the lake's surface. *Only August and already dreary. If only one little ray of sunshine would peek through, it might give me some hope.*

After all her planning, neither she, Kathy or Daniel had been able to convince Matt to attend the reunion benefit concert this weekend. Her dreams had led her here, to construct an elaborate and expensive plan to bring him back to his early friendships. *Why didn't it work? And, what do I do now? Somehow, this just doesn't feel like the end.*

At this point, all Alex hoped for was resolution, whether good or bad. Her love for Matt had encompassed her for so long, face-to-face and in her dreams, she just wanted to be free. She wanted to fling wide the door to their relationship or just finally close it. Somehow she knew the outcome rested at the cabin. Its prominent presence in her recurring dream brought her to make this trek across the lake today. What she was going to do when she got there, she had no idea.

The boat danced over the choppy bay, slicing through white-capped waves. Even though Alex tried to minimize their impact by maneuvering the boat into the swells at a 45-degree angle, spray still flew high on either side of the hull. Her thoughts bounded along with the boat, rising and crashing in parallel with the choppy romance that had led her here.

She imagined herself at 17, standing in front of her new 12th-grade class and seeing Matt for the very first time. Her stomach lurched, mirrored by a physical jolt of the boat hitting an unexpected wake.

Alex took a deep breath scented with pine and fishy lake water and slowed the boat as it approached the familiar weathered dock. She maneuvered the boat up against the bumpers. "Like riding a bike," she said aloud to herself." She turned off the motor and climbed out onto the old dock to secure the ropes.

Alex pulled her curls forward over one shoulder and looked up. Longing and loneliness stirred inside her. Matt's cabin. Would it still even be there after two decades? Peering through the barrier of dense pines, she could still imagine the small, rustic, rectangular structure. She pictured the brick hearth and wood stove within. Strong images of the warm fires she'd seen glowing in it remained, just like the embers of her love for Matt, which she'd never quite been able to extinguish.

Her mind drifted back. Closing her eyes, Alex pictured that almost-forgotten day…Matt's strong arms encircled her while they sat in front of the cabin's wood stove watching the flames and listening to the rain massage the roof. The power of that long-ago memory sent an unnerving chill up her spine and her eyes fluttered open.

She breathed deep in an effort to still her beating heart, wondering if Matt ever came here now. If he did, when would he have been here last? Might he even be here today? "Oh, Alex!" she reprimanded herself in a whisper, "He's not here. God only knows where he is."

She cleared her head with a shake and looked around. In the opposite direction from the cabin, she could just make out a dock she didn't remember being there before. It was just visible some 200 yards around the curve of the shore. She knew Matt's music camp was adjacent to the cabin property, but she couldn't see any buildings from her current vantage point.

Alex suddenly felt the urge to get up to the cabin as quickly as possible. She began climbing the winding, pine-needled path into Matt's forgotten domain. She recognized the path as the snow-laden one from her dream, only warmed by the tones of late summer.

Around one turn, the cabin came fully into view. The smokeless tin chimney still graced the eastern roof, ringed with blackened wooden shingles telling of many fires burned. A stack of cut firewood sat against the far porch railing, but its top layer was uniformly gray from at least a season's worth of weather. She was sure no one had disturbed that wood for a long time.

Stepping up onto the rickety porch, she noticed a layer of pine needles abandoned on the redwood boards. Walking to the outside porch railing, she peered deep into the surrounding woods and listened for sounds of humanity. Nothing but the sigh of the wind in the tops of the pines and a faint screech of an osprey greeted her senses. She searched across the lake to the horizon where the town of Coeur d'Alene nestled against the curve of the bay. Nary a boat in sight. A newly airborne seaplane's engine hummed high above Alex's head, but not even its wake remained in the water. Only crested waves marred the fluid surface of the water. Obviously, for the moment, she was a lone figure in the midst of the forest.

Should I go inside? I've come all this way, apparently for a reason. A twinge of doubt traveled across her consciousness, but she quickly reinforced her current purpose with the reality of her near-death car-wreck experience and the prompting of her cabin dream.

She turned and stared at the cabin's old, screen door, listening for noises from within. Silence. She reached out mentally for direction and guidance on what to do, something she'd begun to practice now that she'd accepted her intuitions. One solitary mental image kept entering her mind, a gray snapshot of the cabin's interior. Along with the vision came a distinct feeling that, trespassing or not, she was intended to go in. Besides, her curiosity was getting the best of her.

Sure enough, the key was still there above the door. Alex was slightly surprised that, in all this time, someone hadn't discovered it up there and made the structure their home for a while, or vandalized the place. She was silently grateful to rediscover this quaint, refreshing refuge where keys didn't often find their way into greedy, destructive hands. *What I wouldn't give for a simpler life!*

Alex held open the screen door and tried the old key in the main door's rusty lock. The door creaked open, letting a soft shaft of muted daylight into the room. She stepped cautiously inside. What met her eyes colorized the gray, mental snapshot she'd carried since her youth. It even bore the same musty, smoky scents so familiar in her memory. Alex's eyes swept from the black wood stove there in the corner on the little raised brick hearth, past the red-plaid blanketed cot and the worn, brown kitchen counter, to the tiny bathroom in the far corner. A rustic presentation, but still offering all the comforts of home. Even the old black rocking chair still sat in its comfortable space in front of the wood stove.

She quietly closed the door behind her and stood in the dim light filtering through the two porthole windows. Her heart pounded harder as she felt the presence of long-ago relationships and experiences, and chased the shadow of Matt's long-ago words. "Alex, I am going to love you for a very long time," he'd said, holding her right there by those windows. *Prophetic. For me, anyway.* Alex crossed the creaking wooden floor and cautiously settled into the old rocking chair. She looked nervously back at the closed door and took long deep breaths to calm her drumming heart.

Suddenly, a ray of sunlight burst from under a cloud and shone directly through the window, illuminating the brick hearth and cheering her.

As trepidation dissipated, Alex sat in the shadow with only the rhythmic rumbling of antique rocking chair runners breaching the quiet. Rocking slowly and rhythmically, her mind roamed back to that last painful encounter with Matt.

October 1978: Alex

*T*hree Fridays after Suzanne's wedding announcement call, Alex found herself in the car on the way to Matt's house for the first time since they'd left for college.

Alex had been thrilled when Matt had called earlier that day to ask her over to his house. She was relishing having a whole long weekend off from publicity and school and she wanted to discuss the previous evening's beautiful engagement party with him, too. He'd seemed short and tense on the phone. He obviously wanted to talk about something serious, probably business related. She'd agreed to come over right away, even though she didn't feel much like discussing business today.

As she drove, her mind reviewed images of the previous evening's party. Mr. & Mrs. Briggs had spared no expense to announce their only daughter's engagement. And, Suzanne had made a good choice insisting Kathy be the event planner, even if it was the intern's first big shindig. Her catering company must have been thrilled implementing their employee's beautiful plan. Alex envisioned Kathy's tasteful touches transforming the Briggs' back yard into an enjoyably warm, glittering fall grove of entertainment and comfort. She had thought of everything, from the huge white canvas tent edged with space heaters, to a harpist. A white wicker arch, artfully hung with twinkle lights, fresh floral swags and large gold taffeta ribbon framed the musician. Alex pictured the tuxedoed caterers behind white linen-draped serving tables and sniffed in remembrance of the delectable food scents that had tantalized her senses.

She scrunched up her nose at the scent that filled her nostrils at the moment: cold lake water tinted with dusty pine needles. The familiar smell of Matt's street. Alex admired the stately homes looming behind wrought iron fences and facing Sanders Beach across the street. The mid-day sun reflecting off the smooth lake water reminded her of how Suzanne had radiated beauty last night as she mingled amidst candlelit tables with her guests. And there was Brett…the twinkle in his eyes rivaled only by the scores of sparkling light-strands hanging in the perimeter pine trees.

Pausing a moment after parking her parent's car in Matt's driveway, Alex enjoyed how good it felt to be reunited with her friends to share this joyful event. She'd only been away at college and publicizing the single for three months, but so much had happened in that time. So much had changed. Even Kathy. The woman had actually been pleasant to Alex last night. She'd also acted friendly to Matt but hadn't been overly attentive to him. Alex would never forget Kathy's apologetic eyes looking up at her, nor her accompanying words. "Alexandra, spending so much time with Matt during his recent…transition…I've realized how much he needs and relies on you. I hope you'll forgive my past jealousy."

At that complete turnaround, Alex hadn't known what to say. All she could do was nod and mumble some comment about being glad they could be friends now. Having said what she intended, Kathy had smiled up at Alex, touched her arm, and left her former nemesis staring after a retreating back. Alex hadn't even had a chance to congratulate Kathy on her beautiful party.

Alex now approached Matt's front door feeling warm and grateful things were turning out so well. Especially with Matt. Last night, he'd barely removed his arm from around her shoulder all evening. She had basked in the attention and soaked up his essence, filling the void left by three months' absence. He seemed so relieved to be having fun. They'd laughed a lot and she'd loved hearing details about all he'd accomplished in the past weeks with his family's estate.

With Buffy's care of his brother and sister, he'd set a schedule to handle all of his current responsibilities: estate calls and paperwork, composing music, and research for his music camp, including finding a team of business consultants. Alex was impressed, and excited for him that his pending inheritance would allow him to move forward immediately with his dream.

Listening to his progress first-hand, Alex pictured him captaining his business endeavors as she'd seen him skipper a sailboat, completely in control of every movement. On one level, it seemed inconsistent with her dreamy young man whose soul wept music. But, that did not matter. She loved the entire package.

Alex rang the doorbell with its familiar beveled glass frame crafted by Matt's mom. It suddenly hit her that Mrs. Roberts was truly gone and a wave of sadness washed over her. *How devastating it would be to lose my own mom.* She immediately stopped that train of thought. This wasn't the moment to give into emotion. Alex inhaled deeply and braced herself for a morning filled with business.

Matt opened the door. She stepped across the threshold and leaned in to kiss him hello, but his eyes flashed and he stepped back.

"Matt?"

He turned immediately and started walking down the hall. "Let's go back to the music library and talk."

She frowned as they walked in silence along white walls reflecting the brilliant colors from Mrs. Roberts' beautiful stained glass. *The house represented so much of Matt's parents' work, it was no wonder he seemed upset in this environment.*

As they moved into the music library, Matt plucked a glass of ice water from the wet bar and handed it to her. He gestured to a table spread with papers, indicating she should sit down.

She put the glass down, sat, and folded her hands on the table. Matt did not take a seat. He just stood next to her with a stern expression, obviously hesitant or unsure how to start the conversation. As she looked up at him, a vibration began humming in her head.

Finally, he took a deep breath and said, "Alex, why do you have music rights and I don't?"

Stunned with this abrupt opening, she managed only to stumble over incomprehensible words.

"Didn't think I'd find out, or what?" he asked tersely.

A flare of anger helped her gather thoughts together. "Matt, we both have rights to the single."

"I don't."

"Yes, of course you do. It's in our contracts."

He glared into her eyes. "I don't have any music rights specified in my contract, Alex. I read my contract thoroughly this morning. No music rights. A quick call to your parents' lawyer confirmed you *do*."

Alex stared back at him in confusion. "*My* lawyer. What happened to using Mr. Post?"

"He's the one who didn't put music rights in my contract." Matt's eyes flashed. "But it was Dan I talked with about the details."

"You never met with Mr. Post about it?"

"No." Matt snarled the words, "Dan said his dad was giving him 'real lawyer experience.' Obviously, he let Dan control the contract more than I thought."

Alex's eyes widened. *Could Mr. Post really have let Daniel control Matt's contract?*

"You certainly know how conniving Dan is, Alex. And you also know how proud Mr. Post is of his son. His entire life, his father has let him get away with murder. That's why Dan is the way he is. Mr. Post turns a blind eye to anything he doesn't like and just trusts him far too much. Wish I hadn't."

"But, no matter how conniving Daniel is, he's been your best friend your entire life."

"So I thought until now. You'd think a friend like that would care more about how he treated me. Obviously, love changes things. Doesn't it, Alex?" He stared at her pointedly.

The hum buzzing in Alex's skull crescendoed and she put one hand to her forehead. "But letting a high school kid handle a legal contract? That could cause big trouble in a law firm."

Matt looked at her as if he thought she already knew all this and said condescendingly, "I'm sure Mr. Post read the contract over for accuracy, but just didn't get involved in the details. He surely thought his son had every detail under control. Which Daniel certainly did." He paused. "Didn't he, Alex?"

She stared at him incredulously. "You think I was involved."

"Of course. It's so obvious now. You've been planning this together since graduation. I remember now how you went off to 'talk things over' with Daniel at the graduation dance. He'd been ignoring me for weeks and, after talking with you, suddenly comes up to me all palsy-walsy again. You clearly worked together to cook up a plan to get back together and take what you wanted from me."

With a siren blaring in her head, all Alex could do was gape at Matt. He began to pace, "I am the ultimate idiot. I'm the one who broke up with you originally. So, I'm the one to blame for you guys getting together in the first place. Yeah, that worked well for you guys. So, why not go further. Just steal the music rights from me, too. I'd never know I was being taken advantage of. I'm just a musical dreamer, a small-town greenhorn. A fool."

Alex stopped his pacing by standing up and grabbing his trembling arm, "How can you possibly...?" she began.

He pulled his arm away and burned his eyes into hers. "Alex, don't even try. I can see now you were working together. Daniel knew I wouldn't read my contract thoroughly, simply because I trusted him to take care of me. You went along with him the whole way. You probably knew I wouldn't want to do the PR, too. That made it perfect for you to make use of the rights with all these publicity stunts and make most of the money."

Alex gasped. "How can you think that?"

"My first clue should have been you being 'over-the-moon' about your royalty checks and me wondering why mine were so small."

Alex tried to speak, but he cut across her words, his voice rising as he spoke. "Dan wanted you to be famous from the start. He knew I didn't want to be, but he went ahead and gave our recording to BJ Starr anyway. For *you*! Not *me*, his best friend. I'm sick of trusting people and having them hurt me! I'm tired of always having to be responsible; the one who has to protect himself from everyone's lack of loyalty." In his fury, Matt backhanded Alex's water glass off the table. It spewed ice water across the luxurious room and shattered against one of the bookshelves into hundreds of shiny crystal pieces. The tinkling crack of one lingering shard of crystal falling to the wooden floor left the room in utter silence. Alex covered her mouth with both hands. Matt closed his eyes and turned away, obviously working to gain control.

After a few moments he turned back around and said in a calm, pain-laden voice, "Why did my best friend turn on me? Why did you have to get into cahoots with him? Why couldn't you really be the wondrous woman I wanted you to be?" He scrubbed both hands through his hair.

Alex could only stare in disbelief. A hundred thoughts went through her mind, but what could she say that wouldn't sound angry, incriminating or stupid? *I am that wondrous woman. I didn't know anything about this. Why don't you trust me when everything I've done is for you?* Alex pressed her palms against her eyes and grasped for a practical line of reasoning. "How is it you never noticed you had no music rights before this?"

"Music rights never came up."

"How could music rights never come up?"

"I just took it for granted they'd be included in the contract. That seemed so obvious. Dan never brought it up, but *you* know he thought about it."

"You read the contract didn't you?"

"Quit playing dumb, Alex. Of course I read my contract." His voice shook. "But, I was so bogged down in understanding the legal verbiage of what was *there*, I didn't think to look for anything missing. It just didn't occur to me. Dan was counting on that. No doubt, you were, too."

Alex swallowed hard and rejected her inclination to verbally lash back at him as anger rose in her. "Look, Matt, are you sure you aren't wrongly blaming Daniel? You've trusted him and called him friend all these years. You really need to talk with him about this."

"I know Dan's potential for things underhanded. I've seen it growing in him for years. I don't need to talk with him. Besides, you two have certainly worked out a 'story' for me. I'm not falling for any of it this time, Alexandra."

"You're convinced your two best friends in the entire world would do this to you?" A burning sensation in her stomach merged with the screeching clamor in her head. "Me?"

"What else am I supposed to think, Alex? You have music rights. To *my* music."

She saw the anger spark again in Matt's eyes and her anger rose to meet his. "It's *our* music Matt."

"Actually it's all yours legally now, isn't it?"

He was not listening! Alex clutched her head in both hands. *But, Daniel's the one who is conniving and deceitful I'm the one who's been by your side the whole time. How can you group me in with him?* She raised her head, realizing he might mistake her frustrated manner for guilt. "We need to talk through this when we're not angry, Matt."

"No, we're talking through it right now, Alex."

"But, you don't want to hear me now. There's so much going on inside you right now with the changes in your life."

"This has nothing to do with my mourning, Alex. No one but architects and artists miss my selfish parents. No one in this family cares much that they're gone. This has to do with *our* future together. Or our *lack* of it."

"But you're not thinking clearly, Matt." Not knowing exactly how to continue, Alex blindly thought aloud. "Creatives seldom think practically, especially when they're freaking."

"Creatives? You mean like some wacky Van Gogh artist who cuts off his ear to send to his former lover?" he scoffed.

"Not that extreme!" She stamped her foot in frustration. "I meant some super talented people who are so busy creating they can't decipher reality when they see it."

"So, you're telling me my head is in the clouds?"

Why did he have to twist her words? "Matt…"

"And what about those of you who are so in control of your emotions that no one really knows what you think? Those who would go to any lengths to control everyone's lives, not just their own."

That stung. Everything she did, she did for him…for them. Her simmering anger roiled to the surface and bubbled over. "Yeah, well, what about those who don't bother to read their contracts and want to blame others for their own stupidity?" Alex bit her lip hard. *Ooooo, she was going to regret that comment forever.* Blurting things like that was exactly why she tried always to manage her emotions.

Matt narrowed his eyes and applied his voice evenly and quietly over searing fury. "Finally we hear your true feelings."

Alex stumbled over her words as she tried to backpedal, her heart hammering in her chest.

"So, I *was* right. You did think I was stupid enough not to figure out I had no music rights. Probably thought it would be years and years before I found out, didn't you?"

Desperately breathless, she pressed clenched hands to her chest. "Matt, I didn't mean to call you stupid. You made me angry because you weren't listening."

"You're right. I am done listening to you. You can expect a letter from my lawyer severing our musical ties. You can also consider this a permanent farewell to my friendship." He pulled her to him and kissed her forcefully. Alex's head reeled until he suddenly pushed her away. He turned and strode toward the hallway. "Now the deal is sealed. You know how to let yourself out," he said over his shoulder.

Alex stood trembling, fingers on her lips, trying to make sense of what had just happened. After a few moments, she wiped angry tears from her cheeks and walked out, leaving her planned future in ruins behind her.

"You've got to go back and talk to Matt when he's not so upset, Lex," Suzanne told Alex later that day.

Alex repositioned the pillows against Suzanne's bed footboard, eyed the black-light posters glowing in the dark corner of her friend's bedroom, and snuffed loudly. "Matt's done with me. He won't trust me now, no matter what I say. Anyway, he needs some time to cool off," she said.

"But he's going through so much right now. He's got to be a total mess inside. He needs you."

"Maybe, but he can't see it. He's too wrapped up in everything that's happening to him."

"How can you be so composed, Lex? You sound like an adult."

"You didn't see me a few hours ago," Alex said, fingering the damp tissue in her hands. Suzanne leaned over and gave her friend a sideways squeeze, as Alex continued, "Anyway, I don't have much of a choice, do I? Someone has to think clearly so this doesn't escalate into a conflict the size of Vietnam."

"But couldn't you just offer to be Matt's friend and to help support him?"

"He doesn't want support, especially mine!"

Suzanne held her palms open and shot her friend a questioning look. "Turn over music rights to him?"

"He doesn't want anything to do with me now." Alex got up from the bed to toss her tissue away. She paused and peered out the window into the dark street beyond. She fingered the beaded tassel of Suzanne's macramé plant hanger overflowing with lovingly tended, trailing vines. "Well, after I left Matt's this morning and cried my eyes out for a while, I fell asleep. I actually reached the shaft of light on the porch in my cabin dream."

"The safe sunlight you've been trying to reach every time you have the dream?" Suzanne asked. Alex could almost hear her friend's mental gears turning it over.

Alex turned away from the window. "It was interesting that as soon as I stepped into the light in the dream, music started."

Suzanne cocked her head "And...?"

"It was me...singing. Only, my voice sounded like the tinkling notes of a music box. It was lovely. Heart wrenching." She laughed lightly, rubbing her puffy eyes.

"Jinkies! What could that mean?"

Alex leveled a look at her friend. "Nothing." She reflected for a moment. "The power of that music hung with me for hours. It was so clear and beautiful."

"So, Matt wasn't even around in the dream at all?"

"Except for his face reflected in the light."

"The safety in the sunlight seemed to be with music, not with Matt? You've never thought it meant *that* before."

Alex refocused on Suzanne with a quizzical expression. "I never thought it meant anything."

Suzanne nodded slowly. "Well, I always thought it was Matt you needed to reach. But you'd never reached the light before, so it was hard to really tell. Still, his reflection was in the light..."

Alex leaned back on the pillows. "Yeah, well, the music was new and very powerful. It doesn't matter, anyway. Music is my refuge. I'm going for it. My own music. My own path."

"You've made up your mind? Are you sure?"

Alex returned to sit on the bed. "Yep. I really think the best way to handle this is to leave Matt alone for a while."

"I don't know..." her friend said.

"I do have some definite things to say to that raunchy Daniel, however," Alex said.

Suzanne shook her head. "So *this* is what Daniel thought of with all that 'contract' talk with Kathy. What a scuz bag. I knew he could be devious, but I had no idea he would ever stoop so low, especially with his best friend."

Alex sighed and a spark of anger reignited in her. "I have a lot of thinking to do before I go talk with him tomorrow."

"What are you going to say?"

"He's going to help me come up with a plan to reimburse Matt...to make things right." She narrowed her eyes, "Or, I'll make sure he goes down in flames."

Suzanne scoffed. "If you're right about what he's done, he certainly deserves flames. Can you imagine the ego?"

Alex nodded in agreement. "Can you imagine Mr. Post letting him run with the contract like that? Not checking to make sure every detail was covered?"

"It actually doesn't surprise me. From everything I saw being around Daniel when Kathy and I were best friends, I'd say the apple doesn't fall far from the tree in his family. You should meet his mom."

"I hope not to have much to do with anyone in the Post family from now on." Alex shook her head. "Well, I'd better get going. I have a lot to think through."

"OK. Try to get a good night's sleep. And call me anytime if you need to talk...about anything."

Alex hugged her friend at the front door and walked out to her car. *How can anyone get through life without true friends? Poor Matt, all he has left is Kathy.* The idea of that chick acting as Matt's closest confidant now, even with Kathy's recent change of heart, tortured Alex. *Oh well, I have more important things to consider. I can't let my emotions rule my thoughts right now. I've got to think rationally, completely control my feelings, until I can fix this situation.*

"You are a creep!" Alex advanced on Daniel with calm fury as soon as he opened the door to his parents' house the next day.

"Whoa, girl! What'd I do to deserve the hairy eyeball?"

"You and your bogus schemes!"

He backed away from the finger pointed at his chest. "What's that supposed to mean?"

"It means I've figured out why you wanted so badly to help me with 'Like the Moon' PR. You were shafting Matt, so he'd break up with me."

Daniel barely suppressed a smile. "I love a sharp girl. And you, m'lady, are a razor."

"Not one speck of remorse. What kind of guy are you?"

"One who has your best interest at heart, Princess."

"Don't you dare call me Princess!" she cried, instantly losing her carefully cultivated calm. She curled her pointed finger in and raised a fist, but he caught her wrist.

"Now don't be calling me names you'll regret, Alexandra."

She reigned in her anger again. "I'm gonna call you whatever I want. And, you're gonna help me fix things."

"With Matt? I don't think so. I think it's time you got a dose of reality, m'lady." He turned a 150-watt smile on her, but it didn't make up for his insufferable condescending attitude.

"You think you know what is right for Matt? For me?" She struggled against his grip, but he held her tight.

"Of course. You'd just be getting back into a relationship that isn't right for you. You'd continue to constantly hit your head against a brick wall trying to get your music partner to sell what you've created. Grow up, Alexandra. I've made it what it's supposed to be." He quickly wrapped her arm behind her back with his so she was pinned against him. His eyes, blue ice fired by conquest, held her defiant gaze for several seconds.

"Let me go!" she hissed.

"Definitely not now. I've waited too long for this day."

She struggled against him until her arm smarted from his tight hold. But he just continued to stare into her eyes.

"Did you think I could honestly be interested in you after the way you've treated your best friend?" she asked.

"Actually, yes. You're better off without him. You needed to see how weak Matt is. He's a dreamer, a fool."

Alex ceased struggling and looked up into the handsome face so close to hers. *Exactly how Matt had described himself. How well did Daniel know Matt to use those exact terms?*

Daniel lifted one side of his mouth into a knowing smirk. "I know him. He may hate me now – and you, but he'll soon find out how much better off he is doing his thing without you. I've actually done *him* a favor, too."

"You pompous…" Her comment was cut off as he quickly placed two fingers across her lips.

"Didn't I already warn you about saying something you'll just have to take back later?"

Alex just stared at him in disbelief.

As his fingers slipped away, Daniel's gaze moved to her mouth. His eyes traced the line of her lips as his head moved closer to hers. Alex resisted, but he moved firmly toward her, his eyes still on her mouth. She struggled again as his face neared hers, but his warmth radiated through her and his musky scent filled her head. She faintly registered her heart beating double time to the tick of a nearby clock.

A sudden familiar desire seared through her, which she worked diligently to suppress. Still, yearning quickly overpowered her while anger swirled and churned to break through its surface. *How does Daniel do this to me? I've gone from calm control, to violent anger, to melting in his arms in the space of a few minutes. I have to get a grip!*

Daniel drew so near their lips almost touched. He closed his eyes and slowly, deeply inhaled. "Deny me," he whispered.

She couldn't. Maddeningly, she was lost. She felt the heat of his lips on hers and his athletic arms tightening around her. His kiss was deep and urgent with a long-denied hunger. Cocooned in his embrace, the pain and cold fury of that other world seemed lost in a mist. Protection and warmth were here. Alex felt as if a powerful ray of sunlight enclosed their forms. Eyes closed, she leaned back her head to allow more of the warmth to shine upon her. Daniel pulled back and smoothed a loose curl from her cheek. She basked in the warm light surrounding them and opened her eyes.

The blatant desire in his azure eyes startled her, causing the imagined golden glow to fade rapidly and its mantle of warmth to cascade to the cold floor. This was *Daniel*, not Matt. He was using their chemistry against her again. She tore herself away and dropped her burning face into both hands. "How can you do this to me?" she moaned. "Matt and I are meant to be together. I've known it since I first laid eyes on him."

Daniel shook his head. "You *are* a tough one to persuade. Things meant to be, shouldn't be this hard, Alex."

She rounded on him slowly. "You're the one making it hard, Daniel Post."

He moved to her and put his hands on her shoulders. "I want to help you fulfill all your desires, Alex. Make you happy. Famous. Wealthy. Together, we can make any life we want. We complement each other."

Alex folded her arms. "But, I don't want a life with you."

Daniel lifted her chin with two fingers, but she jerked away. "Take note of your feelings when we're together, Alex. Don't they tell you how happy I can make you?"

"Yeah, if I want to stay in bed all day." Daniel raised his eyebrows at that, but she continued, "Chemistry doesn't make a good life, Daniel. A successful life takes friendship and common values."

Daniel snickered. "You sound like a mother. You're not becoming a prig, too, are you?"

"Daniel!" Mrs. Post stood at the head of the staircase, frowning down at her son. "What a thing to say!"

The color in Daniel's face heightened. *At least he has the decency to be embarrassed*, Alex thought.

He recovered quickly, and said, "C'mon, Mother. Now, you know I didn't mean you specifically."

"I hope not, young man." She visibly gathered her composure as she started down the curving staircase. "Alex, my dear. It looks like notoriety and college life are good for you." She clicked her tongue. "Why is my bourgeois son holding you hostage in the foyer? Daniel, take Alex into the living room where she can sit comfortably." She reached the bottom of the stairs and approached Alex. "May I get you a warm drink, my dear?"

Every fiber in Alex's body wanted to leave immediately. But she needed to settle business with Daniel. "That would be nice. Thank you, Mrs. Post."

"I'll get it for her, Mother. Just go back to what you were doing and don't trouble about us," Daniel said hurriedly. "How about a cup of our spiced tea, Alex? A special family recipe."

"We do make a masterful cup of tea, my dear. And Daniel brews it up better than any of us," Mrs. Post said, directing a patient smile at her son.

Daniel acknowledged Alex's nod and turned back. "Shall I make you a cup, too, Mother?"

"Thank you, son. I'll be in my sitting room." As she walked by, she laid a hand on Alex's arm and lowered her voice. "My dear, I know you're a new 'public personality,' so you may not have realized this yet. But, relationship issues really should take place in private. Believe me, that little smidgen of advice will save you oodles of pain."

You eavesdropper! A friend's home is *a private place!* Alex silently worked to remain collected. She nodded curtly at Mrs. Post, who smiled and nodded back.

Daniel frowned as he watched his mother glide down the hall. When she was just out of earshot, he said, "Now you know what gene pool I came from." Shaking his head, he bowed slightly and gestured Alex toward a set of carved mahogany double doors. In a mock formal tone, he added, "I'll be with you in a few minutes, M'lady. Make yourself at home."

The living room's heavy soundless doors opened into a large, formal space. Immediately, a heavy scent of rose enveloped her. It wafted up from several large glass potpourri-filled bowls strategically placed around the room. Cream-colored lace edging heavy burgundy velvet draped every window and restricted any exterior light. An elaborate mahogany wet bar backed by floor-to-ceiling wall mirrors occupied one complete side of the room. Gleaming lights illuminated glass shelving and bottles of fine wine and liquor with severe light and shadows. A voluminous, circular, burgundy velvet couch monopolized the center of the room.

I bet a "casting couch" looks a lot like that. Alex moved toward the room's fireplace setting. She took a seat in one of a pair of overstuffed floral armchairs, flanking a matching love seat.

Alex stared into the empty fireplace, wondering whether the sketchy plan she'd devised last night would actually work on Daniel to get everything back on track. Her stomach felt leaden and her heart like a boulder, and she marveled her body could bear the weight. She centered her thoughts on the task ahead: convincing Daniel to help her get Matt back. This wasn't going to be easy. Daniel had achieved his goal now and he certainly wasn't going to want to backtrack. She closed her eyes and concentrated, letting the ideas flow in naturally and calmly, lining themselves up in a progressive order. Easiest steps first, leading to logical action steps. She had formulated her initial outline more clearly by the time Daniel came into the room.

He placed an intricate silver tray with delicate black-and-burgundy flowered porcelain tea cups on the coffee table in front of her and poured them both a fragrant, steaming cup of tea. She sipped a bit, enjoying its relaxing, lingering, tangy orange and clove flavors, and ignored the tremble in her hands.

Daniel left his cup on the table and settled back into the love seat nearest to her chair. He put his hands behind his head and smiled expectantly at her. "So, you obviously have more to say to me."

"We have business to finalize."

"Intimate business? Good thing we're in a private place now." He smirked and leaned forward, reaching for her hand resting on the arm of her chair.

She snatched her hand back. "Absolutely not!"

Daniel shrugged and leaned back into the couch. "Guess we'll save the personal discussion for later." He grinned a disarming smile and his eyes sparkled expectantly.

Alex steeled her thoughts. She needed discipline to deal with this guy. She could not afford to lose control of her emotions again. "As I said, you are going to help me fix things with Matt."

He laughed. "Sorry. Everything is the way that I want it."

Alex cocked her head thoughtfully. "You know your friend Matt really well."

"Yeah. As my dad always said, know your enemy."

Alex's eyebrows rose. *You're calling your best friend your enemy!* But she kept her angry reaction in check. "You also did an amazing job on Matt's contract."

Daniel laughed smugly. "He got everything he deserved."

"Do you hate him that much?"

"No, I really don't hate him. I just always wanted some of what he's got."

"Your dad knew what was going on, right?"

Daniel hesitated before answering. "He knew what he needed to know. He simply didn't question that Matt really wanted you to have the music rights to the song he'd written for you."

"You told your dad that?"

"Yep."

"I bet your dad is really proud of you for handling the contract negotiations so smoothly. And with you still in high school. I can just hear him bragging to his friends."

"Yeah, some of that went on." He smirked.

Alex lowered her eyes and said quietly, "I wonder what the Bar Association would say to you and your dad if they knew his firm was condoning a high-school student practicing law without a license?"

Daniel snorted. "My dad looked over the paperwork and signed off. I didn't sign anything."

"Was your dad in on any of the conversations with Matt?"

"Maybe the first one, but I handled everything after that."

"Really? Negotiating contracts without a real lawyer present."

Daniel's expression became shrewd. "Now, don't go getting all tattle-tale on me, Alex. It's just one little song. You know Matt has tons more hit music in him. You, too, for that matter. This song is just a blip." He flicked his fingers in emphasis.

"This is the one that put us on the map. It's important."

"Yeah, but you aren't going to drag all of us into a potential legal mess over one stupid little song. That would be insane. It could cut off your career before it's even really begun. Besides, your case wouldn't have a leg to stand on."

"You think not? Well, I don't think the bar would look kindly on you doing legal work. Your dad could be in a lot of trouble."

Lines creased Daniel's forehead, but he quickly put on a smile. "You're not going to drag my dad's reputation through the mud for this little contract."

"Nah, I don't think Matt would really want to get involved in anything like that." She smiled at him meaningfully. "Although, it could still be done."

"So, why are you bringing this up?"

"I have a request."

Daniel raised his eyebrows expectantly. "Sock it to me, baby."

Alex grimaced, but continued firmly. "I'd like your dad's brother, the music lawyer in Philly, to introduce me to other songwriters. And I could use your help setting up a fund for all the money Matt would have made by owning music rights to our single. I plan to split it down the middle and give him his half. Only, I don't want him to know it's coming from me just yet."

"The first is a cinch. But the money...I arranged for you to have it. It's legally yours. "

"You're right, and I can do with it what I want."

"And you want to give it to our head-in-the-clouds fool?"

"He can use it to create his music camp."

"He has enough money already for that with his inheritance."

"It's the principle, Daniel. You... And I, unwittingly... We gypped him out of his rightful income." She glared at Daniel who sat forward, leaning his elbows on his knees.

"Alex, I planned for *this* outcome. What makes you think I am going to undo it now? I have made it the way I want it, which works out best for everyone involved. Can't you see that?"

Alex pushed down her rising anger. "Daniel, I know you're used to getting everything you want. Plus, you love showing everyone how clever you are. But, I've seen that underneath your lust for power, you have a kind streak. You couldn't care for Kathy the way you do, if you didn't have a soft spot deep inside somewhere."

Daniel fell back into the love seat, scoffing.

Alex didn't let him interrupt. "You say you want what Matt has, but you don't hate him. Somewhere underneath, you do care for and respect him. Otherwise, you wouldn't have remained his friend all these years."

Daniel smirked at her and put his hands back on his head. "You think you know all about us, don't you?"

She continued, "I know more than you think. At some point, you're going to need Matt in your life and you're going to have to turn to him again as a friend."

"Maybe you're as much of a dreamer as he is," Daniel said, dismissing her comment with a gesture.

Alex leaned toward him. "Tell me, Daniel. When you, Kathy and Matt got together as kids, who made the mischief? Surely you. Followed closely by Kathy? And, who got you out of trouble? I'd say…Matt. It was Matt you turned to when you needed advice, too. Am I right?"

As Alex spoke, she could see Daniel's smug expression falter, but he quickly recovered. "Those days are done."

"Are they?" She fixed him with a penetrating stare. He stared back for nearly a minute, but she was patient.

Eventually, he broke his gaze away and shrugged. "You can think what you want."

Inwardly, Alex gloated. She realized she'd begun to break him down. He'd begun to doubt what he'd done to his best friend. *Now, for the clincher.*

"Daniel, I have to tell you I'm disappointed in you. Not only have you acted less than ethically, you've shafted your best friend and dragged me down with you. You may not care whether Matt hates you or not, but I do care if he hates me. Especially when it's not my doing." She paused. "It's hard to respect someone who's caused all that." She watched his face fall and then steel again. "It would go a long way with me if you'd help me redeem what you've done to Matt and help him not hate me any more." She looked into the flames of the fire in the grate. "I don't think Matt will ever want me back totally, but I need him to be my friend."

Daniel studied his hands for a long time as he pressed his fingertips together. Eventually, he asked, "And what's in it for me?"

"My friendship."

"In what way?"

"You help me with this and I stay your friend. You don't, I walk out of your door today and never again acknowledge your existence."

His jaw tightened. He stood up and pulled Alex out of the armchair and against him. "You can't ever walk out of my life. You know you need me as much as I need you."

Alex immediately forced steel to the surface of her emotions. *I will not let him take me over! I will not be a slave to our chemistry!* She felt his lips pressing on hers, but she did not respond. She simply repeated in her mind, *I will not let him take me over. I will not be a slave to our chemistry.* She kept the words running through her head, squelching spikes of passion trying to eke through her self-imposed emotional encasement.

After several moments, Daniel pulled away. Alex saw concern in his eyes. He tried again, crushing her against him and kissing her ardently. *I will not let him take me over. I will not be a slave to our chemistry.* She repeated the mantra, but her protective emotional wall was crumbling second by second. She held back a strong desire to give in, to match his kiss with equal passion. Just as she felt her will on the brink of failing, Daniel pulled away with real fear on his face.

"Alex?" His voice was shaky.

"I told you I'd walk."

She could see conflict in his face. He turned from her and was silent for a long time, one hand on the fireplace mantel. She could almost hear the debate raging in him. Should he help her and keep her in his life? Or should he stand firm and try another scheme to get her back later? She was sure he had counted on her physical attraction to him to make his plan work. But, she'd just shown him she could resist it. She watched his shoulders drop as he made his decision. But, as he turned around he straightened and a sly spark of defiance glittered in his eyes. "OK. You win."

August 2003: Matt

*T*he morning after the concert brought an overcast sky, with infrequent slivers of sunlight shining through to the water. Matt loved the lake when the light played off and on along its shifting surface. Now brooding gray and then shimmering with dancing sunlight. He slowed the motorboat as he approached his lake properties. As the boat passed by his cabin, he felt a strong pull and looked up at it. His mind flashed on an image of being there with Alex. Holding her in his lap on the old black rocker while the rain splashed on the roof. The image made his heart ache and internal music start up. It was always so. Whenever he thought of her, love songs still composed themselves in his mind. He shook his head to try to clear the insistent notes.

But, the silent music continued. She was in his mind so strongly right now, surely because she was in town. So near. *What was he going to do about her now…?* He tried to clear his head again, but the music wouldn't fade. He decided to ignore it.

As he drove by the old cabin dock, Matt recognized Manny's motorboat moored there. Becka must have called the maintenance man to repair something at the cabin. *I thought Manny rented out his boat to tourists on Sundays. He must be backlogged and catching up on his work this weekend.* He made a mental note to talk with Becka about it.

Matt took a parting look at the cabin with a heavy heart and a head full of melodies as he maneuvered around the point to moor at the Coeur d'Musique dock. He tied off the boat lines and looked up the hill at the beautiful camp he'd created. Beyond the beach and wide green lawn shaded by large pines, his music buildings reigned over the lake. The natural log complex had been constructed from pine trees cut from the property and painted in blues, greens and browns to blend into the environment. Summer flowers blossomed along every wall, and colorful blooms rimmed the yard trees and stone walkway leading to the main building. The handsome, 24-room, two-story dormitory nestled farthest back in the trees. It was eclipsed by the main building with its impressive two-story front windows overlooking the lake. The music in his head only enhanced the beauty of it all.

Matt could just make out the grand piano sitting inside the huge bay window. Intermittent shafts of sunlight through the window showed the warm tones of varnished pine walls and floors. He loved the look and feel of that functional multipurpose room. From the inviting check-in area with its forest-toned overstuffed chairs and rich wooden desk, to the beautiful and acoustics-enhancing Native American rugs hanging on the walls. At the moment, early morning sunlight filtering through the large window gave him a glimpse of the cushioned bench-seating tiered along three of the walls. Matt smiled, thinking of the many wonderful students and audiences who had enjoyed music performances there over the past 15 years.

He felt very happy with what he had created: the buildings, classes, students and the results at the camp. Since his parents died 25 years ago, he'd spent every moment creating his camp, enticing students to attend, building the new complex here near to his family's old cabin. And, today, he had an additional two million dollars to build his programs! He patted his shirt pocket where he'd tucked the royalty check to give to Becka this morning. *Maybe this will fill the recent hollow in my gut.* He hadn't really felt content since he'd seen Alex on that hotel balcony in Santa Barbara.

Whatever that was all about, he couldn't let it bother him today. Humming the unavoidable tune in his head, he walked up the dock and along the winding stone path through the manicured grass. He stopped to pick a couple of withered blooms from the gardens lining the path and deposited them in a wooden trash receptacle just outside the screen door of the main building.

"G'mornin', bro'," Becka gave her usual morning greeting from the front desk as Matt walked through the front door.

"Mornin', sis'," he replied with a smile. "Wassup?" He reached for his pocket to surprise her with Dan's check, but before he could, he stopped at the look on her face. She bit her lower lip in a teasing smile. "You have a visitor."

"This early on a Sunday?" he looked back through the large window down to the dock. "No extra boat out there. Who is it?"

"Suzanne Briggs, I mean Thompkins. Brett dropped her off about 15 minutes ago."

The melody in Matt's head stopped immediately and an odd feeling tightened his stomach. "Really? Did she say what she wanted?"

"To say hi."

"She came all the way from Sedona, Arizona, to say hi?" He shot a quizzical look at his sister. The pressure in his stomach pulsed.

Becka shrugged and raised her eyebrows. "Duh, bro', it's your high-school reunion weekend. I put her in your office."

Matt thanked his sister and started across the large performance classroom. At the far end, Davey was replacing a violin next to its musical brothers and sisters on the instrument wall.

"Hey, dude," Davey said, turning to bump fists with his older brother. He lowered his voice, "What's shakin' with the hippie chick in your office?"

Matt laughed, picturing Suzanne in her typical, flowing, bright-colored clothing. "A high-school friend who's come to visit, is all."

Davey widened his eyes and nodded slightly. "OK, then. Have fun boogieing down memory lane."

"I certainly will. She's a good lady." *Well, at least she* was.

"Don't you mean good hippie?"

"No, she's an advertising writer, not a Flower Child." Matt picked up a polishing cloth to throw at his brother. "Get back to work, kid."

Matt was so happy his siblings worked in the business now, learning the ropes and doing a really great job of running the place, too. *Maybe if I decide to take some time off, they could keep things going for me.*

Matt stopped just outside his office door. Why had he thought that? He wasn't planning on going anywhere. He hadn't gone away in years. His vacation was creating music whenever he wasn't managing his camp. The odd feeling in his stomach now expanded into his chest.

With some trepidation, he opened his office door. Suzanne was standing by a window looking out at the glimpse of lake it framed. Draped in a screaming purple and yellow floral dress, her full frame moved gracefully to him and surrounded him in a bear hug. "It's been too long, Matt."

"That it has," he said, smiling into twinkling brown eyes that lit her round face. He led her by the elbow to a cushy couch in one corner of the office.

She sat and declined his offer for something cool to drink. "We missed seeing you at the reunion benefit concert this weekend, Matt."

"Not exactly my style. You and Brett went, I take it."

"Yes. You missed Kathy's finest hour."

"I'm sure it was all magnificent. Sorry I missed it."

"Really?" Suzanne's expression showed great sympathy, but also some amusement.

An image of Alex's hair shimmering in the spotlights last night snuck into his head. He ignored it. "You live by that intuition of yours, don't you, Suzanne?"

"Indeed."

"Is that what brings you to this neck of the woods on this lovely summer morning? Looking for the King of Rock and Roll?" He winked at her.

"No, long live the King, only destiny," she said, grinning brightly at him as he lowered himself onto the couch next to her.

"Oh, well now, that doesn't sound ominous at all."

"I hope it's not. I bring news of Alex."

Matt leaned his elbows on his knees and folded his fingers together. He dropped his head as he said, "I should have known you'd want to talk about Alex."

"Yeah, well. It's time dreams came true."

He looked askance at her. "What does that mean?"

"It means I was right all those years ago." Suzanne grinned up at the ceiling and continued, "Right that many dreams do come true. Especially Alex's."

Matt stared at her, uncomprehending. "Once I ran away from her dreams, but time showed us that wasn't necessary. Her dreams didn't set our paths. Real-life actions did."

"I'm not surprised you think that, not bothering to talk with her to get the full story after you broke up with her."

Matt tensed, remembering his blind fury the day he discovered he didn't have his own music rights. In more rational moments, later on, he had wondered about Alex's level of involvement with Daniel. But, he could never bring himself to call and talk with her. His life seemed so much simpler without her. "She didn't call me either, you know."

"You told her you never wanted to see her again, remember? She decided it was best to move on."

Indeed she had. But after hearing Alex's speech at the concert last night, Matt now understood how hard that must have been for her.

Suzanne smoothed the folds of her flowing dress. "But that's off the point. I wanted to talk with you about Alex's dreams."

"Last time you did that, the results weren't exactly what you thought they'd be."

"True, but things have changed."

"How?"

"Do you have a couple of minutes? This'll take some explanation."

When Matt assured her he had the time, Suzanne told him about the near car accident Alex had experienced in May and how closely it had paralleled her recurring car dream. She explained how Alex had ignored her recurring cabin dreams for years, but had just recently acknowledged that each installment of her subconscious images had predicted future events in her relationship with Matt.

She pointed out that a couple of days after Matt appeared in Alex's cabin dream for the first time, she'd gotten together with Matt at the Holiday Dance. Alex had seen a tree stump marked with symbols in her dream just days before she'd visited his secret meadow and seen him actually carve in their initials. Just before they broke up in Moscow, Matt disappeared into the forest in her cabin dream. And, shortly after the snowy wedding dress imagery had fallen from her shoulders, she'd proposed to him and he'd been frightened away, only to leave permanently when he found out about the music rights.

As Suzanne painted in powerful pictures how Alex had reacted after Matt's final break-up with her, Matt dropped his head into his hands and lost himself vicariously in his former lover's experience. His heart ached visualizing how she'd gone home and cried until she fell asleep. Suzanne's description made him feel the pull of Alex's dream sunbeam. He swore he heard her voice joined with the tinkling of a music box as she turned upward to view his face in the light.

When Suzanne finished, Matt's hands were trembling. No wonder Alex had followed her gut instinct and left him behind. "Why didn't she believe the signs all along?" he asked, looking up at Suzanne.

"Did *you*?"

Matt pressed his hands against his thighs. "I was afraid if her dreams were true that my life wasn't going to be my own. That Alex and the universe were going to control it."

"Our lives are never our own, no matter what we do."

He stopped to consider this. "But, why are you telling me this now, Suzanne? Obviously, Alex listened and made the right decision to pursue her music," he said, attempting to keep the quaking out of his voice. "She has everything she ever wanted."

"Not really, Matt. She's not happy."

Matt snorted. "C'mon, she's famous. She's rich. She's won awards for making a difference in the world."

"Why do you think she's never been married?"

"Too busy with her career? No good choices among the people she hangs out with?"

"Same reasons as you?"

Matt shrugged. Even though she hadn't seemed trustworthy, he hadn't ever found anyone else like Alex. No one else had inspired even one note to form in his head. "Alex couldn't possibly still be interested in me after all these years, Suzanne." He was fishing for Suzanne's take on what Alex had said on-stage last night.

"Why do you think she planned this benefit concert in Spokane?"

"To raise funds for music education programs?" he prodded.

"Funny she'd choose that. Isn't music education *your* cause?"

"Yes, it is."

Suzanne hesitated. "She hadn't had her cabin dream in years and it came back after the car accident actually happened."

"You're telling me her dream led her to come back here this summer. Not the reunion? Not the fundraiser? Not tax benefits?"

Suzanne nodded at him. "That's right. They led her to come back to you," she said matter-of-factly. Matt felt a shiver run down his spine, but a warm glow from his heart began to replace the empty feeling that had plagued him for months.

"Are you truly happy, Matt?"

He didn't answer, considering his discontented thoughts from earlier that morning.

"That's what I thought," Suzanne said. "There's a hole in your life, just like hers. The universe is showing you the path, Matt. Are you ready to listen this time?"

Before Matt could answer, a knock came at the door. At Matt's call to come in, Becka peeked around the door. I'm sorry to interrupt, but Brett is waiting in the lobby for you, Suzanne.

Suzanne nodded and stood, pulling Matt up by both of his hands until she gazed upward into his face. "Think about what I've said and what it means, Matt. Will you?"

He said he would. How could he not?

In silence, Matt followed Suzanne the short distance out to the lobby. As soon as they came into sight, a broad grin spread across Brett's face. "Look, it's a bird, it's a plane, it's SuperMatt!" he said, one fist clenched over his heart.

Matt laughed. "Holy Superhero, it's Brettman," Matt said, clasping the redhead's hand heartily. "You're here, too?

"Are you kidding? Miss seeing Coeur d'Alene in the summer, not to mention all the potential drama at the reunion and concert."

"You mean Alex arriving with her posse?" Matt asked.

"Yeah, that was cool, but... Well, we were hoping there'd be more. You know... Daniel and Kathy, married. Alex, famous. You, a successful songwriter and music guru. And high tension between everyone." Brett dug his toe in the carpet and looked mischievously up at Matt. "But, ya'll never showed, man. Disappointed!"

Suzanne poked her husband in the chest. "Not helping, Brett."

"I never agreed to attend, you know," Matt said.

"Awww shucks, man, I totally get why. My inner child just wanted to see the fight – that's what Suzanne would say, wouldn't you, hon'?"

She ignored him with a tsk.

"I really didn't want to be part of a fight, Brett," Matt said. "It was better I stayed home."

"Except you didn't," Suzanne said, putting a hand on Matt's arm and smiling knowingly.

Brett's jaw dropped and he glanced in surprise at his wife. His mouth spread into a broad grin while Suzanne continued. "Daniel was in a rare mood after the concert last night. Said he's going to Washington with you."

Matt hoped the rising color in his cheeks wasn't too obvious. "Yeah. He made me an offer I couldn't refuse."

Brett snorted. "Ya'll are kidding me!"

"I'm sure he's not, Brett," Suzanne said. She turned to Matt, "It had to have been a good offer, to make Daniel befriend you again."

Matt nodded and shrugged. "That's Dan."

"And how is it that you bumped into Daniel last night when ya'll weren't even at the INB Center for the concert?" Brett asked with a mock innocent expression.

Suzanne widened her eyes at Brett. "What?" he asked. "It's a perfectly logical question."

Matt cleared his throat. "Had some business with a lighting tech friend of mine there."

"Of course," Suzanne said. "It's always so productive to do business with the lighting guy right in the middle of a performance."

"Your buddy saved you a private seat in the control booth, didn't he, man?" Brett teased.

Busted. Matt smiled apologetically.

"Still as beautiful as ever, ain't she?" Brett lightly punched Matt on the arm.

Suzanne punched Brett in return, not so lightly, and raised one eyebrow at him. She turned again to Matt.

"Go find Alex, Matt. She's trying to do the right thing. You should, too."

Matt nodded and a balmy breeze of hope puffed into his heart. "Thank you, Suzanne. You, too, Brett. I really appreciate you both coming over."

He bade his friends farewell and, from the doorway, watched them walk down the pathway to the dock. Suzanne turned and waved a peace sign at him as they climbed in the boat. Matt smiled.

Recognizing a lilt in his step that had been absent for years, he patted his pocket and went to see how his sister and brother would react to a check for two million dollars.

August 2003: Alex

*A*s Alex sat in the old rocking chair, her mind barely registered the large paddleboat's muffled roar passing by below the cabin. Her mind was swirling with vivid memories as if they'd happened yesterday. *How could 25 years have passed? How could I have ended up here? Famous, rich and, despite my glamorous lifestyle, lonely and totally unfulfilled. My plan failed.*

She rummaged in her shoulder bag for the item that tied her most closely with her past: the small rose-inlaid music box Matt had given her when they were 17. She cradled the music box in her hands and stroked its lacquered surface, dulled across the flower where she'd so often rubbed it. She opened the lid and the crisp tinkling notes of the "Moonlight Sonata" filled the small cabin. As it played through its musical phrase, Alex realized this box held her only remaining music from Matt. Well, that and the few royalties trickling in from their old "Like The Moon Pulls The Tide" single. Alex sighed and glanced around the room.

A sudden beam of light shone through the cabin's porthole windows. Its bright glow beckoned her to take the music box over and place it on a small, now empty, knickknack shelf just under the window. Sunshine glinted off the opened box and Alex immediately recognized the shaft of light. It represented the safe place she needed to reach in her ongoing cabin dreams. The same light she'd seen in her dream 25 years ago just after fighting with Matt.

Suddenly, she flinched at a memory involving that long-ago dream. Part of the music she had heard had been her own voice, but she remembered now that it had also sounded music box notes. And, Matt's face had been reflected in the shaft of light.

Alex looked at the music box sitting in the radiant light and her hands began to tremble. *Did the tinkling sound in the dream really point to this music box Matt gave me, rather than to my own music? Could I really have so widely misinterpreted its meaning?* She collapsed into one of the chairs at the cabin table and put her head in her hands.

She really hadn't been into interpreting her dreams at all back then. She had just reacted to what she felt. At the time, it had seemed right for her to pursue her own music. That had been what she'd rationalized and shared with Suzanne immediately afterward. But, what if she should have paid more attention to the tinkling quality, like the music box that tied her to Matt? What if she *had* been meant to stay with Matt? If that was it, she'd lost a significant portion of her life to an ignorant, willful decision.

She held quivering fingertips against the corners of her eyes. *Oh, Matt! If only I'd been listening. To my dreams. To you. If only I'd tried harder to make you see I was innocent.* She immediately dashed away a tear that squeaked past her fingertip.

Enough, Alex. You're here to see if you can remedy all that, aren't you? Get a grip. Matt wasn't everything. She sighed and closed the music box lid, realizing she probably needed to abandon her plans for reuniting with Matt and move forward with her life. Just because Matt didn't show up at either the reunion or the benefit concert, didn't mean there wasn't another avenue for fulfillment. She had her music and she had her new cause.

She pictured the expressions on Jordan's and Caprice's faces last night as they took their bows and received the audience's enthusiastic response to their inspiring original music. Alex thought of the surprising ticket sales for the fundraiser, the prolific praise from attendees after the concert, and the media interest. Real happiness spread through her. She realized its joyous glow had begun while she was onstage last night, but she had been so focused on her entreaty to Matt, she hadn't recognized it. Suddenly it became clear. *She* was the reason so many gifted children would now be able to pursue their musical dreams. Oh, what a wonderful feeling that was!

But, she couldn't help thinking how much *more* meaningful it would have been to share it with Matt. How could he hate her so much still after all these years, especially now that she'd discovered the value of his own life's work?

On a whim, she moved over to the kitchen counter and clicked on the old transistor radio. It crackled to life only to emanate muted sounds. Alex turned up the volume and inhaled a quick breath as she recognized the music flowing over the airwaves.

...only the spirit of their souls combined, forever entwined.

She draws him like the moon pulls the tide
Into the depths of the most beautiful creation
A place where music plays when flowers grow
Where love hangs like dew in the air
Where energy illumines darkness
And scents of joy fill warm breezes.

How freaky is this? They were playing Matt's and her old single. And, the very first time she'd heard it played over the airwaves had been at this cabin. Without really thinking about it, she lifted the radio to look under and behind it. She didn't know what exactly she meant to find. An Internet connection? A CD player? An iPod? She knew it was just a radio. But it seemed so unbelievable. Why was this song playing at the very moment she decided to turn on the radio here? She stood, immobile, through the end of the song, just listening.

When the DJ came back on and started prattling, an icy finger of anticipation slipped down Alex's spine. Her presence in the cabin, the sunlight on the music box, the song on the radio. The alignment of these things meant something. The only element missing... All of Alex's senses jumped to attention and her eyes flew to the cabin door.

Footsteps approached on the gravel path outside, followed by the subsequent thump of shoes on the deck. Filled with tense expectation, Alex didn't even think to be scared, or even guilty about trespassing in someone else's home. All she could do was stand and watch as a tall silhouette of a man wielding a long, wooden object filled the doorway.

The screen door creaked open, letting in a long shaft of light along with a lean, long-haired figure.

Hazel eyes landed on Alex and widened. "Alexandra Lauren," the man said. His penetrating eyes staying on hers even as he dipped his head in acknowledgement. He straightened and the beam of light haloed his honey-colored hair now touched with gray. His face showed small signs of weathering, but was surprisingly unchanged. One look at him and a very quick, very familiar, surge of intense emotion leapt from deep inside. She caught her breath. "Matt."

He didn't move. He stared at Alex for a long time. Suddenly, he turned away. She was sure he was going to leave and she reached out a hand toward him, about to call his name again. But, he just placed the oar he'd been carrying against the wall of the cabin and turned back toward her. "Somehow, I should have known it would be you."

She shook her head quickly. "How... How did you even know I was here?"

"The boat you rented today belongs to our maintenance guy. I saw it moored over here earlier. We hadn't called him to repair anything over here, so it seemed like I should check it out."

Alex quickly dropped her outstretched hand. "Matt, I... I just wanted to see the cabin again and... Well, the key was in the same place... I just...well, I just let myself in..."

"Yeah, I didn't notice a splintered door or anything. So, I'd actually guessed you didn't ask your bodyguards to break it down for you." He looked around. "Where are they anyway?"

"I only have one bodyguard. And, since I needed a few hours to myself, I convinced him not much harm could come to me on a small-town lake. Especially, if he held the paparazzi at bay in town for me."

"Oh, right. We never have boats break down on the lake. Or," he said pointedly, "untrusting property owners chasing down would-be intruders with wooden oars. No dangers here at all to you. I'm sure he was easily convinced."

Alex glanced at the oar he'd set by the door. *He'd brought that as a weapon?* She cleared her throat. "Well, I do pay my bodyguard's salary. Besides, I can be pretty convincing when I want."

Matt nodded and looked straight into her eyes. "I've been on the receiving end of that." It didn't sound malicious. It sounded almost... *No, Alex, you're imagining things. He's got to be furious with you.*

She flushed. "Matt..."

He held up a hand to stop her. She saw his fingers tremble. *From anger or some other emotion?* "You showed up here headlining this benefit concert to try to make amends with me, didn't you?"

She nodded slowly.

"You've gone to an awful lot of trouble."

She wanted to run to him, throw her arms around him and to gush, *Yes! I've done everything for you. You are the one I've always wanted. I still love you so much. I want you to hold me and never let go.* Instead, she stood perfectly still and said, "It seemed like the right thing to do."

"Hmm," he said. "Suzanne said you were working on that."

"Suzanne?"

"Yeah. We had a little chat."

"You did?" Alex suddenly realized what Matt had implied. "What did Suzanne say?"

"You are trying to do the right thing."

"That's something I've always done."

He shrugged. "Didn't necessarily feel like it from my perspective."

"You were so mad, Matt. You never gave me a chance to explain." Realizing she was twisting her hands, she stopped and stared down at her intertwined fingers.

"Alex, you could have come back to talk with me when I had cooled down, instead of just taking off like you did."

Alex sighed. "That's what Suzanne told me to do. But, I just knew you never wanted to see me again."

"Suzanne always was a wise soul. You on the other hand…just weren't listening."

She and I think the same thoughts almost all the time, Matt. Why don't you think I'm wise? Alex wanted to cry out. She simply said, "Suzanne *is* very wise."

Matt walked over to the wooden table and ran one hand along its worn surface, obviously gathering his thoughts. Alex watched him take in the surroundings: the slight lift of his lips when he recognized "Signed, Sealed, Delivered" playing quietly on the radio, the way his eyes lingered on the music box on the window shelf and his quick glance back at her. *Damn, but he's still gorgeous.* The familiar gait in his walk, the grace in his mannerisms and his beloved facial expressions aroused raw emotions Alex had suppressed for years. She could feel his soul pulling at hers.

"What do you want from me, Alex?"

She couldn't tell whether his penetrating gaze held fear, anger, or excitement. She swallowed. "Mostly your forgiveness."

Was that relief that flickered past his eyes? "You're forgiven."

Alex coughed and stared at him. "What? That's it?"

"Sure."

"After 25 years of considering ways to explain, to make you understand what really happened, you're just going to forgive me with no questions or anything?"

"Yeah. That works for me."

"Are you just trying to get rid of me?"

"Did I say that?"

Does he really forgive me? That easily? Alex took a step forward. "But, the last time I saw you, you hated my guts. You never made one effort to call me. Never even a telegram. No news through our friends. You hate me."

His little dimple played hide and seek as he suppressed a small smile. "Time wounds all heels."

"Right. You didn't respond to Kathy's requests to get involved, or even to attend, the reunion benefit concert..." *Even though it honored your life's work*, her thought concluded.

He smiled a small smile as if keeping a secret. "Almost all true."

Alex let him keep his little secret, whatever it was. Right now, she needed to know what he was feeling. "You lost 25 years of animosity in one day?"

"Not really. It's been falling away for a while. Some things have changed my perception just since last night, though." Matt went over and opened the lid to the music box. The "Moonlight Sonata" tinkling out, clashed horribly with Stevie Wonder on the radio. He closed the lid after a few notes, tracing the worn rose with his finger. "My all-time favorite classical melody." He looked up beyond her. She'd seen that glaze over his eyes long ago whenever he was creating music in his head. As if suddenly realizing she was watching him, he refocused. "Amazing you haven't replaced this little keepsake of bad memories with something much more glitzy and expensive. Something more in keeping with your status."

"You obviously don't know me very well."

"I apparently haven't seen enough of you lately."

Haltingly, she said, "Twenty-five years is a long time to take...to try...to forget someone."

He nodded slowly and asked quietly, "Did you succeed?"

Alex turned and walked to the far cabin window. She looked out at the sun's rays playing hide and seek between cloud formations over the lake. *I can't blurt what's in my heart. He'll bolt.* She cleared her throat. "I keep that music box on my mantle with my Grammy award. They represent the two most important events in my life."

"The nastiest and most glorious of times…?" Matt asked.

"They're the center focus of an epiphany I had a few months ago after I won the Grammy, Matt." He didn't answer, so she continued, "Your music box has always served as an inspiration to me. It represented you. Not just because you gave it to me, but also because, well… It was music stuck in a little box. Like I thought you were. I kept telling myself if I could just make it big, earn a Grammy, I could come back and show you what a little box you'd put yourself in."

His voice sounded wary and he straightened his posture. "So that's the reason for your visit? To say I told you so?"

"Turns out I'm the one in the box." Alex shook her head and looked up at the ceiling. "Fame is like being held inside a container with your music. Everyone around you opens the lid to let the music out and they put you back in the box to control you. All these years when I thought I was the one who was free, it was really you. You were right all along." She turned and looked at him. "I'm sorry, Matt. So sorry I tried to push you into fame when you didn't want it."

"You pushed hard." He watched her intently.

"And it was a very bad time for you to be pushed, I know. I realized that even at the time. But I really was just trying to help." She laughed sardonically, "To do the right thing."

"But you *were* working with Daniel."

"I trusted Daniel's friendship with you. I didn't look at who he really was. I had no idea he was so jealous of you."

"He wanted *you*."

Alex took another step toward Matt. "About that…" She laughed wryly. "Daniel still wants me."

"He's satisfied with Kathy."

Alex stared at him. "How could you have missed the publicity about him kissing me at my big fundraiser in LA? He did that right in front of his satisfactory wife."

Matt put his hands in his pockets and shuffled his feet a bit. "Yeah, he told me about that."

"What?"

"Mm-hmm. He said you seemed unhappy. 'Caged,' is the word I think he used. He also said you asked about me and he realized he wasn't ever going to get you. That was the night he became jealous when his wife fawned over me in an lapse of judgment, and he fully fell in love with what he'd created."

Alex couldn't think of a thing to say. She opened her mouth twice and closed it. Eventually, her mind clutched the most relevant statement to her situation with Matt right now. "I did ask about you… I needed Daniel, and Kathy, to learn what you were doing."

"No you didn't."

"Yeah right, like I was just going to pick up the phone and dial the person who hated me most in the world to ask how he's doing."

"Didn't your dreams tell you what the reality is?"

She tsked. "I didn't know until recently what they…" She realized he hadn't said that with one iota of sarcasm. "Why did you ask me that? You don't trust my dreams."

"Maybe I've learned to respect them, like you have." He paused. "I'm sorry you had to witness that car accident, Alex."

Abruptly, her head jerked up. Even as she said, "How do you even know that?" Realization dawned. "Suzanne!"

"Yep. She's been telling us all along to listen to your dreams, hasn't she?"

"Sure. I just didn't want to believe her. Following such an ethereal guide would mean I wasn't the one really in control of my life."

"You, too?" He moved a step toward her. "Is anyone really in control of their life, Alex?"

She shook head. "No, obviously not."

Matt approached her, slowly closing the space between them. "Let's take control of our lives now. Alex. Let's use your dreams to guide us."

"But…" she stammered. "But, you ran…" Tears prickled her eyes.

"That was a long time ago. We both had lessons to learn. What a shame we had to wait so long to learn them."

Alex stared up into his face, now so near, and an image came to her. Matt and she were applauding a stage full of young musicians taking their bows from a successful show. The happy, grateful looks on their bright faces filled her with warmth. This is what she was meant to do. This was what was going to fulfill her, giving back to the future of her industry with Matt by her side.

He fingered away a single tear falling down her cheek. "We can start by making music together again. Come to Washington DC with me and we'll perform 'Like The Moon…' for the President."

Alex inhaled quickly and covered her mouth with one hand. "But that will mean huge publicity."

Matt took hold of her hands. "I'm going to need it to raise the funds I want. Between Daniel's schmoozing and our 'long-awaited' public reunion, how can we go wrong?"

"You spoke with Daniel?"

"I think he was actually honest with me for once."

"He does seem changed." Alex laughed. "In some ways."

Matt nodded and squeezed her hands.

She gazed up at him and, with a tremble in her words, asked. "Can we be like we were in the beginning?"

He cocked his head. "No. But maybe we can be better."

She lost herself in his hazel eyes and her heart expanded with so much joy she thought it might burst.

As if on cue, the radio DJ commented, "And here's one for anyone out there who's ever experienced love at first sight." The opening strains of "The First Time Ever I Saw Your Face" echoed in the silence of the cabin. Alex's eyes widened. A distant look passed across Matt's face and he smiled. Beginning to move to the rhythms of the song, he swung their joined hands. He gently pulled her close and led them into a slow, synchronized spin. Alex looked up at the only man she'd ever truly loved.

He hummed the melody underscoring the lyrics he'd once penned in code on the back of a senior class photo and suddenly stopped dancing. "You can always give me more Flack, Princess," he whispered, holding her face for several seconds before tenderly pressing his lips against hers.

As she savored his familiar touch, Alex became faintly aware of a bright sunbeam bursting through the window. Its protective glow surrounded them and Alex lost herself to the light, the music and her dream come true.

D.S. al Fine